"I HAVE NO RIGHT TO EVEN THINK OF TOUCHING YOU."

He said so softly I barely heard him, "I would only hurt you, like I have everyone else."

The fire crackled and hissed.

Then he turned very slowly to face me. There was desperation in the depths of his eyes, in the bunching of his jaw, the slant of his mouth. Then his fingers closed around my throat and slid up my neck, where his thumb pressed into my chin, lifting my face toward his. His throat rumbled with a hoarse groan before he admitted, "I want to kiss you."

"I want to be kissed," I confessed, feeling no hesitation, though he looked as wild and powerful in that instant as the rolling fog that had consumed the earth and sky outside the house. I repeated, "I *want* to be kissed, my lord . . . by you."

For a moment neither of us moved, then his hands came up and cupped my face, slid into my hair, and clenched. His dark head lowered over mine and he growled, "Then God help you."

A
HEART
POSSESSED

Katherine Sutcliffe

A TOPAZ BOOK

TOPAZ
Published by the Penguin Group
Penguin Books USA Inc., 375 Hudson Street,
New York, New York 10014, U.S.A.
Penguin Books Ltd, 27 Wrights Lane,
London W8 5TZ, England
Penguin Books Australia Ltd, Ringwood,
Victoria, Australia
Penguin Books Canada Ltd, 10 Alcorn Avenue,
Toronto, Ontario, Canada M4V 3B2
Penguin Books (N.Z.) Ltd, 182–190 Wairau Road,
Auckland 10, New Zealand

Penguin Books Ltd, Registered Offices:
Harmondsworth, Middlesex, England

Published by Topaz, an imprint of Dutton Signet,
a division of Penguin Books USA Inc.
Previously appeared in a Signet edition.

First Topaz Printing, June, 1996
10 9 8 7 6 5 4 3 2 1

REGISTERED TRADEMARK—MARCA REGISTRADA

Printed in the United States of America

For my own Yorkshireman:
My husband, Neil, who has possessed my heart
from the moment we met.

And for his family:
Ellen, Donald, and Adrienne Sutcliffe, and
Charlie and Annie Wheeler,
who welcomed a Yank into their homes and hearts
that blustery Christmas ten years ago.

I love you all.

I thought, O my love, you were so—
As the sun or the moon on a fountain,
And I thought after that you were snow,
The cold snow on top of the mountain.
And I thought after that you were more
Like God's lamp shining to find me,
Or the bright star of knowledge before,
Or the star of knowledge behind me.

—from *The Love Songs of Connacht*

Dearbhrathair don Bhas
fios a chur ar an dochtuir.

Chapter 1

I did not return to Malham easily. It was here, after all, where my despair had begun, my fall from grace. Where the first seed of bitterness took hold of my life until the ache for revenge possessed my every night and day while I languished in that wretched institution, Royal Oaks, in Menston. I might never have survived it—the humiliation, the pain of being interned at Oaks—had it not been for Jerome Baron. Dear Jerome. We had been companions since childhood, and his friendship carried me through the nights and days of black despair when my only companion was grief. Dear Jerome, how he had begged to marry me so I might save myself the awful confinement at Oaks. But though I loved Jerome as a friend, I could not love him as a husband, and told him so. And of course, he understood. He came day after day of my confinement and talked even when I had no heart to listen. He held me close, moments after the flesh of my arm had been seared by the brand that would forever mark me as whore: *His* whore: Wyndham of Walthamstow, earl of this village called Malham.

And then my world came shattering down around me. My uncle, who had committed me at Oaks, died. Without his dismissal I would forever be locked in that godforsaken dungeon.

The shock was too much. For days I slept, weak and near death, but upon opening my eyes I found Jerome there, assuring as always but withdrawn. He confessed that he had carried out my wishes, and I knew then that for the first time in our lives he would not break the vow of secrecy I had begged him to make. I pleaded and wept to know the truth, then, desperate to use any wile to sway him, I cursed him and turned him out. He returned still. Time and again until, despite my anger, I forgave him his silence.

It was during that time that I noticed his illness. What could I do? I held him when he came to visit, though he tried to deny me, afraid the disease would kill me as well. I didn't care. I had lost everything, so what did it matter?

Anguished by my depression, Jerome finally confessed the philanthropic deed he had committed on my behalf, of the arrangements he'd made for my release, and of the money that had passed hands and the officials who were more than willing—for a price—to look the other way as I left my prison. His face bloodless and his chest racked with coughing, he convinced me to return home to Malham . . . to face Nicholas Wyndham. But he warned me too of the dangers, though I covered my ears and called him liar. I was not one to listen to rumors; they were nothing more than twisted truths from twisted mouths. And so I returned to Malham, having lost my dearest friend to death, the only friend who might have celebrated my courage to follow through on my conviction. Here I would end what had begun that spring day on the moor two years before. I vowed that no love I had once felt for the handsome Lord Melham would deter me from my goal.

*   *   *

Dawn crept in on misty feet, smelling of the gray-green lichen on the brick wall where I stood. Wild grapevines cast shadows like entwined serpents over the spongy ground. They brushed the folds of my woolen cape and fluttered like tiny amber torches at the corner of my eye. I swept them away lightly, absently.

Pulling my cloak more tightly around my shoulders, I sank into the shadows. My fingers were numb. So were my feet. I shifted them awkwardly among the bramble, frowning as thorns snagged the hem of my dress and cloak. It is too early to call, I told myself, yet my patience was waning. I had waited long enough, too long, too many weeks and months to act on my and Jerome's plan. "What is one more hour?" I asked myself aloud. Eternity.

" 'Ere now, y' frolicsome bitch, or we'll be havin' trouble afore y' know it!"

I stumbled backward, the twisted trunk of a rowan tree halting my clumsy escape. I stared through its blazing red-orange leaves across the grounds of Walthamstow Manor, my heart climbing into my throat, then easing as I realized the comment had not been directed at me.

A black-and-tan hound, her nose to the ground, loped across the gardens, dragging the short-legged keeper behind her. The animal's chesty baying brought a flash of memory that burned the backs of my eyes.

I slid again into the shadows as silently as possible and made my way down a path overgrown with moss and clumps of tuft-topped weeds. Quickly I swept along, snapping twigs, my footsteps muted by damp leaves that glistened yellow and red and orange in the dim light.

I breathed easier when I reached the foot of the

path. Foolish meanderings, I scolded myself, and looked uneasily over my shoulder. Beyond the treetops Walthamstow's slated dormers peeked through winterstark branches. For a moment I imagined a face there, within the window frame—somber, dark, just a flash of features, then it was gone. *He* was gone. It might have been anyone, I told myself.

Still, the visage had been enough to wrench my breath. No matter what I had told myself since leaving Oaks, no matter what Jerome had told me about Nicholas Wyndham, the future was frightening. Pressing my fingers against my heart, I waited for its frantic racing to ease, telling myself over and over that my reasons for returning to Walthamstow Manor had nothing at all to do with what I had once felt in my breast for Nicholas. Yet my traitorous heart was not so inclined to agree.

There was time to pass so I followed McBain's Wall, skipping among stone rubble, pretending to feel happier than I really was. For whom? I wondered. Because I should, I argued. I should feel happy. I had dreamed of this day. Hadn't I? I had planned for this day. Hadn't I? Indeed.

Malham on the moor was yet asleep beneath the cold, damp blanket of mist. I gathered my cloak about me and, from atop the crumbling dry stone wall, fixed my gaze upon the slumbering town. "Malham." I spoke the name like a sonnet, whispering it to the black-faced sheep that grazed contentedly some distance away. "Walthamstow of Malham, I've come home. Will y' know me? Nay, y'll not. For I've grown up, y' see."

I could not help but smile. Before me was my past, rich in fond memories. And despite the despair of the last two of my twenty-three years, it would carry me a lifetime. Malham, grim and beautiful, her high tops dotted with tumuli and heather, was my future. Turning my face toward the sky, I closed my eyes and repeated:

"Walthamstow of Malham, I've come home."

I would not take the path again. Pushing open the ivy-covered wrought-iron gate I walked carefully up the brick pathway, my cloak scattering the dry leaves around my feet so they tumbled as lightly as feathers in the rising breeze. I stared occasionally through the tree limbs overhead, catching glimpses of bottom-heavy clouds hinting of snow. The air was brittle. My face stung, more from nervousness, I surmised, than from the cold.

The hedge was overgrown, nearly meeting over the pathway. I might have taken that as a warning that things were not as they used to be. Walthamstow's gardens had been once renowned for their spectacular beauty. Folk from nearby villages would take a turn through Malham just to view the floral scenery that blazed around the intricately sheared shrubbery of the lawns. I swept the hedge aside and brushed away the leaves that clung tenaciously to my cloak. Everything must be perfect, I told myself. Everything!

Looking up again, I slowed, then stopped. I hadn't expected . . . I had never ventured so close . . . it hadn't seemed so frightening from a distance. Walthamstow. Three hundred years old. Perhaps she had a right to look rather tattered around her dormers. But I hadn't anticipated such . . . immensity. And a moat. Lord God, a bloody moat. On closer inspection, I realized it wasn't a moat at all, only a rain sink covered with lily pads.

Walthamstow. With all her aged imperfections she was still beautiful beyond my memories or fantasies. Her mullioned oriels winked with leaded and stained glass. Ivy crept up her stone walls, arching over windows and doors, but though streamers had tried their best to cling to the slick slate tiles on the roof, they had failed and now hung like maiden's hair toward the ground. And chimneys. I counted five from my position on the walk. Imagine a fireplace in every room!

I thought to smile at my childish excitement, but then a scream came, shrill and piercing. I stumbled backward, clamping my hands over my ears, shoving the woolen cap of my cape sharply against the sides of my head, hoping to mute the anguished, unending cry. I could not move, and the wail continued until my own hysteria boiled up my throat and threatened to explode at any moment. Then the hands came, squeezing my shoulders so fiercely that pain shot through my arms and sank deeply into my breast. They were weather-raw hands, and twisted. The strength in my knees became water: I nearly collapsed.

" 'Ere now, lass, yer all right. Yer all right!" The hands gave me a shake, and the voice continued, "Shut up yet wailin', 'enrietta, before y' scare the lass out of 'er mind. Fer the love o' God, yer a pain in the arse. Get y' gone, y' silly fowl, afore we pluck and boil yer fancy feathers fer dinner."

The peacock strutted across the walk.

I closed my eyes.

The hands released me then. "Are y' all right?" came the man's gentler voice.

I nodded, feeling foolish.

" 'ere now." He stepped around me, the man I'd earlier seen walking the hound. "The bloody bird is a nuisance. Worse'n any mutt f' scarin' off strangers." His bushy gray brows plunged between his eyes in a frown. "Gum, lass, but yer white as a sheet. Were it that frightenin'?"

"Aye," I said, uncomfortable with my response to the affair. I questioned my own balance, knowing what had caused it and why.

He clucked his tongue. "I've been tellin' the doc that we'd best get rid of t'owd bird, but 'e's quite fond of 'er, I think. Keeps away the riffraff, 'e says. Oh, beggin' yer pardon, ma'am, not meanin' yer riffraff—"

"I understand." Anxious now, I looked toward the house.

" 'oo'll y' be 'ere t' see?" he asked.

Pulling my gaze from the front door, I turned it fully on my companion. He had round, tired eyes that widened as he searched my upturned face. He dragged his hat from his head, and the weight of his once broad shoulders appeared to make him bend at the waist. He shuffled backward.

" 'oo're y' 'ere t' see, ma'am?" he asked again in a more respectful manner.

Opening my clenched fingers from around the crumpled paper in my fist, I took a deep, unsteady breath before replying, "Wyndham."

He glanced at the paper. "Ah! Yer 'ere t' see the doc, then?"

"I don't think so. No. Not the doc."

A gust of wind sliced across the grounds, whipping the hems of the cloak and skirt around my legs. "Wyndham," I repeated a little breathlessly, perhaps a little warily. "Nicholas Wyndham of Walthamstow Manor, I believe . . . Lord Malham." Pleased that I sounded sufficiently ignorant, I tugged the skirts back around my ankles and looked at him again.

He appeared surprised.

"Is something wrong?" I asked him. "Lord Malham's not traveled in the last few days?"

"Nay, lass, the man don't travel much anymore."

"Then he's here."

"Aye, 'e'll be 'ere, I suppose."

We each stood uncomfortably attentive, our faces becoming chafed in the cold. Finally he stood aside and swept his flannel-covered arm toward the house. "Mornin' to y', lass."

With a nod of my head I bid him good morning.

The air stung my lungs as I took another full breath. But it cleared my head. Moving gracefully up the pathway, I neared the massive double door, but slowed when I spied a gargoyle's face, once bronze but now green with age, peering at me through the dried black leaves and streamers of a death wreath. As I had thought the unkempt gardens odd, so I thought the appearance of the wreath unnatural after all this time. I hesitated once, then, flicking aside the dusty satin ribbon, grabbed hold of the cold brass ring in the demon's nose and whacked it soundly against the plate. Every instinct in my body screamed a warning, but I denied them. I had come this far. I would not turn back.

The door swung open. A gaunt man well over six feet blinked at me with kind brown eyes. "I'm here to see Lord Malham," I announced, sounding far steadier than I felt in that moment. "Nicholas Wyndham, please."

There was a moment's hesitation. "Nicholas?"

"Aye."

He considered my reply, appearing a bit dubious.

Then a voice came, rich and deep, from within. "Who's there, Reggie?"

I held my breath.

The butler stepped aside and another man appeared, as tall but not so lean. His hair was chocolate-brown and wind-tossed. His nose was red, as were his cheeks, accentuating the blue of his eyes. He wore an expensive wool coat that fit him perfectly, with wide lapels that thrust outward like a bird's wings, as his collar was turned up to keep the chill from his neck. His broad smile stretched even wider as he acknowledged me.

"Gracious, Reggie, you'll freeze the young woman." He caught my arm and tugged me out of the cold. Then, rubbing his hands together, he teased, "I'm quite certain he's about gaining me new clients. How do you do, Miss . . . ?"

"Ariel Rushdon," I said, relieved. "You're . . . Doc?"

"I am. Stick out your tongue and say ahhh." He laughed as I laughed. Then he said, "You don't look sick. A bit pale perhaps, but—"

"I haven't come to see you," I confessed. I searched about the immense foyer before looking at him again.

"Then you're here to see my sister, I would suppose. What a shame."

"No." As I shook my head the hood of my cape slid back to my shoulders, releasing my hair in a tumble around my face.

I looked again at the paper in my hand, spreading it carefully. My fingers were numb and trembling, whether from cold or nerves I could not guess. Swallowing, I announced, "Sir Nicholas Wyndham: Lord Malham, Earl of Malham."

It was a woman's voice that intruded then. "Nick? Why on earth would *anyone* care to subject himself to that?"

Startled, I spun, my fingers twisting into the paper. The doctor must have noticed. He moved up beside me and kindly covered my hands with his. Looking at me askance, he winked in a charming way that warmed my heart. "Forgive my sister," he pleaded. "Adrienne has an appallingly tenny amount of manners when greeting guests. Adrienne, this is Miss . . . Rushdon?"

"What do you want with Nicholas?" Adrienne asked. She stopped mere feet from me, her hands on her hips. She had the same blue eyes as the doctor, though her hair wasn't quite so dark.

Behind me the butler closed the door against the cold. The sound echoed throughout the house, startling me from my speechlessness. "The notice," I blurted, feeling awkward and less and less confident of my plans as the Wyndhams waited. "I've come about the notice."

"What notice?" Adrienne frowned.

"This notice." I held out the paper for her regard. Adrienne snapped it from my fingers in a manner that conveyed as much irritation as the flash of anger in her narrowed eyes. "It was posted at the Black Bull Inn in Keighley," I managed.

The woman's fine brows knitted in frustration as she stared at the notice. "Oh, for the love of God, Trevor, he's done it again."

"Has he?" He smiled at me. "What has he done, fair sister?"

"Posted these ridiculous notices for a sitter."

"Oh." He winked. "Is that all?"

"Is that all? Is that all!" Adrienne rolled her eyes. "I thought we'd done with that madness last month."

As I looked on, discomfited, I thought I detected a flicker of anger in the doctor's eyes as he looked from me to his sister. "If Nick requires a sitter, I can't see what harm could come of it. Not if it makes him happy."

"But we had these women traipsing through the house for weeks last time, Trevor. It's most annoying, and you know he'll never find another like *her,* so why does he persist?"

"It pleases him."

"It frustrates him, and we both know what happens when he becomes frustrated."

Trevor Wyndham looked back at me, his handsome face thoughtful. Although his manner was careless and almost flirtatious, he exuded an air of self-confidence and breeding that managed to define the line between aristocrat and the common man. "Perhaps this time will be different," he said. "Besides, the young lady has traveled a great distance to see him. I think it's only fair that she is allowed to do so." He turned to the servant. "Where is my brother?" he asked him.

"The conservatory, I believe."

"You'll see Miss—it *is* Miss?"

I nodded, feeling weak but determined.

"See Miss Rushdon to the conservatory, Reggie. I've a client about to give birth. You will excuse me, my dear?"

Wyndham whirled, causing his mantle to billow around his knees. Throwing open the door, he was gone, replaced by air smelling of ice and rain.

I pulled my cloak more tightly round my shoulders and followed the butler obediently, if not reluctantly, down one long, dark hallway after another. They smelled old and musty. Floors of uneven brick were covered by tattered carpets that at one time must have been beautiful and expensive. An occasional oriel offered the only light. Meager though it was, it was enough to brighten the ancient portraits that decorated the wainscotted walls. Pale, oval faces of Lady this and Lady that stared down at me, unblinking and, for the most part, unsmiling. I felt empty inside just looking at them.

I had almost convinced myself that this plan of dear Jerome's was folly, and was on the verge of begging the butler's pardon and escaping when we rounded a corner. Sudden light glowed before us as softly as a candle flame, and again I found myself struggling to calm my racing heart. Pulling the hood up over my head, I pressed my hair back into it. My courage was failing. Dear God, my courage had fled!

I stopped, crumpling the paper in my hand. Foolish girl with your airy ideas, I scorned myself. This would never work. Never. What if the rumors proved to be false? How would he react if he recognized me? Angry? Certainly, for he would know instantly why I had come. Violent? Possibly. The folk in Keighley had warned me—

"This way, madam."

As Reginald motioned toward the room I forced my legs to move, one foot in front of the other. There was still time . . .

"My lord, you've a guest," Reginald announced.

I cautiously entered the room, preparing myself for the possibility—the inevitability—of his reaction should the rumors prove false. I prepared myself for the shock of seeing *him* again.

Nicholas Wyndham stood among great green plants, a trowel in one hand and a watering can in the other. He stared at a yellowing specimen, and his shoulders, though as broad—if not broader—than I remembered, slumped slightly within his white linen shirt.

"Damn," he muttered. "They're dying again, Reggie. The damnable things are dying again."

"I'm so sorry, sir."

"It's this blasted weather. Never any sun. They're accustomed to sun, you know."

"Yes, sir."

He tossed the trowel into a flowerpot, placed the spouted can on the floor, then slapped his hands together. Mesmerized no less than before by the broad muscles of his back as they moved beneath the cloth, I watched the shirt where it bloused slightly at the waist of his tight, fawn-colored pantaloons ... and I thought of running. Far and fast. But I couldn't. Not until I got what I came for.

"Sir," Reginald repeated, "you have a guest."

His head turned slowly.

He appeared disturbed by the intrusion. Thick brows as black as raven wings hooded his gray eyes in a frown; the corner of his mouth turned down slightly in contemplation. I took a step backward, unprepared after all.

"A guest?" he asked quietly. "I have a guest?"

"A Miss Rushdon, sir."

With some effort, it seemed, he shifted his eyes beyond Reginald's stoic face to mine. "Rushdon?" He relaxed and turned to face me fully.

The blow from his eyes was something I had not counted on. Their intensity I could have hardly forgotten. But their impact—how could I have forgotten their impact? I felt my face color beneath his steely scrutiny, and my heart became a wild thing that ran away with my breath, leaving me weak and trembling and uncertain. "My lord," I managed unevenly.

He stared, and with as much force as I could muster, I met his gaze. It was now or never, I reasoned. Yet as he watched me in that moment, unblinking, I knew that the rumors, twisted or otherwise, had not proven false. He did not know me. But though I should have heralded the truth, I could not do it. I had lost him, it seemed, as surely as I had the first time—as if I had ever truly had him. Naught but one question hounded me now. Why?

Nicholas closed his eyes. My presence had obviously

caused him some distress, and with growing trepidation I sensed that he was struggling with his memory. One half of my heart cried, Fight, fight, damn you, and prove all the wagging tongues in Yorkshire wrong. Yet part of me prayed that the idiocy that had turned his past to nothingness would remain.

Pressing his fingers to his temple, the spell appearing to have left him, he again focused on my face. He had the almost excessive good looks of a god, tall and slender but not overly. His hair, now as in the past, looked wind-whipped, giving him a less austere appearance than that of his brother. His skin, like that of all Englishmen, was fair, but had acquired a darkness that was the result of weather rather than sun. The whiteness of his shirt accentuated the aged-oak color and made him look like a shepherd's son.

"Rushdon?" he asked.

"Here about the notice, sir," Reginald said.

He tried to smile, though I sensed it pained him to do so. "The notice," he repeated. "You mean the one in a wad in your hand?" He watched as I took my lower lip between my teeth, and, as if finding amusement in my discomfiture, he smiled a little broader.

"One and the same," I responded, feeling braver.

"Well, I'm afraid, Miss Rushdon, that you have not caught me at my best. Not that I am ever at my best, you understand, but I'm unprepared for an interview."

His voice had not changed. The tone, like gentle thunder, seemed to vibrate inside me.

Standing straighter, he said, "Reggie, will you see Miss Rushdon to the . . ." His thoughts appeared to wander.

"To the library, sir?"

"Ah! Yes, the library. Of course. While I change."

He threw me an apologetic glance. "I won't be long," he assured me.

I had just taken my place in a wing chair when Nicholas entered the room. I was startled by his sudden appearance; in truth, a little disappointed. I needed time to sort out my feelings. Ever since I had made plans to return to Malham, I had wondered if Jerome's dying confession would prove to be true. "Lord Malham will not remember you," he had wheezed into his blood-soaked kerchief. "He's ill. Desperately ill."

And he is, I thought with heart-twisting despair. The vacant eyes were hardly those that had mesmerized my thoughts those many hopeless months; hardly the eyes I had fantasized over since that moment ten years before when he had walked with his rapier grace into my uncle's tavern. I had only been a child then, and he no more than twenty.

He walked swiftly to the desk before me, his stride as graceful—thank God—and with purpose. "Have you been waiting long?" he asked over his shoulder.

I stared at my hands, dying.

"Not long," Reginald responded in a soft voice.

Nicholas appeared ill at ease behind the highly polished mahogany desk. He wore a jacket he had pulled on in haste over his white shirt. The cuffs of his sleeves were soiled and damp. His collar was unbuttoned. Biting back my tears, I looked at his fingers, long, sensuous, and slender, tapping at the tabletop; they were coated with dirt. Hesitantly I looked up.

He offered me a wayward smile, his dark eyes beating into mine. Then, curling his fingers into his palms, he tucked them into his jacket pockets. "Damn, I've frightened you already," he said. "You see, I have this nasty habit of digging in dirt, of late. I can't seem to help myself, for what little good it does me. Everything I touch dies."

The confession appeared to jar him. He rammed his fists harder into his pockets, and the look on his face became angry.

Reginald stepped forward. "Perhaps you would like a sherry, milord." Without waiting for a response Reginald turned for the door.

"Don't forget our guest," Nick replied, his voice edged still with that tone of anger.

"I wouldn't care for sherry," I responded. "Perhaps tea, if you have it?"

Nick eased down into his chair. "Ah, tea. Of course. What would aristocracy be without tea? I am waiting for the day all our blue blood dilutes to the color of urine. Bring the young lady some tea, my good man." He looked back at me. "So, you've come about the notice."

I lifted my chin.

"Take off your cape," he ordered. When I hesitated he added, "It's an old custom: One approves of the merchandise before he makes the purchase."

"I hardly think you are 'purchasing' me, sir. Only my services."

"They are one and the same in this instance. Take off your cape."

Dare I?

He sat back in his chair. "Come now. Are you frightened of me? Perhaps you've spoken to the other young ladies?"

"Others?"

Something, perhaps concern, must have shown in my face. Satisfaction crossed his features and I sensed that he was toying with me on purpose.

"You aren't the first young lady to see me. Did you

think you were? I might warn you, Miss Rushdon, that the others fled the house in a mild state of hysteria."

"And I might warn you, sir, that I don't frighten easily."

He briefly pressed his fingers to his temple again, then wagged his finger in my direction.

I fumbled a moment with the braided frog at my throat, aware that my nervousness was obvious. Too obvious. Without my cloak to shield me, there was always the possibility that he could remember. My face colored with the realization that I hoped he would remember.

Standing, I slowly removed the hood from my head; it dropped to my shoulders, again releasing my hair. The black tresses cascaded in wild curls around my face and over my breasts, and tumbled in disarrayed coils nearly to my waist. The gray eyes assessing me narrowed for an instant, turned as dark as the ashes resting damp and dead within the stone hearth of the fireplace.

"Go on," he said quietly.

The cloak dropped to the floor. I watched the muscles in his face tense, the firm, wide mouth twist, as if he'd experienced a momentary stab of pain. His face grew suddenly pale, paler even than it had been in the conservatory. There were smudges of purple beneath his eyes.

Noticing my distress, he sank farther in his chair, those lips curling sardonically. "Ready to bolt, little girl?" he asked.

I felt as if the stiff, high collar of my woolen dress was choking me. Indeed, I was ready to bolt. But not for the reasons he believed. The feelings I thought I'd hardened my heart against were alive in my bosom, as strong and discomforting as they had been two years before. Throughout the last months I'd struggled to replace the ache with hatred. But how could I hate him? I had known what I was doing then, had entered that room with far less doubts than I harbored now.

"Well?" he prompted.

His look was taunting, daring me to flee. Lifting my chin, I responded, "I think, sir, that perhaps you enjoy frightening people. And," I added, a good deal too forcefully, "I am not a little girl."

Nick's gaze moved over me slowly, from the crown of my lush black hair to my green eyes, to my pale throat and then to my breasts. He stared a long moment, and it was all I could do not to flinch from those intense eyes. There was an aura of carefully restrained power, of forcefulness that emanated from him that I had not experienced before. Then I realized that the moments I'd spent watching Nicholas Wyndham, lord of Walthamstow Manor, Earl of Malham, had been mostly from a distance: from behind doors, fences, McBain's Wall.

He saw the smile start. The slight tucking up of my lips, the lowering of my lashes brought a spark of color to the curve of my cheeks. "Most becoming," he said softly. "I envy your memories, Miss Rushdon. I trust they are pleasant?"

"Not always," I answered truthfully.

"Even bad memories must be better than no memory at all."

I stared at him again, curious.

"You're a very beautiful young woman," he went on. His voice, husky now, was filled with longing. "However, if I decide to accept you for this position you will not be wearing such as that." He pointed to my drab gray attire. "The color doesn't suit you," he added.

This time I flushed with anger. I'd had little choice in my attire.

"Your sherry, milord," came Reginald's monotone behind me.

The servant placed the glass of amber liquid on the desktop, then turned with tea in hand. I took the opportunity to ask Lord Malham sharply, "Have you done with your rather critical inspection, milord, or would you perhaps care to see my teeth as well?"

"I don't paint teeth." Lifting the glass to his mouth, Nicholas arched one black brow at me and smiled.

Reginald closed the door behind me, leaving us alone again. Nicholas studied me as I eased back down in my chair. Balancing the bone china cup and saucer on my knee, I looked down into the steaming brew, concentrated on my heartbeats and thought the air in the room had grown intolerably heavy.

"Who are you?" he asked so suddenly I sloshed tea onto the saucer. "Where do you come from?"

"I am Ariel Rushdon from Keighley. I am unmarried—"

"So I presumed. Curious for a woman of . . . ?"

"Twenty-three."

"You should be married with brats."

Brats. The word disturbed me. I sipped my tea, burning my tongue.

"Are you willing to peel out of those atrocious clothes for the sum of say, three shillings a week, plus room and board, of course?"

"Are you willing to discontinue your insults?" I asked dryly. "Are you willing to swear that your only purpose for hiring me is to pose for your portraits?"

"No."

I blinked and managed a look of total surprise.

"Should I decide to dress you in frills and fripperies

and escort you to the opera in London I will expect you to smile and pretend that you have no idea what they are saying behind their feathered little fans. Because they *will* talk. They talk constantly, behind my back and to my face. They will gape at you as if you were Marie Antoinette prancing about the decks of the guillotine. You will hear stories that will undoubtedly distress you. For example . . ."

He left his chair, hands again jammed into his jacket pockets. I stared at his empty sherry glass, then at his back as he walked to the leaded window and looked out over Walthamstow's gardens. Very slowly the long arms went up. Bracing his hands along the windowsill, he continued.

"I'm a widower, you see. Some will tell you that it's the grief that has driven me into seclusion. Those are the understanding souls, or blind. Everyone in this county knew I loathed my deceased wife." His head partially turned. "Does that surprise you, Miss Rushdon?"

"Yours would not be the first loveless marriage, milord," I responded, knowing it to be the truth.

"Ah, let's hear it for tact."

"Continue," I said.

He took a breath. "Some believe I killed her."

He looked out the window again. The knuckles of his fists were white. "I am hopelessly insane, I am told. Prone to bouts of uncontrollable rage and depression. My dearest brother Trevor therefore has devised these hobbies to keep my hands occupied, so I don't strangle the servants or my sister or do away with myself. Actually, painting has become a fond pastime, but apples bore me. So do vases filled with roses."

He turned suddenly, catching me unprepared. "Ah, Miss Rushdon, you're too kind. Save the tears for one who deserves them. I've not been reduced to Bedlam yet and, perhaps with a little of your consideration, I may be saved the penance of straitjackets."

I turned my face away, chagrined by my emotionalism, embarrassed that he had caught me weeping.

"Do you want the position?" he asked me quietly. There was hope there. I could hear it despite his droll tone of implied indifference. "Should you accept you must be forewarned. The mood to paint may hit me anytime, day or night. Mostly night. The nights are so damnably long, you see, and I—do you want the position?"

I closed my eyes. "Aye. I want it."

There was silence. When I opened my eyes again he was before me. His head, with its thick black hair spilling over his brow, was angled over mine. His eyes, the color of old, old pewter, gazed sleepily at my mouth. I could feel the warmth of his body on mine, so closely was he standing; I could detect the stirring scent of his maleness. It coiled, warm and arousing, in my stomach and breast.

His hand came up to hover about my cheek, and the smell of dirt on his fingers filled my nostrils. Yet he did not touch me; no matter how I willed it, he did not touch me.

"Foolish girl," he whispered. "Foolish, foolish girl."

Chapter 2

Jerome had warned me, after all.

The door beyond us was flung open, allowing a child's wail to pour into the room. I spun and was faced by a woman whose countenance was severe and emotionless as she announced, "Milord, there's been an accident with Master Kevin."

"Accident." The word sounded dry in his throat.

The cry again. It clutched at my heart like a claw.

Nicholas swept by me in a rush. I followed, holding the weight of my woolen skirts in my hands. I allowed the stranger only a glance as I ran out the door, noting with a flicker of curiosity that her severity had not altered in the least. She was stone-faced, and not in the least upset.

My stride could not match Wyndham's; he'd broken into a run. He flashed in and out of the shadows before me, moving easily through the halls. He cut sharply to his right, and I followed, down a longer hallway that was immeasurably darker. Only a sconce here and there alleviated total blackness.

He paused in a puddle of yellow light that spilled out a doorway at the end of the hall, then he disappeared into a room.

Voices came, sounding like a gaggle of goslings frantic with fright. I hurried to the door, squinting against the sudden intrusion of light. The cry was earsplitting now. Yet I could not be certain which jarred me more: that wail or the fear that swallowed me the moment I saw the blood.

"Milord, t'was only an accident. He fell. He only fell!"

"Goddamn you," he hissed.

A short, plump servant, her blond hair tucked beneath a white bonnet stiffened with stays, wrung her hands and pleaded, "Milord, I only found 'im. What was I t' do?"

Gathering my wits about me, I dashed for the child cradled in another servant's arms. "Let me have him," I ordered.

Her eyes round in surprise, the girl argued, "Nay, I will not."

I repeated, "Let me have him." Before the woman could resist me further I slid my arms around the infant and lifted him to my breast. Blood oozed from his cut forehead. His tiny round face was blotched with bright color and slick with tears. The sight weakened me. I sank onto the upraised hearth, the very culprit that had caused the grievous injury. Using my dress sleeve I did my best to wipe the blood from his face.

"He fell," came the cold voice from the doorway.

Nicholas turned. His face white with fury and his fists shaking at his sides, he railed, "By God, you old hag, I've warned you. Had you been doing your job properly, this would not have happened."

The tight skin over the crone's face darkened slightly. It was her only show of anger. "I don't have to take this abuse," she replied. "The child is uncontrollable, milord, as you well know, and I am not a young woman. I have repeatedly asked for help in managing him."

"What the devil kind of woman cannot manage a one-year-old?" he blasted.

"Your wife, for one." One corner of her thin mouth quirked like the tip of a rat's tail.

He took a violent step toward her, and for a dreadful moment I witnessed a hint of the barely leashed rage that had fueled the rumors from Malham to Keighley. "Milord!" I spoke urgently, anxious to avoid the ugly scene about to take place. "Your son needs attention." Kevin's quiet whimpering was the only sound in the room. "Milord?" I pleaded more softly.

He whirled toward me, one hand coming up and raking through his disheveled hair. With a sense of relief I noticed that the frightening anger of moments before had been replaced by concern. Going to his knee, he touched the boy's brow with the tips of his shaking fingers. " 'Tis only a scratch," I assured him.

"Aye, a scratch," he replied. "But my brother should see to it. It might take stitches." He held his arms out for the child. "Come along, lad, and we'll get you cleaned up."

I released the child reluctantly, with a gentle brush of my lips over the wound. The babe buried his little face in Nick's shirt, and all the fury that had hardened his father's features diminished in relief. His tightly pressed lips relaxed in a smile; his eyes closed. The sight was wrenching. I looked away, empty, and in pain.

"Magilacutty, mum. Matilda Magilacutty's m' name. 'is lordship says I'm t' show y' to yer quarters. 'ave y' any parcels? Luggage'n such?" The servant's eyes twinkled up at me, making me smile. She was a cheery sort, as round as she was tall. I liked her immediately.

"I left them at Crown Inn," I told her. "I wasn't expecting—"

She cut me off with a wave of her hand. "Ah, no bother, mum. We'll see to it. Ole Jim'll 'ave someone fetch 'em soon enuff, or 'e'll do it 'imself. Give 'im a good excuse to tip up at t' tavern on 'is way back, if y' know what I mean. Come along now."

I was given the grand tour along the way.

"There's near one hundred rooms at Walthamstow," Matilda boasted. "Give or take a dozen. We ain't counted in a century or so. Some rooms ain't been aired in decades. No reason t' use 'em anyhows. More's the pity for us if they decide to open 'em up. I wouldn't like the chore of cleanin' 'em, I vow. Last we heard, t'owd walls were damp as dungeons anyhows. I shiver just thinkin' on it. Some say ole 'enry the Eighth slept back there, y' know, when he was runnin' amuck and blastin' all the bleedin' Catholics to heaven and back. I'll wager t'owd bugger daydreamed of droppin' Anne's block in a basket from that very room."

The hallway, as always, was dismally dark. I sensed my way along, keeping my eyes trained on the white cap that bobbed up and down before me.

Matilda slowed and pointed with a short, pudgy finger down an adjoining corridor. "Them quarters there are the doc's. There's an entrance from the east garden, so he comes and goes mostly without our seein'. Sometime 'e sees 'is patients there, sometime 'e don't. We don't clean there, y' see, 'cause 'e's got all them gobbledygooks in somethin' called cruc—cruci—"

"Crucibles?"

Matilda's brown eyes widened in surprise. "Well, now, ain't you the clever one? That's t' word I was meanin'. And al—?"

"Alembics."

"Aye," she sniffed. "Alembeaks."

We made another turn, then climbed the staircase.

Once again Matilda pointed down a corridor and explained, "This'll be Miss Adrienne's quarters. She'll be sleepin' now, y'see. She calls it 'er beauty sleep and she won't be disturbed until mealtime. She eats and sleeps and complains t' the doc that his lordship ruined 'er life."

As we turned down yet another hallway Matilda's stride lessened noticeably. Finally she stopped completely. I waited silently as the servant ran her hands clumsily over a table to one side, bumping over a candlestick in the process and clattering a Chinese vase against the wall. A flame gasped in the darkness, smelling sharp and pungent. Its black-gray smoke curled in an oily stream into the shadows, and before the sudden cold draft of wind could extinguish it, Matilda touched it to the candle wick. She lifted the tallow light between us.

"This'll be 'is lordship's quarters," Matilda stated in a quieter voice. "We don't see 'em 'cept at mealtimes. 'e don't like nobody disturbin' 'im, y' see, 'specially when 'e's workin'. That there's 'is studio where you'll be sittin'. That there is Master Kevin's room and yonder is 'is lordship's room."

Looking back down the long row of closed quarters, I tugged my wrap closer about my shoulders. "It's colder here," I said.

"Aye. It's the north side, y' see. The wind from the moor gets in through the copin's and comes barrelin' up the tunnels." She cupped her hand around the candle flame until its frantic dancing eased somewhat.

I moved from the halo of yellow candlelight through the darkness to the studio door.

"It's locked," Matilda said. "No one goes inside but 'is lordship . . . and now you, o' course."

"No one?" I leaned back against the wall, looking up

and down the sequestered rooms. I pointed to the farthest door. "Where does that lead?"

"That were Lady Malham's room, miss, but she never used it. She's deceased, y' know."

I thought back to those tense moments in the library, remembering Nicholas as he stood looking out the window. "How did she die?" I asked.

Matilda, all business suddenly, bustled to the door one down from the studio. "This 'ere'll be yer room. It adjoins the studio, though his lordship keeps that door locked as well."

I noted that only the studio separated my room from Nick's. "I asked you a question," I said.

"She burned t' death, miss."

On impulse I said, more to myself than to Matilda, "That hardly sounds like murder to me."

Matilda looked up, her eyes like dark china saucers in her plump face. " 'oo said anythin' 'bout murder?"

"Why, his lordship himself," I responded calmly.

Ramming the key into the lock, Matilda gave it a hardy twist, then pushed open the door. "This 'ere's yer room," came her voice from inside the enclosure. "I'll 'ave ole Jim bring up some peat for the fire." Turning again for the door, Matilda hesitated, throwing a brief look back over her shoulder before finishing, "Yer on yer own, miss, and good luck."

The first thing I did was to open the heavy crimson velvet drapes adorning the window. I did so with a flourish, scattering particles of dust that danced in the light like sunbeams before settling on my shoulders. The room was tiny but no smaller than I was accustomed to. What mattered most was that it was my own. No palace on earth could have been finer.

The clouds parted in that instant. Sunlight spilled through the lancet window, its spear tip high above my head splintering the rays into dazzling yellow, red, and blue shafts that warmed the back of my neck. I closed my eyes and imagined the many nights I had rested upon my bed at the inn and dreamt of spending one night in this house.

My heart began racing, and I felt queerly giddy. How easily Jerome's plan was working. Almost too easily. Only one thing disturbed me: My feelings for Nick were alive still, and with such a realization there was also pain. It could not be otherwise. I would be forced to hurt him, and although I had set my heart and soul upon the task before coming to Walthamstow Manor, now I could find no peace of mind in doing so. For he was already haunted. The child, it seemed, was his link to sanity. Where would he be when I robbed him of that?

I was certain of my solitude before leaving the room. The corridors, black as pitch and cold as a well, were empty to my right and left. Entering the nursery, I fond life-sized marionettes dangling on ropes from the ceiling. Their polished oaken faces smiled with pleasant mouths that stretched all the way to their red-dotted cheeks. They wore busbies of bear fur. Upon the wall were pictures of lambs; black-faced and smiling, they frolicked among butterflies and birds. Bees frozen for eternity on the paper-and-stone canvas hovered over gardens of buttercups and violets. I realized, with a shocking sense of pride, that Nicholas had painted them all.

I turned round and round, absorbing each wonderful detail. The room was aglow with light. The fireplace at the far end of the quarters hissed at the cold, coaxing away the shivers that had racked me before. Alone in my room, the emptiness of my life had assailed me. But here I was warmed by the fairyland and filled to bursting with hope.

I ran my hand over the rich walnut door of the wardrobe. Unlike the furniture in the rest of the house, it was without the depressing and often frightening symbols of demons. The floors were covered with carpets of Oriental influence. Tapestries of cherubs gave life to the stark walls. And the crib . . . ah, the crib. Ensconced in the center of the floor and draped in yards and yards of the sheerest material that hung in swags from the ceiling, the tiny carved bed drew me nearer, until I ran my hands caressingly over the plump beddings and the porcelain-faced dolls that crowded each corner. There were soldiers in uniform and girls with flowing waist-length hair.

As I carefully lifted one in my hand, voices drifted to me from the hallway. Concerned that I would be found in the child's room without permission, I glanced swiftly about the quarters, but found no means of escape. With my heart in my throat, I hid behind the door.

"How dare you!" came the crone's voice. "How dare you bring that woman into this house so soon after Jane's death."

Entering his son's room, Nicholas strode to the cradle before turning to face his adversary. "Shut up," he said simply. "Just shut up."

"I will not. You've gotten away with murder, Nicholas Wyndham, and before I die I'll see you pay."

Relaxing against the bed, he folded his long arms over his chest and smiled. "So you keep reminding me, Bea, but neither of us has seen any evidence of that."

"The evidence sleeps in yonder cemetery, as you're well aware."

"If you are so certain I killed her, then go to the officials. I'll not stop you."

"Nothing would please me more than to see you hanging from the gibbet."

"Do what you will, hag, but one more mistake where my son is concerned and I will turn you out on your bony backside."

"Ach!" She paced, her thick-soled black shoes thumping dully on the carpet. "When I came here with Miss Jane I had no intention of servicing some little—"

He moved so suddenly she had little time to react. A gasp was all she could summon as he grabbed her scrawny arm and propelled her against the wall. The marionettes danced disjointedly, their heads bobbing to and fro, as Nicholas said, "Never, under any circumstances, will you again profane my son's name. I will tolerate a great number of things, including your annihilation of my character, but you will keep your tongue civil about Kevin, or—"

I held my breath and watched as the woman's mouth parted in a slit of a smile, baring broken yellow teeth.

"You're insane and we all know it," Bea went on maliciously. "Someday you'll get your just reward for what you did to that poor, dear child. She came to you chaste—"

"She was a whore." Like the eye of a storm, his voice remained calm, yet I sensed the maelstrom inside him. His shoulders rose and fell quickly with the effort it took to check his temper. This was no madman, I thought. No madman would take abuse from such as her and remain rational. He continued. "She found pleasure in her lovers' beds, not mine."

"Do you blame her?" The crone's feral eyes bore into his as she needled, "You never loved Jane. It was always *her*, that little slut who worked at—"

"Watch what you say, old woman, or—"

"Or you'll throw another tantrum? Is your head splitting yet, milord? Are you shaking?"

He looked down at his hand. It was trembling.

"It's been awhile, hasn't it, milord? Wonder when it'll hit again. Soon, I wager, by the looks of you. You haven't been sleeping nights—"

"Shut up."

"I hear you pacing. I found those canvases you thought you'd destroyed. They're portraits of madness. You're mad and someday you'll pay for what you did to Jane."

He backed away, and it was obvious from the way he opened and closed his hands that he yearned to wrap them around her neck. I sensed his battle for control and applauded him in my heart when he answered Bea steadily. "I've warned you: Should anything careless happen again to my son, I will hold you personally responsible. Now get out. Out!"

Gathering her limp black skirt in her fingers, the woman dissolved like an apparition, into the dark recesses of the hallway. Nicholas stared first at her, then at his hands, holding them level before him, noting that their trembling had subsided. He then looked toward the door where I hid. Smiling, he said, "She is a hoary old biddy, I vow, and I don't know why the deuce I tolerate her . . . You may come out from behind the door, Miss Rushdon."

I did so but remained against the wall.

Taking a deep breath, Nicholas clasped his hands around his back and took a leisurely look around his son's nursery before bringing his eyes back to mine. "A little old to be playing with dolls, aren't you?" he asked.

"But it's such a beautiful doll," I said. I skimmed my fingers over the wavy blond hair and china face of the toy. Then, not without reluctance, I looked up into Wyndham's gray eyes. His mien was cool, belying the anger and sarcasm I had earlier heard in his voice. But his eyes . . . their unblinking perusal made me flinch.

"Are you convinced yet?" he asked in that taunting, self-mocking tone that disturbed me. He was angry still, and hurt. Perhaps embarrassed that I had over-heard the exchange between him and Bea.

"Of?" The doll, forgotten once again, hung from my hand.

He smiled disarmingly, the way I had seen him smile a hundred times in my fantasies and dreams. Then he threw his dark head back in soft laughter. "Miss Rush-don, you don't look like a simpleton and you haven't, up until now, acted like one. I pride myself on judging character, good or bad, and I surmise there must be brains to go along with that . . . beauty." He moved slowly toward me. Again without his coat, his loose white shirt open to the middle of his chest, he ap-peared warm and masculine and at his ease. I had never considered myself timid, and yet I trembled. My free hand moved backward and sought the solid strength of the wall. I settled against it, praying in-wardly for courage. It came.

"I am not a simpleton," I said.

"Very good. Since it looks as if you have ears, I would imagine you overheard my conversation with Bea. We discussed madness and murder, I believe."

"Yes." I nodded.

"She is thoroughly convinced that I killed my wife."

"Did you?"

He had partially turned. Stopping, he looked at me quizzically, his lips curling in a half smile. "It would hardly behoove me to acknowledge the act."

"Except to assuage your conscience," I told him.

"I can live with my conscience, thank you. What I cannot live with is hanging from the neck or feet at the gibbet in Leeds. It is a most foul affair and one I would not care to subject myself to, if I can help it."

His tone was light, bringing to my mind the many nights I had listened secretly to his friendly banterings at the Cock and Bottle Inn. That memory made me smile.

"Da Vinci would kill for that smile," he said quietly, then added, "Ah, Nick, a poor choice of words."

I stared again at the doll hanging by my side, uncomfortable with the intensity of his gaze, the pagan taunt of his smile. I had once thought him magical and perhaps he was. No. Were it so, he could cure himself; there would be no more talk of madness and murder. The Nicholas Wyndham I had known could not have committed murder. But that Nicholas Wyndham had not been mad.

"What are you doing here?" he asked, startling me from my thoughts. When I didn't respond he continued, "Come now, you know my secrets. I think it only fair that I know yours."

"I was curious, milord. Nothing more."

He walked to the marionettes before turning again. The jester's smiling face intensified the severity of his own. Nicholas's eyes, like chips of coal, were oddly dull considering the room was afire with candlelight. Not for the first time, I questioned my wisdom in coming here.

"Do you like children?" he asked me.

"Yes."

"You were very good with Kevin."

"He's a beautiful child, sir."

There was silence between us. I replaced the doll in the bed, then turned for the door. After the comforting warmth of the nursery, the bleak corridor brought a chill to my shoulders. Without looking back I hurried to my own room, anxious to put distance between myself and the curiosity I saw in Wyndham's eyes. Solitude, however, was not yet to be. As I hurried to close my door behind me Nicholas stood there, his hand on the knob. He said nothing for a moment, then reached into his pocket to retrieve a key. Tarnished with age, it shone dully in the dim light. "Matilda forgot to give you your key, Miss Rushdon."

I took it. He would not relinquish his hold on the door, however, until I looked him fully in the face.

"That is the only key to this room," he told me, his voice low. "Keep it on your person at all times. When you leave this room, lock your door. When you are in the room, lock your door. Especially at night. Should the desire to work surface after hours, I will knock three times. Should I knock twice, ignore it. Should I knock four times, ignore it. Do you understand me, Ariel?"

I did not understand but nodded nevertheless.

Wyndham turned then and without looking back walked to his room, closing the door behind him.

Chapter 3

From my window I could see the distant granges of Malham, dank beneath black ice and fog. Blurry white forms moved in and out of the vapor, images so vague only my common sense told me they were sheep. Beyond the zigzagging row of stone walls perched the township of Malham. Its tumbled roofs clustered about the hollow and were flanked by yellow-green hills whose crests were invisible in the fog. Here and there the stark branches of tall elms pierced the low-lying clouds. Their leaves had fallen to the ground and their trunks were tangled with dying vines of wisteria. Rooks' nests spotted the upper branches. As I watched, several of the large black birds burst from a nearby acacia tree and flew into the distance.

From the window I also looked down on Walthamstow's north garden, with its high walls and stone copings. Wisteria grew profusely here as well. I imagined in spring its blooms might replace the musty odor of the old house with sweet perfume.

On foggy days like today, the flat land looked like an expanse of cotton wool with tufts of trees pushing through it. I looked forward to sunnier days when I might look out on Pikedaw Hill and Scarsdale and the long summit of Malham Cove. The hills would be dotted with sheep and sheepdogs and shaggy-haired ponies. Perhaps I would take Kevin for a ride on one of those ponies.

It was three hours past noon and I had heard nothing more from Nicholas. He had not left his room, I was certain. Jim had arrived with my bag barely an hour after I'd settled in my quarters. From my window I had watched him drive in a pony cart along the winding ribbon of road to Malham. Behind him had bounded a half dozen hounds. Their baying had brought back memories of Nicholas wading through the animals as they frolicked around his legs. "To the hunt, gentlemen!" he had shouted then to his fellow riders. From inside my bedroom window over the Cock and Bottle Inn, I had watched enviously as they mounted their sleek steeds and headed for the moor. Nothing in his behavior then had hinted of madness. How, I wondered, did a man go mad overnight?

Then I reminded myself that two years had passed since I had last walked Raikes Road to Malham. The moor never changed: For over five hundred years the same stone fences had divided the grange into squares of lush grazing pastures. But people changed. Circumstances changed them.

I had no way of knowing the time for certain, but the hour was growing late. Darkness had begun its slow encroachment over the moor. By four o'clock nothing but the twinkling lights of the distant village could be seen outside my window. I yearned for summer, when daylight still flooded the countryside until nearly midnight. Then I was not forced to endure the solitude of my mind for so long a time. For with that solitude came the memory—the one memory that would forever haunt me. Seeing Wyndham again after all this time unleashed the ache, brought that glimmering from the past shining ever brighter and more painful before me.

Nicholas. Whispering the name even now broke my heart.

Nicholas.

Sighing, I closed my eyes and rested my forehead against the glass, remembering that night. Even now I could recall the muted laughter of drunken men coming from my uncle's tavern. But even that had dimmed as I looked up into Nicholas's eyes. "I have to know," came his whisper-soft voice. "Have there been others?"

"No others," I responded.

He kissed me all over, tracing the ribbons of fire's glow with his tongue until my timidity was replaced by passion and the need to give myself to him. He touched the loose strands of my hair, finding pleasure in the way the black curls coiled around his fingers. He then took those curls and brushed them ever so lightly over my breasts until they grew full and ripe, the points hard and rosy, aching for his mouth to claim them. And he did, molding them with his fingers, his tongue, pulling gently with his teeth and suckling like a hungry child.

A strange delight rippled through me, bringing a warm fullness to my loins. As if he sensed it, he slowly ran his hand down low over my abdomen, touching me at the apex of my legs and slipping between my thighs. I shivered, though not with cold, for suddenly my body was aflame, burning with the sweet heat of desire and love. I trembled with the need to be a part of him, to make him a part of me, inseparable in mind and heart and soul, to cleave his body into mine so that the joining would make us as one.

His fingers explored me gently, so gently, sliding inside me until they met my unbreached maidenhead. I gasped and he went still. He kissed me softly, as if in apology, then slid his body over me and against me, spreading my legs with his knees while his mouth went on tantalizing me beyond my control, until I wept with desperate, desperate need.

As his strong, dark hands caught my wrists and pressed them into the bed above my head, he whispered almost regrettably, "I will hurt you only this once, my love. Forgive me."

His entry was swift, complete, drawing from me a sudden cry of pain that was banished the moment he began moving against me. Tears rose unbidden to my eyes, tears of joy and ecstasy and, yes, tears of distress. For even then he belonged to another. The thought of him loving someone else as intimately as he was loving me tore at my heart. I hoped—prayed—that I should die that moment in his arms. For how would I continue without him now?

I opened my eyes to find him watching me. I turned my head away toward the fire, but tenderly he caught my face in his palm and forced it back toward his own. Sliding his thumb over my damp cheeks, he said softly, with a hint of regret, "Did I hurt you?"

I shook my head, unable to speak.

"Aye," he said, "I hurt you and I'm sorry."

I touched his face, memorized its contours, and he began moving once again until the ancient magic crept in upon me, upon us both, drowning out all sight and sound, encompassing us in abandon that was so intense it bordered on pain. Aye, we were inseparable: fused, two parts of a whole come together at last. We strove toward the top and found it together, touched the splendor and held it for several pulsing moments until it settled as softly as nightfall on our shoulders.

"I'll never leave you," he whispered again. "My love, my life, trust me. We will be together as man and wife . . . somehow."

Somehow.

Opening my eyes and shaking free of the memory, I stared out the window toward Malham, and felt my heart break again with new pain.

I had just decided to unpack my valise when a knock came softly on my door. My first instinct was to spring, but remembering Wyndham's order of three knocks and nothing more, I waited. Again the gentle rapping, continuous, before Matilda's singsong voice called, "Miss, are y' there?"

"Aye." I released my breath, laughing at my own nervousness.

"Miss Adrienne has asked t' see y', lass. Come quickly, as she'll most likely be waitin' tea."

Dropping the valise to the bed, I hurried to the door. Matilda beamed up at me, her cheeks dimpling and her eyes narrowing beneath her extraordinary smile. " 'ave y' settled, luv?" she asked. "Are y' comfortable in that room?"

"It's wonderful," I answered. "I can see all of Malham from my window."

We walked together down the corridor, Matilda holding the candle before us. Having forgotten my wrap, I hugged myself tightly as Matilda responded, "Aye, y've a luvely view from that window. Malham is a good township, I vow, and I'm certain y'll like it 'ere. She's changin' ever day, though, and not always for the better."

"Oh?"

"Aye. The Crown Inn used to be the Cock and Bottle, y' know. Ole Kerry Barnes moved in last summer once the proprietor of t' Bottle died. He renamed t'owd place Crown and the ale ain't been near so good . . . so ole Jim says, o' course."

We continued our journey in silence. I did my best to acquaint myself with the surroundings, knowing as I turned one corner after another that I would find myself lost when attempting to return to my quarters. The corridors were like a rat's maze, the passageways shooting off to each side in unending tunnels of darkness. There was nothing there that would help me, so I devoted my energies on the fixtures along the hallway where I walked. As always there were paintings, of women mostly. Occasionally a table was placed against the wall, a mirror above it and sconces positioned on either side. Their light reflecting from the glass further brightened the hallway until we turned yet another corner.

"However will I find my way back?" I asked aloud.

Matilda continued walking, granting me no response.

Our pace quickened. She plodded steadily along, her breath like wisps of miniature clouds tumbling back over her shoulders. I caught a glance of my own breath as well. The cold stung my face and burned the inside of my throat. The tips of my fingers became numb.

I could see in the distance a pair of large double doors. Their sterling silver doorknobs glittered in the candlelight as we approached. Matilda knocked softly and called out, "Mum?"

"Come in."

I closed my eyes briefly as the servant pushed open the door. Matilda then stood aside and nodded for me to enter. I did so without hesitating.

The immenseness of the room was breathtaking. It stopped me short. The ceiling, no less than twenty feet high, was intricately painted. I might have been gazing at a colossal canvas of rolling hills, trees, and blue sky. From the center hung a chandelier of such enormous proportions I could but blink in amazement. At least two hundred candles blazed within the gold-and-crystal fixture.

"It is beautiful, isn't it?"

Startled, I looked around.

Adrienne Wyndham continued to stare at the ceiling. "It was my father's idea, you see. My mother was an invalid and rested day in and day out in that bed." She pointed toward the massive four-poster bed dressing the wall across the room. "The woman was always cold, so by painting the ceiling with scenes of summer he hoped to warm her. The chandelier is from Paris and big enough to cast light to each corner of the ceiling. As you can see, the area closest to the light could be scenes of morning. The far corners, where the light is dimmest, is dusk—won't you sit down, Miss Rushdon?"

I did so.

The door opened again. Trevor Wyndham swept in, throwing his cloak to Matilda, who smoothed it carefully over her forearm. He was smiling in that easy manner that had earlier made me feel less conspicuous in his presence. At no time, however, would I allow myself to forget that my hosts were class, pure to the blood, and I was a commoner. Even to sit in their presence, I felt, was an honor.

"Am I late?" he asked his sister.

"*Au contraire*. You are right on time. How is your patient?"

"Failing, I'm sorry to say. I don't give her a month. Is the tea hot?"

They looked at me.

"Shall I pour it?" I asked them.

Adrienne nodded, pleased. I did not miss the look she exchanged with her brother as I poured the steeped brew into the blue-and-white Meissen porcelain, and it suddenly occurred to me why I had been asked to these formidable quarters. Like all employees who were assigned to the manor, I should know my place. Perhaps they had been concerned that I did not?

"Are you settled?" Trevor asked. I nodded as he took his tea.

"Has Jim returned with your things?" Adrienne asked.

Folding my hands in my lap, I nodded again.

"Won't you have tea?" they both asked.

"No, thank you."

Adrienne sipped her tea before continuing. "I suppose you're curious as to why we've asked you here."

"You want to know more about me, I suppose. I come from Keighley. I lived with my uncle until recently, but he died of consumption. I saw the notice posted—"

"Were you working at the Bull?" Trevor said.

I looked him squarely in the face, aware of the meaning behind his question. "No," I responded.

He returned my appraisal, his blue eyes sharp with interest as they moved slowly over my face. "Have you been ill?" he asked.

My hands tightened within the folds of my skirt. How must I have appeared to him, a doctor? I had seen my reflection in mirrors and knew that the last two years had taken a toll on my appearance. My face was thin, and my eyes, already deeply set, appeared deeper yet. As I looked down at my hands I noted my fingers seemed overly long and the outline of my legs beneath my limp skirts was narrow. I weighed no more than seven stone, and being slightly over five feet and four inches, I was underweight.

"I have not been ill," I answered.

Sliding her cup and saucer onto the table at her side, Adrienne sat back in her chair. "We did not call Miss

Rushdon here to inquire on her health," she remarked flatly to her brother.

Trevor shrugged. "It is a hard habit to break, Adrienne, but you're right." He looked then to me. "We wish to talk to you about my brother."

"I see." Sitting back in my chair, I looked about the room a long moment before facing them again. "Did you wish to inform me that he's mad, perhaps?"

They each appeared stunned.

Smiling a little, I added, "He told me already."

"He told you?"

"He did, sir, and, I might add, I found the idea most amusing."

"Amusing?"

"Lord Malham is not mad. Angry perhaps. Perhaps he's upset over the death of his wife. Grief sometimes drains us of logic, you see. It makes us numb to certain responses. No, madness is irrational. Lord Malham is not irrational."

It was Adrienne who spoke next. Two spots of color blotched her cheeks as she stared at me down her straight, thin nose. "My brother's entire existence is irrational, Miss Rushdon. How can you say otherwise when you don't even know him?"

"I think madness is something that cannot be here and gone. The very idea that he suspects he is mad is evidence of his sanity. A truly mad person seldom acknowledges his condition. That's what makes them irrational, you see."

Adrienne's mouth dropped open.

Trevor lifted one brow and his mouth turned up in a half smile of appreciation. "Well said, Miss Rushdon, but while I would venture to say my brother is not totally mad, I will risk the chance of admitting he could snap at any moment. Which is why we have

called you here. For the past few months Nicholas
has been under a great deal of pressure. His memory
comes and goes with the moon, it seems, and at
times, though they be few, he has been violent. We
would caution you about accepting this commission,
for your own safety's sake."

I looked at my hands. "I am not afraid of his lordship, sir. I do not believe him mad, and I do not believe
he killed his wife."

Again they both sat in shocked silence.

Adrienne pressed her fingers against her temple. "I
feel a headache coming on, Trevor."

"Take a powder. Miss Rushdon, who told you Nick
killed his wife?"

"Why, he did, of course."

"He admitted it?"

"No. He admitted only that people suspected him of
the act."

Adrienne left her chair, spilling her lap blanket to
the floor. Dressed in a powder-blue dressing gown,
she paced to the window and back, one moment
wringing her white hands, the next twisting her fingers
round and round the light brown tendril of hair that
spilled over her shoulder. Trevor remained unmoved
but thoughtful. With one long leg crossed over the
other and one elbow propped on the chair arm, he
absently brushed his lower lip with his forefinger and
contemplated me.

"What shall we do?" Adrienne addressed her brother.
"This kind of thing cannot be tolerated any longer,
Trevor. Something has to be done to stop him before
word reaches the authorities."

"Certainly you don't believe he killed his wife," I
said.

They both stared at me, silent.

"The idea is ludicrous," I added. When they said nothing more I asked, "How did Lady Malham die?"

"In a stable fire," Trevor responded. His eyes still watched me intently.

"An accident perhaps. I cannot believe . . . they were married such a short time . . . He must have loved her—"

"You seem to know a great deal about Nicholas," he interrupted. "How so?"

"Everyone throughout Yorkshire knew of his engagement and marriage, sir. Nicholas Wyndham, Lord of Walthamstow and Earl of Malham, is well-known throughout His Majesty's court, I'm certain."

Trevor laughed. "Ah, my romantic child, did you think we dined with royalty when traveling to London? Perhaps we entertained King George in this dreary old house? We are the bastards of London society, my dear. Too many marriages outside our class, too many debts and too much heresy have, over the last generations, tainted our once spotless reputation."

Gripping the back of her chair, Adrienne rubbed her temple again and pleaded, "Oh, Trevor, please. Not in front of the girl."

"I can see you don't believe me," he said to me.

"Please," Adrienne wept. "Please don't continue."

"Our grandfather was insane. That's when the problems started, you see. He spent his last five years at the Hospital of Saint Mary of Bethlehem in Southwark, London. It is a matter of record, unfortunately, and I understand that many of our so-called equals actually paid money to stroll by his cage and view him. The family name, as you might suspect, could never fully recover. They've all been waiting for the next lunatic to surface and, unfortunately, he has. Nicholas."

Stunned, I sat back in my chair, unable to believe the horrible accusations Trevor Wyndham laid before me.

Adrienne whirled and continued her frantic pacing. "Damn him," she said aloud. "Nicholas ruined what little happiness I might have had with his idiotic babbling about madness and murder. What man in his right mind wants to marry into a family of lunatics?"

Trevor looked sleepily at his sister. "Oh, do sit down and stop the theatrics. Nick did you a tremendous favor by having a spell at your engagement party. Chester Beauchamp would have made you a sorry husband and you well know it."

"I hate him. I hate him, I tell you!" She pounded the chair with her fists.

I jumped from my seat, frightened by Adrienne's outburst. Perhaps it was my nature to comfort the distraught, perhaps merely a habit I had developed over the last months, but I found myself cradling the woman's shoulders in my arms, smoothing back the hair that clung to her wet cheeks while Trevor Wyndham looked on impassively.

"You should not hate him, Adrienne," Trevor said. "He cannot help what has happened to him any more than our grandfather could. We know little of the mind and its afflictions, so, for the time being, patience is a must. He does have his rational moments and during those times we should all do our best to support him. Now, I'm certain we've taxed Miss Rushdon enough."

He left his chair briskly and offered me his hand. I took it, but not before helping his sister into her chair.

Walking me to the door, he said, "I'm sorry to have put you through this, Miss Rushdon. But you must realize that committing your services to this family should take some thought. Our life here is far from typical, not as you might have suspected upon your arrival. Should you decide to stay I will only caution you to take extreme care with Nicholas. His mood swings are unpredictable. Should you experience any problems you will let me know immediately."

I nodded.

Trevor opened the door. "Good night, Miss Rushdon."

The door closed behind me. I stood in the dark, cold silence, my mind whirling in confusion. Perhaps I had misjudged Nicholas Wyndham after all. It seemed the entire world believed him mad—not only mad but capable of murder. Perhaps I did not know him at all, had never known him. Perhaps I had come to believe in my own fantasies, no less fanciful than a child's. No, I did not know him. Had never known him.

I had just moved away from the door when it opened again. I waited, and in a moment Adrienne Wyndham's slim form slipped into the hallway. She stared at me. Her fingers gripped her dressing gown tightly about her throat, and I watched as a tiny stream of breath from her lips dissolved into the darkness.

"Miss Rushdon," Adrienne addressed me in a small voice.

"Yes?"

Adrienne moved toward me with short steps. When we stood face to face, she smiled briefly. "You were very kind," she said. "I fear Trevor has grown too stoic where emotion is concerned. It has been necessary for him to do so, considering his profession, you understand . . ."

"Yes," I responded.

Lowering her voice further, she said, "Help Nicholas if you can. Trevor is determined that the only way to excuse his behavior is to accept it. I cannot accept it, you see, but neither can I help him. I am still too damnably angry at him for leaving me. You see, Nick and I were very close, but since this malady has come upon him . . ." She looked at her hands. "It is like looking at the most beautiful being in your life and suddenly finding him horribly scarred. I simply cannot face him, and that frightens me."

I touched Adrienne's hands, stilling their nervous wringing. "Perhaps he's frightened, too, milady," I said. She looked up.

"Will—will you stay with him? Help him? He's so desperately alone now, except for the child. The child is his life, the only one who can accept him as he is. Were it not for the child . . ."

"Of course."

"You believe in him . . . ?"

"Of course."

Turning back toward the door, she chanced one last glance at me before closing it between us.

Blackness again. The cold settled inside me, yet all I could think of was the child in Nick's arms. I knew then what I must do, what I had to do, for my own sake as well as his.

The laughter came then, soft and low, as cold as the draft that stirred my skirts and made me shiver. He was as illusive as the shadow in which he stood, blacker than black, filling the emptiness of the hallway with his presence and the rich tone of his laughter. As he stepped more into the light I could see he was wearing a dinner jacket of dark green velvet and a shirt of white linen. At his throat he wore a cravat of expensive white silk and upon it, a jade the size of a cat's eye winked in the candlelight.

"You see," he said. That was all. Only "You see."

I stood inside my chamber, listening to my lord's footsteps diminish in the distance. Then silence again.

Once I had craved the tranquillity of solitude, but this soundlessness seemed oppressive, and it made me shiver. I had not realized until that moment how alone I was, yet . . .

I did not *feel* alone.

Shrugging off the bothersome feeling, I changed into my bedclothes and climbed into bed. Staring toward the steady candle flame on my dresser, I convinced myself, again, that what I was doing was right. There would be no turning back.

The candlelight wavered and a thin stream of black smoke coiled up toward the ceiling. And then the cry, long and shrill and painful, sending tremors up my arms and causing my heart to stop. Leaping from my bed, I threw open my window, gasping as a rush of frigid air swept round me. Again the cry, more distant now. To my frightened ear, it seemed as if it came from the direction of the . . . stables.

Forcing myself to smile, I said aloud, "Henrietta. It is only Henrietta." Then closing my windows and drape I crawled back into bed, stared at the steady candle flame, and hugged my pillow to my breast.

Chapter 4

I dreamt again of the darkness. The cloying, suffocating darkness. It washed over me, cold and damp, so I fought out of fear to battle it back. If I didn't hurry *they* would come: the ones with the hands to grip my skirts and arms and legs. They would call me evil and shame me. They would threaten to cut off my hair. They would beat me or starve me. They might even kill me.

"Help me," I tried to whimper. "Oh, help me."

Where was Jerome?

Dead.

"Oh, no. No!" I wept.

I pushed away from my pillow, forcing open my eyes, telling myself that it was all a dream as I rolled my legs from the bed. Focusing on the tiny room, I drew in great lungfuls of cold air that made me cough. *You're safe*, I told myself. No more hands coming at me from the darkness. No more darkness.

The candle flame sputtered. Its halo of orange light flickered erratically about the walls and furniture in the room: a chest of drawers, an armchair, its high back covered with rosebud carvings. They all seemed distorted in size as the light played back and forth in the draft of wind that found its way under the door.

I had just stumbled from the bed, grabbed up a new

candle, and prepared to light it before the other went out when the knock came.

Once. Twice. Three times.

I stared at the doorknob and held my breath.

Silence.

Again. *Knock. Knock. Knock.*

With trembling fingers I swept up the key from the chest and moved swiftly to the door. Thrusting the key into the lock, I hesitated, then twisted it a fraction until the bolt slid into place. I stepped back as the door swung open.

He smelled of mist, of leather and sherry and . . . dirt. The wet hem of his cloak clung to his muddied knee-high boots. His face was chafed red and his hair, curling slightly from the dampness tumbled over his brow.

"Miss Rushdon," came his quiet voice. "I've disturbed you."

"No, my lord." I lowered the candle, feeling those gray eyes travel over my person. It was only then I realized that I'd forgotten to don my dressing gown before responding to his knock. Knowing the sheer material of my nightdress hid little from his perusal, I crossed one arm over my breasts. Tilting my head a little, I looked at him from under my lashes and asked, "Have you a need for me now, my lord?"

One end of his mouth curled up. "Aye," he said, huskily.

"If you'll allow me to change—"

"Don't bother." His hair stirred. So did the tail of his cloak. Hunching his shoulders more closely to his body, he added, "You're fine as you are."

I accompanied him to his studio.

I stood amidst the tented works of art that cluttered each corner of the room, feeling as if I had stumbled into a child's playroom. Swatches of bright and dull paints covered the walls and sheets were tossed randomly over easels and canvases.

"Sit there," came his voice, I sensed rather than saw that he pointed toward the stool near the window. I took my place atop it and stared at the window, my back to him. I watched his distorted reflection in the panes of glass as he discarded his cloak, letting it fall to the floor. Then he stood with his hands at his sides and stared at me.

Feeling panic rise inside me, I asked, "Is there something wrong, my lord?" Only then did I look over my shoulder, where my gown lay threadbare against my shivering skin.

Wyndham's face looked white but for the spots of color in his cheeks. His eyes were the color of cold ash. He pointed to the knot of hair I'd wound atop my head before climbing into bed. "Release your hair."

Lifting my hands, my fingers numb with cold, I fumbled with the combs until the heavy black coil tumbled over my shoulder. When I looked at him again his eyes were narrowed.

He moved toward me slowly, in all his catlike grace, his presence enough to suck the very air from the quarters, leaving me weak and uncertain. I tried to search his eyes, but they were vacant. What memories lingered there? I wondered. What was left, if anything, of the Nicholas Wyndham I once had known?

He stopped, stood beside me a long moment before reaching out and catching a tendril of my hair. My heart raced, and the memories—*my* memories—came tumbling forth. I thought back to when he had touched my hair that first time, and the memory rocked me with an impact no less forceful than it had that blustery spring day on the moor.

"Don't be frightened," he told me. "I have no intention of hurting you."

"I'm not frightened," I assured him before looking back toward the window. I watched him as he studied my profile.

"Beautiful," he said before turning back to his canvas.

I sat on my chair, unmoving, like a bird on a perch. The cold gathered about me, seeped into my skin so my bones ached and my fingers and toes grew so numb it hurt to move them. It was little enough sacrifice, I thought, for the rewards that would eventually follow.

I watched him in the panes, hour after endless hour, and was sorry when the dawn deleted the faceted image on the glass.

He put down his brush and pallet of paints.

Sliding from the stool, I stretched the stiffness from my legs and back and shoulders before venturing toward the easel. His voice stopped me.

"Come away from there," he said.

I smiled to myself, thinking he was only bluffing.

"I said,"—he stepped between me and the canvas—"no."

I stepped away then, as quickly as possible, though in that brief moment the heat of his body had warmed me. I threw my head back, intention meeting his eyes without flinching. But though I tried desperately, I could not. Those eyes, like steel, cut into me like a sword.

"You will never, under any circumstances, take liberties in this room," he told me. "When—if I should decide to allow you to view the painting, I will let you know."

Bully, I thought.

"That will be all, Miss Rushdon."

I turned and left the room, feeling his eyes behind me. I closed the door and waited. Nothing.

Returning to my room, I climbed onto my bed, dragged the heavy counterpane up over my shoulders, and tucked it beneath my chin. My entire body was numb, but it was a numbness that I had grown accustomed to. The cold had never bothered me. It was my constitution, after all. I was thick-skinned like my father. Or so my mother, dead fifteen of my twenty-three years, had told me once.

No, the cold didn't bother me. It was the darkness. I had never, never liked the dark; even as a child, before Menston and its prison of shadows with nothing but the moon to illuminate the bleak stone corridors. Night played foul tricks on my mind, turning chairs into wolf demons that hunkered in corners, waiting to pounce on me if I dared close my eyes. It hid a childhood demon under my bed, with his skeletal hands ready to nab me should I venture off my mattress during the night.

Now I stared at the candle, the vague shapes of chairs more distinct as the early morning mist whirled in clouds against my window. I stared at the candle and wondered what wolf demons possessed Nicholas Wyndham. I would slay them if I knew. I would, I thought, as I had learned to slay my own.

Minutes later I was summoned by Matilda. "Miss Adrienne wishes to see y'," she called from outside my door. "Hurry, miss."

Leaving my bed, I pulled on the same dress I'd worn the day before. I had no others. I raked my fingers through my hair, letting the black curls tumble where they may: over my shoulders to my waist, around my face. Having no ribbon to tie it back, I supposed it would have to do, this maiden's way of wearing it. I laughed bitterly at the thought before whirling toward the door.

Adrienne Wyndham sat alone in the morning room, her brow wrinkled in consternation as she studied the paper in her hand. I stood in the doorway of the slightly shabby apartment, noting the faded Persian rug, as threadbare as my gown, and the discolored silver service placed on the table near her knee.

"This will never do," I heard her mumble.

"What will never do?" came the voice behind me.

I whirled, startled by Trevor's appearance. He smiled down at me as Adrienne said, "Miss Rushdon, come in."

"Yes," Trevor added. "Never dally at Walthamstow. Speak up and let your presence be known."

He took my arm and ushered me into the room.

He continued, "I trust, dear sister, that you are perusing this week's menu. You won't tax yourself?"

"Hoity boy," she came back. Her mood was clearly much lighter than it had been last evening. "You are up and about very early, Trevor."

"So I am."

"Business?"

"Isn't it always?" He took a chair opposite Adrienne. It was a straight-back Jacobean with a faded seat, and flanked by urns of feathery ferns. I continued to stand until he said, "Sit down," and wagged a finger toward a crewel-seated armchair. I took my place in it and waited.

"I spent a miserable night," Adrienne told him. "I didn't sleep a wink." Folding her hands in her lap, she said, "Perhaps a few of your powders . . . ?"

"Absolutely not. You know how I feel about that."

Adrienne lifted one brow and looked at me. "Have

you ever known a physician, Miss Rushdon, who refuses to treat his patients when they are in need?"

"By gosh," he said. "You do me a great injustice, Adrienne."

"Were I fat old Phineas Clark you would heap me with cures."

"Not so. Were you fat old Phineas Clark I would tell you you had dropsy and to cut out the sherry."

A servant entered the room then, a young girl about my age. She dipped first to Trevor, then to Adrienne. "You sent for me, mum?"

Adrienne picked up the paper in her lap. "Our stores are low, miss. How did this happen?"

"An oversight, mum."

I watched the girl's face color.

"Whose oversight?"

The servant chewed on her lower lip and cast down her eyes.

"Ach!" Adrienne announced harshly. "Don't bother to reply. You're covering up for Nicholas. Has he failed again to satisfy our creditors? He has, hasn't he? Now they've cut us off?"

Trevor cleared his throat, glancing from his sister to me.

Adrienne ignored him. "How long must this continue?" she asked to no one in particular. "He is totally incapable as head of the family, Trevor. When will you do something?"

"Leave it alone," he said a bit tiredly. Then dismissing the girl with a wave of his hand, he added, "I'll remind Nicholas when I see him."

"You coddle him too much," his sister said. "You'll make him delicate in the end."

He stretched his legs out and crossed them at the ankles. Tipping his head toward me, so his brown hair slid over his brow, he asked, "How was your first night at Walthamstow, Miss Rushdon? Comfortable?"

"Yes, thank you." Glad the subject of Nick's illness was temporarily forgotten, I began to relax. "We had our first session this morning."

"Indeed?" they said in unison.

"How was his behavior?" Adrienne asked, leaning forward in anticipation.

"Normal," I responded.

"Painting like a demon throughout the night is hardly normal," Adrienne countered. "Did you, by chance, catch a peek at any other paintings in the room?"

I shook my head.

Trevor laughed. "You see, he has won her over already, Adrienne. I applaud your loyalty, Miss Rushdon."

"The truth," I told him, setting my chin stubbornly. "I saw nothing, not even my own portrait."

"I wonder what he hides there," Adrienne said.

Cutting his blue eyes from me to his sister, Trevor admitted, "It is none of our business."

A warning note rang in his words, settling into every nook and cranny in the cluttered room. Finally Adrienne collected her menu, took up her sewing bag from the floor, and announced, "I see I've ventured from my bed too early in the day. I'm fatigued, Trevor. You will forgive me?"

I left my chair. "Ma'am, you asked to see me?"

She looked surprised. "Yes. Yes, I suppose I did." Coloring slightly, she tucked her remnants beneath her arm. "Feel free to move about Walthamstow as you please, Miss Rushdon." With that she spun and left the room.

Then Trevor left his chair. "Your pardon, Ariel, but I have a patient due." He too left the room.

Finding myself alone, I thought there no better time than this to explore my new home.

I met Matilda in the hallway. Her short arms were curled around a pair of rose-painted slops as she beamed at me and announced, "Help's fer breakfast in t' kitchen, luv. Yer welcome t' join us."

I did so, gratefully.

The kitchen, a long room whose walls glittered with copper pans, was the first truly warm apartment I'd visited since arriving at Walthamstow. Servants hustled across floors that had turned black with age, taking turns at the chairs scattered around the antiquated rectangular table in the center of the room.

" 'ere now," Matilda announced. "Where's yer manners, ladies? Say 'ello t' the lass, 'ere."

They all looked around, some peering through wisps of hair, others righting their caps and smearing jammy fingers over their aprons.

Shoving the chamber jars into a frowning woman's arms, Matilda clucked her tongue. "Yer a sorry bunch, gapin' like y' just seen a specter. Close yer mouth, Polly."

A round-eyed woman with gray-streaked hair snapped shut her mouth to a chorus of giggles.

Matilda pointed me toward a rush-seated chair. "She's a mite thin," she said. "Given a few cakes with treacle she'll fatten up."

"She's right bonny," someone said.

I smiled my thanks as Matilda patted me reassuringly on my shoulders. "Aye, that she is. She's 'is lordship's new sitter, y' know."

"Y' don't say," Polly returned. "Finally found one 'e couldn't send runnin' down the road, did 'e?"

I eyed the sweet treacle hungrily as Matilda lathered it over several buttered cakes. "I don't find him frightening at all," I responded.

"You ain't seen 'im in one of 'is moods." It was Polly again. "Becomes a real fright, 'e does. Only one what can control 'im is 'is brother."

"Where you from?" someone else asked.

"Keighley," I answered.

"Me mum's from Keighley. Where 'bouts in Keighley?"

I avoided the question, licking the treacle from my finger. "This is very good. My compliments to the cook."

A middle-aged woman, weighing no less than twelve stone, dropped heavily onto a chair and reared back. " 'e was grave walkin' last eve."

"Give over," Matilda said.

I sucked on my finger and watched the woman rock back and forth in her chair.

"Sure 'e was. I went down to Rockover with Pete. Was on me way home when I seen 'im at the cemetery. Standin' there like a ghoul over 'is wife's grave, 'e were."

"Did 'e howl?" Polly asked, taking a chair herself. Several of the women laughed nervously. I, however, did not. She sniffed and went on. "I'll be expectin' to hear any day that 'e's dug her up and driven a stake through her breast."

"Good riddance," Matilda said. "She were a witch and deserved what she got."

A murmur of agreement followed.

"I, for one, am glad she's gone." The young servant I had earlier met in the morning room poured herself coffee.

Lifting one brow, Polly leaned slightly over the table

and said softly, " 'Cordin' to 'is lordship she ain't. Jane's come back t' haunt 'im."

I sat back in my chair.

Matilda shook her head. "Y'll stop spreadin' such rumors, Polly. There ain't no such thing as ghosts."

" 'oo says?" she responded, looking to each of our startled faces. "Y' can't deny that some mighty strange things 'ave been goin' on 'round 'ere of late. Why, just last week a tin of Miss Adrienne's best tea went missin'. One evenin' it were there, the mornin' it were gone." Narrowing her eyes, she added, "Just yesterday a plate of scones vanished practically under our noses."

"Don't be daft," Matilda scolded. "Ghost don't eat anyhows."

" 'oo says?"

The younger servant repeated, "Well, Jane's gone and good riddance. I could never see what Lord Malham saw in 'er in the first place. She treated Samantha poorly, I vow. That's why Sammy buggered off."

"Samantha buggered off 'cause she seen the murder," Polly argued.

They began a mighty discussion then about Lady Jane's death that made me lose my appetite. I pushed my dish away, with its uneaten cakes and treacle still piled high atop it. I thought of telling those loose-tongued women that they owed Nicholas Wyndham some loyalty. He was their employer, after all. Finally deciding it was no business of mine, I excused myself and exited the kitchen through the back door.

"There goes a strange one," I heard Polly say.

The day was clear. The moor rose green and high on the horizon and the air was sharp with the smell of peat. I drank it in until my head swam dizzily with the musty aroma, until I felt my blood sing in my veins.

The cat caught my eye, black as night with eyes the

color of buttercups. It looked at me steadily, one paw
raised and hooked slightly over its nose. The fur about
its mouth was white with cream. Going down on one
knee, I held out my hand and called, "Kitty, kitty."

It eyed me suspiciously. Finally it padded over, arc-
ing its back as it weaved round and round my hand.
My first friend, I thought, smiling. Scooping him up in
my arms, I continued walking down the path past the
overgrown gardens, where the withered stalks of poppies rattled together in the breeze. I walked several
minutes before turning and looking back.

"Walthamstow," I said aloud. Had I really spent my
first night there? Aye, the first of many, I reminded
myself.

The house rose like a mountain against the sky; from
each of her stone chimneys coiled a wreath of gray-
blue smoke. Her annexes stretched east and west, and
were obscured partially by trees that lifted their leafless
branches toward the sky. A rook perched atop the highest tree, balancing with a flap of his black wings as the
branch swayed back and forth in the wind.

The child's squeal of delight wrenched me from my
daydreams, daydreams too often filled with Walthamstow and Nicholas Wyndham. Again I reminded myself
of my reasons for coming here.

I turned back down the path, clutching the cat to
my breast harder and harder each time I heard Kevin's
laughter. Giving up my patience, I began to run, finally
leaving the well-trod path for one less obvious.

The glass-smooth pond lay serenely against a back-
drop of whip-thin rushes and blooming roses. Any
other time I might have considered the place paradise.
I could do nothing now, however, but stand and stare,
mute in my horror, as the child tottered toward the
muddy shoal and brackish, lily-covered water.

The cat yowled and twisted in my arms as I began to run. "Come away from there!" I called out. My eyes searched frantically for Bea, but there was no one there. Fear blinded me to all but the tiny tottering image in the distance. "Come away from there!" I screamed it now as he stumbled down the grassy incline, his short, pudgy arms waving out to his sides.

I reached him the very moment he fell. He tumbled into my arms and I swept him up, sinking to my ankles in the lichen-covered mud. Burying my face in his fine hair, I closed my eyes and drenched my senses in his musty child-smell. "Oh, Kevin," I whispered. "Kevin."

Opening my eyes, I found Bea standing at the edge of the rose brambles, watching. Her eyes glittered like jacinthe in the half-light; she bared her teeth in a way that reminded me of a jackal.

"Give him to me," came her voice over the croaking of frogs. Her clawlike hands lifted as she plodded toward me.

I shook my head. "Nay, I will not. You were remiss in watching him. He might have fallen—"

"Give him to me."

I clutched him to me. "Nay," I argued. "I shan't. I shall inform his lordship—"

"Go on and tell him. He'll have forgotten by dusk." The crone laughed in her throat. "Sick, sick man. Deranged man, now give me the child."

"But you were remiss—"

"He slipped away. We were picnicking there." She pointed over her shoulder. Then plunging her hand in the deep pocket of her skirt, she pulled out a squirming kitten. "I was chasing the animal, Kevin's pet. You must understand . . ." Her bony head tilted; she watched me from the corner of her eyes.

In that moment I realized how I must have looked,

desperate and clinging like a . . . I staggered toward the carpet of brown wilted grass and placed him upon it. He ran to the hag and I turned away, fixing my eyes on the opaque water until I was certain they were gone.

Only then did I collapse on the ground. I yearned to beat it; I almost did. But the blood on my arms halted the tantrum. With my fist upraised, I stared at the thin bloody grooves running the length of each arm. The cat; I hadn't even realized.

No longer so angry, I sat with arms propped upon my knees and stared at the spider's web crisscrossed between two rushes. I wanted nothing more than to leave this place. But I was bound to it in blood. Dedication to my cause was as great as my need for revenge. Greater, I realized in that moment. Far greater.

What had happened to the hate that had sustained me through those bleak hours in Menston? The hate that had pumped new life into my lungs, even as Jerome took his last dying breath?

Hate then had a face, a name. Wyndham. Nicholas Wyndham. I hated him even as I ached for him, and asked them all: why? Why had he done it? Lied, cheated, and made me a fool. He'd been so good at it, so wretchedly convincing. I had been so certain that he loved me.

As I sat there brooding, immersed in my past, I thought: I hope his conscience has driven him mad.

Chapter 5

Upon entering Trevor Wyndham's quarters I was not a little startled to find his brother there, standing with his back to me, before a window, his hands clasped casually behind him. As I stopped at the door, I heard Trevor's voice clearly from within.

"You were to meet me for cards last eventide, Nick. Where were you?"

"I don't remember. There. Isn't that what you expected of me?"

"How is your head?"

"Cracking."

"You should try sleeping."

"I cannot sleep."

"Have you heard the voices again? . . . Nick?"

"What's it to you?"

Trevor, without turning, moved from one table laden with bottles to another strewn with papers. "You went out last eve, Nick. Do you know that?"

"I told you—"

"You had several pints with Jim at the inn. You two have grown as thick as Damon and Pythias." Trevor looked over his shoulder. "Do you think it healthy?"

The response was a moment in coming. "Leave Jim alone. He is my friend."

"If he were your friend he would not continue to

perpetuate these notions you have. And it is one thing
to feel some sort of gratitude toward him—he did save
your life, or so he says—but I would caution you to
leave it at that. The man has an over fondness for
bitters, Nick, and you hardly need that . . . atop everything else."

I cleared my throat.

Trevor turned. My lord, however, did not.

"Miss Rushdon." Trevor approached me, smiling.
"You're quiet as a cat," he told me.

"I'm sorry."

"No bother." He stopped as he noticed my arms.
"Lord God! What has happened?"

Lord Malham partially turned from the window. His
face was without expression. But I could not turn from
his eyes nonetheless. "The cat," I finally managed.

Trevor took a closer look at the scratches. "What a
bloody mess," he said. "What cat did it?"

"A black one with yellow eyes."

"Belzeebub. The damnable animal is a nuisance, always filching our cream. Come into the light so I can
see you better."

I watched his hands moving tenderly over my arms.
"It isn't bad," I assured him. "But Matilda thought I
should see you."

He flashed me a smile. "Good for her." Then he
reached for a bottle and clean linens. "Push up your
sleeves," he told me.

I looked up from his concerned blue eyes, feeling
my face warm.

He laughed. "What a proper girl you are, and shy. I
assure you, Miss Rushdon, baring your elbows to my
eyes will hardly mar your reputation."

"I'd rather not," I told him.

"Very well, then." He proceeded to touch the lacerations with the soaked cloths. The scratches burned frightfully, and I winced. "There now," he said more softly, "is it too awful, Miss Rushdon?"

"No, sir," I replied. "I can bear it."

"You're a strong lass. Isn't she, Nick?"

I waited for my lord's response, but none came. Finally, unable to refrain, I looked and found him staring at me, his mouth set in a harsh line.

I could not help but notice his appearance. There was a manner of pride, still, in his stance, though his shoulders appeared a little too stiff and therefore formal for this occasion. He wore a jacket of the finest broadcloth, cut closely to his body. His breeches were fawn leather and fit him snugly. He had fine thighs.

"There now." Trevor turned away and dropped the cloths in a basket. "I'll send a portion of this potion with you, Miss Rushdon, so you may continue to bathe your arms."

I lowered the bruised limbs obediently. "What do I owe you?" I asked him.

"Owe me?" He shot me a disarming smile. "Perhaps a bit of conversation some lonely eventide, Miss Rushdon. Nothing more." He handed me the potion. "Cleanse the wounds thrice a day, please, and let me check them this time tomorrow."

I thanked him with a smile and turned for the door.

I had walked only a little way into the hall when Lord Malham's voice stopped me. "Hold up, Miss Rushdon."

I turned.

He stood in the doorway, filling it with his presence, and surveyed me with eyes that revealed none of his thoughts. "Should I help you to your room?" he asked me.

I checked my surprise. "No," I said. "The scratches are on my arms, milord, not my feet."

His face thawed, if only for a moment. He smiled a little, and my heart, traitor that it was, took wing at the sight. I had cracked that veneer of bitterness and anger. As his mouth—once as precious a treasure to me as owned by any king—curled up and dimpled his cheek, I forgot my own bitterness and anger long enough to smile back.

I turned and continued down the hall. He joined me, easily matching my stride.

"I assume you've had time to tour the house, Miss Rushdon?"

"I have, sir."

"Ah. Then you've greeted the help." We turned a corner. His elbow bumped me and he pardoned himself, putting a slightly greater distance between us. "I assume you've been informed, then, on all the gory details."

"If you are aware of their tongues, milord, you could dismiss them."

"Yes I could. But you see, therein lies a problem. No one wants to work for a lunatic. They know it, of course, and bleed my pocket dry because of it." He did not speak again for a long moment. Then, "Are you up to posing again, Miss Rushdon?"

"When and where?" We stopped outside my door.

I looked at him boldly, though my heart was constricting in my chest. Not out of fear—oh, no—he had never frightened me. Not then, not now, despite the gossipmongers, despite his self-recriminations and doubts. "Where?" I repeated more firmly.

His gray eyes pinned me. "There is a pond a short walk from the house—"

"I know it."

"There are roses blooming. In the afternoon there is a nice light—"

"At what hour, milord?"

"Two-ish, I think."

"I will be there." I turned for my door.

"Ariel."

I froze, my name sounding on his tongue like a lover's lament. I circled to face him and met his eyes.

He lifted his head to gaze beyond me. "Thank you," he said. And without looking at me again he turned on his heel and walked gracefully back down the hall.

At two sharp I sat waiting on the marble bench set to one side of the pond. There was no hope of sun. The afternoon shadows were long and gray, and even as I watched, the colors faded from the landscape, turning as bleak as the muted windows of the distant manor house. The moon ascended among the clouds, a seemingly transparent orb that vanished moments after its awakening. With its appearance came an uncanny stillness that left me wishing Nicholas would arrive as he had promised.

Huddling close beneath my cloak, I continued to wait, surrounded by great, dense trees and withered briars that formed a sort of lair to hide me. The air became colder. For some minutes I experienced a heightened anticipation; the feeling that I was about to be joined by someone was so strong I left my seat and stared at the vague path across from me. I saw the leaves of a shrub tremble. The limbs and foliage of a tree swayed aside and yet all else was still.

"Is anyone there?" I called out.

No response.

How dark the day seemed to me. How deep the shadow surrounding me. Suddenly a wild and cold wind rose, sobbing over the distant moor, and, unable to hold in my fear any longer, I grabbed up the hem of my cloak and hurried back to Walthamstow.

Entering through the kitchen door I knew immediately that all was not right. Polly stood wringing her hands, and the young woman who had earlier been confronted by Adrienne stood weeping, a handkerchief pressed to her face.

Then I heard the wail, long and pitiful and full of misery.

Leaving the kitchen, I hurried down the corridor, pulling open my cloak as I ran. The crying seemed to be coming from the same morning room I'd visited earlier.

"You horrible, horrible man," Adrienne cried aloud. "Fiend! How could you do this to me?"

I listened for a response. There was none.

"Monster! You have the heart of a devil!"

My lungs burning, I stopped at the door and looked upon the tragic scene. Adrienne sat on her chair in a powder-blue gown among mounds of white tissue paper, her face streaked with tears. She gripped between her trembling hands a length of exquisite white lace. I was too afraid to look across the room, dreading who I would find there.

My lord Malham.

Tall and dark and silent, his face a cold mask, he stood with his back to the fireplace, as erect and still as the carved caryatids supporting the elaborate Italian mantle. He did not even blink as she railed at him.

"Beast! You are a beast and I would bleed myself dry if it meant separating myself from you completely!"

Spying me then, her eyes flashing and her nostrils distended with fury, she lifted her shaking finger and announced, "Behold the monster, Miss Rushdon; the man you believe is of sound mind and noble heart. He has broken my heart again and—cruel, cruel man, I hate you for doing this to me. I hate you!"

She crumbled before our eyes. I waited, uncertain what Nicholas would do. He did nothing, just remained stolid and unmoving. Unable to bear Adrienne's distress a moment longer I hurried over and wrapped my arms around her.

"There now," I comforted. "It cannot possibly be so bad."

"Why does he loathe me so?" Her shoulders shook as she wept. Yet even as she reproached him, she clutched the lace against her bosom like a treasure. "What have I done that he should want to hurt me this way?"

"What has he done?" I asked.

Opening her fingers, she lifted the material. "A gift."

A gift? "It's beautiful. But why—"

"A *wedding* gift." Her voice broke as she struggled to say, "This was to be my wedding day. I had put it from my mind until . . . *he* ruined it. Spoiled my chances of ever being happy, of marrying the only man I will ever love. And now this. He comes sauntering in here with a gift tucked beneath his arm: wedding lace! Then wishes me happiness on my wedding day. Oh, loathsome, loathsome man, I wish you had died in that fire with your spiteful wife. Then you both could have burned in hell for an eternity!"

I turned my face to his. Eyes like cold, hard stone fixed me.

"Behold the lunatic and monster," he said quietly, his lips twisting just short of a smile. Turning then, he walked out the door.

I summoned Trevor from his apartments. Both of us helped Adrienne to her quarters. Her weeping filled the long corridors and echoed deep into Walthamstow's closed-off chambers, and I knew, wherever Nicholas had gone, he could hear her.

Adrienne's apartment was overly warm. Light from smoldering wood-ash radiated from the hearth, from the chandelier overhead, and from a dozen lanterns set about the room. Trevor tossed aside the faded mulberry curtains that draped from the tester of her bed, and we settled the distraught woman onto her banked pillows.

"Adrienne, you must try to calm yourself." Trevor squeezed her hand in concern. "I'm certain Nick meant no harm."

"Meant no harm! Why do you continue to excuse him?"

"It's his memory, darling, he simply forgot—"

"Forgot that he shamed me? Ruined me? Has forever made me a spinster?"

She lapsed into a crying fit again. "I wish I need never have to put eyes on him again! He has hurt me abominably and I shall never forgive him!" As Adrienne continued to weep into her hands, Trevor turned to the mahogany table beside her bed. He poured water from a ewer into a glass, then into the glass poured a tiny phial of powder. He gave it a quick stir with his finger, then lifted the glass up to her mouth. She gulped it down quickly, then relaxed on her pillows.

Standing away from the bed, Trevor looked at me, his dark-brown eyebrows drawn severely over his nose. "What has brought this about, Ariel?"

I picked the lace off the floor where Adrienne had thrown it. "A gift, sir, from your brother. A wedding gift."

He took it in his hands and studied it with pressed lips before crumpling it in his fists. "Damnation, it's his first flareup in a while. I had hoped . . ." Looking directly at me, he asked, "Will you stay with her a while? I've a patient waiting."

I could hardly refuse.

When he had gone I took my place beside Adrienne's bed on a Chippendale stool with cabriole legs. In a moment her weeping had dissipated to little more than an occasional shuddering breath. I began to relax, and thought her asleep until she startled me by saying:

"No doubt this is all my mother's fault." Her head rolled. She blinked sleepily at me, her blue eyes pale and slightly puffy. "My mother was a witch, you see, as stern as a pope and as unbending as a dictator. My father often said, 'Watch my sons; as men they will harbor gross hatred for all the female gender.' It has happened, as I see it. Nicholas hated my mother, his wife, and now me. He would like nothing better than to destroy us all, I think."

I realized it was the powders talking: I knew their impairments as well as their benefits. But I listened nevertheless, enthralled.

She covered her forehead with her arm. I thought in that moment that she was a very pretty woman, her lashes pale brown and her skin unblemished like a white cameo.

She sighed. "My mother died in this very bed just days after my brother's marriage to Jane. They were still on their honeymoon in London. When she grew ill we sent Jim to fetch him home, but of course Nicholas arrived too late. He came moments after she took her final breath." She indicated a certain place on the floor near the foot of the bed. "He stared upon her still face and called her 'bitch.' Poor, poor Nickie. How I pitied him in that moment. Even more than I pitied my mother. He had given up everything, you see. Everything he had loved in his life to please her—my mother. Why must we struggle throughout our lives to please our parents? Oh, Nickie, if you had only waited. You should have known that marrying Jane would never have been enough to win the dragon-lady's approval."

I sat upon my stool, the bottom of my shoes resting lightly on its claw-and-ball feet, and the heart in my breast drew up into a hard, brittle knot. I turned my gaze from Adrienne's waxen face and stared at the window, my eyes full and burning with tears. Understanding drummed in my head and I too hated Lady Millicent Wyndham for what she had done to Nicholas . . . and to me.

Adrienne's voice came more softly then, and slowly. I brushed away my tears before facing her again.

"My beautiful, beautiful Nickie, so fair and gentle. He was the only one of my brothers who pampered me. George and Eugene and Trevor thought me no more than a nuisance and scolded me if I ventured too close to their treasured belongings. Not my Nickie. He would have cut the heart from his breast and given it to me if I had asked for it. Then. But when Father died—oh how she clung, wrecking his youth and using her sickness to get from him what she wanted."

She drifted peaceably, her lower lip quivering only slightly as she murmured, "Too young to hear this burden of nobility, this wretched title—lord, lord—hardly a man and knowing so little of life. Too many responsibilities and her dragging him down. Then Jane came. Wretched woman. Handpicked by Mother. Just like Mother, making demands of Nickie, of me, moving into this house, calling herself *Lady* Malham and taking more than he could afford to give her. I hated her. Cruel, vicious woman like my mother. I told him . . ."

Her head rolled back and forth. Slipping from my chair, I soothed her warm, smooth brow with my hand

and said, "Hush now, milady. He didn't mean it. He wouldn't hurt you intentionally."

"I told him . . . I hate her . . . I wish she were dead . . ."

My hand paused.

"Dead," she repeated, her word a whisper through her dry lips. "God forgive me . . . I wish she were . . ."

I pulled the counterpane up over her knees but no farther. Folding the length of white lace, I tucked it beneath her pillow, then quit the room.

I did not stop to think where I was going. I only went, mayhaps out of instinct, less out of common sense. I traveled mindlessly through the cold, dark corridors of Walthamstow, letting my thoughts muse over what had transpired these last awful minutes.

How Adrienne had disliked Nick's wife. Perhaps dislike was even too light a term. She had hated Jane because she was so like her mother, had hated her for making Nick so unhappy, had hated her for usurping her place in this house.

Passing through the kitchen, I spoke briefly to Matilda and Polly. Then, exiting the house, I followed the path I had walked earlier, continuing beyond the pond, past the magnificent orchard of cherry and pear trees. In my mind I recalled sitting at the foot of the hill near town in hopes of catching a brief glimpse of the young earl himself. It all seemed a lifetime ago, Nick's sauntering into my uncle's tavern and biding his time over warm pints and Havana cigars, while I could but crouch like a timid mouse in the shadows and watch him. I had known then that we would touch, for he was lonely and I was alone. And like the nightingale who waits patiently for its turn to sing, I waited until my season, anticipated my nights filled with laurel-sweet winds and song and Nicholas—always Nicholas.

The baying of the hounds brought my mind back to the present. I tucked my hands into my cloak and marched, head up, beyond the dog runs.

Jim looked round, his arms full of rakes and ropes and hoes, as I walked into the garden shed. His hair was grizzled and his paunch hinted of too many pints of ale, but his face was as friendly and pleasant to look upon as it had been on the morning of my arrival to Walthamstow.

"Good evenin' to y'," he greeted me.

"Good evening," I returned, smiling. "I am looking for the stables."

His brown eyes widened in surprise. "Will y' be needin' an animal?" he asked.

"I won't."

He watched me with curiosity, then caution. After a moment he proceeded. "I'm supposin' y'll be here t' see the *new* stables?"

I hesitated, suddenly aware of how odd my request would appear. I decided then that if Jim was indeed Nick's Damon, he would be willing to help me. I shook my head. "The *old* stables, or what is left of them."

He fixed me with eyes as sharp and searching as a hawk's. "There's nowt there, luv, but rubbish. It burned, y' know."

"I'm aware of that." I pulled my cloak closer about my shoulders.

He slowly began to unload his tools, then without another word he left the shed and walked off down the over-grown path running at an angle to the kennels. I followed at a distance. What drove me to stand among the scorched pilings and stone I could not guess. But some instinct told me it had all started here: the madness and mayhem that was crippling my lord's mind.

It was an eerie place in the half-light of approaching

dusk. Hidden from Walthamstow by horse-chestnut and gooseberry trees, the rubble was as bleak to look upon as death itself.

Looking up from beneath the hood of my cloak, I watched Jim as he ambled about the cinders, flaking the crisp ash from a timber with his toe. He hunched his shoulders against the cold north wind and stared at a particular spot. I sensed, in that awful moment that it was the place Jane had died. And I could not help but stare myself.

Finally Jim turned. Running one rough, red hand over his mouth, he asked, "Have y' seen wot y' come t' see, Miss Rushdon?"

I hesitated, then pushed on. "Were you here that eve, Jim?"

"Aye, I were."

I waited.

"Like hell it were," came his quiet, thoughtful voice. I found myself straining to hear it over the sudden gust of wind. "All the poor animals trapped there. The flames must have singed the very bottom of God's feet, they reached that high t' heaven. All them fine horses gone. It were a tragic loss, I tell y'."

"Jim," I said, "I know about Lady Jane."

"Ah!" Scowling, he shook his head and again looked toward the massive beam that lay partially burned through on the ground. "So the gossip-tongues 'ave been at y' already. Don't surprise me none. They'll be fillin' yer head with tales of hobgoblins and demons within a fortnight. A shame it is that they've got nowt else to' do besides ruin a man's fine reputation."

"Do you believe them?" I asked him outright.

"I only know what I found when I came here: flames risin' from perdition and blisterin' the sky, and my friend—his lordship—standin' just there and starin' like a dazed man into the flames."

"Do you know him well, Jim?"

"Aye, I know 'im. Not long, mind you, no more'n three year, but we've been close, like this." He held up his big clasped hands for me to see.

"You saved his life?"

He looked surprised. " 'e told y' that, did 'e?"

"In a manner."

Jim nodded. "Fished 'im out of that watery death, I did, thinkin' 'e were already a corpse, frozen through. 'e lay with 'is shoulders and 'ead out o' the water and the rest of 'im surrounded by ice. I took 'im back to my 'ouse and there 'e lay for a fortnight, shiverin' and talkin' out o' his mind with fever. When 'e finally came to, 'e couldn't remember who 'e was, where 'e'd been or where 'e was goin' when 'is horse fell through the ice. 'e went on that way for a month; it were then we became friends."

I sat down upon a stone and drew my legs up under my cloak. Pacing back and forth before me, Jim continued.

"Mind you, I knew 'e were no peasant like me. 'e'd been wearin' fine clothes when I fished 'im out of that ice. And 'is way of speakin' were of the titled folk. In a way I 'oped he wouldn't ever remember. 'e became like a son to me. I won't lie by tellin' y' otherwise. Then one mornin' it come to 'im who 'e were, though he still 'ad no recollection what 'e'd been doin' travelin' to York. 'e insisted that I return to Walthamstow with 'im and, as you can see, I did. I were a poor man and proud, but I ain't afraid t' work. 'e saw me set up 'ere and gave me a job and more wages than I'd ever see raisin' sheep."

"Did he love Jane?" I asked.

He stopped his pacing and looked at me, his face strange in the pale light. We stared at one another without speaking. Finally he spoke. "There were only one woman 'e loved and she haunts 'im t' this day. Faceless she is to 'im now, though the loss of her gnaws at 'is insides . . ."

I came to my feet, my heart thumping with impatience. With hardly a breath's space between us, I turned my face to his and beseeched him in a voice grown hoarse and unsteady with anticipation, "Tell me who he loved, Jim, tell me now."

"Why does it matter, lass? She's dead, y' see. Dead and buried and cold in the ground, buried in some pauper's grave north of 'ere. 'e blames 'imself f' her death, too, poor lad. 'ad I known, 'ad I only known those days 'e lay fighting 'is fever on my bed and callin' out 'er name—"

I grabbed his arms and shook him. "Tell me what name he called, my friend, I must know."

"Maggie," he responded. "The lady of milord's heart was Maggie."

Dropping my hands, I stumbled backward. The wind whipped the hood from my cape as I leaned my face into the falling icy mist and wept, "Maggie." Turning, I fled back to Walthamstow.

Chapter 6

I stood shivering in my room, that blessed sanctuary with its locked doors that kept the world at bay. Outside the winter storm raged, hurling sleet against my window, howling like a banshee around the pointed dormers and eaves of the ancient house. I was at a loss. What should I do? My preconceived notions about Nicholas Wyndham had been driven to dust. He had loved Maggie, had wept her name in despair as he lay struggling for his own life. And yet, she was lost to him, in mind if not in heart.

How could that be? I asked myself.

I left my room with candle in hand, hesitating in the hallway. To my right the corridor stretched into an abyss of darkness. To my left ... the door of Wyndham's studio was open, beckoning me, tempting me, and I told myself even as I approached the threshold that I had no right to intrude; I had been ordered to take no liberties in his studio. Yet, with every minute I found my need to learn this family's secrets growing more urgent.

The door gave with a slight creak as I entered, lifting my flame to better illuminate the shadowed interior. Swallowing back my fear, I stepped inside and closed the heavy door behind me.

The room, so bright and friendly that morning, took

on a different appearance now that daylight had again turned to dusk. Standing in my halo of light, I studied each hulking canvas as if it would suddenly grow eyes and fangs and leap at me from its shadow. Imp! I chastised myself. There is nothing here but paint and linen stretched over simple ash-wood frames. I lifted my chin stubbornly and ventured farther into the room.

Harboring hopes of finding my portrait, I headed straight for the covered easel in the center of the room. Yet as I lifted my hand to sweep away the cover, I hesitated. And with my hesitation, the wind slashed at the windows so they rattled an ominous warning.

The candle flame flickered and died. Within the cavernous four walls of the room, I stood in blackness. And there I waited, listening to the frantic pounding of my heart in my ears. In that moment I wished for Nicholas. Frightful, harsh, belligerent Lord Nicholas Wyndham, Earl of all Malham. Fiend. Murderer and lunatic. Yes, I wished him with me; rather I suffer beneath any cruelty he might subject me to than succumb to my idiotic fear of darkness.

Think! I told myself. Were there werewolves hunkered in the shadows when I first trespassed in this room? None. Were there ghouls? None. Vampires? No! No! I took a deep breath and focused my eyes on the deepest shadow, focused until the strain on my eyes brought a pain to my head.

If only the wind would cease its roar, its unrelenting rampage over the moor! It bludgeoned the walls and whipped the limbs of the chestnut tree so hard against the window so I was certain the panes would shatter at my feet. I threw open the curtains and was surprised to find a moon set among the scuttling clouds. She appeared only momentarily, but long enough to brighten Walthamstow's grounds in ice-blue light.

The light spilled through the window and into the room. As I turned, I swept my desperate gaze over each corner to assure myself that no demon lurked there. How wrong I was. Within the elaborate moldings over the door perched a gargoyle, his snout pulled back in laughter, his slitted eyes staring at me and mocking my fear. In reflex I stepped back.

The chestnut tree thrashed its bare branches from side to side, casting long, twisted shadows across the floor. Focusing my eyes once again on the solitary canvas in the middle of the room, I forced my legs to move and approached it. Quickly! Before the moon's light is cast away—before I am found out—before I die of fright.

I flung the covering away and stared. Full black hair spilled around the girl's shoulders, to the middle of her back. Who was she, this faceless, dark haired waif, surrounded by baskets of heather and yards of pearl-gray fabric? It was not I. I had sat upon no moor with heather. Perhaps this was the portrait of another.

I ran to a far canvas and exposed it.

The moonlight waned, and again I was blanketed in darkness. I dropped the sheet as if it were a hot coal, curled my fingers into my palm, and pressed my hand against my palpitating heart. What had I seen there? *"Portraits of madness!"* came the crone's words to my mind. Horror, yes. Terror, undoubtedly. But madness? What else would I call it? What sort of mind would set forth to paint portraits of such unspeakable evil? Of skeletal hands reaching from flames while scathing eyes stared out from faces shorn of flesh?

How I suffered in that moment! Upon arriving at Walthamstow I had prayed that Nicholas Wyndham's madness ran true and deep. That his madness would blind him to reality so I might be allowed to act upon my crime and run, never to return. Alas, it was not to be. For with each hour that I spent within Walthamstow's walls I became more and more concerned for his state of mind. How could I feel otherwise, knowing now how he felt about Maggie? That he had loved her; that he loved her yet. Had his feelings perhaps driven him to this brink of irrationality?

I wondered, there in the dark with the wind and sleet pelting the house, with the smell of turpentine making my head reel. With the gargoyle looking on, I crouched upon my heels and wondered what I should do. All instinct warned me to leave, to take what I had come for and disappear into the night like a thief. So, gathering my courage about me like a mantle, I stood and turned for the door.

That was when I heard the laughter.

At first I thought it a wailing of the wind. But no. No simple wind ever sounded so. It occupied every black corner of the room. It froze me in my place. It filled my breast with heart-stopping fear and my mind with imaginings too awful to declare. Unable to bear the sound a moment longer, I ran from the room, dropping my candle on my way and never bothering to retrieve it.

I did not stop to think where I was running until I found myself in the bright, warm confines of Kevin's room. Standing inside the door, I basked in the brilliance of light, feasted with my eyes on the cheerful faces of dancing sheep and the welcoming hiss of the fire in the distant hearth. Here I was safe from demons and madness and—

"Ah, Miss Rushdon, I see you're still here," came Nick's voice. Startled from my reverie, I spun around, searching out the deep-timbred voice that I knew too well.

He sat in a high-backed chair of simple design, his long legs spread slightly, his right arm curled possessively around Kevin's shoulders. Kevin, with his back resting on his father's chest, slept in peaceful oblivion.

"You will join us?" my lord said.

I recognized the directive and hastened to his side. I noticed then the open door beyond us. In that small, stark room, in a chair similar to the one Nicholas lounged in, sat Bea. Her eyes, like tiny round beads of glass, watched us intently.

"Ignore the hag," he said.

I turned my face from her as I was told.

The earl ran long fingers through his son's hair before looking up at me. I was struck in that instant by their similarities. Wounded by them. My lord Malham looked young and yet old, the skin of his face unlined but for the deep creases between his eyes. And his eyes, how they touched me, warmed me yet made me shiver.

He stared at me a long while, absently rubbing his chin round and round the top of Kevin's head. Finally he asked, "Have you searched me out to tender your resignation, Miss Rushdon?"

I thought the query odd, so I frowned. "Why should I do that?"

"I thought by now you must have realized the folly of accepting my employment. Tell me, did you enjoy your tour of the stables?"

My heart thumped in my breast.

His hand stopped its stroking. "Well?"

"Very much, milord." I looked away.

"Look at me." When I did so, he continued, "God, how sick I am of people diverting their eyes when I walk into a room. Is there something distasteful in the way I look, Miss Rushdon?"

"Well—"

"Have I grown a wart on my nose?"

I covered my smile with my fingers. "No wart, sir."

The cold gray of his eyes suddenly danced with warmth. "That's better," he said more gently. "You made me smile earlier in the day; I've returned the favor." He pointed to a stool covered in a frayed brocade cushion. "Take that seat and sit before me."

I pulled it to his feet.

"Closer," he directed.

I tugged it closer, nearly between his knees, and took my place upon it.

"Tell me, Miss Rushdon, what you think of my son."

I looked into the angelic face and felt my cheeks warm. My throat grew so tight with emotion I barely managed to speak. "I think, milord, that he is the most beautiful child ever created."

My lord's thick black lashes lowered, and I perceived a trembling of his eyelids. "Yes," he responded in a subdued tone. "I pray on my knees that he will grow to be stronger than his father in heart and soul and mind. I pray that this . . . disease that inflicts me will not be inherited in his manhood."

The quiet crackling of the wood-ash glowing red in the hearth was the only sound in the chamber as we watched Kevin sleep. I yearned in those moments to never leave this room, or the child or man. Having put rumors and portraits of madness from my mind I was content to wile away my years never straying from this very chair.

"Ariel," came Nick's soft voice, and I loosed myself from my daydreams and looked to his eyes. I felt a softening in my heart, a spinning in my head that was neither new nor unusual; I had experienced it a thousand times in his presence.

"Sir?" My words were steady.

"You have a melancholy look on your face. Are you sad?"

"I am distressed, milord."

"Tell me why."

"I cannot understand your malady. What brought you, milord, to hurt your sister this morning?"

"I'm a lunatic."

"I deny it."

"I'm a monster."

"An absurdity."

He caught my chin in his long, hard fingers; his eyes bore into me like the sharp, shining steel of a double-edged rapier. Leaning toward me slightly, his mouth coiling like a whip around his words, he said, "Little fool, you have eyes; open them. See me for what I am. I am a liar and a rakehell. I entertain myself by luring hearts and breaking them. I'm a lunatic from a long line of lunatics. I'm a murderer—"

"Stop!" I leapt to my feet and covered my ears with my hands. "I won't hear it."

"Then you are an idiot," he said calmly.

Lowering my arms, I looked at him fiercely. "I fear you are right, sir, but that is my prerogative."

"Sit down, Miss Rushdon."

I obeyed him. Sitting very still, I continued to watch the child. My gaze drifted occasionally to my lord's fingers, their slow circular movements in Kevin's hair mesmerizing me. I wanted to lift my eyes to his, but I dared not. Oh no, that would have been disastrous. For I felt such expansion in my breast at the sight of father and son that one look into his stormy eyes would have been my undoing.

Suddenly Nicholas stood. Gently he placed Kevin in his bed and tucked his blanket about him.

Walking to the nursery door, he paused, half turned and commanded, "Come along, Miss Rushdon."

With some regrets I joined him.

We entered a great room with a high-pitched ceiling with such magnificent moldings I could scarcely contain my appreciation. The walls were dark with wainscotted paneling, but glowed with light from the peat fire in the hearth.

I waited just inside the room as Nicholas approached his desk. As if undecided, he stopped and pressed his fingertips onto the smooth, mahogany plane for several moments. I noted with distress a slight sinking of his shoulders and a drop of his dark head.

I had opened my mouth to speak when he turned again to face me. His face looked pale, as it had that first morning of my arrival to Walthamstow. His eyes were sunken and dull, his eyelids heavy. "Come here," he said in a low voice.

Dare I?

He leaned a little against the desk. He tried to erect his shoulders. "Having second thoughts, waif?"

"No, sir."

"Then come here." When I had done so, keeping a respectable distance between us, he pointed to the open ledger on his desk. "Can you read?" he asked me.

"Enough to get by, milord."

He looked pleased. "Then tell me what you see written under today's date."

Turning the open book toward me, I studied the scrawl. "Adrienne's wedding day," I read aloud.

"There. You see, I didn't imagine it."

"But, my lord," I closed the book, "surely you knew those plans had been canceled."

"I thought I did. Yes. Yes, I knew it. Dear merciful God, I knew it."

I looked at the toes of his boots and asked in a whisper, "Then why?"

His sudden laughter sounded fierce and savage. "Why? It was that gift. That goddamned bolt of lace. I don't recall buying it, Miss Rushdon. When I found it wrapped in paper and ribbon and placed there on my desk I actually imagined I'd dreamt the entire humiliating scene at my sister's soiree. It wouldn't be the first time. I oft times imagine things, as you will learn should you continue to live here. I live in a constant state of confusion, and when I found the gift . . ." His voice dropped, defeatedly. "I simply did not think. I did not reason. On impulse I grabbed it up and—God in heaven, I would rather wrench my arm from my shoulder than hurt Adrienne."

"Then tell her so."

He looked at me askance. "Little innocent," I heard him say. "You see before you two men. Lord Malham, Wyndham of Walthamstow, earl of this village called Malham, would never hurt his sister, but the other— ah, the other, what would he do? Hmm?" He lifted his hand and placed it on my cheek. "There is madness in me, I won't deny it. It is there in my head now, swelling against my temples until the pain drives me to oblivion. Those are the hours I dread, when blackness falls in on me and I can account for nothing, not even my name. When nothing exists but flashes of faces and voices; when I am dependent on family and friends— sparse as they are—to inform me of my activities when I'm rational enough to care."

He dropped his hand, and the cool rush of air that replaced it seemed to blister my skin. I yearned to grab the beautiful hand back and press it again to my face, to turn my mouth into it and drink in the texture and smell of it until I was overcome. But most of all I yearned to heal him.

He prowled the room slowly, time and again pressing his fingers to his head. He walked to the bowed window behind his desk, and there stood for some time, staring out into the wet darkness. It seemed to me in that moment that he spent his entire life looking out on a world that was familiar and yet foreign to him. What did he seek there? Penance? Truth?

And then it struck me. It struck me as he lifted his hand and pressed it flat against the frosty pane of glass. The blow winded me, squeezed the breath from my lungs so I was forced to lean upon the desk for support. It was not the gardens on which he looked, nor the village of Malham or the moor beyond. It was himself: the reflection of the stranger he had become.

I fled. Back to my room, through the cold and darkness to my solitude I ran, closing my door and locking it. I cannot do this, I vowed. I will go now. Go and never look back.

I unlocked my door again and flung it open. I walked with purpose back to Kevin's room, stood outside the door and looked upon the distant cradle at the sleeping child. I approached him on tiptoe, casting a cautious eye toward the room where the jackal resided. I listened, then moved with caution along the wall, peeked around the doorframe. Just as I thought. She still sat in her chair, her bony hands clasped in her lap, her head fallen forward in repose.

I hurried to the bed, eager to act on my plan. Kevin lay on his back. I stared at him a long moment: his fair complexion, his cheeks like apples. My heart hammered in my breast as I slid my hands around him. His dark hair slid over his forehead, revealing the cut above his brow. Only then did I think of Nick, of his hands trembling in worry as he gently touched the boy's head.

The moment was as painful as any I had ever spent. As black, as shameful. I was rent by my own self-ishness.

Replacing the lad in his bed, I returned to my room and there spent the next few hours in such miserable indecision I forgot even my fear of darkness, and hardly noticed when my candle wick sputtered and went out. The sleep I was able to summon was neither peaceful nor restful. I tossed and turned on my mattress, rueing the promises I had made to myself and Jerome. Poor Jerome. He should have left me buried at Menston, for all the good my purchased freedom had brought me. I was without courage. I was confused. I was yet in love with Nicholas Wyndham, shacked by heart to a lunatic. Alas, my despair was complete!

Chapter 7

He came for me that midnight.

At the sounds of his knocking I rolled from my bed, the key still clasped tightly in my fist. Even as I felt my way to the door I heard him pacing. He did not hesitate as I opened the door, but swept across the threshold and walked directly to the window. Throwing open the drape, he stood silhouetted against the silvery glass.

I waited, discomposed by his state of mind.

"Were you sleeping?" he finally asked, and I noted a difference in his voice.

"Yes, milord."

"And are you a sound sleeper?"

"Yes, sir."

"Then you heard nothing? No footstep? No voice in the hallway?"

"Only yours, sir, when you knocked on my door."

I saw his breath condense like a fog upon the glass. Then he leaned his head against the pane, indeed, pressed his cheek against it as if its bitter cold would somehow soothe his feverish state. "No footstep. No voices. How can that be?"

"Were you bothered by these things?" I asked him.

"They woke me."

"Perhaps it was the help. Matilda or Polly or Bea—"

"The hag is asleep. I checked her."

"Then—"

"It was my wife."

I dropped the key. In the dark it sounded like a crash of cymbals. Falling to my knees, I swept my hand over the floor until my fingers brushed against the key.

"It was my wife," he said more loudly. He turned from the window, and though I could not see his face I knew he had spotted me where I knelt on the floor. "It was my wife," he said yet again.

"Your wife, sir."

"Are you going to tell me that I imagined it?"

"I can hardly tell you anything, sir, since I did not hear it."

"Then you are saying, since you did not hear it, that it was all a figment of my imagination?"

"No, sir. I simply did not hear it."

"Then you will insist that it was the help."

"Insisting *anything* to your lordship would be overstepping my limits. I shall never do so, sir, in your presence."

"Of course you won't, Miss Rushdon, you will huddle by the fire come morning, perhaps in the kitchen, perhaps the butler's pantry, and you will run off at the tongue—"

"No I shan't. I am not a talebearer."

"But you don't believe me."

Standing again, I thought of lighting my candle. Arguing with a shadow was disconcerting to me.

"Well?" Lord Malham continued. "If I tell you I heard my wife calling my name from outside my bedroom door, will you tell me I'm a lunatic?"

"No, sir, I won't. Idiot I may be, but I am not daft."

Now he became silent.

Finally he moved closer. I could better see his face:

it appeared haggard. His hair tumbled, blacker than the shadows, over his brow. His white shirt was open.

"Miss Rushdon," he stated. "Do you oftentimes sleep in your clothes?"

"If the occasion suits. And you, sir?"

Silence again. I watched a pale gray vapor leave his mouth as he took a breath, then released it. *Dragon!* I thought.

Gripping my skirt in my fingers, I asked, "Will you paint, Malham?"

He considered my question before replying. "In five minutes." Stepping by me, he disappeared into the hallway.

In five minutes I had taken my place on my perch. Nicholas had taken up a clean canvas, a pallet of fresh, glistening paints, and begun to work. Again, he turned me slightly away from him. I could not help but ask: "Sir, why do you disregard my face in this matter? Is it so unappealing?"

His head came up. His eyes peered at me over the top of the canvas. *"Au contraire,"* he responded. "You have a most appealing face."

I basked in the compliment. Then I said, "But you have some preference to the back of my head. My hair, perhaps my shoulders are more to your liking?"

His left eyebrow arched.

I closed my lips and looked toward the window. Half an hour passed before I spoke again. "Sir, I have an idea. Perhaps it was not Bea or Matilda or Polly you heard outside your door. Perhaps you dreamt you heard your wife."

"I wasn't asleep when I heard her voice the second time, Miss Rushdon."

"But perhaps, sir, you thought you were awake. Oft times my mind lapses—"

"I was awake, miss, and sitting up in my bed."

"In that case I will make this suggestion: Mayhaps it was the wind." I glanced at him from the corner of my eye. "Could that be possible, milord?"

"No."

Until that moment I had forgotten the laughter I had heard during my secret visit to this room. Had anyone tried to convince me at the time that the awful sound was nothing more than howling wind, I would have devoutly denied it.

In that moment Nicholas dropped his brush. I watched as he stooped to retrieve it. I noted then that the candle I had earlier dropped lay near his foot. To my discredit I blushed.

Wyndham straightened, rolled his brush between his fingers, and scowled as he contemplated the canvas. I looked again at the candle. I looked again at him. His eyes, cold and hard as lead, assessed me. It was a queer look that he passed me, not so fierce that I was frightened, yet threatening. Sitting straighter, I looked back toward the window. He continued his painting.

At half past ten in the morning I stood inside Trevor's office, my sleeve rolled up to my elbow. The potion on my arm stung at first. I fixed my eyes on the small man wedged in a chair between shelves of medical books and a table stacked high with papers. His elbows were propped on his knees, and his head rested in the palms of his hands. As he groaned I looked at Trevor and said, "He appears to be in pain."

"He'll wait his turn," he snapped. Then, bathing the welts one last time, he muttered, "Silly old bugger has been in three times this week for his bloody bowels and head. I've bled him so he's weak-kneed and still he comes back."

I was stunned by his tone of voice, but I didn't show it. "Have you tried calomel?" I asked. Then realizing what I had asked, I bit my lip, fixed my eyes on the moaning patient, and held my breath.

If Trevor heard me at all, he didn't let on. He turned to the table, recorked the bottle, and threw the linens onto the floor, missing the basket.

" 'ere, doc," came the gent's weary voice. "Me 'ead is splittin' and me guts no better. Is there 'owt you kin gi' me whilst I wait?"

"I'm no miracle worker," Trevor answered, too abruptly for my liking.

Rolling down my sleeves, I approached the old dear, noting his color was off and his eyes were slightly glassy. He looked at me rather pitifully and shook his head. " 'e's gonna bleed me agin. I've little blood left in me as it is."

I looked around as Trevor approached, a knife in one hand and a cup in the other. I took the gentleman's hand in mine. "You'll be very brave, won't you?"

"I won't be squealin' like a pig if that's wot y' mean. But I'll be tellin' y' this. I'll be bloody glad when Doc Brabbs returns. 'e's been off too long, I vow. Why, Mary Francis took to 'er bed a fortnight ago and ain't been up agin. A pitiful sight she is and growin' softer by the day. I'll vow she won't see the new month if Brabbs don't get back."

Trevor slammed his cup onto the table, took up his knife, and fixed his blue eyes on his patient's face. "Where do you want it this time, Donald? The throat, perhaps?" When I looked at him, surprised, he smiled and shrugged. "Very well, then, you old bugger, give me your head. I shall make this as painless as possible."

"Would you like me to warm the cup for you?" I asked Trevor.

An abrupt nod was his response, so I proceeded to heat the small glass cup over the fire until it grew uncomfortably warm to touch. Over my shoulder I watched the indisposed old gentleman lower his head nearly to his knees, closing his eyes as Trevor welded the silver sharp-edged blade back and forth before his face.

"Are you ready, Mr. Dix?" Trevor asked.

"Aye," the man mumbled.

"Is that cup prepared?" Trevor called.

"Aye," I responded.

"Then hasten it to me now." With a flick of his wrist, he slid the knife into the flesh of Mr. Dix's forehead.

I almost stumbled in my haste to press the four-ounce cup onto Mr. Dix's brow. Immediately the article adhered to the patient's head. The vacuum created by the cooling of the cup drew blood in a rush from the incision.

Trevor turned away, offering no encouragement at all as his patient paled and shuddered. Sliding my arms around Dix's shaking shoulders, I soothed him. "There, sir, this will undoubtedly cure you. Have faith."

"I am bled dry of faith," he said.

"There, there, it will soon be over."

He angled his face toward me. "Yer a kind lass."

"No sir, not kind."

"Aye. Gentle and kindhearted."

"Hush now." I smiled and smoothed my hand over his brow. "You are delicate now and prone to sentimentalities."

"Yer a right bonny lass."

"Sir. Mayhaps you're better? There. I see color in your cheeks."

"Have ye a husband, lass?"

My eyes widened.

"I've a son yer age, y' see."

"I am not in the mind for marriage, Mr. Dix, but if I were, I'm certain a son of yours would be far too good for me."

He clapped his hands. "She's modest too! Doc, where did y' find her?" Forgetting in his reverie the glass sucked up against his head, he centered his sparkling, if slightly feverish, gaze on his physician, who eyed me in return.

"She belongs to my brother," Trevor said, and I noted the slightly upward tilt of his mouth as he continued to survey me. "I agree she is quite the philanthropist. And, aye, she is bonny as well."

I was not accustomed to this appreciation. It made me blush.

Sensing my discomfiture, Trevor went immediately to his patient, and I hurried to the door, stopping only long enough to bid each gentleman a good day.

Upon entering the kitchen, I was heartened by Matilda's good cheer. She sat me down at the table and plunked before me a heaping bowl of steaming porridge swimming in butter and sweetened with treacle. I was given toast and blackberry jam, a cherry tart, and coffee.

Around me the others hustled to prepare a much heartier breakfast for their employers. Ham sizzled over a fire, cakes rose in fluffy mounds in the brick ovens. Adrienne's highly treasured Chinese tea steeped in a white china pot of painted cupids and pink rose garlands.

Just then Polly entered the room through the outside door, her apron bulging with eggs. The wind whipped in around her, whirling with leaves and the snowflakes that had begun to fall from the heavy sky. "Lud," she

said, "it's cold as a well digger's arse out there. We'll
be snowed in by evenin'."

Matilda jumped for the tea, hovering her arms
around it like a mother hen protecting her chicks.
"Close the bloody door; y' know what milady's like if
'er brew is cold."

"Ah, she's gettin' as flaky as 'er brother," someone
mumbled. I was soon to learn the young woman's name
was Kate.

"I beg your pardon." I stared into my porridge as I
spoke. The hustle and bustle about me paused. Then,
certain I had their attention, I said, "I think you should
not make light of Lord Malham or his sister. They pay
your wage, do they not?"

They gaped at me. Glancing at each one somewhat
sternly and stirring the cream into my porridge, I stated
firmly, "They deserve your loyalty. Without their consideration you would be no doubt involved in some sort
of occupation that may or may not be so comfortable,
or respectable, as this one."

Matilda cleared her throat. "She's right, ladies, I've
told y'—"

"Give over." It was Polly. Having placed her eggs on
the table, she fixed her eyes on Matilda and screwed
up her mouth in a way that likened her countenance
to that of a tit-mouse. " 'e's daft. 'e ain't even human,
if y' ask me. 'e aught t' be locked up, considerin' wot
'e done. I'll warrant 'ad it been me or you who committed the same crime we'd 'ave been bound up at Leeds
long ago." She punctuated her remark with a sharp
nod of her head.

Irritated, Matilda countered, "Y' got no proof, y'
cheeky girl, that 'is lordship were involved in 'er ladyship's death."

" 'e were there now, weren't 'e?"

"So what?"

I looked back and forth between the two, discomforted by their heated opinions. Their voices were rising and I was certain they would be heard soon by the Wyndhams. I looked to Kate as she joined in.

"Well, it were 'igh time someone did somethin' to stop 'er philanderin'. She were makin' a mockery of 'er position. She broke Miss Adrienne's heart by forcin' 'er out of 'er own quarters and puttin' 'er on an allowance. And she made no bones about the gents she was seein' on the sly. Why, I heard with me own ears, 'is lordship accusin' 'er of adultery and 'er admittin' to it. Flung it in 'is face, she did, at the top of 'er voice. Said 'e had no right upbraidin' 'er for 'er affairs after wot *e'd* done."

Matilda huffed. "His lordship can't be held accountable for what he done before he married Jane. It were no business of Jane's at any count."

Kate's eyes grew round as saucers, and her look of disbelief was obvious. "Well, 'e made it Jane's business, didn't 'e, by allowing that wasted man into the house." Kate looked down at me. "It were just as well. It were common knowledge milord and lady were married in name only. Never once did they spend a night together—as 'usband and wife—in this house."

Matilda very nearly hopped now in her exasperation. "Y'll be hushin' such gossip, Katie Smythe."

"But it's true, Tilly, and y' well know it." Kate looked at Polly for substantiation, then back at me. I had begun to rise from my chair, grasping the table edge to support my wobbly knees as Kate narrowed her eyes and said, "It's no secret, y' know. It ain't as if Jane 'erself didn't weep to the entire world that Wyndham 'ad shamed 'er. It were no secret that Master Kevin is—"

I had closed my eyes when the room suddenly rang with tomblike silence, and I knew even before I opened them and spun around, that Nicholas would be there.

Recovering my composure, I dipped slightly and met his gray eyes without blinking. A slight but unmistakable shudder ran through me at his studied nonchalance. For an instant I questioned whether he had overheard Katie's remark, then as quickly I dismissed it.

"Come along, Miss Rushdon," he said.

I moved woodenly to his side, and did not look back at the mortified women.

I entered the breakfast room behind him. Pausing in the doorway, I waited, wondering what course I was to take next. Adrienne sat at one end of the breakfast table, her fingers absently tracing the brass inlay that decorated the rosewood veneer. Trevor, seated to one side of his sister, stirred his coffee and glanced up from the text he was reading as Nicholas announced, "Miss Rushdon will be joining us."

Taken off guard, I questioned him. "Sir?"

Dropping into his chair, he pointed to a place beside him.

My cheeks burned as both Trevor and Adrienne studied me curiously. Squaring my shoulders, I said, "My thanks, milord, but no. My position is in the kitchen and I—"

"I said"—he looked at me, his gray eyes threatening—"sit down."

I obeyed him.

Nicholas regarded his brother and sister with a challenging look. "I find it necessary to separate Miss Rushdon from those vipers in the kitchen. If either of you find some problem with my decision, speak now. No?" He sat back in his chair like a king regarding his subjects, and twisted his lips in a smile. "You're think-ing, 'Humor him.' Wise, very wise. I'm in no mood to deliberate on my decision at this moment."

Polly bustled through the doorway then. She stopped when she saw me.

Nicholas looked savagely at the stunned servant and said through his teeth, "Serve her."

Curtsying in compliance, Polly hurried out of the room, only to return a minute later with the same breakfast I had begun to eat earlier. As the woman thudded the bowl of congealed porridge before me, his lordship announced, "Get that foul rubbish out of my sight. If I am not totally out of my mind that is ham I smell roasting."

"Aye, milord."

"She'll have ham, then. And eggs. And some of that black gold otherwise known as tea."

Polly snatched the porridge from the table and disap-peared out the door.

Silent, I looked about the room, noting Trevor had gone back to reading his book. Adrienne, appearing to shrink in her chair, clasped her hands in her lap and stared at Trevor as he continually stirred his coffee. "Do you mind?" she snapped in an edgy voice.

Without looking up, Trevor tapped the spoon on the cup rim then set it aside.

"Thank you," she said.

Although I was aware that Nicholas watched me, I could not manage to face him. I wondered why he was doing this. I was not comfortable in these people's presence any more than they were comfortable in mine.

I had just worked up my courage to excuse myself when Polly and Matilda reentered the room with the food cart. As they went to the task of dishing out the food, Reginald entered brusquely and handed Trevor an envelope. With his white-gloved hands clasped, Reginald considered me at some length before centering his eyes on the limewood mirror adorning the wall behind me.

Trevor scanned the letter, then threw it on the table. "Praises, the old man has returned. I wager Mr. Dix will be on Brabbs's doorstep within the hour complaining that I sucked him dry of blood."

Adrienne slumped in her chair. "Must we discuss this over our meal?" she asked in a weak voice.

Trevor smirked. "I've charged him a pence for my services. No doubt I'll be paid again with a blasted sack of cornmeal." He looked at me and his smile became friendly once again. "Brabbs will be interested to hear about you, Miss Rushdon. I'm certain Dix will be crowing of your kindness to everyone in Malham."

There was silence again. I did my best to eat the luscious food placed before me. But I wasn't hungry. I realized I would somehow have to get to Brabbs as quickly as possible. It would not be an easy feat. To reach his house I would find it necessary to pass directly through Malham.

Adrienne spoke then. "Miss Rushdon."

I looked at her directly, thankful for some cause to avoid the doctor's eyes.

Adrienne's delicate hands carefully spread white butter over her thinly sliced Sol-et-Lune bread before she regarded me. "I shall be riding out today. If my brother is agreeable I would like you to attend me."

"Where are you going, Adrienne?" Trevor asked.

"Beck Hall. I'm to luncheon with Melissa."

"Why do you request Ariel's company?" Nicholas asked.

A long moment of silence passed. Adrienne continued chewing the bread and dusting the caraway seeds and sugar from her fingers before reaching for her tea.

"I asked you a question," he said. Sitting back in his chair, he smiled. "Oh yes, you're not speaking to me again because of yesterday. I have apologized for that."

Adrienne continued to sip her tea.

Nicholas glanced at me with a slight tightening of his mouth. "Very well," he suddenly announced. "If you cannot find the words with which to answer me—"

"As you recall," Adrienne began quietly, silencing his forthcoming ultimatum, "you sent any companion from the house in a fit of tears a little better than a fortnight ago."

Nicholas paled.

"You frightened the young woman out of her senses with your tales of ghosts. I am surprised we have managed to keep what little help we have."

His eyes came back to mine. As quickly he looked away.

"Such idiotic foolishness." Adrienne's cup rattled as she replaced it on the saucer.

Shoving his breakfast plate away, Nicholas said, "I could use a drink."

"So could I," Trevor joined in. Shutting his book, he placed it aside and volunteered to fetch them both a sherry. Excusing himself, he left the room.

I spent the latter hours of morning preparing for the trip to Beck Hall. I recalled it clearly in my mind. Small compared to Walthamstow, it was yet grand to passersby, its gardens tended regularly and blooming with seasonal flowers. Ofttimes I had daydreamed of visiting there.

At one hour past noon I was summoned to join Adrienne. The front door stood open, and beyond the steps awaited the grand post chaise, its gleaming, black-lacquered doors ensconced with the Wyndham coat of arms. All at once, a strange delight inspired me. The nervousness that had racked me throughout the morning was forgotten.

"Ariel?"

At the sound of my lord's voice, I stayed my step. I slowly turned to face him.

He stood in the shadows of the foyer, a shadow himself dressed in black. "Where are you going?" he asked me.

I stepped forward to better see him. His port was erect, but his countenance looked desperate and confused, like a child who discovers his last friend has deserted him without explanation. Pulling the hood of my cloak up over my head, I responded, "My lord. You have granted me permission to attend your sister to Beck Hall."

"Did I?" came his quiet voice.

"Aye, milord. At breakfast. Have you forgotten?"

His silence was an admission that took my breath and twisted my heart so painfully I was forced to blink back my tears. I looked away and continued to the chaise, praying he would not call me back. I could not face him when he was like this.

With relief I sank back into the chaise's leather cushions. As Reginald closed the coach door, I shut my eyes, momentarily forgetting Lady Adrienne at my side.

"He's getting worse," she said softly.

I inched the burgundy velvet casing from the window as the coach got underway. Only then did I release my breath.

I continued to watch the countryside as we advanced toward Malham. We passed the common pastures of Grisedale and Pikedaw. Swinging off Raikes Road, we skirted the outlying shops of the village and continued over Monk Bridge. Finally, we entered Malham East, its common granges and pastures cultivated with lynchets. I knew the moment we swerved onto Hawthorn Lane. Looking out across the rolling moor of rough brown grass and the sedges growing along Millstone Grit, I was assailed with memories both happy and sad. Jerome and I had frolicked about these very pastures as children. I missed my friend deeply at that moment.

Hearing Adrienne sigh, I relaxed in my seat.

"I wish to apologize for my behavior yesterday," Adrienne announced. Burying her hands in her fur lap muff, she eyed me from beneath the brim of her hat. "You were very kind, Ariel."

I returned her smile somewhat shyly.

"I would like to thank you in some way."

"That isn't necessary," I told her.

"You must understand how I felt."

"I understand," I assured her.

We rode in silence before she continued. "I feel you must know. This morning Trevor and I discussed committing Nicholas to Saint Mary's."

I looked away, seized with sudden panic. "No," I whispered.

"You think us unkind."

"He is not mad. Forgetful, perhaps—"

"His memory lapses are only a small part of his ailment, Ariel. At times his moods grow severely dark, and I fear not only for our safety but his as well. And there is the child to think of."

I turned suddenly, terror-struck by the quiet insinuation. "You think him capable of harming Kevin?" My heart pounded in expectation. Her awful silence was more than I could tolerate. "Well?" I demanded. "Have you some reason to believe he would harm the child?"

"No." Closing her eyes, she rested her head back on the seat. "He loves the boy more than his own life. No. He would never harm the boy."

"Yet you would send him away from the boy. Would that not equal death to your brother?"

"Yes. It would destroy him completely."

"And what of the child? What would happen to Kevin without his father? Would you entrust his care to Bea? Knowing how she loathes him? He would wither and die from lack of love."

Adrienne looked at me, her eyes sad and her smooth face pale with cold. "I am fond of my nephew."

"But you are neither his father nor his mother."

"He has never known his mother, so that is of little importance. Besides . . ." She took a breath. "Oftentimes I think the child has a great deal to do with my brother's illness. It is Nick's guilt, you see, over the death of Kevin's mother that is driving him to ruin. I firmly believe that."

I forced myself to look out the window.

The halt of the coach silenced any further remarks on the matter. We had arrived at Beck Hall.

Chapter 8

We returned to Walthamstow just after dusk. After excusing myself from Adrienne, I waited in my room until I was convinced that milady had returned to her quarters. Then I struck out for Malham.

Color had faded completely from the landscape as I approached the tiny village. Dark as it was, I could still make out the distant steeple of the church and the oblong structure of old Malham Hall, with its walls of crucks and stone and wattle. The snow was falling harder now, swirling about my shoulders, whipping this way and that. I shivered, not so much from the cold as from my dread. It seeped into the marrow of my bones, into my heart and there battled my better judgment. Perhaps I was making a mistake by returning here and facing the same man who had sent me to Menston two years before.

I continued my journey down the bridle path, closing my eyes occasionally as the wind whipped the falling snow into my face. My hands and feet grew numb and my lungs ached from the cold. But I was determined now. No climate would turn me back. No threat from a man who had once been a friend would deter me from my goal.

I took the footbridge over the hemp beck, pausing momentarily to peer down into the freezing stream.

I could barely make out the retting flax stalks that lay discarded or forgotten from summer. Farther I traveled, along the outskirts of the village, my eyes roving over each familiar landmark: Cromwell Cottage, South View Cottage, Dixon Inn. I crept closer to the inn. I went up on my tiptoes and peered through the mullioned window into the low-ceilinged tavern, just as I had done when I was a child. As always, the miners from the colliery sat about tables, their work-callused fingers wrapped around mugs of warm ale, their clothes and faces still dusty with the residue of their labor.

I carried on to Finkle Street until I reached Deadman Lane. There I stopped. I told myself, *Carry on, carry on. There is nothing here for you now. He is gone. Jerome is gone. Make do with the memories.* But I couldn't. The many hours I had spent at that humble cottage drew me nearer. I could almost hear Jerome's brash laughter, his good-natured teasing ... his first declaration of love. The recollection brought tears to my eyes. How I ached to confide in him now.

Weakened and shaken by my sorrow, I stumbled to the house and sank against its stone wall. How I longed to press my face against the glowing panes of glass in the window and feast my eyes on this stark but cheery interior. I could imagine Rosine Baron, Jerome's mother, stooping over the fire with her poker, her simple pewter pots and dishes dully reflecting the light from the hearth. This had been a kind of home to me. I did not realize until that sad moment how much I had come to miss it.

The wind howled over Pikedaw Hill. Forcing myself to leave the cottage, I trudged through ankle-deep snow up the road to Lavely Lane. There I looked upon Friars Garth and the house of Doctor Brabbs.

As I huddled there I thought—hoped—some passerby would dissuade me from knocking. But, save for the tumbling sleaves of ghostly white snow, there was nothing astir on that inclement night but me. Taking a deep, burning breath, I banged upon the door.

I waited.

I banged a second time; I waited again.

I heard the lock grind. The door inched open, pouring warm yellow light across my face.

"Who is there?" came the voice grown hoarse with age.

"It is I," I said.

"Speak up. I'm deaf, you know. Who is there?" He opened the door a little more.

I pulled my cape more tightly across my shoulders and stepped farther into the light. I saw his twinkling hazel eyes assess me. "Brabbs," I said, "I am freezing."

The night wind swept over the bracken moor and died, moaning in the distance.

"Blessed saint," I heard him whisper. "Mayhap the foul wind plays tricks on my ear."

"No trick," I told him.

"Mayhap, then, it is the snow."

"No snow," I assured him. "Brabbs," said I, shivering and numb, "I am cold. Will you not allow me in?"

He flung open the door, allowing the snow to scatter around his feet. He opened his arms. "Lord God. Lord God. Ariel Margaret Rushdon, the sight of you is enough to shock an old man to his grave. Maggie, you're alive."

I swept through the molded doorway into his arms. He clutched me to his chest and rocked me side to side. "Maggie, Maggie." He sobbed before releasing me, then slammed the door closed against the cold and leaned against it for support. Without turning, he said in a weakened voice, "If you're a ghost come back to haunt me—"

"No ghost," I replied. "No wind or snow or figment of your aging mind. But haunt you I will. I will haunt you until your dying day because I loved you. I trusted you with my secret—"

"Stop! Stop!" he entreated me.

"Nay, I will not." Sweeping my cloak from my shoulders, I threw it to floor. "Look at me, Brabbs. I am flesh and blood—no specter of death."

He looked cautiously over his stooped shoulder. His eyes widened. "Lord God, I cannot believe it. I don't know you. You're not my Maggie, my childlike Margaret with laughing eyes as green as Ireland and cheeks as pink as heather. Nay, you're nothing like her. Go away! Go away, wraith! Your eyes are too dull and your cheeks too sunken to belong to my Maggie."

"Aye, my cheeks are sunken and my eyes dull. Living night and day in dungeons will do that to you."

Facing me completely, he sank back against the door. "Lord God. Merciful God, I am dreaming. He told me you were dead. Jerome stood in that very place you occupy and wept into his hands that you had died in that miserable, wicked place." His gray brows hooding his eyes, he slowly began to circle me. "Answer me this then. What day and hour were you born? Quickly!"

"At one stroke past midnight in the year of our lord, seventeen and seventy-seven."

"Your mother's name."

"Julianne."

"And your father's?"

"Eric."

"Were there brothers and sisters?"

"Aye. One, but she died at birth."

"And?"

"My mother died with her."

"And where is your father?"

"Dead. He died at the colliery when I was ten."

"And—"

"I came to live with my uncle." I turned to face him. "I lived for the next ten years in the quarters over the Cock and Bottle Inn. I used to attend you when you made your rounds. I dusted this very house and swept these very floors. I begged you to teach me of healing, and you promised you would someday."

He wept into his hands.

"When I was sixteen I confessed to you that I was in love with Nicholas Wyndham. I told you that I dreamt of marrying him, that I *would* marry him. You laughed and said you would dance at my wedding. For ten years I watched him come and go out of my uncle's tavern, always remaining hidden, certain he would find me too plain or too young. You convinced me I was beautiful. You and Jerome. You called me princess; said I deserved no less than a prince."

He dropped into a chair. "If I could only do it over—"

"I convinced Jerome to help me. Following his instructions I planned that meeting on Cove Road. Precisely at noon I met Nicholas Wyndham face-to-face for the first time where the road branches to the north and south. In my hand I carried baskets of heather and daffodils. I wore a dress of pearl-gray muslin . . ."

My voice trailed off as I recalled the first moment I turned my eyes up to Wyndham's. "My wish came true. He fell in love with me that day."

"I should never have allowed it," my old friend declared.

I frowned into his grieving eyes. "Aye, you might've

told me about *her*. Of Lady Jane Blankenship who was doing her best to nab him."

"I didn't want to hurt you."

"Hurt me! Was I not hurt to learn of his betrothal to Jane? A betrothal that came not two days after he had declared a love for me?"

"Then it is Lord Malham you should be shaming, Maggie, not me."

"Nay, I'll not shame him. I shame myself. I shame you and I shame Jerome. Had I known about Jane before—"

Brabbs came out of his chair. "You knew about Jane when you climbed in his bed, girl. Where was your pride then?"

"Pride!" I railed. "You preach to me of pride: a man who tosses aside friendship and confidences like they were cinders. I trusted you—"

"What was I to do? When your uncle come to me with the suspicions of your problem . . . what was I to do?"

"You might have sent me anywhere. Anywhere but Royal Oaks in Menston. It is housed by lunatics—"

"There was nowt else to do, lass." He sank defeatedly back into his chair. "After your uncle died I tried writing letters to the institution, but I heard nothing. Nothing! Then Jerome showed up, barely alive himself. He told me you were dead. Had died in that miserable place during your ordeal. Oh, Maggie, Maggie, how I suffered."

His sobbing tore at my heart. I sank to the floor and hugged his knees. "Do you think I haven't suffered?" I asked him, more gently now.

He stroked my hair. "It must have been a wicked place."

"Aye. Wicked. I was so ashamed by being interned

there. I hated you. I hated my uncle. I hated Nicholas. Why me? I asked myself a thousand times a day. I had always been a good girl. All I ever wanted was Nicholas, and even wanting that I was willing to let him go, for I knew the ways of nobility. He had to marry Jane. It was agreed upon between their families."

"And yet you went to him."

I closed my eyes, remembering. "Aye, I went to him. Is it not ironic that his engagement celebration was spent in my uncle's tavern?"

"How did you manage it?" he asked me.

"I paid off the wench that Wyndham's friends had purchased him for the night. I took her place."

"He should have turned you out."

"He tried."

"He is not without fault, lass."

I sighed and stared into the blazing inglenook fireplace. "His only fault was allowing me to believe I stood a chance. He promised me that night, swore to me that he didn't love her, and I believed him. He vowed he would find a way to break the engagement. He set out to York the following morning with that intent . . . I did not see him again for weeks. When I learned of his return to Walthamstow I waited, certain he would come to see me. He didn't."

"That is when you left for Menston."

"Aye," I answered softly. "While he stood at the altar marrying Jane Blankenship I was hearing the iron doors of Royal Oaks Institution slam on my future."

"But you're here, lass. You've come home now and—"

"Not for long," I told him. His hand grew warm and heavy on my head. Closing my eyes, I admitted, "I'm here to take what is mine; then I'll be gone."

He hesitated before replying. "There is nothing Maggie, nothing here that belongs to you. Your uncle left you nothing."

"I did not return here for clothes or coin or keepsakes."

"Look at me."

I shook my head.

"Look at me!"

I did so.

"Tell me; where are you staying?"

"Walthamstow."

"Lord God!"

"He doesn't remember me."

"That doesn't concern me. But this crime—"

"Crime!" Roused to something like passion, I threw his hands from me and stumbled to my feet. "Crime, sir? Is it a crime to take back from a thief what rightfully belonged to me in the first place? The child is mine! Mine! Taken from my bed and breast less than twenty-four hours after his birth! Taken by a well-meaning friend—"

"Maggie, think of the child. What can you give him?"

"I am his mother!" I pounded my chest. "I am his mother! Do I love him less because I have no home? Because I am poor? Uneducated? What does that have to do with what I feel in my heart? He is my flesh, my spirit—"

"He is Wyndham's as well!" He left his chair. "Tell me, girl; y've seen them together: Does Nicholas love him any less than you?"

I turned away and sobbed convulsively. It was as if some great, terrible wound had burst inside me and flooded me with all the pain and anger and grief I had pent up since first being shut inside that wretched asylum at Menston.

Brabbs enclosed me in his arms, gathered me to his

chest. "Hush. Hush, Maggie, and listen. You cannot take the child. If you were caught you would lose him again. You would suffer greatly at the hands of the courts. You gave him away—"

"Nay! He was taken from me!"

"Hush," he repeated. "Now tell me this. Did Jerome act in total duplicity? Did you never agree that he would place the child in a capable home? Look at me, Maggie, and answer truthfully. Was such an agreement made?"

"Aye. But—"

"Then he acted in good faith, lass."

"Cease speaking to me of faith," I told him. Pushing him away, I paced the room.

"Maggie," came his kind voice. "Come and sit down with me. I've made mulligatawny for my dinner. We'll discuss this dilemma, perhaps work something out."

"There is nowt to work out," was my answer, though I looked toward the aumbry where rested a platter of bread and a ewer of posset. The warm milk and ale beverage, smelling of spices, caused my stomach to ache with hunger.

"Come on." He fetched another bowl from the cupboard and placed it alongside his on the table. Turning his grizzled face back to mine, he smiled. "Maggie-mine, when have you ever turned down my mulligatawny? It used to be your favorite."

I tried to resist again. "The hour is late, Brabbs."

He poured me a mug of posset. "One hardy drink and bowl of soup and then you're gone. I'll fetch my timbrel and we'll get you back to Walthamstow in half the time it takes to walk it."

I did not refuse again, for my appetite was awakened and keen. Brabbs sat across the table, his hazel eyes steadfast on my face, though we ate in silence. I sensed his curiosity: I was changed from my former self in both appearance and personality. But I avoided his appraisal, staring occasionally toward the fireplace. I was in no state of mind to speak of my experiences at Menston. My thoughts, instead, were on Nicholas. And my son.

When Brabbs had finished his soup, I sat back in my chair, closed my eyes briefly with sleepy contentment, then asked, "In your opinion, is Nicholas mad?"

"I do not know, girl."

"But you must have heard—"

"Only rumors. The man is reclusive."

"But surely his brother—"

Brabbs threw up his hands. "His brother is as likely to continue this profession as I am to be appointed King of all England. Would you like more posset, girl?"

I shook my head.

"Trevor has a keen head on his shoulders, I won't deny it, but he lacks the sensitivity it takes to be a dedicated physician."

Thinking of Mr. Dix that morning, I mentally agreed.

"George might have made a fine physician. Aye, he would've at that, come to think on it."

I had forgotten George Wyndham, the second-born son of milord's parents. I recalled Eugene Wyndham as well, who was slightly older than Trevor—Trevor being the youngest of the Wyndham sons. "They are still in the colonies?" I asked.

"Aye, they've set themselves up nicely in Boston." Scraping his chair away from the table, Brabbs fixed me with his eye and said, "It's back to Walthamstow with you before this storm gets worse. I'll get my cart. Settle yourself before the fire and warm up while you can. I'll be back in two shakes of a lamb's tail."

I watched him pull on his woolen cloak. "Brabbs?"

He turned to face me.

"I have but one question, and I'll put it to you straightforward. Do you think he killed her?"

The wind rattled the glass in the window.

"You know him better than I, girl," he finally replied, then turned for the door.

I stopped him again. "Were you summoned to the house the night she died?"

"Aye," he replied without turning to face me again.

"You saw her body?"

"What was left of it."

"And how was Nicholas?"

"He was like a man in a trance. It was several days before the shock began to wear off. The worst of it started then, I fear." He opened the door and looked out on the swirling snow and darkness before stepping out into the night.

I donned my cloak, then warmed my hands before the fire before leaving the house myself. Standing inside the fenced toft, I looked about the gardens where the dried stalks of poppies and sweet williams lay mostly hidden by the blanket of snow. Then Brabbs appeared with his horse and cart and I climbed aboard.

We passed directly through town, by Common Ewe Moor and Pinder Ing at the foot of Lavely Lane. Twice we met horsemen, and twice I huddled more deeply into my wrapper. Once we passed a stooped figure standing beside the road, and as Brabbs slowed the cart and allowed the wasted figure to pass, I noted the familiar profile of my old friend, Rosine.

Halfway across the road she stopped, lifted the hood of her cape slightly to better see me. I did not hide though my instinct told me I should. I could not hide from Rosie.

What emotion did I see there within her weakened eye? A tear of recognition? Of memory? Of forgiveness? A smile touched her mouth and then she was gone behind a flurry of snow. The cart rumbled on. I heard Brabbs say quietly, "She's been ill."

A half an hour passed before we arrived at Walthamstow. I had no desire to leave my old friend. I looked at him and smiled. He returned my smile and hunched his shoulders against the cold.

"Maggie-mine," came his shivering voice in the darkness. "Answer me this: If it's only the child you've come for, why have you not taken him and gone?"

I climbed from the cart.

"Maggie . . . ?"

I looked up at Brabbs, allowing the snow to fall lightly onto my face. "Because Nicholas needs me," I said. I turned to the house and thought, *Because I love him*.

With the admission came an unexpected release. I was free to love Nicholas Wyndham again because I understood now. He had loved me. He might have returned to me but for some cruel twist of fate that had caused his horse to fall through the ice. The accident had left Nicholas partially without his memory. But could such a trauma be affecting him still?

I turned to look down the road. Brabbs was no longer visible to me, swallowed by the darkness and snow. I turned back for the house.

I cannot guess how long I trudged my way along the path before realizing the snow had been trampled before me. But the footprints, though fast filling in with fresh snow, were there. I bent to study them curiously, and followed them as they wound away from the house and into the trees.

The snowdrifts, much deeper at the edge of the

woods, sufficiently hid the tracks from my sight. I continued to search for several minutes before giving up. Turning back to the house, I paused to take in Walthamstow's enormity. I recognized this wing even in the darkness. It was my lord's quarters. I stared up at his window, then toward my own.

What made me stand in the frigid, blinding snow and stare at that dismal portal I do not know. But stare I did, as if compelled never to take my eyes from it. Then I saw it: a shadow against the window, a silhouette, blacker even than the darkness surrounding me. Someone was in my room.

My pulse stopped. Plunging my hand into the pocket of my cloak, I closed my fingers around my key. Had I remembered to lock my door? Yes. I vividly recalled locking it. My mind raced frantically. I had taken every precaution to destroy any evidence that could somehow link me with Royal Oaks. But what if I had overlooked a scrap of paper or article of clothing?

I backed into the tree line, suddenly aware that whoever stood at my window and looked down into the garden could see me as well. Deeper into the trees I descended. Then the ground gave beneath my foot, and though I made a desperate grab for some harbor to save me I felt myself tumbling backward into the chasm of black and white that reached with icy fingers to envelop me. My head struck the ground, and my world dissolved into darkness.

I awakened gradually. Snow covered my face and clung to my lashes. How long had I lain there? Odd that I should feel warm encased in this frigid shroud. I looked about me. The snow was falling less steadily now. Occasionally the ethereal moon would dash its

light over the snow, throwing shadows on the ground
where moments before none had existed.

My head ached. I closed my eyes briefly before struggling to sit up.

At first I thought the movement to my right was
nothing more than the wind whipping the snow into
some odd formation. Perhaps the snow on my lashes
played tricks on my mind. I rubbed my eyes, then
looked again.

The apparition was gone.

What had I seen? My first impulse was to call out.
But to what? Certainly there was nothing—no one—
there now. The vision had been vague, like a wisp of
gray smoke here one moment and gone the next.

I struggled to my feet and steadied myself against a
tree until my world quit tipping to and fro. Then I
continued on my journey, slogging my way unsteadily
through the shin-high snow that had by now turned
my feet into blocks of ice.

The kitchen was a welcome haven, dark and warm.
The coals in the hearth glowed eerily beneath the
drawn peat. I huddled before it, not yet ready to retire
to my room and yearning for company—Matilda or
Kate or even Polly would do.

Then, suddenly, I sensed that I was not alone. I
slowly turned and stared into the darkest shadow. Yellow eyes stared back at me.

"Belzeebub," I whispered. "Here, kitty."

She stretched and yawned and padded over to me.

I took the cat in my arms, smiling to myself as its
contented purring filled the room.

"Ariel?"

The sound of my name spoken so suddenly in the
quiet startled me.

Adrienne entered the room. The powder-blue of her

gown looked white in the semidarkness. "Have you been out?" she asked me.

I could hardly deny it. "Yes."

"I looked for you earlier . . ."

"Is something wrong?"

She wrung her hands. "It's Nick. There—there's been—Oh! Oh, Ariel, it was just awful. Awful!"

I dropped the cat to the floor and hurried to her.

"What are we to do?" she asked me. "I have never seen him so—so desperate. He hardly knew me. His own sister—and he hardly knew me."

Taking her cold hands in mine, I told her, "You must try to calm yourself and tell me what happened."

She shook her head and briefly closed her eyes. "We should have seen it coming. The incident with the lace yesterday should have warned us." Looking at me directly, she asked, "What madness has possessed him, Ariel? He paces the floor and argues with himself. He insists his deceased wife has come back to haunt him. Oh dear God, what are we going to do?"

"Where is he now?"

"With Kevin."

A weakness befell me. I dropped Adrienne's hand, turned for the door, and hurried down the corridor.

The candles along the bleak hallway were unlit. I groped my way along, bumping tables and knocking chairs. My eyes traversed each corner and cranny. Black—all black—I was suffocating in it.

I came to a foyer and stood like some wayward voyager uncertain which road to take. The darkness confused me. I chose the hallway to my right. The air was colder, the darkness more impenetrable. But I hurried on, so intent on my mission I was unaware that the opulent carpet beneath my feet had given way to stone until the echo of my footsteps rang out.

I stopped.

The abysmal darkness surrounded me. Dampness crept through my clothes and clung to my skin like the fear gripping my heart.

Panic seized me. Foolish girl, I scorned myself. There is nothing here but dust balls and perhaps a mouse or two. Close your eyes and when you open them again the black will seem less dense and frightening.

I tried it.

Pray, it did not work! The fathomless depth and measureless distance of the corridor promised nothing welcome. I backed away, slowly at first, making certain each step was solid until I once again felt the cushioned softness of carpet beneath my heel. I spun then and ran, frantically waving my hands out before me. I passed through the foyer: Yes, I reckoned, I should have turned left and not right.

I hurried up the stairs.

Where were the bloody servants?

Were I mistress of this bleak, dim dungeon I would line the walls with girandoles. The candles would never, ever be allowed to die!

Reaching the upper landing, I paused. Blessed relief! The hall was not dark. A warm glow suffused the port-colored carpet that lined the floor. A gilt-wood chair against the wall reflected candlelight from its gold-leafed arms and legs. I viewed these things like a child who had lost her way in the wood, and by some quirk of good luck had found her way home again. I hurried toward Kevin's room, my fear of the dark overridden again by my concern for my son . . . and his father.

I approached the door.

"Jane's come back," came the crone's voice. "Back

to make you pay for what you did to her. Murderer. She's calling out from her grave this very moment, milord. Listen."

I stopped and held my breath, doing my best to cease the noisy thud of my own heart against my ribs. The walls creaked as wind roared through the eaves and drove snow and sleet against some distant window. A mournful sound, to be sure, but wind it was and nothing more.

Rallying my spirits, I entered Kevin's room.

Bea sat before the fire, her shoulders curled away from the back of her rocker, her fingers twisted like gnarled branches about the arms of her chair. Her thick-soled shoe thumped against the floor as she rocked.

The child slept soundly in his bed. Nicholas, his back to me, stood at Kevin's bedside, watching him sleep.

The thump of Bea's foot quieted as I called out, "Lord Malham?" Nicholas, however, did not move.

I refused to acknowledge her. Instead, I walked quietly up to my lord and touched his arm.

"Yes." The acknowledgement whispered, he tucked the blanket more gently about his son. "What is it?"

"Come with me from this room, sir, and I will tell you."

"Come with you?" He lifted his face to me, and his look was fell. He focused on my face a long moment as if he were attempting to recall my features. And then—what?—enlightenment? confusion? Perhaps it was alarm that widened his heavy-lidded eyes for an instant, then it was gone. Settling back against the bed, he smiled.

"Will you come with me?" I asked him. I took his hand in mine in the most brazen way. But I was not dealing with a rational person. I could see it in his eyes, his smile. He was not himself.

His fingers tightened over mine. Backing away, I said, "Come along, sir," and he obeyed me.

Chapter 9

"Perhaps you would like to paint?" I asked him.

He towered above me, his downcast face gray in the half-light. Then his hand came up slowly and his fingertips drifted over my shoulder. "You've been out," he stated. I heard him swallow in the silence. He asked then, "Why?"

"To see a friend, sir."

His brows drew downward. "Friends. I recall having friends—yes, I can recall that much." He passed his hand over his eyes and looked away.

Squaring my shoulders, I walked to the studio door. He followed.

I moved to the center of the room while Nicholas stood at the threshold, his features hidden from me by shadow. I removed my cloak and dropped it to the floor. "Will you light the candles, sir?"

He moved like an automaton to the table and there fumbled with flint and candle for some minutes before accomplishing the feat. I watched as he lit each of the many tapers about the room until the quarters glowed cheerfully with golden-yellow light. Smiling, I hurried to a clean canvas, swept it up from the floor, and placed it on the easel. I lifted brushes and a pallet for his paints.

His eyes moved carefully over my face. What did he

see? I wondered. Were those opaque, steel-gray pools acknowledging the same gauntness of my cheeks that Brabbs saw? Did he assess me in the way of an artist . . . or a man?

My blood warmed as I fixed my gaze on his mouth. Even in the bleakest of moments, when my despair had threatened to break me those months at Menston, the memory of those lips had filled me with both anger and longing. Now I was forced to face reality. I had continued to love Nicholas Wyndham as surely, as desperately, as I had hated him for deserting me.

No longer could I deny the truth to myself.

"My lord," I forced myself to say, "will you paint now?"

I held my breath as he approached me. He wore the same black coat and white shirt that he'd worn earlier in the day. About his neck hung a loose cravat. As he reached for the brushes in my hand our fingers touched. We stared at each other for a long moment before I forced myself to brush past him and climb atop my perch.

Turning my back to the window, I faced him fully.

His movements were hesitant at first; perhaps clumsy. But by the end of the first half hour he had fallen into the ritual with zest, losing himself completely in the colors he lavished on the canvas. Yet his eyes rarely strayed to my face. When they did, they were troubled. He would stare at me long and hard, then delve with renewed vigor into his work, his face becoming rigid and flushed with emotion. Brushes scattered over the floor at his feet and splashed vibrant pigments on the tips of his boots. He took no notice.

I should have suspected the explosion that followed, for his movements had hinted of frustration. But I was too caught up in my memories and fantasies.

I was lurched back to reality as he grabbed the canvas from the easel and hurled it across the room, where it crashed against the wall.

"Damn!" he shouted.

I leapt from my stool, my fingers twisting into my skirts, quaking visibly from surprise as he paced restlessly about the room.

Raking his fingers through his hair, he paused before the window and gazed through the icy panes of glass. "My paintings rival Antoine Watteau in realism and yet my fingers grow dumb and my eye blind when I attempt your likeness."

"Mine, sir?"

"Aye, yours, miss." He whirled to face me, his eyes like smoldering gray coals. Then he looked at his hands. "God help me, are they going the way of my mind?"

I tried to force a smile into my voice. "Your hands are steady, my lord." Then I hurried to the canvas, gently lifting it from the floor. Staring down on the featureless face, I studied the swirling black hair. Though shorter, it was much like mine, but the richness of color and the vibrancy of the shine far surpassed my own. "A face with no eyes? No mouth?" I laughed gaily. "Am I so nondescript, milord?"

His dark head snapped up. "Are you mocking me?" he demanded.

"Mock you, sir?" Tilting my head, I looked again at the canvas. "Whoever she is, she is very pretty. I think I'm envious."

He slowly crossed the room and stood at my side. It was all I could do not to lean into his frame, to soak up the heat of his body. For indeed his very presence sapped my strength, left me weak and breathless and yearning. In the absolute hush that claimed the room

I could hear plainly the deep draw of his breath as he watched me.

"Envious," he said in a quiet response. And then he touched me. Nicholas took my chin in the crook of his finger and gently tipped up my face. He studied it: my eyes that glistened with tears and all the unspoken words I longed to say; my mouth that parted—half in fear, half in expectation—and quivered with the memory of his kiss; my cheeks, blushing now in shame and—

"Foolish child," said he. "The paint on that pallet dulls in comparison to the beauty I behold at my fingertips."

"Beauty? No, sir, I am not beautiful. I am not even pretty."

A slight pressure of his fingertip drew me closer. His dark head tilted. "Are you not afraid of me?" he asked softly.

"No."

His eyes assessed me: my face, my shoulders, my hands—searching perhaps for some evidence of my lie. Dropping his hand, he turned away. "Who did you see in the village? A friend, you say?"

"Aye, a friend."

"A man?"

"Yes, a man."

"Ah." He stared out the window. "And what would you say if I forbid you from seeing him again?"

"I would say, sir, with all respect, that it is none of your business who I see." I replaced the portrait on the easel and picked his brushes off the floor. "Will you continue to paint?"

"Are you in love with him?"

I responded with silence. I did love Brabbs but not in that way.

"Are you about to marry some shepherd's son and leave me?" He waited; his shoulders rose and fell with a breath. "I should hate to see you go, I think."

With every nerve of my body unstrung in that moment—that eternity—I watched Wyndham's profile as he gazed at the glass. Oh, how I loved him in that instant. How I loved the sweet vulnerability I heard in his words, the unspoken hint of fondness. I had heard it before, a lifetime ago.

Was it too much to hope that somehow the spark of love for me that had once warmed his noble heart had been rekindled? The idea made me light-headed. Or could it be that deep in his mind, some buried memory of what we once shared was struggling to surface? I was determined to know.

"I suspect this a lonely place. Walthamstow, I mean."

"A prison, madam, and yes, it is lonely."

"You should go out more."

"And give the gossip mongers something more to prattle about? I don't think so." He smiled at me warmly.

"But you drink at the tavern with Jim. Do you find it a pleasant place?"

"Not often."

"Then why do you go there?"

He shifted one shoulder in a careless response, and I thought, this is getting us nowhere. I decided on a more direct approach. "Did you go there to escape your wife?"

He pursed his lips.

I asked myself in that instant, why not tell him who you are, admit your identity, your purpose for returning? The very thought, however, brought fear to my heart. I was a stranger to him, after all. Unfamiliar now with the feelings we once shared, he would suspect my motives. I could take no chances that he would banish me from my child.

Too, I was a dead woman to him. If it were true, if he was so unstable to believe his wife was haunting him, what would he think of me? Cultivating the love he had once felt would take time. During my term behind Royal Oaks's barricaded doors, I had seen many an infirm mind snapped completely by an impatient hand or tongue.

Oh, but I could not take that chance. I would not take that chance. I lost him once, and the breech had left me desperate and broken.

Putting aside the brushes, I bid him good night. He did not respond, just continued to stare out the window as I quit the room.

I spent the next two hours in my room. After hurriedly inspecting my belongings and finding no evidence of intrusion, I reassured myself that there was nothing there that could place me again at that wretched hospital in Menston. I carried the only evidence on my person: A brand, RO, had been burned into the flesh above my elbow.

Sitting in a French fauteuil with tapestry upholstery, I stared at the flickering tallow light on my dresser and listened to Wyndham pace about his quarters. As he prowled his room like a caged cat I began to share his sister's distress. He spoke on occasion, and it was then that I tipped my head and held my breath in anticipation of some reply. There was nothing, only the moan of the wind and the scrape of ice-bound branches against my window.

At midnight the wind stopped. The silence grew as heavy as the darkness outside my window.

Had I dozed? A singular noise brought my head up. Sliding from my chair, I watched the knob of my door turn slowly to the right. I looked toward the key on my dresser and held my breath.

The lock held.

"Who is there?" I called out. The words rang like an echo in a well. "Speak up," I said. "Milord, is that you?"

The knob, glittering in the dim, wavering light, slid back into place.

My ears ached with the strain as I waited. There! A movement in the hall. I swept up the key and ran for the door. One thrust and the lock grated. I threw open the door and . . . nothing.

How could that be?

I returned to my room and took up the candle. Running into the dark corridor and cupping my hand around the frantically dancing flame, I hurried down the hall, beyond my lord's closed door to Kevin's room. Lifting the light over his sleeping form, I assuaged my panic with his peaceful presence. I tiptoed then to Bea's door. She lay in her bed, still as a corpse on a catafalque.

Perhaps I was letting my imagination run away with me. Perhaps I had only dreamt that someone meddled with my door, as I had earlier imagined someone's presence by the pond. No doubt I was letting Polly's tales of ghosts get the better of me. Still, having returned to the hallway, I wavered in indecision. I thought to rap on Wyndham's door, indeed, had raised my hand to do so when it was thrown open.

I had witnessed madness. I had experienced terror. But the look I perceived on my lord's face as he came at me was beyond either, and it was frighteningly familiar.

The candle slipped from my fingers to the floor as I stumbled backward. My arms came up to ward off his hands—too late! His fingers closed about my throat, as cold and hard as steel.

By some miracle the candle at my feet continued to burn, sending a coil of black smoke into the air. Wyndham shoved me against the wall and hissed, "If I didn't kill you before, I will kill you now! God, how I loathe you. In the name of all Christendom, if I have to burn in hell myself I'll end this madness now, Jane!"

Jane!

Though his fingers dug into my throat, I managed to cry out. "Nicholas, I'm not Jane! Not Jane! Jane is dead; she is dead!" I gasped for breath. "Please! It is I! Maggie! Maggie! God help me!" For a split second his eyes cleared. He shook his head.

His hands left me so suddenly I sank to my knees on the floor. When at last I turned my face up to his, I knew not what to expect. Coming down on one knee, he grabbed my shoulders and shook me. "She was here. I saw her out my window earlier. I heard her voice in this very hall. I smelled her perfume. I saw her, I tell you. Jane is here, she's alive! For God's sake, why won't you people believe me!"

Before I could respond he stood again and turned back to his room. Stumbling to my feet, I followed.

Clinging to the door frame, I watched helplessly as he swept up his fur-lined mantle from the floor and swung it around his shoulders. "What are you doing? Milord, you aren't going out? It's after midnight and—"

"Out of my way." Barreling through the doorway, he shoved me aside and said, "As God is my witness, by morning's light I'll have proven that my bitch of a wife has come back. I vow midnight tomorrow will see us *both* burning in hell!"

Standing in the hallway, I watched helplessly as Nicholas disappeared into the darkness.

"Lunatic!"

Startled by the crone's scratchy voice, I spun to face her. She crouched on the floor in her crumpled muslin gown, holding the candle. Tipping up her pointed chin, she cackled a laugh that echoed throughout the empty rooms surrounding us.

"I warned you, didn't I?" Melted wax dripped over her gnarled fingers as she lifted the light between us. "I warned you he's mad. He were nearly mad when he killed her, and now his conscience has driven him over the edge. Well, I say good riddance! I hope his soul burns in hell."

Stepping forward, I swung my palm across the woman's cheek.

She sagged completely to the floor, her arm thrown up to protect her. "Wicked girl!" she cried out. "Wicked, wicked, girl. I'll see you dismissed for this. You'll pay. I'll see you pay!"

I ran to my room, grabbed up my cloak, and reentered the hallway. Through the darkness I saw a familiar image approaching.

"Gum, wot's 'appenin' 'ere? Lud, you old bitty," Matilda said to Bea, "wot y' doin' on the bloody floor?"

I grabbed Matilda's shoulders. "Fetch help, Tilly. Nicholas has to be stopped." I left her gaping down at Bea.

Exiting the house through the kitchen and pulling my cloak tightly about my shoulders, I entered that dim and misty night, oblivious to the snow that fell fast and cold against my skin. I had but one thought, one fear, and that was Nicholas's safety. Sinking to my shins in the snow, I plodded on toward the stables. Too late. Wyndham came out of the darkness, his booted legs wrapped about his horse's heaving sides, the tail of his mantle flying behind him in the rising wind. The beast nearly trampled me: I threw myself aside and into the snow as he thundered by me.

I called out his name, then scrambled to my feet and ran as fast as the snow and my strength would allow. I ran until my lungs burned and the wind cut my eyes and I could barely see. Until I fell onto my hands and knees and forced my lungs to take one more excruciating gasp of air. Then I climbed to my feet and ran again.

Reaching the bottom of Raikes Road, I noted the tracks veer to the right, away from the village.

"Where is the moon?" I asked aloud. Oh, for one thread of silver light to brighten my path. I lifted my face and searched the sky, blinking away each tiny flake of snow that drifted onto my lashes. "God, give me the strength to see this through," I prayed, then moved on toward the stone and wrought-iron entrance to the cemetery.

Amid the velvet darkness were shimmering relics of angels, their marble wings outstretched. I listened hard, and heard in the intense stillness a scraping noise. There! Beyond that pile of stone overlooking the mausoleum. I forced myself to move. Silence again.

I was certain that each soul who resided here had arisen from his earthly bed to watch me. My temples throbbed painfully. Topping the rise, I searched. Oh! how bleak and void was this desolate acre! How cold!

I tipped my head into the frigid wind, but it drove me backward, stole the breath from my lungs so I was forced to shield my face with my arms to regain it. I struggled forth, slipped, then continued. Onward! My mind bade my numb body to move. And then I saw him. Though horror shook my limbs I roused my rebelling senses and stumbled forward. I could not speak at first. I could not breathe. Throwing myself onto my lord's procumbent form, I struggled to lift his face from the snow.

Wretched fate that had brought my beloved to this! I swept the wet stuff from his eyes and cheek. I rolled him over.

Was he dead? Tearing the mantle from his breast, I pressed my ear against his heart. My hope soared. There was life there yet, thank God. Then I noticed the shovel at his side and the dark, damp clods of brown earth that stood out against the blanket of white around us. With a trembling hand I reached and nudged away the refuse from the marble headstone partly hidden by snow.

Jane!

I removed my cloak and placed it beneath his head. Lying down and pressing my body against his, I wrapped my arms and legs around him and waited.

Presently I heard a voice. "Ariel;" it called. "Ariel, are you there?"

I sat up and cried out, "Here."

A figure lumbered toward me. I tried hard to make out the face. Jim. My lord's friend. I wept aloud in relief. "Jim, I am here. Nicholas is here. Come and help us!"

Before long he stood above us. "What's this?" he exclaimed.

"Will you help us?" I asked.

He dropped to his knees beside us. His face, gray and damp, looked hopelessly dejected. He shook his head. " 'e warned me. I should've listened. I might've stopped 'im. This'll do it, I fear. They'll take 'im away now."

My heart almost died within me, but I rallied again.

"Then we shan't tell them. Why must they know?" Taking encouragement from his silence, I continued. "We will take him from this inhospitable place. Fill in the grave and tamp the earth and only you and I will know." Crouching now, I attempted to lift Nicholas from the ground. "If I must, I will drag him from this place myself. All I ask is that you will speak no more of this. Vow it now!"

He reached and caught my arm. "Why are y' doin' this?"

"He needs our help."

"Y've troubled 'im, girl, since y' came here. He told me so 'imself. Go on, then, catch his feet. I'll take 'is shoulders and—"

His sudden silence threatened me. I looked up and caught my breath. Trevor stood at the top of the rise, his face mostly hidden by the fox-pelt collar of his mantle.

"What, by all that is sacred, has happened here?" he said.

Neither I nor Jim responded.

Trevor approached, grabbed up my cloak from the ground, and threw it into my arms. "Put that on before you freeze, then tell me what has happened to my brother."

Still I remained quiet.

"Very well, keep your bloody silence. Matilda has already informed me of his bout of insanity. Come here, Jim, and help me. My carriage is outside the gate. We'll carry him there."

They stooped and lifted him. Carefully they trod back up the rise and hurried toward the gates.

I entered the carriage before them, took my place on the seat, and prepared to nestle Wyndham's head in my lap. I held it gently while his brother counted his pulse beats.

"What has happened?" I wondered aloud. "There is no injury—"

"The grievance is mental, I fear. I suspect a total collapse." Trevor peeled off his wet gloves. "I've suspected the breakdown for some time, though I admit this is somewhat sudden. Something must have triggered it."

"He thought he saw his wife," I responded.

"That is nothing new. He's experienced that hallucination since the fire." Leaning back against his seat, he said, "I'll pen a letter of inquiry to Doctor Conrad in London. There are certain measures that must be taken before we can have Nick committed."

Jim, who sat in stony silence at my side, flinched at the words. But no more than I. Panic seized me.

We arrived back at Walthamstow and found its windows blazing with light. Reginald waited there, and Matilda and Polly and Kate and a score of servants whom I had never before seen. I removed my cloak and gently placed it over my lord's face. I could not bear to subject him to these gaping eyes and curious minds. I knew their thoughts; I knew their sharp and vicious tongues. I would protect him the best I could.

I accompanied Trevor and Jim to Nicholas's room, but as I thought to cross into those quarters Trevor stopped me, closing the door in my face. I turned and found Matilda weeping quietly in the dark.

"Wot's t' do?" she asked in a small voice. "They'll take 'im now; that's for certain. Wot a pity."

"What could have happened here?" I asked the question for myself, but it was Tilly who answered.

" 'e seemed right after dinner. 'e were lookin' for you, miss, wantin' to paint, methinks. 'e had a drink with 'is brother and sister then 'e went for a walk ... It were so sudden, just like the night Lady Malham died." She blew her nose into a hanky. " 'e come back from 'is walk a different man. 'e looked ill, 'e did. Complained 'is 'ead was poorly. 'e 'ad another drink and went to look in on Kevin." Without waiting for a response, she turned and waddled down the hall.

I closed my eyes briefly, then returned to my room.

Chapter 10

"You asked to see me, milady?"
      Adrienne looked up from her book and smiled.
"Come in and sit down, Ariel. Please." When I had done
so, she closed her reader and sat back in her chair. "I
was just practicing my French. I'm considering a trip
abroad, perhaps in spring. Have you ever visited Paris?"

I shook my head.

"Quel dommage!" she exclaimed. "Paris in spring is
like heaven. Tell me: Would you like to go there?"

"To Paris?" I thought a moment. "To be truthful, I
have never given Paris much thought. Besides, I think
my going to such a place is highly unlikely."

"But if it were likely?"

"I don't know."

Adrienne placed her book aside. Folding her hands
in her lap, she took a deep breath and began again.
"Considering the circumstances—"

"Circumstances?" I interrupted.

"Since your continuing in your present position is
highly unlikely, I thought you might consider the position of companion to me. I—"

"Ma'am."

Her fingers twisting together, Adrienne avoided my
eyes. "I hope you'll consider my offer, Ariel. I've come
to enjoy your company. You've been—"

"You have not asked about your brother for three days."

She stared at her hands. "As I was saying—"

"You have avoided all discussion about his well-being."

"I—"

"Don't you care?"

At that moment Reginald entered the room. With a look of relief, Adrienne addressed him.

"Ma'am," he said. "Lady Forbes has arrived."

I stood and prepared to leave. Adrienne, however, was not to have it. "Please stay. Perhaps then you will understand."

In that moment, Claudia Forbes arrived. A stout woman in her early forties, she swept toward Adrienne, a flutter of bright satin and feathers, her arms thrown wide to embrace Lady Adrienne in a tremendous hug.

"Oh, my dear, you look wonderful! Wonderful!" Claudia exclaimed, then she dropped into the chair and released a huff that I was certain could be heard in the next room. "We missed you last week. The Wakefield soiree was marvelous! So sorry you couldn't make it." Her tiny round eyes found me then and perused me at length.

"I was not up to a journey to York," came Adrienne's tired response. Then, with a smile, she introduced us. "I was just speaking to Miss Rushdon about accepting the position of companion to me. Pamela left me, you know."

"I heard. She's applied at Breakton."

Adrienne paled noticeably.

I took a chair and looked out the window on the thawing countryside. Though snatches of gossip came to me occasionally, I pushed them aside in deference to my own thoughts. Three days had passed since Nick's breakdown; three days he had been locked in his rooms and all but Trevor had been forbidden to see him. I knew he was well cared for. Food was brought to him three times a day, though each time it was returned to the kitchen uneaten. Peat was taken in regularly, so I knew his room remained warm.

Why, then, was I not satisfied?

Because I felt that *I* could help him, yet I could not see him. I could not touch him.

"I suppose there will be no representation of Walthamstow at the races at Middleham this spring," came Claudia's words, intruding on my thoughts. I looked again at Adrienne. Her eyes were troubled. "Of course not," Lady Forbes continued. "How thoughtless of me. Your animals were all killed in that terrible fire last summer. What a shame. Such splendid beasts they were too."

There was desperation in the glance that Adrienne threw me. Weakly she responded, "Yes, they were."

"I must admit, York is positively roiling with the gossip. Why, one evening at charades Paul Hurst even enacted the terrible scene. It was all quite wicked. Here, what's this?"

Our attentions were momentarily diverted toward the door as Kevin toddled into the room. I was first from my chair, though I instantly checked my parental instinct and allowed Adrienne to sweep him up in her arms.

Cradling Kevin's wee, dark head against her shoulder, Adrienne said, "Bea is neglecting her duties again. I'll have to speak to her."

Lady Forbes leant back in her chair. "I must commend you, my dear, you show great consideration to that boy, considering."

"Considering? Pray tell, Claudia, what is there to consider?"

"That he is illegitimate, of course."

I thought I had grown to know Adrienne, but I was wrong. In that instant her demeanor turned as brittle as ice. Rounding on her pompous acquaintance, she declared, "How dare you?"

"I—I beg your pardon?" she responded.

"How dare you come into my home with your wicked, wagging tongue and cast aspersions on my brother and this beautiful infant. The child has caused you no harm, has committed no crime and yet you would besmirch his innocence. Madam, you may leave my house. You are no friend to this family, and certainly not to me!"

"Well, I never—"

"I know now why you came here; I should have guessed. You want nothing more than to gather rumors and send them flying to every corner of Yorkshire. Well, you'll find no gossip here. My brother is well and happy and without suspicion. The child you behold in my arms is an accomplishment of pure devotion. He was born to a young woman who cared for my brother enough to sacrifice her chastity and fine reputation for no more motive than love. Get out, I said. Get out!"

Having staggered to her feet, Lady Forbes quit the room.

Adrienne sank into the chair, rocked Kevin in her arms, and pressed her trembling lips to his brow. "Sweet child, my own flesh and blood." Lifting her eyes to mine, she said, "Now you know, Miss Rushdon. Another of our secrets is laid open for ridicule. Go on, if you must; judge us."

"Must I?" I retook my chair and watched fondly as

Kevin's aunt squeezed him gently. "Your love for Kevin is undeniable," I told her. "He's very fortunate."

"It is I who am fortunate. Each time I hold him in my arms I bless the girl who gave him birth. I pray for her soul and hope she finds peace in heaven. And the poor man who brought Kevin to us—I wonder to this day if he survived his illness."

He did not, I knew.

"I shall never forget the eve that poor, racked fellow entered our home with Kevin, and the child but days old. Jane tried to turn them back out into the cold. Oh, it was a dreary Christmas Eve. When the young man placed the babe in Nicholas's arms I began to believe in miracles again."

I could not help but ask, "What was your brother's reaction?"

"Disbelief. He said he knew no such person as 'Maggie.' He didn't remember, of course. His illness had begun to distort his mind even then, you see."

"Yet he accepted the child as his own. Why?"

"He didn't at first. It is that marvel of bonding, I think, that convinced him, though I and Jim helped as well. You see, my brother confided in me once about his relationship with the girl, though he was very protective of her and would divulge nothing more than her first name. I suspected they would marry. Indeed, he traveled to York to break his engagement to Jane so they might do so."

"But he didn't break it."

"There was an accident. Near Weatherby his horse went down. It was fate that Jim happened by. Nicholas was submerged to his shoulders in freezing water."

"That's when his illness began?"

"When he returned he knew nothing more than his name and his family. He had no recollection of why he was traveling to York." Adrienne appeared thoughtful. "I had already noticed behavior changes in Nick, but I assumed it was due to the demands of my mother that he marry Jane. They argued bitterly. He began to spend more time at the tavern. Perhaps the liquor was altering his moods. Yes, he began changing even then, I think. The fall from his horse only exaggerated his problem."

Leaning forward, my elbows on my knees, I asked, "Do you mean that he had already begun to lose his memory before the fall?"

"Yes. I recall several instances when he forgot an appointment . . ." Her brow creased. "I teased him about it. Nick's memory was always so sharp."

"Were there physical changes?"

"He complained of fatigue. And there were headaches."

"Did he take medication?"

"On the contrary. Nicholas has never believed in such remedies. He never believed in bleeding, either. He always teased Trevor that if he ever came at Nick with a razor he would thrash him."

"Then tell me this: Since the fire and the death of his wife, has his mind deteriorated further?"

"Definitely."

"But he has his good days."

"Yes. Oddly enough, however, it's during those clear days that he seems to be most troubled."

"Explain 'clear.' "

"His mind is sharp."

"But he has no memory."

"Oh, he has memory, but there are dark areas. He explained it once. He said, it is like staring at the sun, then looking away. For a few brief seconds that image remains before his eyes, then it vanishes. When his mind is sharp, forgotten images come and go, but they are here and gone so quickly he cannot grasp them."

"Odd," I said. "Tell me, has he ever glimpsed, even for a second, Maggie's image?"

"I cannot say. He rarely speaks to any of us any longer. He sinks deeper and deeper into his quandary."

Silent, I watched her stroke my sleeping son's head, and I was shaken with envy. "Shall I carry him back to the nursery?" I asked her.

"No. I'll summon Bea—"

"Please." I left my chair and stood above her. Extending my arms, I said, "It would give me such pleasure . . ."

Our gazes met. We smiled. In that instant our friendship was born. Accepting the child, I turned toward the door.

"Ariel?"

I stopped and faced her.

"How *is* Nick?"

"I cannot say as I have not seen him."

"Not once? Is that Trevor's directive?" When I nodded, she looked away. "It's begun, then," she said so softly I barely heard her.

"Meaning?"

"His confinement, of course. It's what I dreaded most."

"It's what you wanted."

Her face colored. "Not true. I don't hate him, no matter what he's done. I think he never intentionally meant to hurt me. Yes, I'm certain of it, and if there were anything I could do to help him, then I would do it."

"Do you mean that?"

She came to her feet stronger and more determined than I had ever seen her.

"Then do this," I told her. "Convince Trevor to let me see him."

Eternal minutes slipped by as she watched me, then the child in my arms. When her keen eye came back to mine, she nodded.

Adrienne was true to her word.

"I would like to see Nicholas," she announced to Trevor over the shrill crying of the child, whose cheeks were burning with fever. I stepped away from their discussion, hoping to appear as disinterested as possible. It was then that I spotted Mr. Dix, sitting again on his perch beside the bookcase. He looked up and smiled as I approached.

"I see the bleeding didn't help," I told him.

"Put me off me food, it did," he responded.

"Is it your head again?"

"It's me gut. It were always me gut but I don't see what bleedin' me bloody belly button is goin' t' do t' help it."

I pressed my palm against his forehead and asked as quietly as possible, "Have you seen Brabbs?"

" 'e's out with Mary Francis. 'as been for two days. She's about gone, y' know. Slipped into sleep two days ago and ain't come out yet."

I tipped his face up and looked into his eyes. "What was Mary's ailment?"

" 'er sight was goin', her legs were gone, and, if you'll forgive the reference, so was her 'functions.' "

Porphyria. I told him to open his mouth and stick out his tongue. "Did you say she suddenly lapsed into this sleep?"

He did his best to nod.

"Unusual," I said.

"Me tongue?"

Laughing, I shook my head. "Your tongue is fine, Mr. Dix." Lowering my voice, I added, "But if I were you I would hasten from this house as quickly as possible least Wyndham break out his jar of leeches."

"Wot about me gut, lass?"

"You have intestinal worms, Mr. Dix. Go home and take two doses of calomel in water: one in the morning and one at night for five days." As he slipped from his stool, I asked, "Has Doc Wyndham seen your friend Mary?"

"Aye, the doc seen 'er last week. 'e were always good at ridin' out when she needed 'im."

"Did she call him out regularly?"

"Twice a week, usually."

"Was she in pain?"

"Oh aye. 'e give 'er laudanum for that." Lowering his voice, he said, " 'e might not be the doc that Brabbs is, but 'e's a kind heart and does 'is best." Opening the door, he pulled his scarf up around his ears and stepped out into the sunlight. I walked a short way out with him and looked out over the line of trees at the edge of the garden. For the first time since the incident at the cemetery I thought of the night I had followed the tracks into those trees. Lightly touching the bump on the back of my head, I reentered the house.

The child was still crying and wiggling on his mother's lap as I approached Trevor and Adrienne. I heard him say, "I really don't have time to argue with you, Adrienne. I've told you, for your own sake, just stay away from him. You would only upset yourself."

"I should be no more upset than I am now," she responded. She glanced toward me, then back to Trevor. "I would like to see him."

"You shouldn't be alone with Nick, Adrienne. He's not responsible for his actions."

"Ariel will be with me." She held out her hand. "Please. I would like the key."

The child let out an ear-piercing scream. Trevor grimaced, dug into his vest pocket, and withdrew the key. "If he shows any signs of violence—"

"Then we'll leave." She took my arm as we turned and left the room. Once in the corridor and up the stairs, however, Adrienne wasn't so stalwart. "I'm not certain I can do this, see him this way."

I marched determinedly to his door and held out my hand for the key.

"Oh, I cannot bear it," she said, covering her face with her hands.

"You may remain in the hall," I replied. "Now please, give me the key."

"But what if he's violent?"

"He won't be."

"But—"

Resolutely, I turned to face her. "He is not a lunatic. I refuse to believe it. Confused, yes. Angry, yes. Frightened? Most assuredly. But I am as confident of his nature as I am of my own. Give me the key, *please*, and let's put this matter to an end quickly."

She pressed it into my palm.

I turned for the door. Yet my hand shook. I can't deny it. Nor can I deny the many hours I had lain awake in the solitude of my room, remembering his face when he thought I was Jane. Such hatred had glittered in his eyes. Such loathing I had heard in his voice. The man who had wrapped his hands about my throat was hardly the man who had made love to me so sweetly two years before.

I turned the key, and in another moment I was within the apartment.

The hour was near noon, yet within these cloistered

quarters darkness prevailed. I was forced to wait until my eyes adjusted to the change before moving farther into the room. And what a grand room it was, with soaring ceilings, velvet draperies, and ancient tapestries along the walls. Centered between two windows was a high bed of intricately carved walnut.

An odd silence surrounded me, a silence filled with expectation. The bed was empty, as was the chair behind the great desk. Not until I turned did I find Nicholas. He sat in the shadows on an uncomfortable looking *caquetoire* with a hard high back. He watched me.

I looked for signs of distress. There were none, so I approached him, cautiously at first, doing my best to see through the shadows. "My lord," I whispered. "Are you well?"

He did not respond.

"He doesn't know us," Adrienne said quietly behind me. "He doesn't even hear us."

I saw his eyes widen at the sound of his sister's voice. "He hears us," I said.

"I cannot bear to see him in this pitiful way. What shall we do?"

"You will begin by keeping such comments to yourself while in his presence. Then you will do us a great favor by leaving us alone."

"But that's not possible. Trevor said—"

"I know what Trevor said." I faced her. "Adrienne, he needs companionship now, not solitude."

"Then let me stay as well."

"I'd rather you didn't."

"Very well, then." She backed toward the door, her eyes never leaving her brother. "You'll call me if there's any change?"

I closed the door behind her and locked it. Facing

my lord, I took a deep breath, squared my shoulders, and approached him again. There was something far too familiar in the glazed eyes staring straight ahead, in the lethargic manner in which he responded to my presence.

"Here now," I said loudly, "this will never do, sitting solitary in this room like a bloody Cistercian monk from Fountains Abbey." Bending over him, my face near his, my hands propped upon the *caquetoire*'s bowed arms, I asked, "Can you hear me? Aye, I know you can. Can you stand?" I pulled him up by the lapels of his dressing robe until he stood unsteadily before me. Wrapping his arms around my shoulders, I began walking him around the room. Finally, after nudging the chair toward the window, I placed him into it and flung aside the oppressive draperies, spilling brilliant light into the room.

At once, Nicholas lifted his arms to shelter his eyes.

"That's what you get for living in a cave," I told him. Then I opened the window. The cold wind smacked him fully across the face.

"That should do you," I said. I opened all the windows, allowing the room to grow brittlely cold while I climbed into his bed and pulled the coverlet up around my neck.

I saw him glower at me several times from behind his arms and I told him, "If you're cold, milord, get up and close the window. If the light hurts your eyes, shut the drape." But he continued to sit in his chair until his entire body shook and his lips turned blue.

I, meanwhile, continued to talk. I talked at length on the duties of a physician, mostly because the subject had always been of great interest to me. I told him that once I had worked in a hospital (of course I did not mention Oaks by name or *why* I had gone to that wretched institution in the first place), and that I had been allowed to assist some of the most influential and learned physicians outside of London. I added, with a sheepish smile, that I could no doubt teach Brabbs a trick or two.

Then I spoke of Walthamstow, because I knew it was a devotion we both shared. "I love its dark windows and ponds reflecting the winter-gray welkin. I love the rooks and jackdaws that nest in the thatched roofs of the field houses. I love each ewe and lamb that graze her pastures. And," I added more softly, "I love you."

A melancholy came over me then as I watched him shiver and look out the window. Leaving the bed, I sat upon the wide windowsill, drew my legs up to my chest, and rested my chin on my knee. The air was cold. Sunlight reflected from the snow on the trees, and water dripped quietly from the leaves of the house.

Through the bare branches of the distant wood I could see Malham. Closer still, I saw Jim, with hounds in harness, making his way through an arched gateway; I watched Polly hurry from the henhouse with her apron full of eggs. Then I looked back at Wyndham. His eyes regarded me.

I cannot convey how I felt in that moment, the subject of his intimate perusal—and it was intimate, desirous and beguiling as a lover's. It flushed me with warmth, stirred within me an ache so painful and yet so wonderful I had to bite my lip to keep from weeping aloud. I was no stranger to that look. No indeed.

"Lord Malham," I addressed him, aware my voice wavered. "Are you feeling better?"

He continued to stare. Finally he moistened his lips slightly with his tongue and responded, "I'm bloody cold, love."

I leapt from the window, grabbed the counterpane

from the bed, and spread it across his lap. Going to my knees beside him, I asked, "How are you feeling?"

"Tired. How long have I slept?"

"Do you remember going to sleep?"

"I remember trying to wake up."

"And you couldn't?"

He shook his head and an ebon strand of hair spilled over his brow. I swept it back with my fingertips. "What is the last thing you remember, milord?"

"Painting . . . something wasn't right. The face was wrong, all wrong. I became confused . . ." He closed his eyes and rested his head back against the chair.

"Nicholas, what do you dream of when you're asleep?"

"Nightmares."

"Of?"

His eyes opened. "I dreamt of seeing my wife again. I dreamt of following her to the cemetery and of digging up her grave."

"Is there anything else?"

"There was someone standing over my bed." His voice became hoarse and tight. "And . . ."

"And?"

"Bells."

I sat back on my heels. "You heard bells?"

"Small ones. Very, very small—God, my head hurts." He rubbed his temple, turned his face to one side, and said, "Close that damned drape. The light hurts my eyes."

I did so with a flourish before facing him again.

"I'm freezing," he said. I flew about the room, slamming closed each window and drawing the drapes. Then I hurried to the hearth and fanned the embers until a fire crackled and warmed my hands. When I returned to his side his eyes were closed. There was a smile on his lips.

"Imagine," came his quiet, sleepy voice. "Imagine my waking from a nightmare to find you perched like some trembling little passerine on my windowsill."

"Imagine," I whispered. "Just imagine."

Chapter 11

I stayed with Nicholas throughout the day, watching as he slept fitfully in his chair. He roused occasionally, opened his eyes, sat up, and looked about the room. Yet his consciousness was brief, and again he laid his head back and drifted to sleep. I had seen this behavior many times at Oaks. I recalled overhearing a physician speaking to the relative of a severely depressed patient: "Sleep is the way of the body to avoid further stress and confusion." That was often true: I had experienced it myself. Depression, however, was not the only cause of such behavior.

I dozed, and when I awoke a chill touched my bones. The fire had died. Rubbing my eyes, I started as a knock on the door sounded in the silence. I quickly left the bed, withdrew the key from my pocket, and unlocked the door.

Trevor brushed past me, a tray of food in his hands as well as a decanter of sherry. "Put some lights on in this bloody tomb," he said. As I hurried to light the candles, he asked, "How is he? Behaving himself, I hope."

"Of course," I responded.

"You may leave now."

"I'd like to stay."

Trevor looked my way briefly before sliding the tray onto a table beside Nick's chair. "You must be hungry by now, Miss Rushdon. Matilda has a wonderful kidney pie just out of the oven."

Eyeing the pastry-covered stew on the plate, I felt my stomach rumble.

Having pulled a chair up before my lord's, Trevor sat into it before looking toward me again. "Go on and eat, Ariel. You're too thin as it is." At my continued hesitance, he smiled. "Very well, then, come here."

I hurried to him.

"Has my brother awakened at all?"

"Yes. Just after noon."

"Ah! Progress, then. Tell me, how did he appear?"

"Remote."

"How do you mean? Did he know you?"

I thought a moment. "I believed he knew me at first, but I'm not certain now."

"But he spoke."

"Oh yes. Definitely."

Nicholas opened his eyes and looked at his brother. Trevor sat back in his chair. "Welcome back to the living, my lord. Haven't you grown weary of sleeping?"

"I haven't been sleeping," he said.

"No?" His blue eyes twinkling, Trevor glanced at me and smiled. "Tell me, then, what have you been doing all this time?"

"Thinking."

"Now that, my good man, can be utterly dangerous. Are you hungry?"

"Famished."

"I've brought your favorite dinner: kidney pie with Tilly's special crust."

Nick pushed the counterpane from his lap as he attempted to stand.

"Here, now," Trevor told him. "What are you trying to do?"

"Get up."

"Sit down and let me feed you."

"No." He stumbled and grabbed the back of his chair. Nervously I stood my ground, encouraged by his show of independence. Trevor, however, was not inclined toward patience.

"For God's sake, Nick, sit down before you hurt yourself."

"I'm not a damned invalid. Yet. Let me alone." Trevor reached for a spoon but had no more than lifted it from the tray when Nicholas flung out his hand, knocking it from his brother's fingers. Before either I or Trevor could recover from our surprise, he whirled, caught the table of food with his foot, and sent it shattering to the floor. "And I don't want your rotten food. I'll tell you what I want: I want out of this miserable 'tomb,' as you so aptly called it. I want out now!"

Slowly Trevor came to his feet. "That's not possible," he said.

"Why?"

"You aren't rational."

"Meaning?"

"You are a menace to yourself and others."

"Whom have I hurt?"

In a softer voice, Trevor said, "I think right now you would like to hurt me. Wouldn't you?"

"Aye, very much. But I haven't, have I?"

"Touché."

"Give me the key."

"The door isn't locked."

Nicholas turned for the door, and though I stepped forward and opened my mouth to protest, Trevor lifted his hand, palm up, to silence me. His eyes and the shake of his head said, Let him go.

And he did go, out through the door and into the darkness.

"Why," I asked Trevor, "did you let him go? He is obviously overwrought."

"We shouldn't make demands on him, Ariel. It would be dangerous to do so."

"So you truly think he's dangerous?"

"You saw for yourself."

"So what purpose do you have of letting him go, if you believe he is capable of hurting himself or others? Would you have the entire village of Malham seeing him this way?"

He shot me a fierce glance and I realized I had overstepped my limits. But he dismissed my blunder with a flip of his hand. "We're all upset. Seeing my brother like this grieves me more than you know."

"Have you spoken to Brabbs concerning Lord Malham?" I asked him.

"Certainly. Many times. He agrees with my prognosis and believes Nick should be put away."

I did not like that term: "put away." It made Nicholas sound like an animal without human feelings. I kept my opinion to myself, however. Trevor had forgiven my earlier error. He might be less gracious next time.

Adrienne entered the room then. Wringing her hands, she looked at her brother, then to me. "Polly said she saw Nick—"

"Aye," he interrupted, "he's gone." Kicking aside the tray at his feet, he started for the door.

"What will you do?" his sister asked.

Without responding, he left the room.

An hour later I stood in Brabbs's house, warming my hands before a fire. I had roused him from a nap and now he stooped over a bowl of cold water, rinsing the sleep from his eyes.

"It was a long vigil," he declared as he reached for the linen I held in my fingers. "Mary Francis is at peace now. God rest her soul."

"She died of porphyria?"

"Aye."

"Her death was quite sudden for porphyria."

He peeked at me from behind his linen. "What do you know about porphyria, girl?"

"There were cases at Oaks. The sight is usually the first to go, then the power of locomotion and the control over the bladder. It is very painful and brings forth a very slow and agonizing demise. The victims at Oaks were interned there because they soon became a hindrance to their family, and, of course, an embarrassment." I lifted one brow to punctuate the remark.

"Did you come here to discuss Mary Francis and porphyria, Maggie, or to exaggerate my guilt?"

"Neither. I've come here to discuss Nicholas."

His look became dark. "Ah."

"I understand you feel he should be locked away."

"Do I?" He threw his linen down and turned away.

"Don't you?"

"I have made no prognosis on the case. He is not my patient."

"Certainly you have an opinion. I rarely recall you ever being without one."

"This line of questioning leads me to believe there has been some alteration in his behavior." He stooped toward the fire and prodded it with a poker.

"Your mind is yet sharp, sir. Yes, there has been. Four nights ago he was found attempting to exhume his deceased wife's body. He then collapsed and has slept deeply for the last three days, rousing only upon occasion. This noon he spoke briefly with me."

Rounding to his chair, Brabbs sat onto it and crossed his legs.

"You don't appear surprised," I told him. Indeed, he seemed totally preoccupied with his thoughts.

Finally, he looked up. "Well? Tell me your opinion, girl. Certainly you have one."

"Do I?"

"I see it in the stubborn angle of your chin. In the glint of your green eye. Forgive me, Maggie-mine, but you have had more experience with feeble minds than have I. I am quite adept at rendering remedies for dropsy or—"

"Porphyria."

"But the mind is an enigma. We cannot open the skull, withdraw the organ and point to an area and say, ah, *there* is the cause of his howling at the moon, any more than we could say this matter is what separates a man with conscience from another who is without conscience. There is good and bad in all of us: agreed?"

"Aye."

"Ofttimes look to the soul and less to the brain, for it lives and thrives as surely as this matter." He thumped his temple.

Frowning, I shook my head. "You sound like the vicar."

"The soul cannot be healed by calomel or James's Powder. You must look to a higher power than mine for that."

"Whatever inflicts my lord has nothing to do with his soul. Indeed, if it had he would have been cured days ago, for each night in my bed I have invoked the help of the Holy Spirit to conquer this awful malady before it destroys him."

"Then pray longer and louder, Maggie. Mayhap, He will hear you."

"We both know God does not always listen."

"So now you are practicing sacrilege as well as medicine."

I ignored the remark.

Lifting his face, he watched me for several minutes without speaking. Finally, "Tell me what you wish to hear."

"Is Nicholas truly insane? Yes or no."

"Possibly."

The response rocked me. Propping my hand against the mantel to steady myself, I stared down into the fire. "Then you feel he should be locked away as was his grandfather? You think him that unstable?"

"His grandfather? Oh yes. I recall it now; I had completely forgotten . . . Well, no worry there. His grandfather's mental incapacity had nothing to do with some malfunction of the brain. Simply put, he was a randy old bugger and his indiscriminate philanderings eventually caught up to him. He was diseased with *Treponema pallidum.* No doubt you saw a few cases of that while at Oaks."

"But Trevor said—"

"I'm well aware of what Trevor said. Of course the family won't admit to it—it's quite an embarrassment, you see—but I am the physician who diagnosed the malady. Indeed I witnessed the signing of the documents, along with several members of Wyndham's family, that interned the old man to Saint Mary's." He poked at the fire again, giving me time to consider this new information. He sat back and continued. "It isn't an easy feat to commit someone of the late Lord Malham's peerage. There were stacks of documents to complete, as well as testimonies to hear."

"Testimonies?"

"Certainly. There must be a sum of no less than twenty witnesses to attest to the fact that, without a shadow of doubt, the unfortunate victim is mentally incapacitated and no longer able to function in a normal or rational way."

"But you say the treponema was the source of his problems."

"Without a doubt. He suffered with it for years: fever, loss of weight, and finally a breakdown of the nerves. I understand in his final days he was stricken totally with ataxia."

"Well," said I, at a sudden loss for words. I maintained a grave silence for some minutes before speaking again. "You say there must be witnesses willing to declare a man to Saint Mary's? Then I surmise that the more people that see the victim in a state of delirium, the more likely he is to be put away? Yes? Damnation!" I swept up my cloak and turned for the door, calling back over my shoulder, "Good eventide, Brabbs."

I returned to Walthamstow but I did not reenter the house. Instead I made my way down the garden path, beyond the frozen pond, beyond even the kennels to Jim's stone-and-wattle cottage.

I knocked on his door.

"I said," came the gruff response, "I ain't seen 'is lordship, so bugger off."

"Jim!" I whispered loudly as possible. "It is Ariel. If you will please—"

The door was yanked open an inch or two. Seeing Jim's grizzled face peer at me from his dark quarters, I smiled and spoke frankly. "He is here, I think. Will you let me in?"

"Let her in," came my lord's voice from within the room.

Heartened by the sound, I stepped gingerly in from the cold.

Lord Malham sat beyond the frail rushlight in the shadows with a tankard of what smelled like mulled wine in his hand. A heavy blanket hung about his shoulders as he reared his chair against the wall. "Take her coat," he told Jim.

Jim did so, giving it a shake before laying it out over a chair in front of the fire. "Welcome to me 'umble 'ome," he said, "such as it is."

I looked about the comfortable but stark surroundings. No doubt the cottage was old, to judge by the remnants of the hob of clay in the center of the floor where once the fires were built. But years ago the house had been renovated and the open fire replaced with an arched fireplace and chimney built of stone.

"Perhaps Miss Rushdon would care for wine," Wyndham said. Jim hurried to fetch it.

Lifting the tankard nearly to his mouth, Nicholas said, "Have you come to coax me home, Miss Rushdon?"

"No, sir."

"Then you've come to convince me of my folly."

"No."

"Perhaps then you just enjoy wandering about the freezing nights dressed little better than an urchin."

"Sir," I said, "this is all I own."

"Pitiful. We'll have to do something about that."

"Does that mean you intend to up my wage?"

"No."

"Well."

"Come over here and sit down beside me." At my hesitation he narrowed his dark eyes and frowned. "Have you suddenly decided against me? Perhaps you're convinced now that I'm a lunatic?"

"Lunatic is a strong word, milord. It has a macabre connotation, I think."

"Ah! Well, then, what about madman, barmy, imbecile, mooncalf . . . daft?"

"Daft is more dumb and you are not dumb."

"Confused? Demented?"

Nodding, I said, "I like confused."

Offering me a lupine smile, he lifted his tankard in salute and said, "Then confused it shall be from this moment on."

Jim handed me a tankard of the pungent wine. I wrapped my fingers around it, warming my hands. I did not, however, take the chair beside Wyndham. In truth, I did not trust myself to reside so closely to him. To have him look so appreciatively at me unraveled my senses.

Jim must have noted my thoughts, for he quickly lifted a hayfork and a passel of rake teeth from off a stool and placed it behind me. "There now, lass, sit you down and stay awhile. I've only me wimble for companionship afore milord came by."

I glanced down at the bore bit.

Nicholas lifted his tankard and in a baritone voice he recited: "And when the husbande sytteth by the fire, and hath nothing to do, then may he make them redy, and toth the rake with dry withy wod, and bore holes with his wimble."

Swiping up his mug, Jim joined: "Yokes, forks, and such other, let bailiff spy out. And gather the same as 'e walketh about; And after, at leisure, let this be 'is hire, To beath 'em and trim 'em, at 'ome by the fire!"

"Ha!" they exclaimed in unison, then throwing back their heads, they gulped their wines.

I laughed, finding joy in their boyish behavior.

Wiping his mouth with the back of his hand, Nicholas dropped his chair to the floor and motioned toward me. "Ah, Jimmy, behold: *cette jeune fille magnifique aux cheveaux noirs comme le jais*, as my sweet sister would say it. Her laughter is like music. I have never heard her laugh . . . or perhaps I have: I cannot remember."

They burst out laughing again, and I thought, Lud, they are caught in their cups.

Nicholas slapped his knee and said, "Come here, Miss Rushdon, and sit on my leg. You are perched there like a bloody sphinx. Have you never seen a man enjoy his drink? Don't you approve?"

"I have and I do."

"Perhaps a man of my peerage should not so indulge?"

"You have every right, sir. However, it would behoove you, I think, to keep your voices down lest your brother find you out."

His eyebrows shot up. "Jimmy, I believe we have a *soubrette* in our midst."

"To *soubrettes* with green eyes!" the man responded, and they drank again.

Rocking back in his chair once more, Nicholas fixed his gaze upon me, watched as I drank timidly of the wine and blushed at his evident interest in me. Not that I was at all displeased—heavens no!—only discomforted; I was not, after all, accustomed to such blatant appreciation. He eyed me like a hound would a vixen, with a glint in his eye and his teeth showing in a smile.

"Tell me," he suddenly said, "where have you been this eventide, Miss Rushdon?"

"To Malham." I spoke into my cup.

"What? Speak directly to me, Miss Rushdon. There. Repeat what you said."

"To Malham, sir."

He pursed his lips almost angrily before saying, "Do I not recall your telling me of some shepherd's son that you had smitten there?"

"No, sir. I've smitten no shepherd's son there or anywhere."

"But you mentioned you're in love with him."

"No I didn't."

"Then I must have dreamt it."

"Assuredly."

"Have you ever been in love, Miss Rushdon?"

I barely nodded, then drank my wine.

His chair hit the floor. In two strides he stood before me, grabbed my wrist, and pulled me from my stool. I followed obediently as he tugged me to the light before the fire. The pressure of his hand on my shoulder demanded that I sit, so I descended to the floor and curled my legs up under me. He followed suit, but with one black-clad knee bent up to his chest and his silk-draped arm looped around it.

Laughing, I said, "Lord Malham is feeling better, I think. He's up to games now."

"Beg to differ. Lord Malham's two sails to the wind," he responded. "But that is besides the point. I asked you a question, Miss Rushdon, but the shadow and wine hid the response. Have you ever been in love?"

I looked around at Jim. "He's very personal, don't you think?"

" 'e's a bloody nosy bloke, but that's nobility for y'." He winked an eye at me and smiled.

Looking back into the gray eyes that took my breath away, I said gently, "Aye, my Lord Malham. I have been in love."

His eyelids drooped a little as he looked at my mouth.

"Now it is my turn," I asserted, and his eyes came

back to mine. "Have *you* ever been in love, Lord Malham?" I waited like an expectant child for his response, doing my best to ignore the lure of his beautiful mouth, with its teasing corners. By the soft glow of the fire his features took on the tenderness of a child's. "Well?"

"Yes," he finally responded.

"Who was she?"

"I'm told her name was Maggie."

"You don't remember?"

He shook his head.

"Then how do you know you loved her?"

"Because I still love her. Do you think that odd? I do. I cannot understand how I can continue to love someone whose face I cannot remember. Can you?"

He watched me with a whimsical gaze. Looking away from his features and into the fire, I pondered that thought for some time. Finally I said, "I believe I can and I will try to explain. I was eight when my mother died. I loved her deeply. I love her deeply still. Yet when I attempt to bring her face to mind I cannot do it. Those features are lost to me. I cannot tell you the shade of brown her hair was, or even the color of her eyes. Her tone of voice is a mystery to me. But I recall how she made me feel: happy and content and . . . loved. Those spiritual things are what remain with us forever. In some small way they make us what we are. Do they not?"

There was a dreamy expression on his face when I raised my eyes back to his. "She must have loved you," I said. "She gave you Kevin."

A soft hope bloomed in my heart. Stirred by the spirit that loved him still, my feelings leapt warm and vibrant like the flames in the hearth. Very slowly his hand came for mine. His fingers wrapped gently about my wrist, lifted my hand, and pressed my trembling palm upon his unshaven cheek. "Ariel," he whispered. "Heal me."

I leaned closer to him. "How? Tell me how and I will do it, my lord."

"Make the nightmares stop."

"What sort of nightmares? Perhaps if you confront them . . . ?"

"Fire."

"You dream of fire. The fire that killed your wife?"

"I see myself hitting her. She falls and doesn't get up."

He turned his face and breathed softly against my palm, then lightly touched the tip of his tongue to my hand. The love I felt for Nicholas was so intense at that moment that it was very nearly painful. And the awful realization struck me: I did not *care* if he murdered his wife, if he had somehow been driven by that hateful mistress to violence, if he raised his hand and struck her that fatal blow. I loved him that much.

Shamed by my weakness, I turned my eyes away.

"Ariel?" His voice touched the skin of my temple. "Look at me."

I could not. I would give myself away.

"Ariel."

Don't touch me, I thought. Don't speak to me, don't look at me . . .

He brushed my cheek with his.

God, oh God, what was to become of me?

"Don't turn away," he said. "I need you. You're the only one who doesn't look at me with accusing eyes. You and Kevin. I don't know what I did before you came here. What would I do if you left . . . ?"

It was all spoken in deep, husky whispers, warm and arousing and moist like a summer mist against my ear. Then as quickly he pulled away.

I watched from beneath slightly lowered lashes as he tipped his shoulders toward the fire and held his hands up to the warmth. "I've asked too much," he said finally. "Forgive me. You came to Walthamstow to sit for portraits and nothing more. You shouldn't like to become involved with my problems. I shouldn't ask it of you."

"But I am involved," I responded. "Perhaps I could help if I understood fully?"

"What is there to understand? I am losing my mind and in a fit of rage I killed my wife."

"But you cannot remember killing her."

"I remember striking her."

"Is the memory sharp?"

He shook his head. "The few memories I have are never sharp."

I turned and looked at Jim. "You said for several weeks after his accident he had no memory at all?"

"Didn't even know 'is name, lass."

"But he eventually remembered." Jim nodded. "Yet he had no recollection of what he was doing on his way to York?"

"Didn't even recall that 'e was goin' t' York. Didn't know that until we returned 'im to Walthamstow. 'is mother and the doc and Adrienne are the ones who told him 'e was on 'is way to see 'is betrothed, to make final preparations for the weddin'."

"Then he didn't remember Jane?"

Nicholas said, "The first time I saw Jane she was a total stranger to me."

Jim looked thoughtful before saying, "The doc called it am . . ."

"Amnesia?"

Both men looked at me, surprised. "Aye."

"And your memory of her never returned, my lord?"

"It did. Two days before the wedding. My head was splitting, as it often does, and she walked into the room where I was sitting. I looked up and the memories came rushing through my head like a gale."

"All memory?"

"Only hers, though that is when I began having flashes of others."

"Do you still experience these flashes?"

"They come and go."

"What are they like?"

A frightened look passed over his features. His hands clenched as he stared into the fire. "At first they are normal, or *seem* normal, though in an instant they change into something so horrible only a twisted mind could imagine them."

"Like nightmares?"

He pinned me with his eyes.

"At what time are you most likely to experience them?" I asked.

"Anytime. Day or night."

"Do they follow a pattern? Can you predict when they will begin?"

Leaning forward, propping his elbows on his knees, Jim said, " 'e'll have 'is few good days, then 'e gets 'is moods and 'e starts forgettin' again. 'e starts complainin' again about 'is 'ead and 'is nightmares come on."

"Do you ever seek treatment for your head, my lord?"

"Never."

" 'Ceptin' a shot or two of sherry," Jim teased good-naturedly.

"Aye," Nick responded, smiling at his friend. "I do seem to have a weakness for that, don't I? But it's the only thing that stops the pain and the nightmares."

We sat in silence then, listening to the fire snap.

Soon Nicholas got to his feet, held down his hand to me, and helped me to stand. Taking up my cloak, he placed it gently around my shoulders. "We're off, then," he said to Jim in a subdued voice.

Jim lifted his tankard to each of us, then Nicholas took my arm and we left the cottage.

I lay awake that night, tossing and turning, staring at my candle flame and listening to the wind moan outside my window. As the distant case clock chimed twice, I sat up in bed. How I hated that lonesome hour. My mother had always said that souls left their bodies with the turning of the tide, when they most craved release from their misery and loneliness. I shivered.

Leaving my bed, I moved to the window, scratched the icy condensation from the glass, and peered out into the wall of fog that roiled between me and the ground. I heard the hounds howl. Then the wind rattled the window so suddenly that I jumped back in alarm.

A strange disturbance overtook me, that same feeling of expectation that I had experienced before. Drawn toward my bedroom door, I unlocked it and stepped into the hallway. All was still. A single candle burned steadily at the end of the corridor. Finding some courage in the light, I walked down the hall to my lord's door. Cautiously I turned the knob. The door opened, creaking very lightly in the quiet.

Again I looked back down the hall, checked the burning candle, then entered my lord's darkened chamber. Silently I moved across the room and eased back the drapes, allowing a sparse light to spill over the floor. Then I approached the bed.

He slept. I heard his breath coming unevenly and deep. I touched his brow, and found it damp, then saw the bottle of sherry on his bedside table. I picked it up.

A movement caught my eye and I turned toward the door. As I watched it slowly close, the sense of some presence overtook me again, chilling me until I grew weak and trembling. Replacing the sherry on the table, I moved again to the bed, reached out for Nicholas, and shook him.

No response.

"My lord," I whispered, and shook him again. "My lord, wake up."

He slept.

"Nicholas." *Please, please, wake up!* I shook him yet again, saying aloud, "Malham, if you please . . . ?"

When he did not move, a new fear overtook me. I took his shoulders in my hands and called his name over and over, my foolish terror of the dark choking me nearly soundless. I could not wake him and, cursing the sherry, I backed away into the corner, my eyes searching out the shadows while my mind battled with silly superstition.

Finally forcing myself to move, I walked slowly to the door, opened it slightly, and peered into the hall. I did not notice until I stepped into the corridor that the candle on the distant table was no longer burning.

I continued down the hall, my eyes searching every shadow until I came to my room. My door was closed and I vividly remembered leaving it open. I glanced at the knob and took a breath. Reaching for the doorknob, I turned it as quietly as possible. My candle, too, had been extinguished. The room lay in total blackness.

Cautiously I continued, moving to the dresser, my senses attuned to any sight or sound or . . . presence. Running my hands over the dresser top, I located flint and candle, then fumbled with them, striking and striking until my fingers became raw with the effort.

At last the flame sputtered and danced. I grabbed

up the candle and lifted it before me toward every corner, every shadow, the window, my bed, under my bed. Nothing. I flung the door open again and stepped into the corridor. Nothing.

Finally I returned to my chamber to climb into bed. For the entire night I listened to the wind chant outside my window, and I prayed for an early dawn.

Chapter 12

The next morning at ten I stood in the Great Hall wondering why I had been summoned here. Perhaps Nicholas had experienced another one of his spells. Recalling his apparent state of unconsciousness the night before, I would not have been surprised.

I had spent those many sleepless hours considering my lord's illness. More and more his lethargy and confusion reminded me of certain patients at Oaks. One thing was for certain: He was hallucinating. Hallucinations were not uncommon among the mentally disturbed at Oaks, but such symptoms did not normally show up except in the very advanced stages of mental collapse.

"Ahhhhh!"

Hearing the high-pitched shriek, I felt the blood drain from my face. I spun around in time to see Kevin run by the door. He let loose another wail that vibrated the *craquelle* goblet on the table against the wall.

"Bloody hell, is it a wonder I'm a lunatic?" Nicholas, in his long-legged stride, bypassed me on his way to grab Kevin. As he swept the child up and tossed him across his shoulder, he turned again to me, laughing. "I wager half the souls in Saint Mary's were put there by children."

"It's like music to my ear," I replied. I laughed myself

as Nicholas suspended Kevin upside down by his feet. "Here now," I scolded gently, "the blood will rush to his head and make him dizzy!"

"Like father, like son."

I shook my head in exasperation and went for the lad, taking him up in my arms. Turning my back on his grinning father, I returned to the Great Hall and sat down by the hearth. "I take it Bea is napping again," I said.

"Her day away," Nick replied. Stopping at an ornate vase stand that held a decanter of sherry, he poured himself a drink before turning to face us again. He was still smiling.

"Unusual," I said.

Nick looked down his person and said, "I am?"

"I meant the stand. It is rather . . ."

"Vulgar?"

I bit my lower lip and smoothed Kevin's hair. "Unusual. But it is very pretty wood."

He turned to eye the furniture. "Walnut and ebony sculptured by Andrea Brustolon sometime in the seventeenth century. I'm certain you can appreciate the fine detail used on the chained negroes. And of course you recognize the river gods Charon, Cerberus and Hydra?"

"Certainly."

"I thought the old man, bearded to his genitals, looked like he could use a drink. So I replaced Jane's Sevres potpourri vase with my sherry decanter. He hasn't stopped smiling since."

"And of course Lady Malham was all for the idea?"

"Certainly. She was a jolly good sport about it all."

We laughed together.

Nicholas took a chair across from me and sipped his drink while I wrapped my arms around my son and hugged him to my breast. This was joy, heaven in its

most sublime. To freely cuddle my child was a dream
that had often brought me as much misery as hope.

I looked back at Nicholas. He watched me with a
faint hint of curiosity, and something else, an emotion
that was too fragile to name. In that instant I half
expected him to leave his chair and touch me.

"I asked you here for a reason," he said. "I'm taking
Kevin out. We would like you to come." As I hesitated,
he added, "I thought I would take my paints. There is
a rise above the cove that would make a perfect setting . . . I've been meaning to capture my son's likeness
on canvas, but that may take some doing unless he's
asleep. Perhaps if you held him . . . The day is clear
and warmer and—"

"I would be honored, sir," I replied.

In one fluid motion he stood, moved across the
room, and lifted a garment from the back of a chair.
Facing me, he opened it wide and said, "This should
keep you warmer."

I eyed the fur-lined cloak speculatively.

"It may be a bit large but it will provide more warmth
than that pitiful wrap you wore last evening. Come
here and try it on."

I lowered Kevin to the floor and approached him
slowly. "Sir, it is much too grand."

"Nonsense. It is doing little good for anyone locked
away in a trunk."

"It was your wife's?"

"Mother's. But she never wore it. Not once. In fact,
it arrived from London long after her death. I'd like
you to have it."

"Have it? Oh, no, sir, I could never accept it. It's
much too beautiful. It wouldn't be proper." Guilt consumed me as I noted the disappointment in Wyndham's eyes. He approached me nevertheless and placed

the wrap about my shoulders. Then he turned me around.

"It suits you, you know. If you won't accept it as a token of my appreciation, then consider it loaned to you as long as you live here." As he pulled it closed beneath my chin, the fur collar framed my face in softness. Nick's hands lingered along my jaw. His look of yearning so bewitched me I could find no strength to speak. Finally he pulled away and said, "Be ready on the hour, Miss Rushdon."

"I look forward to it, my lord."

We spent the day on the Cove overlooking the common fields of Malham East. Nicholas painted while Kevin squirmed in my lap. And the following week, we picnicked in a little cave in Grey Gill behind Cawden, allowing Kevin to splash his hands in the bracingly cool waters from the Tarn Watersinks. I took profound pleasure in my son's squeals of delight. And Nick's carefree laughter filled me with happiness and hope, for his mind seemed to grow sharper every day. Rarely did he find the need to reach for sherry. Here was no madman, I thought, no sick fiend, but a gentle, loving man who wanted nothing more than to sample the simple pleasures of living. Here was the man who had once run with me hand in hand across the moor, who had lain with me in fields of heather and made love to me with gentle words and tender caresses. I remembered the fire of desire in his eyes, then, and I recognized that look again. He wanted me. And I knew it was only a matter of time before he came to claim me.

Inclement weather returned with a vengeance, as howling winds and roiling snow clouds forced us all to remain indoors. Nicholas once again became more reclusive, venturing into the bosom of his home and family only upon occasion. And then it was only to fetch more sherry.

One evening, on my way to the kitchen after having put Kevin to bed, I overheard my lord speaking with his brother in Trevor's office. Curiosity compelled me to linger in the dark hallway and listen.

"Where were you last eventide, Nick? You were to meet me for cards at ten."

Silence.

"Did you forget?" Trevor asked him.

My heart quickened as I awaited the response. For the last week Nicholas had taken such pride in the fact that his memory had not failed him.

"Well? I waited in the Hall until half past."

The response finally came. "In truth, Trevor, I was feeling inordinately tired. I took to my bed to sleep."

"Sleep? Come, Nick, just admit you were tipping up with Jim. I came to your room when you didn't show and knocked on your door. When I got no response I went in and found the room unoccupied."

"Unoccupied." It wasn't a question. "This was at what time?"

"Half past ten."

I delayed no longer and hurried from the room. Finding Tilly hard at work on Adrienne's favorite haverbread, I sat in a chair before the fire and watched intently as she kneaded the dough and prepared to bake it on the oven backstone.

"Tilly," I finally said, "were you about last eventide?"

Her round cheeks glowing from exertion in the overly warm room, she smiled and mopped her brow with her dress sleeve. "Aye, lass, I were here until midnight. Miss Adrienne got a sudden cravin' for Sol-etlunes and I was turnin' 'em out 'bout then. By the time I took 'em to 'er she were asleep."

"I turned in early myself," I said. "Tell me, did you see his lordship last evening?"

Her hands stopped her rhythmic punching and rolling as she collected her thoughts. " 'e were with Master Kevin until nine. Aye. Then he sipped a few sherries with Miss Adrienne. That's it. I heard 'em talkin' about 'er goin' t' France. She mentioned somethin' about your goin' too, come t' think on it."

"Oh? And what did Lord Malham respond?"

"Well . . . t' tell y' the truth, luv, 'e weren't happy about it. They got into a real tiff, come t' think on it. O' course they normally do these days. Miss Adrienne, as you're aware, is keen on speakin' 'er mind to his lordship. Then somehow the conversation came back to his wreckin' 'er chances of marriage. 'e come burstin' out of the room lookin' black as a thundercloud and carryin' 'is sherry. Said 'e was turnin' in and didn't want to be disturbed."

"Did he go directly to his room?"

"I got no way of knowin', lass. 'e took to the backstairs two at a time and I didn't see 'im again till mornin'.' "

"And how did he seem this morning?"

"Poorly. Though 'e perked up when y' come round, I vow." Passing me a pleasant smile, she teased, " 'e's sweet on y', miss. We've all seen it. 'e's been a different man since y've been 'ere. More like 'is old self . . . the way 'e were before Jane come."

I tried to ignore the skip in my heartbeat, but my blush gave me away. Tilly only giggled and returned to her haverbread as I excused myself and withdrew from the room. I went directly to the Great Hall where I found Adrienne just restopping the sherry decanter. At my greeting she jumped and spun to face me.

"You startled me to death, Ariel." Her smile quivered as she took a breath.

I glanced down at the generous glass of sherry on the table. "Is that drink for you?"

"No," she said, "I can't abide sherry. It troubles my sleep and leaves me with a wretched headache. No, I was just about to take my brother a peace offering. We had words last night and—"

"I know."

Her smile faltered. "He's been complaining about his head this evening. He asked Kate to fetch him the decanter but I thought that excessive after last night."

"I'm on my way to my quarters," I told her. "Shall I take it to him?"

A long moment passed before she responded. "Oh. Oh well." She glanced at the drink. "Certainly, I suppose that would be fine." She lifted the glass to me with shaking hands, sloshing the sherry onto her fingers.

Taking the drink, I looked her in the eye and said, "Good eventide, my lady," then left her staring after me.

I took the stairs carefully. Having made my way through the cold, dark corridors to Nicholas's room, I stood for some time in the shadows, recalling Adrienne's obvious nervousness at being found with the sherry. With growing suspicion I stared down at the glass and listened to Nicholas pace behind his closed door. Then lifting the glass up in the darkness, I said, "Mayhaps you'll have pleasant dreams tonight, my lord." Turning the glass up to my mouth, I drank the sherry down.

*   *   *

Bang! . . . *Bang!* . . . *Bang!*

That awful sound! "Go away!" I cried. "Please, please, go away!"

Bang! . . . *Bang!* . . . *Bang!*

I sat upright in bed. The suffocating darkness gripped my mind so painfully I wanted to scream.

"Ariel! Ariel, are you in there? For God's sake, will you answer me? Dammit, Ariel, are you there?" *Bang . . . Bang . . . Bang . . .* "Ariel, open the door!"

Rolling to my knees, I pressed my back to the wall and covered my ears. "Go away! Leave my alone! I'm not a whore! I'm not! Stop calling me that!"

"Ariel, it's Nick," came the calm voice. "Please, love, open the door."

Nick? the word broke my heart. "I don't believe you." I sobbed. "Nick hasn't come for me. You're lying. You're lying! You've lied before. He hasn't come. He hasn't!"

"Open the door, Ariel. The door. I promise you it's Nick. Open the door and see for yourself."

Pressing my hands to my breast, I stared at the door. My body shook with cold, yet oddly my flesh was slick with sweat. Cautiously I slid from the bed and moved to the door. I closed my eyes and fought the nightmare that refused to relinquish its hold on me. I was back at Oaks, that wretched hole where strangers stared at me through bars in the wall, where they called me whore and said the child inside me was the devil's spawn. I had sinned and would suffer in this hell until I died, they said. Oh God, help me!

"Open the door so I can help you."

"I—I can't. It's locked!"

"Get the key, love."

I backed to the dresser and ran my hand across it. Then, key in hand, I moved woodenly to the door and fumbled with the lock before stepping away. Closing my fingers about my throat, I strained to see through the darkness. *They* had done this before—the insane ones—they had told me Nicholas had come to rescue me from this suffering.

The door swung open. *He* stepped through the shadows, his eyes hard and gray and blazing with the same fire he held in his hands. With a strangled cry I collapsed on the floor.

I became vaguely aware of being carried in my lord's arms through the hallway, into his room, and, once there, into his bed. His large, warm hands cupped my face and his thumbs lightly brushed the tears from my cheeks. Sitting down beside me, he smiled into my eyes and asked, "Are you awake now?"

I nodded.

"Look how you're shivering. You're wet through. Are you ill? Hurt?"

"No, my lord."

Raking a hand through his unruly hair, he looked away. "You frightened the devil out me when you cried out. Then I couldn't get into the bloody room . . ." He stared at the floor. "Perhaps we should reconsider locking it . . . or make some other arrangements . . ."

"There were dreams, awful dreams. I'm sorry, I didn't mean—"

"Hush." He tipped up my chin. "I understand dreams, Ariel. I know what they can do to you."

Shakily I attempted to sit up.

He seized my shoulders. His hands were warm and gentle against my skin, and I shivered. He began talking in a soft murmur.

I watched drowsily as he formed the words, noted the sudden flash of white teeth as he smiled. I saw his grim, gray eyes as they shifted to my shoulder, where the thin strap of my tattered shift drooped. His gaze wandered, lower and lower still, over the frail material where my breasts shimmered damply and the gown clung to their rosy crests that rose and fell rapidly with the force of my breathing.

Lifting his hand, he trailed one finger down the coiling black tendril of hair that lay against my breast. The tentative gesture was as arousing and frightening to him as it was to me. I felt desire in his sharp exhalation of breath against my face. I saw it in the narrowing of his eyes and in the sudden tightness of his throat.

Timidly I lifted my hand and laid it flat against his chest. The fine lawn shirt grew damp beneath my palm. The beat of his heart vibrated against my fingers.

"Sweet innocent," came his words, warm and deep against my temple. "Look at me."

Basking in his presence, I turned my face up to his. Lifting his hand, he laid it tenderly against my cheek and I thought, Was this the sort of man who would—could—hurt another? Never!

He said gently, "What is it about these features that causes me to yearn, even in my weary state, to fetch brush and paint from yonder room and capture their likeness on linen? And yet when I do, I cannot grasp them even long enough to place them on canvas."

I drew in a long breath. "I cannot say, milord."

He skimmed my lower lip with the pad of his thumb, very slowly. Time stopped, as it had that spring morning on the moor when we'd shared our first kiss. Our breath mingled as he brushed his lips against my cheek.

"Sweet, sweet innocent," he murmured in my ear. "Would you let me love you, knowing what I am?"

"And you are?" I looked up into his eyes.

He lifted one brow and said, "Mad."

"Nay, my lord, not mad. I won't believe it! You listen too much to rumor—"

"But I killed her."

"No!"

"Aye, I did it. I remember doing it." Roughly catching my face in his fingers, his mouth hovering over mine, he said, "I learned she was spreading herself beneath other men, making me a laughingstock among my peers. I remember striking her—" He squeezed his eyes closed as pain washed over his features. Then his lashes fluttered and he looked at me again. "She's not the only one, I'm told. There was Maggie . . ."

I touched my fingers to his lips, hushing him, but he turned away, left the bed, and moved toward the fire. He stood before the hearth, his face downturned, allowing the orange glow to silhouette his troubled features. "I have no right," he said so softly I barely heard him, "no right to even think of touching you. I would only hurt you, like I have everyone else."

Leaving the bed, I moved unsteadily up behind him. *Touch me*, I longed to say. Instead I only lifted my hand and smoothed it up his rigid spine to his shoulder. His head fell back so his soft, shadowed hair brushed my fingers. "God," he whispered, "you make me forget all that."

The fire crackled and hissed.

Then he turned very slowly to face me. There was desperation in the depths of his eyes, in the bunching of his jaw, the slant of his mouth. Then his fingers closed around my throat and slid up my neck, where his thumb pressed into my chin, lifting my face toward his. His throat rumbled with a hoarse groan before he admitted, "I want to kiss you."

"I want to be kissed," I confessed, feeling no hesitation, though he looked as wild and powerful in that instant as the roiling fog that had consumed the earth and sky outside the house. I repeated, "I *want* to be kissed, my lord . . . by you."

For a moment neither of us moved, then his hands came up and cupped my face, slid into my hair, and clenched. His dark head lowered over mine and he growled, "Then God help you."

It was, in that instant, as if my body left the earth. For as his mouth possessed me with an overpowering fierceness and hunger, I wrapped my arms around his neck and pressed my body against his. Adrift on a rush of desire as I had never before experienced, I opened my mouth under his, groaned as he slanted his mouth in one direction over mine, then another. His hands ran over me, urgently then gently, dancing hot and cold against my flushed, sensitive flesh, making me gasp and tremble with anticipation. So long I had waited, I had dreamed . . .

He kissed me until the breath became painful in my throat, until I was driven to plunge my hands beneath his shirt and press my fingers into his damp, hot skin. I rediscovered the supple firmness of his flesh, the iron hardness of his shoulder muscles that flexed with each movement. And at last, when he finally tore his mouth from mine, I buried my face against his chest where his shirt was unbuttoned and inhaled the musky scent of him until passion rose like driving wind in my mind.

"Please. Oh please . . ."

I said the words aloud, not meaning to, not even realizing I had until he took my face again in his hands and turned it up to his. I thought with a faint despair that he would turn me out, perhaps scorn me for my wanton needs, my desire to please him. But the words formed by his smiling mouth were simply: "I want you."

Then he lifted me in his arms and carried me to the bed.

The air was colder there, the room darker. Yet as he laid me into the downturned covers and lowered his body onto mine, I knew only the satisfaction of finally attaining what was mine, what should have been mine two years before.

A soft cry of desire escaped me as Nicholas buried his mouth against my throat, my shoulder, and moved up again to my ear. The material of my shift was a frail barrier to his exploring hands as he eased the material over my shoulders, his fingers gently caressing my breasts until they throbbed and ached under his touch. There was no reality in that moment beyond the two of us, and I caught my breath when his warm tongue curled intimately around my breast, until my body arched up to his mouth and the desire to give myself to him completely consumed me.

The touch of his chest against my breasts sent a burning wave of need through me and I gasped. Often I had dreamt of his holding me again, as he had that one time before, but those were merely fantasies. I seemed to soar with a wondrous pleasure that was only enhanced by his movements against me, his crushing me to him so fiercely I could hardly breathe.

When finally he pulled away, his eyes were dark with questions. To assure him I curled my arms around him, pressed my hands flat against his shoulders, and molded my legs over his. I made a soft moan of pleasure as his hand ran down and up my thigh, slowly, slowly, his fingers warm as they caressed, explored, until the sweet torture grew and I feared I would drown in it.

He moved to his knees, and I watched as his long fingers expertly flicked open the buttons of his shirt, slowly released his breeches, and peeled them down his hips. He looked magnificent to my admiring eye. His legs spread wide between my thighs, he kneeled over me, his eyes roving over my breasts and down, down until his intimate perusal brought a different sort of fire to my skin. Once I had hidden myself from him but not now. I knew he loved me; whether he realized it himself yet I could not guess. But I saw it in the sudden glow of his eyes; I felt it in the tender touch of his hands.

Then desire eclipsed all, demanded an insistent response. Reaching out, I took him in my hands, worshipping the hot, hard flesh that had driven me beyond boundaries once. I loved him with my hands, my lips, in all the ways I had fantasized those many lonely months when I had only a memory to guide me. I heard him groan and felt him shiver. And when his fingers twisted into my hair and pulled my head back sharply, I became breathless with the raw, savage desire I saw in his face.

Sinking back on the bed, I watched the candlelight play over his features, saw the slow ripple of his flesh and sinew as he leaned over me. His form blocked the dim, dancing light and cast cool shadows over my fevered skin. With his mouth set in a tight, determined line, he shifted my legs, and I felt that part of him touch me, throbbing, straining with passion and heat. But still he held back, his eyes on mine, his lips brushing mine until I whimpered and clawed his hips.

I lost my breath. My heart beat rapidly beneath his palm and my skin grew flush and moist with wanting.

He kissed me again, invading my mouth with his tongue, swirling it inside me and plunging rhythmically until I cried aloud for mercy and gasped for breath. And all the while he pressed the length of his body against mine, his chest to my breast, his stomach to mine . . . his hips moving sensuously upon mine so the hard rise of his desire scored my damp, tender flesh with heat. When he pulled away I trembled with longing.

"I have to know," came his soft, urgent words in my ear, "only because I don't want to hurt you. I have to make certain . . . have there been others, love?"

I replied without blinking, remembering the first time he'd asked me that question. My answer then had been different. "There has been only one man in my life, my lord."

His eyes met mine in surprise and some disappointment. "Did you love him?" he asked.

"I loved him more than my own life," I answered. I saw him swallow and, lifting my hand, I laid it gently upon his face. "But no more than I love you." Sliding my hips fully beneath him, I finished, "My lord."

Naked he rose up over me, his dark, penetrating eyes locked on mine. The fire beyond us caused his skin to glow: wet and gold and . . . intoxicating. I wanted to drink it in. His head lowered and his lips brushed my breasts. I closed my eyes, buried my hands in his hair as he bent to take each nipple in his mouth, first the right, then the left, his tongue worrying each straining, aching rosy peak into a hard bud of desire. And the throbbing started, the delicious pulsing that beat through my body and centered deep and low in my groin. I turned liquid inside, burning with desire, melting with need, but though my body arched and lifted in invitation, though I called—nay, wept—his name, he held back, tantalizing me with his mouth and hands until my blood coursed like fire in my veins and I became frenzied with white-hot rapture.

When I thought I could take it no longer, he entwined his fingers with mine, rocked slightly forward on his knees, and in one slow, exquisite motion sank into me. His head fell back; his hands flexed, griping mine painfully. I didn't care, for I knew how he felt: as if he would explode inside, as if he wanted to cry.

I did cry.

When he noticed, a look of fear crossed his features. I felt him stiffen. "I'm happy" was all I said. Then I lifted my arms and legs up around him to prove how happy I was.

He moved inside me again with a sigh of relief, at first hesitant, then confident, then finally with such urgency I could do nothing but respond in the same way. The glory grew and he was mine, all mine, in heart and mind and soul. *I will never let him go again!* I wept to myself as the pressure mounted, dragging me upward on sensation, my body seeking, demanding, straining toward fulfillment. I clutched his sweat-glazed shoulders that moved forward and back with each thrust of his hips against mine. I felt it growing inside him as well. I knew it in the animal growls he made in his throat, in the violence that seized his body until he rode me with such ferocity the room seemed to spin into a blur around us.

It happened for us both in that instant, as it should, as it had in the past, lifting us beyond the sublime, the infinite. With a sob of passion he twisted his fingers in my hair and went still, as did I, feeling our bodies throb as one.

Several moments passed before we relaxed, yet he didn't leave me. I wouldn't let him. I held him to me like a child with a treasured toy, selfish, full of love and joy that no one could ever take from me again. I felt his heart pound against mine, felt the sweet stirring of his breath against my temple. The slick, warm tip of his tongue brushed my ear as he moistened his lips, then the words came, deep and sleepy and disbelieving.

"I don't understand . . . how one day I am nothing but blackness and hopelessness. Then you come along and I feel . . ."

I turned my head slightly and looked up into his glowing eyes. "And you feel, my lord?"

"Saved." He closed his eyes. "God, I adore you."

Chapter 13

I sat before the fire with Kevin in my lap rocking him gently, smiling down into his cherubic face. I sang him a lullaby about puppies and lambs and butterflies. I told him the story of *Cendrillon*, of the beautiful young woman who met her handsome prince at a gala ball and swept him off his feet. I realized the babe could not understand me, but it didn't matter. This was *my* fairy tale, and it was coming true.

Looking up, I met my lover's eyes. Propped on his elbow, he watched me somewhat cautiously, searching my face the best he could through the gray shadows of early morning. There was an intenseness about his eyes that disturbed me, a tightness about his mouth that made me wonder if he regretted our lovemaking throughout the night.

"Good morning," I told him.

The response was a moment in coming. Then he smiled. "Yes, it is. I can't recall a finer one."

"I hope I didn't disturb you. When Kevin awoke I brought him here before Bea could take him. You don't mind . . . ?"

"No."

"I've been singing him lullabies."

"I heard."

"He seemed fascinated."

"I suspect no one has ever sung him one."

"But that's terribly sad! My mother often sang to me."

"He doesn't have a mother."

My eyes misted as I looked down on my son's face. "Ariel."

I forced my gaze back to my lord's, afraid the tears clouding my vision would spill down my cheeks and give away my emotions. Wyndham's dark hair spilled over his forehead nearly to his eyes, and his lids were slightly heavy. He watched me unblinking, his face set like stone. Then his lips parted, and he spoke with utmost equanimity.

"Marry me, Miss Rushdon."

I blinked and the tears fell. I hugged Kevin more tightly to my breast. "It is not necessary, sir, to—"

"Necessary? Is that what you think? That because of last night—"

"Is it not?"

He sank back to his pillow and stared at the ceiling. "Aye," he finally said, his voice weary. "Perhaps. Yes, dammit, because of last night, and all the mornings I awoke thinking of you and wishing . . . despite this numbing pain in my head the thought of you remains. God, even in my nightmares your face comes back to haunt me. When I think of you the pain goes and nothing else matters. Not the madness. Not anything. Is that selfish of me, Miss Rushdon? Rushdon. Even the name brings turmoil to my head, and heart. The sound has grown more powerful to me every day until I find myself penning 'Rushdon' on paper over and over again and staring at it as if it holds some deep and mysterious secret that I cannot quite fathom."

Coming up again on his elbow, he looked me in the eye. "Do you know how long I looked for a sitter?

Weeks, months. I interviewed woman after woman, hoping to find the one who matched the haunting image in my mind of the perfect woman. I turned them each away, until you. And I knew the moment I saw you that you would be the one to help me. Come here, Miss Rushdon."

I did so, still holding Kevin in my arms.

Nicholas pulled me down on the bed beside him, brushed his son's cheek with his finger before looking again to me. "I have never hurt him. Whatever madness or sickness or cruelty that forces me to become what I become is not strong enough to make me harm what I love most." He lifted his hand to my face, cupped my cheek in his palm, and brushed away a lingering tear with his finger. "I would never lift a hand against you. Come live with me, Ariel. Share with me your sweetness. Comfort me in my madness and I will cherish you for as long as I live."

I had never loved him more than I did in that moment, for never had he spoken to me in so gentle a tone. Never had he looked at me with so fond an eye. I felt glad beyond mortal boundaries, and my smile told him so.

"Well?" he said, and the tender glint in his eye flashed with sudden passion and impatience. "Will you sit there and smile and keep me in suspense? Answer me, Miss Rushdon—Ariel—and be quick about it or . . ."

"Or what, my lord?"

"Or I might be forced to press that beautiful body down into this bed and make love to it again."

"Then it would behove me, sir, to hold my tongue awhile longer, I think." As his eyes widened in pleasure, I laughed and leapt from the bed. Backing toward the hearth and pressing Kevin's head to my shoulder,

I told him eagerly, "Aye, Lord Malham, I will marry you, but on one condition."

"Name it."

"That we are wed in secrecy. That no servant, or your brother or sister be informed of the marriage until *after* we are banded and the vows are spoken."

He appeared thoughtful, then with a grin he kicked the counterpane from his hips and came off the bed. "Agreed," he replied.

I saw Nicholas very little the next five days. Remote as he often was, he rarely left his room, calling me only once to the studio where, for some six hours, he attempted to paint my likeness. In the end he only smashed the portrait against the wall and bellowed for me to leave the room, for I was driving him totally "confused." I then began to worry that he had forgotten our pledge. He had made no mention again about marrying me.

On the sixth day I returned to my room, having spent the afternoon with Adrienne, tutoring, or attempting to tutor her in French. Since I knew little to nothing about the language it was not an easy feat. For hours we sat in the Great Hall while she recited phrases from her reader; I think she believed she would convince me to attend her on her voyage to France.

Entering my room, I stopped. Piled high on my bed and dresser and stacked on the floor were dozens of bolts of material: velvets, satins, silks, in every color imaginable. Draped over the back of my only chair were yards of lace and ribbons.

"I like the emerald velvet," came the voice behind me. "It will go beautifully with your eyes." I spun. Nicholas, his hands in his pockets, grinned with one corner of his mouth and said, "We will be married

Tuesday next at Burnsall. I have found a vicar there who will perform the ceremony without posting banns. Mind you, he'll have a new chapel for his efforts . . . Have you some witness who might attend you in this rather secretive, momentous occasion, my dear?"

"Aye." I could hardly speak.

"Will that give you time to stitch up something suitable?" Raking my dress with his eyes, he frowned with distaste and added, "God, I hate that dress you're wearing."

I lifted my chin in response.

He turned and walked casually down the hall. I heard him say, "Saucy wench." Then laughing to myself, I closed my bedroom door, hugged myself in happiness, and thought Tuesday next seemed a lifetime away.

I set to the task of forming me a creation of green velvet to wear on my wedding day. I had all that I needed: scissors, thread, pins and needles. Wyndham had forgotten nothing. He was better, I thought. There had been color on his cheeks and a twinkle in his eyes.

I worked through the afternoon, sketching the dress, then cutting it out. By dusk the floor was scattered with yards of emerald velvet and a satin lining of a slightly darker color. Tired and hungry, I put my sewing aside, locked my bedroom door behind me, and started for the kitchen.

As I passed Trevor's office quarters I noticed a light burning beneath his door. Since Trevor had traveled to York five days before and was not due back until tomorrow I was curious. I walked quietly over and peeked in.

Adrienne, with her back to me, searched Trevor's bottles and phials, holding one up to the light, then another as she attempted to read the inscription on the label. Beside her on the table was an open book.

Then, as if suddenly sensing my presence, she slowly turned to face me. Her eyes widened at first, then she relaxed. "Dear God, I thought at first that you were Trevor. Ariel, dear, you must stop walking about so quietly."

"I'm sorry."

"No matter." Relaxing somewhat, she threw a casual look about the stuffy quarters, centering her eyes on the dingy yellow skeleton suspended by ropes from the ceiling. A noticeable shudder passed through her. "I don't blame my brother for taking a holiday. This is such a depressing place."

"There are worse," I said. "I'm certain Bedlam would make this room seem as pleasant as a holiday in York." When Adrienne made no response, I walked farther into the room. "Forgive my speculating," I said, "but I sense Trevor's purpose in going to York was not strictly for holiday."

She bumped the table at her back, rocking the bottles so they clattered together. "I don't know what you mean."

"I understand there are necessary legal steps that must be taken before committing someone like Lord Malham to St. Mary's. Papers must be drawn up, a court date set."

Her mouth opened in a soft gasp.

Stopping at the end of the table, I glanced down at the open book, then back at her. "Are you ill?" I asked.

"Yes." She pressed trembling fingers to her head. "Actually I am. My head is splitting again and I thought . . ." Slamming the book closed, she smiled. "I suppose I'll have to wait until Trevor returns. You won't say anything about my being here, will you? He's very particular about people coming in when he's not present."

"No," I said. "I won't tell him."

"Good. Well, then, shall we have dinner?" Sweeping by me, she left the room. I followed at a considerable distance.

We were surprised to find that Trevor had already returned. He stood with Nick in the foyer, his face chafed with cold and his brown hair wind tossed and slightly damp. Throwing open his arms, he embraced Nick with a great hug, then slapped him on the back.

"By God, Nick, you look wonderful. Are you feeling well?"

"Very well," my lord responded. "You're home early."

"I completed my business a day ahead of schedule."

Adrienne, holding her brown skirts slightly in her hands, glided gracefully toward her brothers. She offered Trevor a small kiss on each cheek before responding to his last comment. "I was under the impression that you were going to York on holiday, Trevor. What sort of business were you about?"

"Investments. But we'll talk on that later. I—" His eyes widened with pleasure as he finally spotted me. "There you are, hiding in the shadows like a little mouse, Miss Rushdon. Come here and tell me hullo."

I did so, hesitantly. When I was close enough to touch, he grabbed my arms and turned them over, examining the scratches that were now no more than thin white lines on my skin. "Healed well, I see. They'll leave no scars. What a shame if they had permanently marred such beautiful skin."

Feeling myself blush, I stepped away and returned his smile with some effort. I sensed that his journey to York had more to do with arrangements to commit Nicholas to St. Mary's than it did with investments.

In that moment, the door behind Trevor burst open and several servants filed in carrying parcels.

"What's this?" Adrienne asked. I detected a little girl's enthusiasm as she perused the gifts.

"When have I ever traveled to York or London without returning with gifts? Shall we all go to the Great Hall where it's more comfortable?"

Excusing myself I turned for the door when Trevor spoke up again. "Miss Rushdon, you'll join us, of course."

"No, sir."

"But I have something here for you."

I stopped abruptly and turned to face him. "For me, sir?" I looked briefly toward Nick. He looked at his brother, one brow lifted in curiosity. Then he looked at me.

"Nick asked me to pick up something for you, Ariel." Trevor spun on his heel to Reginald and extracted a great bundle wrapped in tissue paper and ribbons. Dropping it into my arms, he winked and said, "Come along to the drawing room and out of this frigid foyer. I want to see your face when you open it." He grabbed my arm and moved me toward the hallway. Glancing back over my shoulder, I met my lord's eyes in question. He looked quickly away and pressed his fingers to his temple.

Adrienne was atwitter as we entered the room. She babbled good-naturedly with Trevor, wanting to know all the gossip: "Is it true that Virginia Briggs is consorting with someone in Parliament? Is the price of tea really going up?"

"Virginia Briggs has consorted with every eligible and ineligible man in Parliament, my dear, and with little doubt the cost of tea is going up again. The East India Company is robbing us blind."

"Why, those dastardly Chinese! Whatever will we do? The price is exorbitant already."

"There is rumor—and rumor is all it is at this stage—that China is considering closing its doors to foreign trade sometime in the future. I ran into Lord Melbrook outside the Ministry and he tells me the British Committee is considering a plan for growing tea in India."

"India!" Adrienne sat back in her chair.

"I think there may be worthwhile investment opportunities there," Trevor pointed out. He looked toward Nick, who was frowning still and rubbing his brow. "What do you think, my lord? If push comes to shove with China, perhaps we might dabble in the tea business ourselves. I understand Earl Grey—"

"What is in the package?" Nick asked, cutting Trevor off.

They all looked at me, and the bundle in my lap.

Trevor, who had been poised casually by the fire, his elbow propped against the marble mantle, stared at Nicholas in something like shock. Crossing the room, he placed a gentle hand on Nick's shoulder and said softly, "You asked me to get it for her. Don't you recall?"

Nick's refusal to respond was a response in itself. Sitting forward in his chair, his elbows on his knees, he pointed one unsteady finger at the package, looked to my eyes, and said through his teeth, "Open it."

I began doing so, slowly. In truth, my mind was not on the gift in my lap but on my lord's eyes, more distressed than they had been in days. Finally the tissue laid open. I stared down at the folds of exquisite green satin that made up the finest gown I had ever seen.

"Don't you recall, Nick?" came Trevor's voice. "You mentioned to me you were tired of that drab dress she was always wearing, and that you wanted to paint her wearing something bright and beautiful. You asked me to visit Madame d'Eliza Varden, knowing she would be able to come up with something on short notice. Truth is, I would have been home yesterday, but the gown took longer than Madame anticipated. Of course we had to estimate your measurements, Ariel, but I think you'll be pleased. Why don't you go and try it on. I'm certain Nick is as eager to see how it fits as I am."

I looked at the dress again, knowing now how Adrienne felt when gifted with the wedding lace. My heart raced with despair. Nick had forgotten that he'd requested the garment, and with that lapse I was reminded that his illness had not miraculously cured itself. For that I loathed the dress. Yet I wanted to press it to my breast because he had gifted it to me for no more motive than love.

Unsteadily I left my chair, spilling paper around my feet. My own mind tumbled in a state of confusion, not knowing how or if I should accept such an extravagant gift. Finally, Nicholas sat back in his chair and said quietly, "Of course. I remember now. Certainly you should go and try on the dress, Ariel, as a favor to me."

I returned his smile, then left the room in gratitude. For the time being, I would be allowed to calm my fractured nerves before facing my lord again.

I entered the foyer and found Brabbs standing just inside the door, speaking with Reginald. I walked directly to him and took his arm, dismissing the butler with a smile.

Reggie bowed slightly to Brabbs and said, "I'll tell Mr. Trevor you're here."

"Give me ten minutes with Brabbs alone, please," I told him.

As he nodded and walked away, I turned to my friend. "You're just the man I want to see. I've news, Brabbs."

His eyes fell on the dress in my arms. "What's this?" he asked.

"A dress." I pulled him toward the nearest doorway, ushered him into the room, and closed the door behind us.

His eyes were still on my bundle. "So, it's come to that, has it?"

"To what?" I scowled and placed the dress across a chair.

"What did you have to do for that, Maggie? I never thought it of you. I never thought you would sell yourself for—"

"How dare you even insinuate such a thing," I interrupted. "The dress is a gift and only a gift. Besides, what should it matter to you?"

"It matters," he said. "He's the last person in this world I care to see you with, lass."

"I cannot believe this! Are you telling me that you truly believe the rumors as well? Do you truly believe him insane?"

"Insanity is a well enough ploy to hide behind, Maggie. Grand crimes are committed in the name of insanity."

"Are you telling me that you believe he killed his wife and has completely fabricated the story of his illness?"

He caught my shoulders and spoke in a quieter voice. "Maggie-mine, if it's only the lad you want, take him and get out. I'll help you if I must, but I can't stand seeing you throw your life away on such as he! You'll end up hurt, lass, or worse."

"Nay, he would never hurt me."

"How can you say that? He broke your heart by marrying Jane. Then when he tired of her he killed her. Maggie, get out while you can, before it's too late!"

I shoved him away. "I can see you're no friend to

me, Brabbs. If you were you wouldn't be saying these things about the man I love and am about to marry."

"Marry! Merciful God, Maggie, what are you saying? You're not about to marry the murdering scoundrel."

"I am," I responded, with a lift of my chin. "And he didn't murder anyone. I'll never believe it."

He turned away, shaking his head. "I've heard love makes you blind to reality but I didn't realize it robbed you completely of common sense." He faced me again. "Even if he were as righteous as a pope, Maggie, you still got no place in this house. They're different people, lass. They're a different class. You'll never fit in. He'll resent you soon enough and *then* where will you be. Down at the cemetery no doubt, buried by Jane."

Snatching up my dress, he shook it at me and said, "Is a bit of fluff like this worth your life, girl? Is it worth the humiliation you'll feel when his friends turn up their nose at you? You're nowt but a peasant, Maggie, and that's all you'll ever be. Get your pretty head out of the clouds and face reality."

I calmly took my dress from his hand, though my heart was beating furiously. Smoothing the crumpled skirt against me, I said with restrained emotion, "I brought you in here to ask a favor. I am to be married to the man I love Tuesday next in Burnsall, and I am in need of a witness."

He caught my chin in his hand and tipped up my face. "I'll witness the marriage, Maggie, but I won't be happy about it. I'll be prayin' until the moment you finish your vows that something happens to stop it."

I left him staring after me as I quit the room. Lifting my skirts, I fled up the stairs into the same cold and darkness that I had once abhorred. No longer. The brittle coldness soothed the hot anger flushing my

cheeks. The darkness hid the scalding tears of anger
and frustration streaming from my eyes. I ran down
the corridor to my room, and once there slammed the
door behind me.

At my feet lay the remnants of my wedding dress. I
fell to my knees and brushed my hand over the velvet,
cursing openly as Brabbs's accusations burned through
my mind. Was I the only person in the world fool
enough to believe Nicholas Wyndham innocent of insanity and murder?

Stumbling to my feet, I stared at my reflection in
the mirror, then, gently laying my gift on the bed, I
promptly removed the worn gray garment I was wearing
and kicked it aside. Carefully, I stepped into the emerald satin, struggled for some time to fasten each in-
tricate button up the back of the bodice, and when
finished, closed my eyes briefly before finding the courage to look again at my reflection.

Oh! was it really Maggie? Was this stranger I beheld
truly the same wasted and plain waif who moments
before had looked little better than some ragamuffin
wandering the streets of London? Were those eyes really the same? How green they were now, perfectly
matching the dress. How they shone!

My hair looked startlingly black about my pale face.
Spinning, I grabbed up a length of green ribbon, pulled
my hair over one shoulder, and with my fingers began
twisting it and the ribbon into a braid. Bending closer
to the mirror, I blinked, unable to believe the sight of
my own reflection. I turned slightly to the right, then
to the left, smoothed my hands down the bodice of the
dress, lightly touched the modest, embroidered décolle-
tage and trailed my fingers down the close-fitting
sleeves that came to the wrists.

I dropped to my knees, and with a trembling hand,

picked up the scissors laying to one side of my wedding dress. Then I lifted the abhorrent dress I had worn during my nightmare internment at Oaks and slashed it to pieces.

Chapter 14

I prayed the next five days for fair weather. Tuesday dawned clear, but soon a fog formed so close to earth I could barely see the treetops outside my window. Pressing my forehead against the icy glass pane, I listened to the distant baying of the hounds while contemplating my future as Lady Malham.

The servants, with the exception of Matilda, had already changed toward me. Now they hushed as I walked into a room. They eyed me speculatively, their lifted brows and pursed lips evidence of the disapproval they felt over my relationship with the Wyndhams. When they learned of the fabrics Nicholas had bestowed on me, Polly conveniently let it slip that they had belonged to Jane, that they had been stored since her death in a room in the old wing. She'd made a point of shivering on my behalf and saying aloud, " 'Tis bad luck t' wear anythin' belongin' t' the dead, y' know. Y'll end up sufferin' the same fate, I vow."

Recalling those words, I turned from the window and stared at my wedding dress. I thought, perhaps Brabbs is right. Perhaps I am a fool for believing in Wyndham's innocence, in his sanity. But there was no way to prove either unless I had some sort of control over his circumstances. And *that* is what I dreaded most. If I was wrong there might well be a new Lady Malham in Malham Cemetery very soon.

I arrived at Brabb's house at just after eight.

"I don't understand why you just didn't ride to Burnsall with *him*," he said.

Ignoring the barbed tone of his voice, I asked, "What do you think of my wedding dress?"

"It's green. It aught to have been white, but considering the circumstances . . ."

"Watch your tongue, Brabbs. You are talking to the future Lady Malham."

He bristled at that.

I continued. "Nicholas and I decided that our leaving together would only raise suspicions. The help is whispering already, you know, and I'm quite certain Adrienne and Trevor believe we've become close."

" 'Close?' Is that what it's being called now?"

I turned away. "I don't know why you hate him so. I don't recall your feeling this way toward him before."

"That was before he took a virgin and ruined her."

"You were the one who sent me to Oaks, Brabbs, not Nicholas."

"It was your uncle who sent you," he responded hotly. "There was nowt I could do about it."

I listened as he shuffled and banged about the room like a child in the throes of a tantrum. "Brabbs," I said, "calm down and think. Your reason for continuing to hate Nicholas is absurd. Had I truly died in childbirth your anger would be justifiable. But as you can see I'm still alive and—"

"Not for long," he snapped. Grabbing up his cloak, he swung it around his shoulders.

"I will never believe Nicholas is mad!" My patience at an end, I glared at him in frustration. "As a physician, surely you can understand his basic problem. His initial loss of memory was brought on by some kind of physical or emotional hysteria. It is the brain's way of shutting out any stress that could further injure it."

"Bloody hell," he groaned. "There you go again telling me my business."

Hurrying across the room to the shelves of medical texts lining the wall, I drew one out and slammed it onto his desk. "See for yourself. It is there in black and white for any layman to read."

He shook his head. "I regret the day I ever taught you to read, Maggie."

"Don't change the subject," I said, thumping the book with my fist. Hunching his shoulders, he buttoned his cloak. His gray brows drew down in a frown, and I knew I had him. "Think, Brabbs. Nicholas is not totally without his memory. He knows who he is. He knows his family, his history. What he cannot recall are those stress moments: the night his wife died, and Maggie. The brain could be blocking recall of both because they bring about a certain trauma. And such a condition can cause abrupt hallucinatory images that become momentary visual impressions. This all could be partial cause for his confusion."

He squinted one eye at me and said, "Could be? Partial? Is some common sense in that pretty head telling you that that might not be the case? Are you telling me that there might be other reasons for his apparent illness?"

I walked again toward the fire and ventured softly, "For a moment let's forget Nicholas completely. You are called out to see a patient who is suffering head pain, rigors. His family tells you he has become explosive on occasion, violent, moody, sleeping more than usual. He's suffering nightmares, hallucinations; what

would be your prognosis?" He turned away. "Brabbs!"
I beseeched him.

"Are you going to marry the bastard or not?" He
called out. "If you are we'd best go. It's goin' to snow."

The small church, its gray stone walls barely discernible in the fog, perched on the hillside overlooking the
village of Burnsall. As Brabbs's buggy rattled over the
drive I caught a glimpse of the chapel's towering crucifix jutting through the dreary mist. Occasionally a flash
of leaded glass winked from an arched window overlooking the village.

After stopping outside the weathered rock wall surrounding the church, Brabbs hurried around the buggy
and helped me to the ground. I could hardly make out
his troubled features through the fog as he said,
"There's still time, you know. We can turn round and
go back to Malham if that's what you want."

"It's not," I responded.

He shoved open the wicket for me. Its rusty hinges
creaked, exaggerating the quiet solitude of the sacred
grounds surrounding us. He held my arm as we made
our way down the cobblestone walk. I noted the gray,
leaning headstones in the nearby cemetery, obscured
mostly by mist. Several sheep grazed among the grave
mounds, nibbling dead grass from beneath the snow. I
could hear the tinkling bell about one's neck as it
pranced somewhere in the distance.

The front doors of the chapel were slightly ajar.
We entered.

How quiet. How still. Then a movement near the
front of the church caught my eye. And another, and
yet another. The clergyman moved toward me, his
white surplice ghostly over his black cassock, his loose
full sleeves billowing as he opened his arms.

"Miss Rushdon?" he whispered. Or so it seemed. My ears hummed with the silence.

"Yes," I responded. Then I saw Nick. He stood with Jim near the chancel, his face pale, his black hair damp and tousled, his wide shoulders sporting a black mantle that swept to his knees. Sketching a slight curtsy, I said, "My lord, I'm sorry we're late. There was a problem with a wheel . . ."

He moved toward us with spectral grace. As he neared, I noticed his gaze was fixed not on me but on Brabbs. He examined my friend with expressionless gray eyes, then his lips pulled back against his teeth, and he growled, "Get out."

I felt Brabbs tense behind me.

Stepping forward, I said, "But, my lord—"

He nudged me aside and looked down into Brabbs's face. "You bloody bastard, what are you doing here?"

"Please, sir," the priest intruded, "remember where you are, Lord Malham."

"I asked you a question," Nick said.

"I'm delivering the girl to Satan," he responded.

Nick drew back his hand and slapped Brabbs across his face. I sprang for his arm. "Stop!" I cried. "Why have you done such a thing?"

His piercing eyes took in my frantic features. "Who is he to you?"

"My friend. My only friend in this world. If you hurt him you hurt me. He has never harmed you—"

"No? He comes to my home in a fit of rage and accuses me of murder, of killing Maggie, not to mention my wife, and you say he has done nothing to harm me? He threatened to take Kevin away from me, Ariel."

I looked back at Brabbs. "Is this true?" I asked.

"Aye, it's true," Brabbs responded, rubbing his

cheek. "It's true and I'd do it again tomorrow given the same circumstances."

"Here, now." The clergyman stepped between them. "This is a place of God, gentlemen. Remember, my lord, why we are here. This is your wedding day, sir. It should be a happy occasion for us all." He stepped up to Nick and took his arm. "Please, Your Lordship, for the sake of your bride-to-be."

Nicholas gave Brabbs one last withering look before turning to me. Forcing myself to remain calm, I took his arm and walked with him through the nave. A white bolt of doubt sluiced through me as I recalled the sudden violence in his manner, the viciousness in his tone toward Brabbs. I could yet feel the pent savagery in the flexed muscle beneath my hand. How much would—could—he take before snapping?

Once reaching the chancel, Nicholas turned to face me. His hands came up, fumbled a moment with the fastening of my cloak, then slipped the garment from my shoulders and tossed it onto the pew behind me. Dropping his hands to his side, he stepped away and ran his gaze over my dress.

"Nice," he said. "Very nice." Then looking back to my eyes, a smile twisting one corner of his mouth, he added, "But you might try smiling, my love. This is your wedding day, is it not?"

My throat was suddenly tight. I tried speaking but couldn't. I felt a sinking sensation in my stomach as if I had unexpectedly stepped over a cliff in the dark and was plummeting into the very pits of hell. For certainly at that moment I felt as if I were looking into Satan's eyes.

As my lord's hands came up slowly and released his own cloak, Jim stepped up behind him and slid it off his shoulders. My breath left me, for I had never seen him so handsome, or so threatening. His coat was of rich olive-green velvet embroidered with black silk fleurs-de-lis. His satin breeches were of the same color. Beneath the coat he wore a white lawn shirt, and white lace ruffles cascaded down his chest and from beneath the cuffs of his coat. The dress I had made now seemed too simple, too plain, and I suddenly felt a wave of humiliation wash over me. I recalled Brabbs's reminding me that I was not of Wyndham's class. I had never felt it so acutely as I did in that moment.

Nicholas took my hand in his firm fingers, slowly lifted it to his lips. With his kiss I felt my reservations begin to thaw, and I smiled. "Shall we get on with it, my lord?" I was pleased to hear my voice sound steady.

"By all means," he responded. He turned to face the clergyman, pulling me closer to his side.

"Shall we begin?" the minister asked.

I looked up at Nicholas as he nodded.

The minister stood before us, an open Bible in his hands, a small gold ring placed on one of the pages. His resonant voice echoed about the sacred chamber as he began the service with a prayer. I listened intently, repeating each Amen the minister whispered.

The room became colder as he ended his prayer. The hem of the minister's cossack fluttered in a sudden breeze as did my skirt and the thin wisps of hair I had curled about my face. The reverend paused and looked about the nave before asking, "If anyone knows any reason why this man and woman should not be lawfully joined in marriage, speak it now or forever hold your peace."

I saw Nick's head turn toward Brabbs. I held my breath.

As the reverend's fingers nervously nudged the ring about the Bible, the seconds clipped by, seeming like hours. Brabbs shifted from one foot to the other; from the corner of my eye I saw a thin wisp of vapor leave his mouth as he released his breath.

"Very well," came the minister's words.

I closed my eyes in relief.

After we repeated our vows Nicholas slipped the ring onto my finger, looking down into my eyes as the minister said, "By the authority vested in me and in the name of God Almighty, I pronounce you man and wife." Gently shutting his book, he smiled at my husband and added, "My lord, you may kiss your bride."

The cold tip of Nick's finger caught my chin and tipped up my face. He brushed the corner of my mouth with his lips, then he turned away.

There were documents to sign. By the time we were prepared to leave the church, a light snow had begun to fall. We stood on the steps outside the nave, waiting as the Wyndham coach was brought up from the stables. Pulled by coal-black beasts with arched necks and high-prancing hooves, the ebony post chaise stopped before us.

My husband stood at my side, the clouds around us intensifying the cold gray of his eyes as he looked out over the countryside. He smoothed his leather gloves over his hands before looking down at me. "Lady Malham," he said. "You may bid your friend adieu now."

My heart set up a rapid pounding in my breast as I turned to Brabbs. He looked suddenly older, his eyes sadder than I had ever seen them. "Be happy," he said, but before he could take me in his arms Nicholas clamped his gloved hand on my shoulder and pulled me away.

Through the mist and snow I saw the chaise door open. My lord caught my arm in a firm grip as I lifted my skirts and mounted the steps into the coach. Then Nicholas mounted behind me.

Settling back into the leather cushions, I took one last glance out the door before it shut in my face. I glimpsed Brabbs and Jim walking to Brabbs's buggy. "Jim is not coming with us, my lord?"

"No" was his simple response.

With a crack of a whip, the coach lurched into motion and I settled again into my seat. Nicholas sat directly across from me, his legs casually open, swaying slightly with the motion of the chaise. "So," he said, shattering the quiet. "How does it feel to be *Lady* Malham, Lady Malham?"

I looked to his face, expecting to find some humor there. I was met instead with grim gray eyes and a deep furrow between his arching black brows.

"Grand, I think, sir."

"You may discontinue speaking to me in that subservient manner. You are an equal now, remember."

"Yes, sir. I mean, yes, my lord . . . yes, Nicholas." I bit my lip. This is going to take some doing, I thought. Looking back to his chilly eyes, I said, "Sir. Have I displeased you in some way?"

"What do you mean? Do I appear displeased?"

"Yes, you do. You hardly seem gay about our marriage. Are you angry because of Brabbs?"

"I wonder what you are doing with him."

"He's only a friend. A long-time family friend."

"I don't like him."

"I'm sorry."

"I don't want you to see him again."

My heart stopped. "But—but he is my friend. I love Brabbs like—"

His eyes suddenly flashed like fire, cutting off my words. A muscle quivered in his cheek as he said, "As my wife you are to obey me, Ariel. If I decide to drag you kicking and screaming to the top of the cove and tell you to jump, you will do so. Do you understand me?"

I felt the blood drain from my face. Hot anger burned in the pit of my stomach. "Nay, I do not understand! You are my husband, yes, but not my master, if I am indeed your equal. If being your wife means I am to live night and day under the thumb of a tyrant, you may turn this coach about and return me to Burnsall. We will dissolve this marriage now before we both come to regret our rashness." I made a move toward the door.

"Sit down," he ordered me.

I moved again.

He caught my arm and shoved me back in the seat.

The rumble of the coach-wheel and the clop of the horses' hooves sounded eerie, echoing against the wall of fog that swirled around us. Nicholas neither moved nor blinked as he apparently considered my words. Then, taking a deep breath, he relaxed into the seat and flicked open the buttons of his coat. "Do you like the ring?" he asked, his voice yet tight, but his tone more congenial.

My nerves, however, were still on edge. Instinctively I closed the fingers of my right hand over the wedding band. "Aye, I like it," I snapped.

One end of his mouth curled up. "It belonged to my grandmother on my father's side. It's a big large, I see."

"A bit." I spun it around my finger.

"I'll have it measured and cut down. Unless, of course, you wish for me to turn back for Burnsall. I won't stop you again if that's what you want."

I did not respond. At that moment I did not know what I wanted.

Nicholas looked out the window, lost in thought. His handsome face was partially in shadow, chin, mouth and nose barely visible; broad, high cheekbones were lit by dim daylight and his eyes were dark and grave. I was stunned, as he began to softly recite in a deep and melodious voice:

> I thought, O my love, you were so—
>   As the sun or the moon on a fountain,
> And I thought after that you were snow,
>   The cold snow on top of the mountain.
> And I thought after that you were more
>   Like God's lamp shining to find me,
> Or the bright star of knowledge before,
>   Or the star of knowledge behind me.

He looked in my eyes and smiled. "It's an old Irish love song."

"I know."

"You're part Irish, I think."

"Aye," I responded. "My mother was from Ireland."

"I knew it. The hair and the eyes gave you away . . . come here, Ariel. Come here, I won't hurt you." When I didn't budge, he pressed his lips and frowned. "Very well, then. I'm sorry I hit your friend. Does that appease you?"

"Little."

Lacing his fingers over his flat stomach, he rested his head back on the leather seat and stared at the roof. "I reacted rashly where Brabbs was concerned. I admit it. But sometimes, Ariel, I cannot help how I act. I'm sorry. You knew that before you married me. I warned you."

I stared at my wedding ring and whispered, "Aye, you warned me."

His head came up; a wave of dark hair spilled nearly to his eyes. "Regrets?" he asked.

"In truth, it is not how I dreamed of my wedding day."

He leaned toward me suddenly and caught my face in his fingers. "I've made you cry," he stated angrily. Shifting onto the seat beside me, he curled his arm around my waist and lifted me onto his lap. Cupping my face in his palm, he frowned. "I'm sorry if I hurt you. Do you think I would intentionally cause you pain? Well? Answer me, dammit, and stop trembling there like a sparrow with a broken wing."

He curled his fingers more gently around my chin, tipping my head back, and the sweet ache of love bloomed anew in my heart and blood as I looked into his dark eyes. Tilting his head to one side, he brushed his mouth against mine, once, twice, then with a low growl he covered my mouth completely with his. Melting against him I opened my lips, submissive as he thrust his tongue into my mouth and crushed me to him so fiercely I gasped.

My husband. The ecstasy brought by my silent repetition of those words beat inside me with as much passion as his kiss. I did tremble, but with longing and not fear.

Grasping my shoulders, he lifted his head and looked into my eyes. "Do you know," he began in a voice thick with desire, "that when we made love the other night, it was like the first time for me. My god, I've wanted you since. I want you now."

I felt his hand move up my back, expertly unfastening the bodice of my gown. Loosened, it fell forward over the swells of my breasts, partially down my arms, trapping them against me. Then he tore it away from my breasts completely, releasing me into his hand. As he rubbed his palm gently across my nipple I closed my eyes, feeling the sensitive sphere swelling and hardening with desire. "My lord," I finally managed, "do you think it wise?"

"Wise and necessary," he murmured. "Very necessary." Then he buried his face against my breast, took the high, hard point in his mouth and circled it achingly slow with his tongue. Gently, so I barely noticed, he shifted me about until I straddled his lap. He spread his legs farther until I lay pressed intimately against the rise of his need, then he slipped his hand under my skirt and touched me.

He felt me flinch but continued, weaving magic with the rhythm of his fingers until I was whimpering and grinding my hips against his, all reason gone, driven away by this swirling, drowning sensation inside me. "Make love to me, Lady Malham," I heard him say, and through passion-drowsy eyes I looked down on his face, a face too handsome to be real. Despite the cold outside the coach, a tear of sweat rolled down his temple, and, pressing my mouth against it I drank it in, thinking it sweet as honey. "Make love to me," he repeated, and, catching my hands, he dragged them down to his breeches.

I flicked the buttons open, one by one, and, once releasing him into my hand, I raised up on my knees, positioned him against me and sank onto him. His hands twisted into my dress, my hair. Burying his face against my breast, he smothered the sharp gasp and low, savage growl that wedged from his throat. Then, plunging his hands beneath the velvet skirts of my wedding dress, he gripped my buttocks in his fingers and pressed me up and then down until the ancient rhythm came naturally to us both.

He felt strong as steel and as soft as velvet inside

me, filling me, driving me with each swivel of his hips against mine to certain madness, until I lost all control, all thought of propriety, and abandoned myself to the pleasure and the gratification of pleasing *him*. And the tension mounted. With each deep thrust inside my body I scaled one step closer. The torment flooded me, building as it did for him, until he was gripping my dress in his fingers and pressing his head back into the seat, his eyes tightly closed and his face immobile with the same exquisite pain as mine.

I buried my hands first in his hair, then his shirt, twisting my fingers into the fine lawn, shredding it with my nails, moaning, moving until we tumbled together over the barrier. Waves of sensation swept over us, a spiraling, exploding sky of stars that caused us each to cry out in surrender, to cling together until we were drained and limp and complete.

We rode that way for some time, satisfied with the closeness of just holding each other in our arms, not quite ready to give it up. Here we were alone, sheltered against the madness of the outside world. There was no madness here, none but the maddening love we felt for each other in that moment, so intense it bordered on despair. My head on my husband's shoulder, his arms around me, I closed my eyes and allowed the gentle rocking of the coach to soothe my feverish state.

Perhaps we both slept. When I opened my eyes I discovered that he had, at some time, righted my dress and rebuttoned my bodice. Breathing in the virile scent of his flesh, I lifted my head and met his eyes. He looked at me sternly at first, and my heart turned over in fear. Then he began to grin. In a low, silky voice he said, "There'll be no going back to Burnsall now, you know."

"I know."

"You're mine."

"Aye."

"For better or worse."

"I vow it."

"Do you still love me?"

"I do."

"Then say it. I have to hear you say it."

"I—I love you, my lord husband, now and always."

He took my face in his hands. His eyes burned into mine. "Swear it."

"I swear."

The coach stopped. We heard the footman jump to the ground.

Nicholas took my hand fiercely in his. "We're home," he said.

Chapter 15

The flush of color in Adrienne's face died, leaving her cheeks very pale. She looked anxiously from Nicholas to Trevor, and then to me. "Married, you say," were her words. "To each other?"

Nicholas stood before the fire, his eyes on his sister as he rotated a glass of sherry in his hand. There was a certain mischievous belligerence in the tilt of his lips that made me wonder if this marriage had been perpetrated more in the name of spite than in love. Dismissing the thought, I looked at Trevor.

He regarded me openly from his satin-lined *bergere*, lifting one brow as my eyes met his. "Well," he said, "this should certainly give the tongues something to wag about."

"They are wagging already," Nicholas said.

Trevor smiled.

I, however, did not. I found it more and more discomforting to sit in these peoples' presence while they assessed the circumstances of our marriage. I wasn't a little surprised then when Trevor asked:

"Ariel, my dear, are you pregnant?"

"No," Nick responded. "In any case, that is none of your concern."

"Just attempting to understand," Trevor responded.

"What is there to understand?"

Leaving his chair, Trevor walked to the fireplace to face his brother. "You have known each other a month, Nick. Less than a month, actually. And considering your present state of mind—"

"Not to mention the difference in our backgrounds," Nick snapped.

I looked away, embarrassment burning my cheeks.

"There is that obvious difference," Trevor continued. "But that is the least of my concern. After all, this is not the first time a Wyndham has married outside his social standing. No, my concern, Nick, is your health. You are fully aware of what you've done?"

"Fully. I have married the woman I love."

I closed my eyes, savoring his words.

Trevor turned away, his hands thrust deep into the pockets of his broadcloth jacket. "Love. For God's sake, man, you can hardly tell me your name from day to day. How do you know if you love her or not?"

"I know."

"As you love sherry? It's a crutch to get you through the night, or from one miserable hour to the next. The sad truth of the matter is you wanted someone to lean on, who made you feel like a man again. You've used her despicably, Nick, and you should be ashamed of yourself." Trevor turned to face me. I continued looking at my husband, however, waiting for him to deny his brother's accusations. Instead he stared down into the fire, his fingers clasping the sherry glass so tightly I expected the fragile crystal to shatter at any moment.

Trevor stopped by my chair. With hesitance I met his eyes. "I'm sorry, Ariel, but there are certain matters I must discuss with my brother. You'll excuse us, I hope. Perhaps you and I and Adrienne will talk later?"

Before I could leave my chair Nicholas slammed his glass onto the hearth with enough force to send shards of crystal throughout the room. Grabbing Trevor by the lapels of his coat, he hissed, "Goddamn you. Have you forgotten yourself, young brother? Have you forgotten whom you are addressing?" He shook Trevor furiously. "Ariel is now my wife. My wife! And since I am still lord of this manor she is to be addressed accordingly as *Lady* Malham. *I* still have sole responsibility for Walthamstow, and if at any time I am unable to carry out those responsibilities they will revert to my wife. *I* will give her directives and no one else. You and Adrienne and every parlor bitch working on this asylum will answer to *her.* Is that clear?"

I left my chair, frightened beyond measure at the anger I witnessed before me, disturbed even more because I was the cause of it. "Please," I cried. Grabbing my husband's tightly clenched fists, I attempted to wrench them from Trevor's clothing. "My lord, he meant no offense, I'm certain. Let him go for my sake."

Little by little Nicholas unclenched his fists. Trevor stepped away, his face white, his chest rising and falling with emotion as he attempted to straighten his clothing. His voice shook as he managed to respond, "My apologies. I certainly meant no disrespect, Lady Malham."

Adrienne, having left her chair, looked from her brothers to me. Her dress, being a vivid scarlet taffeta, flushed her face with color. With coldness in her voice she remarked, "I suppose this means I'll be asked to leave my quarters again. Understandably you'll want the largest and most comfortable rooms for your own."

"Nonsense," I exclaimed. "Please, nothing here will change. This is your home and I have no intention of becoming a nuisance—"

"Nuisance!" Nicholas roared. "Ariel, you are my goddamned wife. If you want to tell these two to leave the

grounds entirely, then they will be obligated to do so."
He grabbed my arm and propelled me toward the door.

Within five minutes every servant at Walthamstow
was lined up across the Great Hall's wooden floor,
Polly on one end, Bea on the other. Polly wrung her
hands in her apron and eyed Nicholas through thin
wisps of hair while Bea clutched her skirts and mumbled to herself, looking ready to spring should my husband decide to make any murderous move toward her.
In truth, he looked dangerous, the light from the candles about the walls playing strange tricks on his face
as he paced back and forth across the room.

The snowy ruffles down his chest were a sharp con-
trast to his skin, making it look as swarthy as a gypsy's.
With his hands on his hips, his olive-green coat caught
behind his wrists, he glared at each servant a full minute before he pointed to me and announced, "Lady
Malham."

Not a servant moved, but I noted their surprise (and
in some cases outrage) as they shifted their gazes to
mine.

"Well," he suddenly thundered. "You have just been
introduced to the new Lady of Walthamstow!"

The women bobbed up and down. The men bowed.

"Very good. Now, get out of my sight."

They dispersed quickly, bobbing to me again as they
left the room. I waited until we were alone before turning to Nicholas. I watched in silence as he walked to
the Brustolon vase stand we had laughed about only
two weeks before. I could sense his mounting frustration as he stared down at the cut-glass decanter of
sherry.

With no warning he swept his hand across the bottle
and sent it shattering to the floor. Before I could clear
my mind of its shock, he took hold of the walnut-

and-ebony table and sent it crashing against the wall. "Crutch! By God, I should go back and thrash him, Ariel." He spun to face me. "Now they're trying to convince me—convince you—that I don't know my mind enough to recognize my own feelings." He frowned and his look became fiercer still. "You don't believe that, do you?" he asked me.

I shook my head, thinking it better to say nothing than to risk the chance of agitating him further.

He turned again and looked down at the puddles of amber liquid on the floor. Then his hand came up and he pressed his fingers to his temple. "Crutch," he repeated more softly, and he lightly moistened his lips with his tongue. "God, is that what it's become?"

I advanced toward him cautiously, gripping my skirt in my fingers. "Of course not," I said. "You don't need the sherry, my lord. Do you?"

He pressed the butt of his palm against his head. "No. I don't need it. It's just that . . ." His voice trailed off and again he stared at the floor.

"It's what, Nicholas?"

"It helps my head."

"Would it help your head now?"

Closing his eyes, he nodded.

Stopping beside him, I reached up and touched his face, brushed his temple with my fingers. "I love you," I said. "I don't mind being a crutch if that's what it takes to heal you. You asked me once to heal you. I couldn't then, but I'm your wife now. I think I can help if you'll let me."

A fine film of sweat beaded over his lip; he wiped it away with the back of his hand.

Pressing my body against his, I smiled brightly and touched my finger to his lips. "Will you let me help?"

He nodded, though not without reluctance.

"Good. Then we'll start with the sherry. I don't think you should drink it anymore."

"But my head—"

"We'll find something else for your head. I'm certain Brabbs has something that may help."

He scowled at that, making me laugh. "Something lethal, no doubt," he said.

"I'll drink it myself first."

Nicholas began to smile.

I had changed out of my wedding gown and back into my green satin dress, and was making my way to the kitchen to oversee the preparation of my lord's tea when Trevor approached me. He bowed slowly, bestowed on me a lazy, chagrined smile, and said, "Lady Malham. A word with you?"

I smiled back. "His lordship may stand on ceremony, but I do not. Please don't continue embarrassing me by addressing me so. It is Ariel."

He fell in beside me as we continued down the hall. "So tell me, . . . Ariel. Understanding that every woman has her own ideas about the running of the house, I'm certain there will be changes about Walthamstow. Where will you begin?"

"I will line the walls with girandoles. Walthamstow will never be allowed to dwell in darkness again."

"Then?"

"I may consider opening the rest of the house." His pace slowed. I looked around, surprised. "Is something wrong?"

"That may be a grand undertaking. Those rooms have been closed for nearly a century."

"You're probably right. It was only a thought." I continued down the hall, began my descent down the stairs, holding the banister tightly with my right hand. Trevor caught my arm, offering assistance.

"For what it's worth," he said, "welcome to the family."

I flashed him a smile.

"I hope you didn't take exception to anything I said earlier, but you must understand our surprise over this sudden marriage."

Reaching the first floor, I smoothed my skirt before facing my brother-in-law again. He regarded me warmly, a faint smile turning up one end of his mouth. "I understand," I told him. But as I began to turn away, he caught my arm one last time.

His blue eyes were full of concern and a measure of sadness. Clasping his hands behind his back, he stated, "I hope you realize fully what you've gotten yourself into, my dear."

"Of course I do."

"Do you? You saw a glimpse of his temper with me this afternoon. Ariel, he can be extremely violent."

"I'm well aware of that."

"I would hate for you to get hurt."

"He won't hurt me."

Trevor stepped closer, so close I could detect a faint hint of liquor about him as well as something else, a slightly floral scent that stirred a vision in my mind of a summer garden. His words, however, were not so pleasant when he finally spoke. "Jane said the same thing just before she died. Regardless whether or not they loved each other, she trusted that he would not hurt her."

I turned away, angry, and continued to the kitchen. Trevor stepped around me, blocking my path. "The man is not rational, Ariel."

"I disagree, sir."

"For God's sake, lass, open your eyes to reality."

"They are open." I attempted to step around him.

"He murdered his wife."

"Show me proof."

"He's admitted as much."

"He's admitted nothing more than striking her."

"Then how else would you explain the burning of the stables?" As I attempted to step around him again, he caught my arm. "He struck her, then set the stables on fire to cover up the fact that he'd killed her."

Jerking my arm from his grip, I demanded, "If you are so certain he is a murderer, then why have you not called in the authorities?"

"Why—" He shook his head in disbelief. "The man is my brother. Regardless of the heinous crime he's committed I don't wish to see him hanged."

"Yet you and Adrienne would rather see him interned at Saint Mary's? Sir, that is a fate worse than death. It would be a living hell—"

"I personally want nothing of the sort. But if it comes to that, I'm certain they would treat him kindly considering his status."

"Kindly!" I stepped away, unable to believe what I had heard. "They are treated little better than animals in those institutions. They are caged—"

"Only in very severe cases, I understand."

"They are beaten and starved. They are subjected to the mistreatments not only from the employees, but from patients as well. They sleep on stone floors without the benefit of a single comfort, other than a pile of straw. And that, if they are fortunate, is swept out once a fortnight, and only then because it is rank from rot and offal. Sir, do not tell me that such an existence is better than death, it is not, and I will not allow *anyone* to subject him to that fate when it is not necessary."

Only then did I realize that I had begun to cry. I turned my face to the wall while I attempted to regain my composure.

"Ariel." Gently catching my shoulders, he pulled me around to face him. "I'm sorry. I didn't mean to upset you. Perhaps I didn't realize how much you truly care for Nick. He's a very fortunate man and I envy him." Gathering me up against his chest, he squeezed me tenderly and rocked me back and forth. "There now, everything will be fine, I'm certain. Of course I'll do our best to see Nick remains with us if that's what you want."

"It's what you and Adrienne should want as well," I said pointedly. Pushing him away, I looked him in the eye. "It is what you want, isn't it?"

His blue eyes widened slightly in surprise. Then he laughed. "That's an odd question. Certainly, if Nick were to suddenly recover from whatever irrationality is plaguing him—"

"He will."

Trevor frowned. "You sound certain."

"I am."

"Do you have some direct communication with God?" He smiled, but I detected a certain sarcasm in his voice that gave me pause. "If you have," he continued in a lighter tone, "I'd appreciate your putting in a good word for me."

Returning his smile, I said, "If you are as innocent as my husband, sir, then you should have no problems entering heaven when the time comes."

I left him standing in the corridor as I continued to the kitchen.

Matilda greeted me with open arms, her face beaming with pleasure. Crushing me to her ample bosom, she exclaimed, "It's right. I told me mates, 'That one's special. She'll bring light to this old 'ouse, y' mark me words.' And y' have!" Then, as if suddenly realizing what she was doing, she jumped back and giggled. "Saints alive, wot am I about." She curtsied. "Yer ladyship, I should be sayin', wot bring y' down in this hot old dungeon when y' should be spendin' time with yer groom?"

Dropping into a chair before the fire, I replied, "Spare me all the formalities, Tilly. All I want's a cuppa tea and a bitta friendly conversation."

"Well then, y've come t' the right place. Will y' be 'avin' scones with yer tea?"

"Nay, I'll not. I'll eat with his lord—my husband." Resting my head back against the chair, I smiled. "I cannot believe it, Tilly. I think I shall awaken at any moment and discover this is all a dream."

"It's real enough, lass. I take it yer happy?"

"Aye, I'm happy." Turning my head, I watched my friend scurry to the fire, where she placed a pot of water. "I'll make him happy."

"I know y' will, lass. Y've done that already."

"Have I?"

"Aye. Y' don't know wot he was like afore y' came, y' know."

"How was his relationship with Jane?"

"Aw, they didn't 'ave no relationship, mum. No, mum. They lived in separate ends of the 'ouse. T' my knowledge they were never even . . ." She bit her lip, then finished, "Well, you know . . . intimate."

"Did Jane have lovers?"

Tilly held the inverted teapot over the rising steam, warming the pot properly before adding tea in heaping spoons into the container. Carefully she poured the boiling liquid into the china pot and replaced the lid.

"Well?" I said. "Did she have lovers?"

Again Tilly turned away. "Did y' say y' wanted scones, mum? I believe we 'ave a few left. I declare we've 'ad 'em go missin' again."

"Tilly."

She stopped in her tracks and slowly turned to face me. "Why is it so important for y' t' know, mum? Y' know how I feel about gossips. It ain't my way; I leave all that up t' Polly and Kate and such. Not t' say that I don't listen, y' understand. There's nowt that goes on in this owd house that Tilly don't know about, but—"

"I take it she did. Did Nicholas know about them?"

"His lordship knew, or at least suspected that she was seein' another man on the sly. I heard 'em arguin' over it enough. Yer husband demanded a divorce, but she wouldn't 'ave it, y' see, 'cept on one condition."

"And that was?"

"Walthamstow. She wanted it all: house, grounds, money. 'Course he wouldn't give it to 'er. Walthamstow has always belonged to the Wyndhams. It always will, I reckon."

"Did you see or hear anything the night of Jane's death?" I asked as Tilly disappeared into the larder. She reappeared with a china cup and saucer in her hand, then began to pour out my tea.

"We all heard the row. It were awful. I get the shakes just thinkin' of it. His lordship had been drinkin' the afternoon in the Great Hall. He were on his way back to 'is quarters when he run into Jane. She were dressed for ridin' and smellin' like a rose garden. He accused her of meetin' her lover and she didn't deny it."

"And he followed her to the stables?"

"Aye. After she wagered he didn't have the backbone t' stop 'er. It were almost as if she were purposely tauntin' him into a lather. Ooo, it were awful. The woman was screechin' like a banshee the entire way t' the stables."

"But you say no one actually witnessed the confrontation in the stables."

"No one but Samantha. Aye, I'm certain she seen it. That's the only explanation why she buggered off like she did. Not a word to no one, just disappeared sometime durin' the night, takin' her few belongin's with 'er."

I thought a moment, then asked, "Why are you so certain Samantha was at the stables? Did you see her afterwards?"

"She told me she were goin', that's why." Tilly placed the tea in my hands before plunking her fists on her hips. She shook her head. "She were dallyin' with one of the grooms, y' see, but 'is lordship let 'im go the week before for mistreatin' one of 'is horses. She got a message to meet Billy there at eight sharp."

"Then there should be two witnesses. If Billy—"

"Billy never showed, but that ain't unusual. 'e weren't reliable, y' see. 'e were down at the tavern boozin' at the time. When Jim went down to question 'im 'e denied ever sendin' a note to Samantha. But it'd be just like 'im to have sent it and forgot that 'e sent it. 'e liked 'is ale, y' see, and on more than one occasion left Samantha waitin' on the green for 'im t' show. Samantha were a lovely girl and too good for that lad, but she continued t' see 'im, regardless."

Tilly must have sensed my disappointment. Fondly she placed her hand on my shoulder. "Wot's done is done," she said. "Ain't it best t' forget it?"

"Perhaps," I responded. "But I can't believe Nicholas, no matter how provoked he was, would murder his wife in cold blood."

" 'is lordship ain't 'imself, luv. Y' know that."

"Aye, and he never will be until the truth is known." I placed my cup and saucer on the table, then left the chair and faced my friend. "I have to know the truth, Tilly. Somehow I must learn how Jane died, for my own sake as well as my husband's. When Nick is cured we'll have to come to grips with the tragedy in one way or another."

"Then yer sayin' y' won't be lettin' the doc and Miss Adrienne send 'is lordship off to Bedlam?"

"Certainly not. Nicholas is no more insane than you or I."

Her round eyes widened in surprise. "Then you don't believe that 'is accident caused 'im to change?" she asked.

"Accident? No, Tilly, I don't think his accident has much to do at all with my husband's behavior."

"Then wot's 'appened to 'im, mum?"

"I can't be certain, Tilly, although I have my suspicions. Perhaps later, when his lordship is better, I'll look into the matter more thoroughly. Until then would you do me a small favor?"

"O' course, mum. Anythin' you want, mum. Tell Tilly wot it is."

"For the next few days I would like you to bring my husband's food tray directly to me. Allow no one else to seize it."

"That sounds simply enuf."

"Do not let anyone else tamper with his food or drink in any way."

"No one gets by me, mum, when it comes to pre-parin' yer meals. But does this mean y' won't be dinin' with the others?"

"Aye. For the next few days my husband and I will be acting like newlyweds. We're retiring to our quarters and don't wish to be disturbed for any reason."

Ducking her head, Tilly giggled and said, "Now ain't that nice. I'm certain 'is lordship is gonna be a different man now that y've married 'im. Yes, mum, we're goin' t' see the true master amidst us again just any day."

Smiling, I said, "I hope so Tilly. We'll just have to have faith."

I thought: *I only hope I have enough faith to see this through. I have to believe, to trust. No matter what happens from this moment on, I must continue to have faith.*

Chapter 16

The hag regarded me with caution as I stooped to pick up my son. Lifting Kevin in my arms, I smiled into his green eyes and said, "Come to Mother, my darling." Kissing his cheek, I turned to Bea and said, "You're suddenly very quiet, Bea. Is anything wrong?" I taunted her and took open pleasure in doing so.

"Y'll be sorry soon enough," she said.

"I doubt it."

Her head tilted as she sidled closer to me, so close the musty smell of her aged skin filled my nostrils. "He'll kill you, girl. He's possessed by madness—"

"Don't be absurd," I told her. Cradling Kevin closer, I said, "I forbid you to talk in such a way."

"He killed my darling Jane. My beautiful Jane." She smiled, showing me her teeth. "Would you like to see her?"

I shook my head and stepped away. "Nay, I do not. Why should I?"

"You should know her: You've taken her place in this house. She was a real beauty, fragile as a buttercup. It wouldn't take much to strike her down." She backed away, lifting her hand and motioning me to follow.

I did follow, oddly hypnotized by the crone's words.

Reaching the doorway to her bedroom I stopped, refusing to enter. As my eyes took in the room my skin crawled. Jane's possessions lined every corner of the quarters like treasured objects in a museum. A white nightgown adorned a mannequin, spilling from its armless form to a puddle of exquisite lace on the floor. Pearl-backed combs and brushes were placed neatly across Bea's dresser, as well as cut-glass perfume bottles of every shape imaginable. But it was the portrait on the wall that riveted my attention.

Bea took the canvas from the wall and, turning back to me, held it up before her. "Jane."

I held Kevin more tightly to me, but no matter how I willed it I could not take my eyes from the portrait, and the slashes running vertically over Jane's face.

"He did this; took the portrait he'd painted and slashed it with a knife. The next night he killed her." She ambled closer. "She's a beauty, ain't she?"

She is indeed a beauty, I thought with a sense of desperation. I wanted to turn and flee the room, but I remained, my feet like lead and my heart barely lighter. I studied Jane's childlike features, noting she appeared far more delicate than I had imagined her. Perhaps it was the milk-white skin, the baby-fine blond hair that Nicholas had so skillfully portrayed with the brush that made her appear so. Her eyes were blue and large and deep. Her lips wore a curl that was both sensual and aloof.

"She looks very young," I said.

"Only nineteen. She were a babe when he killed her."

"I forbid you to continue saying that, Bea. I'm not so patient as my husband. I'll see you away from Walthamstow if you pursue that allegation."

"Only telling you for yer own good, lass. You'll be next if yer not careful."

I backed away, shaking my head.

"Keep yer eye open," she said. "It comes on him when you least expect it."

Unable to tolerate another moment of the woman's presence, I left the room. After returning Kevin to his bed I made for my own quarters, arriving just as Polly and Kate marched through my doorway, their arms burdened with my own belongings.

"What's this?" I asked.

" 'is lordship's orders, mum," Kate replied. "We've been instructed to move yer clothes into the master's bedroom."

My face colored as I met Polly's appraisal. Her eyes narrowed with malice before a sudden look of fear washed over her features. I knew, even before I turned, that my husband had joined us.

He addressed me in a quiet voice. "Lady Malham. I hope you are agreeable to these accommodations."

"Whatever pleases you, sir," I replied in a tight voice. His eyes studied me unblinkingly and a quivering began in my heart and stomach that unnerved me. Dear God, the seed of doubt and fear that Bea had planted inside me had begun to germinate into something tangible. My husband's presence frightened me. And he sensed it.

"I looked for you earlier," he said. "Where were you?"

"The kitchen."

"After that."

"With Kevin."

"Ah." He slid his hands into the pockets of his jacket while looking beyond me to Kevin's room. "I have an appointment in ten minutes with Trevor." His eyes came back to mine. "I would like you to join us. We'll be discussing business, no doubt. You should become acquainted with that aspect of Walthamstow. It may be tedious and somewhat boring but it's necessary."

"Very well, my lord. Whatever pleases you."

We walked together down the hall. When we turned the corner, Nick's pace slowed. His hand came up and brushed the small of my back. The touch was like a knife blade through my insides. I gasped, ashamed of the sudden doubts that made me yearn to take my son and flee the man I had married that morning out of love.

He stopped before me, blocking my path. I found myself backing away no matter how I struggled to stand my ground. "Something's happened," came his quiet voice. "Tell me what's happened."

"Nothing."

"Ariel—"

"Nothing!" Throwing my head back, I met his eyes, dark and sharp as flint as they regarded me. There was no escaping. He saw my lie for what it was and without uttering a word he forced me to speak the truth. "Very well, then." I spoke as bravely and straightforwardly as possible. If I was to be the next Lady Malham in Malham Cemetery this was as good a time as any to go about it. Rather now, in daylight (dim as it was in that bleak tunnel) than at night in my sleep when I least expected it. "I spoke with Bea and she showed me the portrait you did of your wife."

"You are my wife," he answered without inflection.

Frustrated, I shook my head. "Jane!" I exclaimed. "I saw the portrait you did of Jane. Will you tell me why you slashed it?"

Wyndham stood up straight before replying. "Better it than her, I should think."

"That is no consolation. Bea tells me she died the next night."

"You mean I killed her the next night."

"Precisely."

"So. Do you finally doubt the wisdom of marrying me, sweetheart? Have they finally beaten some sense into your pretty head?" Like a striking snake his hand came out and caught my face, tilting my head back so roughly I flinched and grabbed his wrist. His dark head lowered over mine so closely I could feel his hot breath against my cheek. He said through his teeth, "A little late for regrets, isn't it, Lady Malham?"

"I said nothing of regrets," I responded with passion.

"No, you don't have to. You have that same look of fear in your eyes as everyone else in this house." Releasing me, he leaned against the wall at his back and closed his eyes. "Aye, I slashed the portrait. I slashed it because she asked me for Walthamstow. Asked? Let me rephrase that. She demanded Walthamstow. She told me she would have it one way or another."

Nicholas looked at me and said, "I told her that night that I would see her dead before she took one rock from this estate." Noting my concern, he lifted one brow in surprise. "You mean the gossips haven't tattled about that one? It was one of our better arguments, actually. I was nearly driven to kill her then. But I had never lifted a hand against her, you see, and I was still sober enough to keep a rein on my temper. When she left the room I simply picked up a pallet knife and shredded the canvas." His features relaxed somewhat and he closed his eyes. "I'm sorry, Lady Malham, if that's not what you wanted to hear." Without looking at me again, Nicholas pushed away from the wall. We continued down the hall in silence.

The office suited my husband. Imposing and elegant, its linenfold carved walls gleamed with layer upon layer of fragrant beeswax. Mullioned windows overlooked Walthamstow's east gardens and the pond I had frequented when I first came to the estate.

My lord saw me to a high-backed, brass-studded leather chair before the window. Beside me on a walnut trestle table were placed platters of sausages en brioche, canapes, petits fours, and fruit tarts. Tea steeped in a sterling silver pitcher.

"Welcome to high tea," Nicholas said. "Become accustomed to it. Enjoy it. It's a tradition of the ton, you see. No doubt you'll be invited to a few once word of our marriage reaches my peers. They'll want to inspect you, certainly, so they can vividly visualize your face when they are stabbing you in the back with their gossip." He picked up a petit four and bit into it. "It's safe to eat, sweetheart," he said. "As you can see, I haven't poisoned it yet."

Before I could respond, Trevor entered the room with a decanter of sherry. He stopped abruptly upon seeing me. "My lady, I wasn't aware you would be here. My apologies if I've kept you waiting."

I returned his smile, acknowledging that the formality was more for my husband's benefit than for mine.

Nicholas turned toward the desk, a great scroll-carved piece of oak that looked as aged as Walthamstow. I recognized the Wyndham escutcheon emblazoned upon it.

"Sit down," Nicholas ordered his brother. "I want to get this bloody meeting over with as soon as possible."

"Understandable. This is your wedding day." Placing the sherry on the desk, Trevor reached for the liqueur set to one side and picked up two glasses. "A toast then to your marriage, my lord."

Nicholas slowly took his chair, his eyes on the decanter. I knew a time would come when my husband's willpower would be tested but the knowledge did not lessen my anxiety. Nicholas was angry with me, and I would not have been surprised had he accepted Trevor's proffered toast just to hurt me. Too, I knew he needed the drink. His head had been aching him terribly. If I was correct in my prognosis, the pain would be crucifying him by now.

He sat back in his chair, his face moist with sweat as he watched Trevor pour the first sherry. But as Trevor began to fill the second glass, he said, "No, thank you."

Trevor tipped up the decanter and looked at his brother with surprise. "No? Good God, Nick, are you ill?"

Nicholas shook his head, then looked to me.

Releasing my breath, I smiled in encouragement and said, "Perhaps my lord would care for tea instead."

Nicholas nodded and Trevor laughed in disbelief. "Tea? Nicholas drinking tea? I thought I'd never live to see the day. Very well, then, have your tea, dear brother. But if you don't mind, I'll drink my sherry." Lifting it to his mouth, he drank it down without taking a breath.

Appearing paler suddenly, Nicholas closed his eyes as I hurried to pour his tea. I placed it before him and stood at his side, ready to offer support should he need it. Gently laying my hand on his shoulder, I said, "You seem overly warm, sir. Shall I remove your coat?"

Slowly he left his chair and I slid the finely tailored jacket off his shoulders and down his arms. The white lawn shirt he wore beneath the coat clung damply to his skin, defining the tense muscles of his back and shoulders.

Instead of returning to his chair, he began to pace, impatient to get on with the affair. Finally, after pouring himself another sherry, Trevor relaxed in his chair. "I won't beat about the bush, Nick. I've asked to see you because an opportunity has arisen that I feel would be of great benefit to us."

Nick stopped before the hearth, his back to his brother, his eyes on the glowing red coals of the peat fire. He did not respond.

Trevor, clearing his throat, twisted slightly and looked back over his shoulder. "My lord, if this is a bad time—"

"There is never a good time, sir, so get on with it."

Trevor glanced at me, and I saw in his blue eyes a flash of anger that was gone so swiftly I thought I had imagined it at first. But the sudden set of his mouth gave away his irritation at being treated so rudely. In truth, I could not blame him. Nicholas could cut to the bone with his abrupt manner when he was not in a sound state of mind, and, suspecting the discomfort he must be experiencing at that time, I thought of suggesting that their conversation be delayed until later. I was not given the chance, however.

"As I mentioned earlier," Trevor continued, "I spoke to Earl Grey while in York. He is planning an expedition to China and there is some talk of forming a partnership of sorts with Twinings of London. Earl Grey has kindly offered us an opportunity to join him in this venture."

"For how much?"

"Depends. We could become full partners for fifteen thousand pounds. However, for a much smaller percentage—"

"No."

"But—"

"I said no."

Trevor turned away, his face burning as he stared at

the decanter on the desk. "I wish you would at least hear me out," he said finally.

"The last time I heard you out we lost twenty thousand pounds in a mine investment that caved in on our heads."

"The vein looked good. How could we know it would give out so quickly?" He reached for another sherry. "Jesus, Nick, you're being unreasonable."

My lord massaged the back of his neck. He closed his eyes. How I yearned to shield him from the pain he was experiencing, from the ordeal he would soon face. I would somehow have to prepare him, make him understand what was happening. But only after I was certain. I must be certain that the cause of Nick's nightmare was an addiction to opium.

Trevor left his chair. With his hands in his pockets, he faced his brother again. "Then perhaps you will consider advancing me more of my allowance. That way the monetary burden, should the venture fail, will be totally my responsibility."

This time Nick turned. With his gray eyes bright as quicksilver, he stared at Trevor intently before replying. "Forgive me if my memory has failed me again, but did I not advance you five thousand quid only a month ago?"

"I had debts to pay, if you recall."

"And you paid them."

"I did. I am free and clear of any monetary obligations."

Silence yawned between them, growing ever wider as the seconds ticked by. Doing my best to concentrate on my tea, I nibbled on a tart and listened as the tall case clock down the hallway chimed the half hour. As my husband returned to his desk to remove a ledger, I chose to peer out the window at the gardens, hoping my apparent disinterest would alleviate the tension in the room. It didn't. The longer my husband studied the ledger the more intense the anticipation became. Although Trevor remained quiet, the muscles in his jaw worked furiously with impatience.

Finally Nick looked up, his eyes dark, the ends of his hair wet with perspiration. "Very well. I will see you another five thousand. But mind you, this will have to do you until the year's end."

Smiling, I released my breath, recalling again why I continued to love him despite all the obvious reasons why I shouldn't.

Jubilant, Trevor leaned across the desk and slapped Nick on the arm. "Big brother, you've never let me down. I'll forever be grateful."

Sitting back in his chair, Nick grinned, though I sensed it pained him to do so. "That should keep our sister in tea for a while," he said.

"It will! And speaking of our sister, I would not venture too far from that chair. I understand she will be hitting you up soon for that trip to Paris. Perhaps you and Lady Malham should consider joining her. It might do you good, Nick, to get away from this dungeon. God, for a bit of fresh air. London would suffice for lack of anything better. Sometimes I actually envy Eugene and George their freedom in the colonies."

"Oh, I don't know. Living among barbarians who wear little more than feathers on their heads hardly seems enviable from my position."

Trevor laughed. "Perhaps you're more civilized than the rest of us. Who knows, it might do you good to experience the wilder side of living."

"Perhaps," my husband responded in a tired voice.

Trevor, his brow furrowed in concern, leaned on outstretched arms onto the desk. "Nick, are you all right?

You've looked gravely ill since I entered the room. Your color is bad and you are sweating profusely."

"Put away your medical text, sir; my head is splitting as usual, but I'll survive it. I think." His attempt at humor fell short as he winced with pain. His hands, resting upon the desk, doubled into fists.

Trevor looked around at me. "How long has he been this way, Ariel?"

I considered my brother-in-law's expression before replying. "Since our return to Walthamstow, I think."

"Nick, you should've come to see me. If you would only let me help—"

"Keep your damnable leeches to yourself, Doctor. I'll not have one of those wretched bloodsucking little creatures anywhere on me."

"There are alternate cures."

"Oh? Like Bedlam, perhaps? No thanks, Trev, I'll throw myself off the roof before I let you and Adrienne do that to me."

Affronted, Trevor abruptly stood upright. "You don't have to talk like we have some malicious intent to be rid of you. We only want what's best for you in the end."

"Do you." It wasn't a question. Then his eyes came back to mine, hopeless, defeated . . . resolute. Oh God, I thought. I love you. Trust me. I'll never leave you. I'll never let them take you from me. I'll be your crutch for as long as you want me. For as long as you need me. Don't give up, I thought. Just don't give up.

Slowly releasing his breath, Nicholas looked back at his brother. "Of course," he said. "Now if you'll forgive me, I've kept my wife waiting long enough. This is our wedding day, after all."

"Certainly." Trevor turned to me. "Lady Malham, my congratulations again. I trust you'll continue to stop by my office on occasion. My patients have grown quite fond of you. Especially Mr. Dix."

"Thank you, sir. I shall do so at every opportunity."

Bestowing my husband and me one last smile, Trevor left the room.

That night in our room I sat on the floor before the fire, watching the flames dance with each wind that spiraled down the chimney. Outside, winter had set in again with a vengeance, whipping ice and snow against the windows, moaning in the eaves. Nicholas lay with his head in my lap. Beside him on a blanket slept our son. I was content with whatever temporary peace had enfolded us for the moment.

Sensing my husband watching me, I looked down into his eyes. "I'm slipping over the edge," he said, "and I can't seem to stop it any longer."

I stroked his temple with my fingers and did my best to smile. "Let go. I'll catch you when you fall."

"I'm afraid of hitting the bottom, afraid of what I'll become . . . Why has this happened to me?"

"I don't know."

"You won't let them take me."

"Certainly not." I brushed my fingertips gently over his lashes, closing his eyes. "Sleep, my lord husband, while you can. I'll be here when you awaken."

His voice was groggy as he said, "Aye, but will I know you?" Then he drifted to sleep.

I watched the fire until the coals turned gray and the case clock in the hallway rang out in the silence. I found my solace by holding my husband, by watching my son sleep. It was a vision I had carried in my mind for the last year. If need be, this memory could last me forever.

I had no doubt now that my husband was an addict;

unknowingly, but an addict nevertheless. Someone in this house had turned him into one. My first objective was to release him from his dependency. I believed the pain he experienced in his head was a combination of the drug and his mind's effort to recover the past. With that release, I hoped, his memory would be totally restored.

But what then? I asked myself.

He would know me for the impostor I was: I had come to Walthamstow intent on revenge, intent on ruining him, on hurting him, on taking away my son—his son—and never returning.

Would he understand? Would he forgive me?

That was my dread, my desperate, heartbreaking fear, more powerful even than the possibility that he was a murderer. Murder, after all, could be committed in an instant of violent passion, leaving the perpetrator bloodied but remorseful. But revenge? Cold, passionless, premeditated intent on destroying. Aye, I was guilty. If he turned me out I would go . . . and never look back.

Chapter 17

I thought I was prepared.

I wasn't.

I saw Nicholas through the first three days of his withdrawal without leaving his side. Each time he looked at me, his eyes questioning *why?* why are you doing this to me? I turned away and wept. For him to think that I was the cause of his pain was almost more than I could bear.

Little by little the tremors ceased. The hallucinations became less frequent, the pain in his head less intense. But little by little he changed, withdrew. Again I was becoming a stranger to him, and I feared my greatest worry would be realized. Perhaps his loss of memory was permanent and had actually had nothing to do with the drug. Perhaps the man I had grown to love those years before no longer existed. Perhaps, I thought, he never had.

The fourth evening Nicholas slept soundly enough that I allowed myself to leave his room and venture to the Great Hall, prepared for a barrage of questions from his family. I had refused them entrance to our quarters when they pounded on our door demanding explanation. Facing them now would not be an easy task. But I was certain now that *someone* in this house was slipping my husband an opiate, and I was determined to learn who was doing it and why.

Upon my entering the room, Adrienne came out of her chair. "It is about time," she said. "What in heaven's name is going on up there? What are you doing to my brother?"

"He's been ill," I said. "He's better now."

"Ill? What do you mean? If he's ill then why haven't you allowed Trevor to see him?"

"It was my husband's request," I said.

"You're lying," she stated boldly. "You've made this illness all up. To think I trusted you at all. You're just like Jane, I think. You want to keep him to yourself, afraid I'll convince him this marriage is a farce. Well, I will if given the chance. I shan't allow you to usurp my position in this house like she did."

Pouring myself a cup of tea, I closed my eyes in weariness before saying, "I'm sorry you feel that way, Adrienne. I had hoped we could be friends."

"No doubt I'll be ostracized even more now by my peers. When they learn the new lady of Walthamstow is nothing but a common little—"

"That will be all," Trevor ordered. I looked around, placing my cup on the Chippendale game table beneath the window. Trevor stood in the doorway, his eyes fixed on his sister. "My apologies, Lady Malham, for my sister's ill manners. Suffice it to say she is overwrought with concern." Satisfied he had successfully shamed Adrienne into silence, he entered the room. "How is my brother, madam?"

"Sleeping."

"He's had a total breakdown, hasn't he?"

Adrienne dropped into the chair and pressed her kerchief to one eye. "Of course he has. For God's sake, Trevor, don't be so imbecilic."

"Are you all right?" Trevor asked me, his voice kind. "My God, Ariel, we've been out of our minds with worry. You can't possibly cope with something like this by yourself."

"I am coping well enough."

He caught my chin and tipped up my face. "Is that a bruise on your cheek? Ariel, has he been abusive?"

I pulled away. "He hasn't," I answered truthfully. "He hit me by accident. He was in the throes of a nightmare. My husband is well," I assured him, wishing I felt as confident of the matter as I sounded. "Given another two days of bed rest I'm certain he'll be as good as new." ·

Trevor crossed his arms over his chest, lifted one brown eyebrow, and smiled. "You *are* lying, of course, and I know it. We've anticipated this breakdown for some time. I'm just sorry it's happened now, just as he's married again. It must be very difficult for you."

I glanced toward Adrienne, then out the window at my left. I had no energy to argue. I was drained from my ordeal and already I regretted having decided so soon to face my in-laws' curiosity. Perhaps, if I had been more confident of my husband's total recovery, I could have faced their accusations with more certainty. But I was not. I was feeling decidedly defeated and hopeless, and at that moment I wished I had never returned to Walthamstow.

I was relieved when Reginald entered the room. He looked first to Trevor. "Sir, your appointment has arrived. I have shown him to your office."

Taking my hand and giving it an affectionate squeeze, Trevor said, "We'll speak on this further, Ariel. Until later, ladies." Spinning on his heels, he left the room.

Uncomfortable and unwilling to subject myself to further abuse from Adrienne, I too excused myself and made for the door. Just outside the room, however,

Reginald stopped me. "My lady, Dr. Brabbs is here to see you. He wishes to speak with you privately."

I followed him to the smallest drawing room on the east wing of the house. There I found Brabbs standing beside a spiral-legged table, looking out the window. As he turned to face me I knew immediately that something was wrong.

"Lady Malham. Rosine Baron is dead," he said. "I thought you would want to know."

I stared, my sudden grief choking me speechless.

Dropping his hat onto the table at his side, Brabbs opened his arms. I yearned to fly into them, to bury my face in his damp topcoat, but fatigue and despair stayed my step. Shakily I lifted my hand to him. Too late he obliged: I collapsed onto the floor.

"Maggie! Maggie, for the love of God, child!" He scooped me up in his arms and hurried me to the black-walnut settee across the room.

I felt again all the grief of Jerome's passing. I had loved Rosine like I had my own mother. She had been a mother to me those many years after my father's demise. Now she was gone. They were both gone. My world was shrinking day by day.

Sweeping a tangled web of black hair from my face, Brabbs touched my forehead, my cheeks. "Merciful God, look what he's done to you already," he said. "Maggie, you're hardly more'n a wisp of air."

"Please," I begged him, "do not chastise me for 'owt foolish. You have just told me my friend has died." I began to cry.

Pressing a kerchief to my face, he shook his head. "Maggie-mine, there are more to your tears than Rosine's passing. Tell me what is wrong."

Giving into my grief, I wrapped my arms around his neck as I had when I was a child, and wept against his chest. "What am I to do? They don't want me here. I only wanted to help, now they are blaming me. Even Nicholas has withdrawn. He won't touch me. He called out Maggie's name in his delirium, not mine. He loves Maggie and not me—"

"Lass, do you hear yerself? You *are* Maggie—"

"Nay. Maggie is dead. She is buried in his memory and will forever remain, so it seems."

He rocked me and soothed me, but he didn't understand.

"He is loving the image in a reflecting glass but hating the one who makes it!" I sobbed again.

"Tell me what has happened."

I pushed my way from the settee, rubbing my eyes. "I was right. Someone has been slipping him some form of opium in his drink or food. Someone *is* trying to do away with him." I walked to the window and looked out on the snow-covered grounds. "I thought—hoped—that once rid of the dreadful drug he would be his old self again. I was wrong. The sharper his mind becomes, the more he withdraws. He looks on me with suspicion and distrust, as if he believes I am somehow responsible for the pain he's experienced of late."

"He's told you this?"

"Nay, he hasn't uttered a word. He doesn't have to. He just stares at me with those damnable gray eyes as if I were some specter from hell sent here to make him suffer."

"I'm certain you're makin' too much of it, Maggie. You always had an over-imaginative mind."

"The opiate was no product of my mind, sir."

Brabbs's response was a moment in coming. "Do you realize what you're claiming, Maggie? You're claiming someone here has some unseemly intentions toward his lordship. Who would do such a thing? And why?"

Facing him again, I met his eyes and lowered my voice. "Adrienne is highly excitable and *very* bitter because Nicholas ruined her chance to marry. She constantly harps on it and never lets him forget it for a moment. Bea loathes him because she suspects he killed Jane. I've heard her vow numerous times that he'll pay for his crime. Then there is Trevor. Being a physician he is most capable of getting his hands on the opium."

Brabbs shook his head. "He gets all medication from me, Maggie. I would know if he were using an unaccountable amount of laudanum. And what reason would he have to want to kill Nicholas? He is not in line to inherit. At his death Walthamstow would pass to George in Boston."

"Aye," I responded thoughtfully. "Trevor has been very kind and supportive since my arrival." I looked at Brabbs. "Finally, of course, there is you, my friend."

He did not move, but stared at me with expressionless eyes that were faded with age.

My heart ached but I continued. "I had not suspected you until the morning of my marriage, when I learned of your intense anger toward Nicholas. Now you have just told me that you are the only one who has charge of the opiate." Silent, I waited for him to deny the charge. When he did not, I said, "I could understand, perhaps. I was—am—like a daughter to you, as you are like a father to me. You blamed Nicholas for the ruination of my innocence and finally my death. You wanted to destroy him. Since you are frequently to this house to see Trevor, slipping opium in some form into my lord's sherry would seem an easy enough task."

His head dropped slightly as he stared at the floor.

"Will you deny it?" I asked him.

"Would it do me any good?" He looked at me again, a tear in his eye. "Maggie-mine, if a deed or thought is a crime, then I am guilty. I have murdered him over and over in my dreams for the last two years." He stood then, and with shoulders back, walked to the table and picked up his hat. "I can see I am no longer welcome here. Good-bye, Maggie."

I watched, wanting to call him back, but unwilling. It seemed I had forsaken the one person who truly loved me for one who did not know me, who apparently did not care to know me—who did not love me and perhaps never had. But I had married him—Wyndham, Earl of Malham, Lord of Walthamstow—for better or worse. And I did, regardless of everything, love him.

My friend walked to the door and stopped. Without turning, he said, "Think with your head and not your heart and you will realize the plain truth: Jane is dead. Her skull was crushed, her body burned. The madness that killed her is deep and true and more deadly than any opiate ever was. You might soon be wishing you'd left him sedated, Maggie. You may have released a monster."

The words struck cold fear to my heart. I harbored in my mind the portrait of Jane, of tilted, china-blue eyes and hair as gold as summer sun. To picture her struck down so brutally was torturous to me. To think my husband may have done it brought me immeasurable pain.

Doubt! It continued to plague me, no matter how many times I assured myself that Nicholas was not capable of murder. Yet he had struck her. He remembered striking her. Passing my hand over my eyes, I ran for the door and into the hallway. Brabbs was gone.

The cold crept in on me and chilled me to my bones. My spirit was low, lower than at any time since my internment at Oaks. My head ached. I was lonely. That morning I had two friendly acquaintances in this world: Rosine Baron and Brabbs. One was now dead; the other hurt beyond measure.

I continued down the hall, anxious now to return to my room. In the distance I saw the open door of Trevor's office. My stride lessened. Nearing the doorway, I held my breath and listened.

Peeking around the door frame, I searched each corner of the dim, musty quarters. Finding no one in attendance, I entered the room. With a distrustful eye I viewed my cluttered surroundings with new interest. I pondered each crucible. Studied each alembic. I lifted and sniffed and tasted each bitter phial and pungent powder I found hidden or otherwise.

I was about to leave this quarter when I heard a rustle of material, a soft footstep nearing the office. I looked about, searching escape. I found it: the door leading to the courtyard and out of the house. Quickly! Some instinct told me I must not be found here alone. I grabbed the door handle. It would not turn. I tried again, gritting my teeth and throwing my weight backward. The door opened. Stepping into the twilight and closing the door behind me, I waited, holding my breath.

The bolt shifted across the door, locking me outside.

A soft, cold drizzle covered my face as I listened, heart racing and flesh quickly turning to ice. Moving toward the window to my right, I tugged away the withered streamers of ivy that clung tenaciously to the brickwork, then I cautiously cleared dirt from the pane and did my best to peer into the room, through the slight opening between the partially closed drapes.

I beheld a form, decidedly feminine and dressed in white, moving gracefully among the lengthening shadows. Unable to see, I cried to myself: *Stand still for one moment, blast you, so I can tell who you are.* "Damnation!"

Pushing away from the wall, I began running the best I could through the ice and snow.

The night air, though brittle, was very still. A peculiar mist covered the grounds, luminous as it reflected the patches of snow against the frozen earth. Odd, for there was no moon.

Behind the bank of fog the hounds wailed, the mournful sound echoing beyond the toolshed and centering, it seemed, in the hollow where the old stables had been. I regarded all this with only partial interest, however, for my intent was to get back inside Walthamstow as quickly as possible and return to that chamber before its intruder disappeared.

I burst through the kitchen doorway, causing Matilda to drop the joint of pork she was preparing. Polly threw up her arms, strewing pudding batter across the table. "Lady Malham," Tilly cried. "Wot's happened? Wot're y' doin' outside in this weather without a—milady, is 'owt wrong?"

"Out of my way!" I exclaimed.

"Lud," Polly expelled, "she's gone daft as 'er 'usband, I vow."

I ran down the hallway, knowing my way well enough now to avoid the furniture and loosened bricks about the floor. I turned one corner. The shadows lengthened. I turned another. My footfalls rang out in the silence. When I finally reached the chamber, the door was closed. Gripping the knob with one hand and bracing my other palm against the door, I took a breath . . . and shoved it open.

Empty.

"How can that be?" I asked aloud. Slamming my fist

against the wall in frustration, I returned to the corridor. To my left the hallway ended at a wall. The only way out was the way I had come.

I waited until my heartbeat slowed before turning back up the hall. Then I saw it, a white piece of material resting just outside the office door. I bent and picked it up.

I hurried away from the chamber and back to the Great Hall. Alone, I sat down at the secretary, pulled the tallow light closer and spread the square out for inspection: a woman's handkerchief of delicate, laced-edge linen. I ran my finger lightly over the embroidered scroll in one corner, and as I lifted it to my face the faint scent of flowers touched my nostrils. The fragrance stirred some recollection in my mind, but though I tried I could not recall where I had smelled it before.

I considered my alternatives. The handkerchief must have belonged to Adrienne, as there was no one else in the house who could lay claim to such a pretty piece of lace and linen. I could pretend that it did not exist, or I could confront its proprietress and ask her why she was milling—again—about her brother's office. Deciding on the latter, I made my way to Adrienne's quarters.

She was reclining on her bed reading a leather-bound copy of Jean Jacques Rousseau's *The Social Contract*. She looked up, startled, as I entered without knocking, then calmly closed the book and placed it aside. "Oh dear." She sighed. "You have finally come to evict me."

"No. I do not want this room, Adrienne." I meant it.

"Well, then, you have come to tell me that from this moment on I am to be on an allowance. I understand. Just tell me what meager stipend is to be allowed me and I will do my best to adjust."

I felt my anger desert me. "Nay, I've no such news.

I hope for both our sakes I am not so hard-hearted as the former lady of Walthamstow."

She tilted her head. Her soft brown hair spilled over her shoulders.

"Why are you here, then?" she asked.

I had momentarily forgotten the handkerchief. Looking down at my hand, I answered, "To return you this."

Her eyes shifted to my hand. "What is it?"

"Your handkerchief, of course. You dropped it in the hallway."

She slid off the bed and approached me, took the kerchief and inspected it. "This is not mine," she said.

"I beg your pardon?"

"Simply, it is not mine." Pulling her own handkerchief from the cuff of her sleeve, she crossed the floor and held it out to me. "Mine are plainly monogrammed, as you can see."

I felt my anger rising again.

"Perhaps," I said severely, "you have one that is not monogrammed."

Adrienne stepped back, surprised at my vehemence over something so trivial as that handkerchief. "Would you like proof?" she asked.

She lifted one brow in a way that reminded me of my husband. That resemblance made me all the more determined. "Yes," I told her. "Show me."

She crossed the room to a high, narrow chiffonier and pulled open a drawer. "See for yourself. There is not one square of linen here without my monogram: AW."

There were no less than three dozen handkerchiefs but I inspected every one of them. Finally satisfied that Adrienne was telling the truth, I gently closed the drawer and turned back to face her. She had returned to her bed.

"My apologies, Adrienne. But if the handkerchief does not belong to you, then whose is it?"

"Where did you find it?"

"Outside Trevor's office."

"Well, then, it no doubt belongs to one of his patients."

I saw through that excuse immediately. "Someone capable of owning this finery would not be traveling to Walthamstow to see the physician. He would call on her."

"You're right, of course. Why don't you ask him?"

I could hardly do that, considering the circumstances.

"Why is it so important?" she asked.

Looking down at the dainty, fragrant material, I said, "Perhaps it isn't. I fear I've become over-emotional on the issue. I beg your pardon."

"You need not beg me for anything any longer," I heard her say. I looked up. "You are Lady Malham now, remember."

"And ill to death of hearing it, I must confess."

That surprised her. Adrienne leaned back on her pillows and frowned. "But you are in an enviable position."

"Am I? Tell me why."

"Walthamstow is yours."

"Why should I want her? Her chambers are drafty and cold and her grounds are continually covered with mist. While Malham basks in sunlight this estate broods in the clouds. I have not experienced such dreariness since I left . . . Keighley."

"Then why did you marry my brother?"

"Why?" I walked to the bed and leaned against one of its towering four posters. "Why?" I repeated. "Is it not clear to you yet? Madam, I love your brother."

She looked embarrassed. Turning her face from me and staring at the china bowl of dried rosebuds near her bed, she asked softly, "How can you love something like that? He is barely human any longer. The man who was once my brother no longer exists. He is gone. Gone! Why can you not accept that?"

"Why are you so eager to accept it?" I asked her pointedly. "I will tell you why. For the same reason you covet this house, these rooms, your friends' opinion of you. They bring you prestige and envy, and each gives you a feeling of power and worth. You thought Nicholas perfect before, a shining example of a flawless gem you could dangle before your friends. You are no better than your mother." She gasped and covered her face. "You hated your mother because she manipulated him, yet you use him in the most selfish ways and now, because he is less than perfect, you cast him aside because he embarrasses you."

"Stop," she cried.

"Do you know why I love him? Because he *is* human. He saw the ugliness in the world and acknowledged it. He saw the beauty in simplicity and loved it. He should have been king, madam, housed in a palace. Instead you would house him in a cage at some asylum. Well, I shan't let you do that to him, Adrienne. If I must, I will take him away from here. I will auction off this house and everything in it you hold so dear, and I will take my husband to Boston to live among barbarians. I have no doubt that they are more civilized than your idolized ton."

I ran from the room to my own quarters. I struggled with the lock on the door before it gave, then, gaining entrance, slammed the door behind me and leaned against it.

My husband, sitting before the fire, turned his head

and looked at me. What did I see there? Suspicion. Confusion. Anger. And all directed at me.

"Why are you locking me in here?" he asked.

"To keep them out."

"Them?"

"Them! Them, damn you! The one or ones who did this to you."

He looked again at the fire and said, "There is no one doing anything to me but you."

I covered my face with my hands. "Don't say that. Please don't say that. I'm trying to help you—"

"By locking me away."

"You're confused, husband. It's to be expected. Soon everything will be crystal clear again. I promise you."

"I trusted you," he said, and the coals in the hearth shifted, spraying the floor with embers.

The hour was late. I sat by the fireside, sewing my newest creation: a simple black taffeta that I planned to wear to Rosine's funeral on the morrow. As I sewed, I glanced occasionally toward my husband, asleep in our bed.

Hopelessness burdened my heart. Finally placing the material aside, I blew out the two wax candles standing on the table beside me, then climbed into bed. I kissed my husband's brow and vowed to him again. "Tomorrow things will be different. You are growing stronger every day. You *will* be your old self tomorrow. Have faith." Then I lay back on my pillow and closed my eyes. Soon I drifted off to sleep.

In my dream, I saw again the twisting path, snow-covered and rutted by carriage wheels. Raikes Road. I followed it, oddly floating above the frozen terra firma until I came to the split in the road. No. No, I did not care to follow. Not there. Let me go back to Walthamstow, if you please! my mind pleaded. Yet I was compelled onward through the stone and wrought-iron gates of Malham Cemetery.

I felt the cold mist swirl around me, touching my face, clinging to the frail material of my sleeping gown. I strained my eyes but saw only the still marble faces of angels whose eyes followed me on my course. They whispered. I heard their tiny, melodious voices singing, *"Amen. Amen. She has come."*

I floated onward, looking down on the snow-covered mounds, on the slate-topped roof of the burial chapel and the mausoleum. The clouds broke. A dim moon shone through, lighting the clearing on the ground.

A man stood at the edge of the mist with his back to me, his shoulders covered in a black mantle that spilled to his ankles. I heard the scrape of iron and gravel and then saw the open grave at his feet.

From the mist came the mournful sound of a woman's weeping. A ray of moonlight spilled onto her as she stood at the edge of the grave, dressed in black, her downcast face covered by hat and veil. I suddenly understood. It is me, I thought. I am mourning my friend, dear Rosine. I felt the grief in my throat, and yet I could not cry. I reached and placed a cold hand upon the shaking shoulder, offering comfort; still the vision shook.

"Amen. Amen."

Suddenly I was airborne again, helpless like a leaf in a tide, rising then drifting back to earth. I rested in a satin bed surrounded by flowers, and thought: At last. Peace.

"Amen."

The weeping continued. The woman stood *above* me now. As the breeze lifted her veil I knew the wasted flesh, the weary eyes. Rosine. Rosine Baron! Confused,

I attempted to struggle from my bed. This is not right, I cried. There is some mistake! But I could not move. Some weight pressed me down. Heavier and heavier it became until my breast ached and I fought to breathe.

Then the man appeared, looking down onto me. His eyes were hard and gray as steel. "No!" I screamed. "Nicholas, it is I!" I lifted my hands but the earth rained down onto me, filling my nostrils and mouth. I twisted and raked my face with my hands.

The moon cast its timid light onto the cold marble fixture above me, illuminating the wretched name. JANE.

"Amen. Amen," the angels sang. *"She has come."*

Chapter 18

I sat upright in bed, gasping for air. The door of our bedroom was open and my husband was gone. Throwing the covers aside, I jumped to the floor, and without benefit of a dressing gown, ran from my room into the hallway. At its far end a single candle burned on a table.

I looked left and right, listening for sound, then went for the candle and with it wandered down the corridor to the top of the stairs. There I waited, cursing the loud pounding of my heart that drowned out all other noises to my ear.

I heard a door slam. Footsteps rang out in the silence. I held my place, watching both left and right. Then I perceived a figure in the distance. Closer it came until finally I recognized Trevor.

"God in heaven," came his voice. "Ariel, what are you doing out here?"

"Nicholas is gone," I told him.

He cursed under his breath.

"He must have taken the key from the pocket of my dress."

"What the hell does he think he's doing?" he demanded.

I had never seen Trevor so angry. I backed away.

"Have you searched the house?"

"No."

"Then we'll being here. I'll send Jim down to the cemetery just to make certain. Go put on some warm clothes before you freeze. Quickly!" He stepped by me and descended the stairs.

I returned to my room to dress, donned my cloak, then left the house, intent on joining Jim on his trek to the cemetery.

He came at me from the darkness, a blur of white that froze the scream in my throat before I could expel it. My lord wrapped one arm around my shoulders and clamped his hand over my mouth. I swooned against him in relief.

"You won't scream," he said.

I shook my head in response.

Dropping his hand from my mouth, he caught my arm. "Come with me," he said.

Rebelling, I stood my ground. "Why and where?" I demanded.

"To the stables."

"*Why?* What are you doing *there?*"

He stared down at me, his eyes deep and shadowed, his black hair stirred by the wind. "Jane," he said.

My heart tripped. "What?"

"I followed Jane to the stables."

I close my eyes. I might have collapsed from despair but he caught my arms again with a violence that wrenched me from my lethargy.

"Husband," I said. "Jane is dead. You saw her buried in Malham Cemetery."

Nicholas continued to stare, making no move or sound to indicate that he had heard me. Still gripping my arm, he started down the path, beyond the kennels and tool shed, past Jim's house, to the burned stables.

When finally we stood at the edge of the charred remains, I was too numb to think.

Unaffected by the cold, my husband paced before me, moving in and out of the shifting mist. "There is no one here," I said.

"I heard her calling my name outside our door," Nick insisted. "When I opened it, I saw her standing at the end of the hallway. She wanted me to follow and I did. She led me here."

"You imagined it."

He kicked a charred timber angrily. With his hands on his hips, Nicholas stared at the sky. I considered telling him the truth now—the entire truth, that there was more to his illness than a simple dependency on sherry, that his hallucinations were brought on by addiction to opium, but in his state of mind, would he believe me? Somehow I had to find substantial proof of who wanted to destroy him in such a way, and why they were doing it. Only then would I reveal my assumptions.

As he took up his pacing again, I begged him, "Please come back to the house. You will fall ill from the cold."

I turned back for the path, hoping he would follow.

That is when I saw Trevor and Jim approaching at a fast pace. I opened my mouth to speak, but the sudden look of terror that crossed my brother-in-law's features froze my words, and I spun to look behind me.

Brabbs's words came back to me: *"Jane is dead. Her skull was crushed."*

My husband stood holding a massive stone in his hands. Numb with terror, I stumbled backward into Jim's arms while Nicholas stared at me, first in confusion, then realization, and finally disbelief. He dropped the rock and looked from me to Trevor and back again.

"So," Nicholas said, "you believe it too. I wondered how long it would take you to come around to their way of thinking." Trevor reached for his arm, but he shoved him away. Then Lord Malham returned to Walthamstow without me.

He locked me out of our room so I was forced to return to my old chamber. I was to learn later that my husband's drive to cure himself was much stronger than even I believed possible. For he did not turn to the sherry as I feared he might. But neither did he turn to me, and that was as painful as watching him struggle alone with his ordeal.

In the morning, as was my custom, I went directly to Kevin's room, but found the door locked. I pounded the door with my fist for long moments before it barely opened. Bea's black eye glittered at me through the crack.

"Why have you locked this door?" I asked her.

"His lordship's orders."

My heart stopped. "What do you mean 'his lordship's orders'?" I asked. She remained silent. "Speak to me, Bea. What do you mean by that?"

"You ain't allowed in," she said.

I leaned against the door, panicked but Bea's weight held me back. I heard her chuckle. "I told you. He's a devil, I swore, and now you've got on his black side. You'll regret it. He'll kill you just like he did my Jane." She slammed the door in my face and locked it against me.

I pounded on the door. "Damn you," I said, "let me in to see my son. I demand it." Enraged, I ran across the hall to my husband's room. He was not there. I made for the studio then, and rushed in.

Lord Malham stood in the center of the room, impeccably dressed in black, a snow-white ascot about his throat. About him were strewn the many canvases he had painted throughout the previous months. On the easel beside him was another, draped by a cloth.

I watched as he tugged kidskin gloves onto his hands. The movement was controlled, arrogant. He half turned and fixed his eyes on me. "Lady Malham," he said coldly. "I've been expecting you."

His eyes were clear, clearer than I had seen them since my return to Walthamstow. I moistened my lips and forced myself to breathe.

One eyebrow drew up and he smiled, a macabre curl of his lips that hinted of mockery. "Have I shown you my paintings?" he asked, his voice soft. "I'm certain there are several here that will interest you." He made a beckoning motion with his hand and I followed him, hypnotized by the cadence of his voice, the odd, steely light in his eyes. *This is how Satan would look,* I thought. Tall and dark and alluring enough to make even the most Christian-hearted soul follow him into the pit of hell for want of his love.

"Well?" he seemed to whisper. "What do you think?"

I forced my gaze to the paintings along the wall.

"Do you think the British Museum would be interested, my sweet?" he asked.

I stared at the one painting I had witnessed before: hands reaching out from the flames, eyes wide in terror. Madness . . . *Pandemonium.* I shuddered.

"I painted whatever came into my mind. I realize now that they were simply shadows of memories. That's why all my painting sessions were preceded by, and followed by headaches." He moved up behind me and caught my arm. "I'm in the mood to paint again, my love. Have you objections?"

"None, my lord."

He took the covered canvas from the easel, then led me back to our bedroom. Then, grabbing up my cloak and spreading it over my shoulders, he guided me into the hallway and out of Walthamstow. The chaise was waiting, its solemn driver, as usual, standing attentively to one side of the door.

Soon we were on our way. My lord sat across from me, as he had on our wedding day, and I could not help but recall the intimate moment of consummation we had shared then. Nicholas had that same desirous look in his eyes, and though he remained as still as stone I knew he too recalled the moments, and the movements. I closed my eyes and prayed very hard— that he would take me in his arms again. Here. Now. Desertion breeds desperation, and I feared he was leaving me, in heart and mind.

When the coach stopped and the door was opened, I looked out on the distant ledges of Malham Cove. With some hesitance I took the driver's hand as he helped me to the ground. Nicholas followed, the canvas under his arm, then ordered the driver to bring the chaise round and wait at the foot of the hill. He then took my arm and propelled me toward the cove.

Malham Cove. No trees lined its limestone cliffs. Its sheer, razor-sharp edges plunged two hundred feet to the rock-studded valley below. From where I stood upon the clint, I could clearly see the footpath winding up distant Sheriff Hill. A solitary beam of sunshine broke through the clouds and reflected off frozen channels of rainwater fissuring the limestone. With the spring thaw, those icy rivulets would surge and plunge with awesome force to the beck below.

I sensed when my husband moved up behind me; I smelled the lemony scent of his cologne and the damp wool of his mantle.

"I enjoy it here," came his words in my ear. The tips of his gloved fingers brushed the side of my neck and my breath froze in anticipation. "I think it is the closest to heaven as *I* will ever get. You can touch the clouds on rainy days." He pointed toward the distant opening of the gorge. "After a rain there is a rainbow that bridges those cliffs . . . Have you ever seen it, Ariel?"

His hand then shifted to catch my waist. He pulled me over to a plateau covered with last summer's dead grass, covered the ground with his cloak, and said "Sit down."

I did so. Nicholas stood at the edge of the cliff, silhouetted against the pewter sky. Too close, I thought. He is standing too close to the edge.

"Do you know why I brought you here?" he asked.

"To paint, I suppose," I told him, my eyes still on the ledge. "Or to prove that you still control everything at Walthamstow. Including me. Are you about to tell me to jump over the edge, sir?" I looked at his eyes again. "Well?"

"Will you jump if I tell you to?"

"You won't."

"Are you so certain?"

"Aye."

"You thought me capable last eventide of bashing in your skull with a rock."

"Only for a moment. Are you never without doubt, husband? Did you ever doubt, standing in that chapel in Burnsall, that I married you for love's sake alone?" I saw his thick lashes lower. "Aye, you doubted me because it is natural to do so. In the end you trusted that my feelings were true so you went on with the marriage. Show me a man who does not falter occasionally in faith and I will show you Jesus Christ."

I climbed upon a rock beside him, took his face in

my hands, and looked him straight in his eyes. "Husband. I cannot tell you if you killed your wife. Mayhap we will never know. I trust, however, that if you wanted to kill me you would push me now over this cliff. It would be simple enough to say I slipped."

His fingers closed around my wrists. We stood that way upon the edge of the world, one foot from eternity, eyes locked, hair and clothes whipping in a sudden blast of wind. Then, with a muttered curse, he shoved me away, spun on his heel, and strode to the canvas he had thrown on the ground. I watched, transfixed, as he picked it up and turned again toward the cliff.

"My salute to faith," he said through his teeth. Then he hurled the canvas over the edge.

"Blast your faith, Maggie, it will see you buried here in a fortnight."

I turned from Brabbs, my downcast face covered with a length of black veil. I had waited until Rosine Baron's few mourners departed before approaching her grave. Holding my hand open over the trench, I watched the dirt sift through my fingers. "I should not have told you," I responded.

"Why did you go there with him? You're tempting fate, lass. After last night you should know that."

"He did nothing to me last night or today. He's rational now, Brabbs. His mind is growing clearer every day."

"That's no guarantee. He could have a setback any time; you know that."

"I don't think he will." Lifting my black skirt, I walked among the mounds of earth, taking care not to catch my hem on the rose thistle growing along the path. "I would like to be alone, Brabbs," I said over my shoulder.

"I won't have it. I want you to come home with me, Maggie, before it's too late."

"Had he any intention of harming me, he had the opportunity at the cliffs."

"He wasn't about to send you over the edge with a witness about, was he? He was just lulling you into a false sense of security, so when the time comes—"

"What reason does he have to want me dead?" I spun to face him.

"What reason did he have to kill Jane?"

"I can give you a dozen."

"Reason does not justify murder."

"I am tired of discussing it."

"What if he's realized who you are, Maggie?"

I dragged the veil from my head. "What are you implying?"

Brabbs rubbed his roughened hand over his face and shook his head. "What if he never had any intentions of marrying you, girl? You know for yourself that institutions like Oaks are full of unwed young women who believed the fol-de-rol whispered in their ear by some lord of their realm." I turned away. He grabbed my arm and turned me back. "Perhaps his intentions of marrying you were genuine enough: He was feeling isolated and friendless and desperate, but you said yourself, his mind is clearing, Maggie. Bits and pieces of his memory could come back to him at any time. What if he realizes who you really are, and that you've duped him?"

"I haven't." I yanked my arm from his hand.

"But you did. You did! And you know it. You came here with the sole purpose of revenge, Maggie. I can imagine you and Jerome with your young heads together, planning how you would make the great and mighty Lord Malham of Walthamstow pay for ruining you. Here is a man capable of murdering a woman who wanted to take nothing more than a bloody house. In God's name, what is he going to do to the woman who wanted to take his son?"

I would speak no more on the matter and told him so. Finally, his patience at an end, Brabbs left me alone at the graveside and returned to Malham.

I stood on that bleak hill, surveying all around me. I could yet see the mourners moving together down Raikes Road, the vicar following at a distance like a shepherd guarding his flock. In my solitude I recalled sitting once at Rosine's side while she held open her hand to me. In her palm were seeds. "It's all that's left of last year's crop," she told me. "Bury it and it will come forth anew, stronger and more beautiful than before . . . Ain't it miraculous, Maggie?"

"Aye," I whispered, smiling at the memory. "It *is* miraculous, Rosie."

A half dozen rooks perched atop the highest limbs of a distant elm, their feathers ruffled and their wings slightly spread as they balanced in the breeze. As I watched them a serenity overcame me, and I closed my eyes. For a moment I too was at peace.

It was then that the familiar sense of being observed crept over me. And in that instant the sharp grate of iron and gravel pierced the quiet. My breath froze. Slowly I opened my eyes and turned.

The man stood at the grave side, his back to me, his shoulders draped in a black mantle. He stooped, slid his shovel into the earth, and, without facing me, tossed the dirt onto the coffin. I backed away, the heel of my shoe sinking into the muddy hillock of another grave.

"Here, now," I said, "can that not wait, sir? I am not done mourning the deceased."

He continued, unwilling to respond.

My forehead became clammy with fear. Twisting my veil in my hands, I slowly moved away, keeping my eyes on the man, listening to the dull thud of earth on wood as he filled the grave. Not until I reached the bottom of the hill did I release my breath and scorn myself for my ridiculous fantasies. That was when I noted the figure standing some distance from me, watching me, and I was certain she called my name. "Ariel!"

Yet though the voice was decidedly feminine, I could not see the face or the form of the one who watched me. I did not respond—hearing my name called by this stranger was disconcerting—but lifted my skirts and fled the cemetery.

Upon reaching Raikes Road, I paused to look back. *She* was there still, keeping her distance. I turned and continued a brisk pace up the road, wishing now I had agreed to Trevor's request that I take the chaise. Before rounding the last bend toward Walthamstow I slowed and looked back one last time. She was gone.

Relief left me weak and feeling foolish. I was letting Brabbs's monitions unnerve me. That, coupled with my dream and my husband's overly fervid imagination about Jane, conjured threats when none existed. I continued my walk with much less haste, considering my morning journey to the cove and Nick's reasons for taking me there. I stopped, the recollection coming to me as clear and cold as a sudden moorland wind. How could I have forgotten? As Maggie I had once met Lord Malham at that very place. I had perched upon that very rock after a spring rain, admiring the rainbow that bridged the cliffs of the gorge. Around my skirt hems grew heather. I wore a pearl-gray dress . . .

The portrait.

My blood felt like a fire inside me as my husband's words came back to me: *"I realize now that they were simply shadows of memories . . ."*

The portrait had been of *Maggie!*

I began to run. Reaching Walthamstow, I rushed up the stairs. There was only one way to be certain. If the portrait was there, then I could put my suspicions aside. I stopped first at Kevin's room, finding the door still locked. I turned then for the studio, held my breath as I entered, and glanced about the room. I found my own portrait, and with growing trepidation I noted its eerie likeness to the girl on the cliff. I sat upon my perch like Maggie sat upon her rock, staring out over the valley. *Shadows of memories . . .*

The portrait of Maggie was gone.

I backed toward the door. My lord's hand upon my shoulder stopped me.

I did not turn at first, but glanced with caution down at the gloved fingers squeezing my shoulder. *Remain calm,* my reason told me. *There is no cause to fear him yet.* "My lord, you frightened me."

He drew me back against him. "Sorry, but one more step and you might have trod on my toe."

"Then you've been standing there for some time?"

"Watching you . . . You don't mind, I trust. It's one of the few pleasures with which I can selfishly reward myself." With one hand he swept my hair aside. He pressed his warm mouth against my neck in a kiss, then said, "I've missed you. Where did you go?"

"I told you. A friend died."

"Brabbs?"

I shook my head.

"A shame."

Unable to withstand the tension any longer, I spun

to face him. His disheveled hair spilled over his neck-cloth. And his eyes: like storm-clouds with the sun behind them. The hint of cold wind clung to him as well as the scent of fresh, rich earth. A fear pressed in on me and clutched my heart.

"It was you," I stated softly. "It was you at the cemetery."

His eyes narrowed.

"You followed me—"

"I've been with Jim."

"Nay, you were there." I tried to back away. He closed his fingers around my nape and held me fast, the soft tips of his glove pressing into my skin.

"I was with Jim," he repeated. "We walked back to Pikedaw Cliff. It seems we lost some sheep over the edge because a fence is down." Slowly releasing his grip, he stepped back and began peeling off his gloves. "I saw you walking up Raikes and called out to you. I guess you didn't hear me."

I searched his face for the lie.

When he touched my cheek with his hand his fingers were cold but steady. "It occurred to me as I hurried home to see you that we haven't made love since our wedding day. I think"—his mouth curved in a smile—"that such behavior is hardly befitting newlyweds."

"You've been ill."

"So I have. But I'm better now. Much better. Like my old self. Does that please you, Lady Malham?" Before I could respond he stepped up against me, pressed his thumb into the tender skin beneath my chin, and tipped up my face. All reason vanished. My fear melted into white-hot desire, though I tried to struggle and turned my face away. His mouth brushed the corner of my lips, my cheek. Then his hand gripped my jaw and forced my face back to his. As his hand buried

into my hair and dragged me down, my eyes closed
and I thought:

*God help me, but I love him. Despite it all ... I
love him.*

Chapter 19

The following morning I ventured out into the cold dawn, intending to distance myself from my husband's presence. He was changed toward me; I could hardly deny it. He'd made love to me almost angrily throughout the night, withholding the tenderness he'd shared so freely with me before. I had detected suspicion as he looked at me. Once leaving me and standing by the window, he'd said softly, "Perhaps I *am* insane. Perhaps I *should* spend the rest of my days in Bedlam, but I swear to you I will not go there without a fight. Be warned, my love, that if I must I will stop at nothing to save myself from that fate. *Nothing.*"

He had warned me, and I must heed that warning, no matter how much it distressed me to do so. He regarded me as a threat to his freedom, and if Brabbs was right—if he suspected that I was Maggie—he might consider me a threat to our son. Already he had forbidden me from seeing the child.

I wandered Walthamstow's grounds, hoping the brisk air would revive my spirits as I continued to consider my circumstances. As I rounded the corner of the house I stopped. Through the mist I saw an apparition. The cloaked and hooded figure moved with wraith-like grace through the fog, away from Trevor's office door, down the path, and around the distant corner of the house. At dawn? Compelled by curiosity, I walked swiftly to the point where she'd rounded the house and found . . . nothing. She'd vanished like smoke in the mist.

I returned to the office entrance. Once there I did my best to see into the room through the window. The office was dark. I tried the door. Locked.

Returning to the house, I flung my cloak over the stair rail before grabbing up the nearest candle. I hurried to Trevor's office, and found no evidence that it had been occupied that morning. The wax candle on the desk was still cold. No fire burned in the hearth. Perhaps the visitor was simply a patient of Trevor's who had arrived too early to see him, I told myself. Yet some niggling doubt stirred in my subconscious. The image of the cloaked figure in the cemetery the day before came back to me with chilling clarity, and with it the frightening sensation of presence that had haunted me since my arrival at Walthamstow.

I returned to my quarters. My husband, however, was no longer in the room.

I hurried to the kitchen, confident that the help would know my husband's whereabouts. Matilda was busy raking the glowing coals from the ovens, preparing the back stones for a day of baking haverbread. Smiling, I watched her plump backside sweep from side to side as she stoked the embers.

"Good morning," I said, laughing as she hopped in surprise off the floor.

"Gum, lass," I heard her say. "Are y' about givin' old women apoplexy?"

"I've nowt better t' do," I smiled. "Have you seen his lordship recently?"

Her eyes widened as she came up right. " 'ave y' been out?" she asked.

"Aye. For a walk."

"Well then, that explains it. 'e's off with Jim to Pikedaw t' repair a wall."

"It's quite early for that, isn't it? And what's my husband doing toting stone when he's paying the help to do it?"

Hooking the boiler over the fire, she shook her head before facing me again. " 'e were never one t' sit around when work was t' be done. 'e and George and Eugene were always about some chore. Not like Trevor, y' understand, who thought such labor was beneath 'im."

Pilfering a scone from a tray, I bit into it and said, "Then perhaps I will walk out to Pikedaw to see him."

Tilly pursed her lips in contemplation.

"Is anything wrong?" I asked, swallowing.

"Beg pardon, mum, I suppose it ain't my business, but if I were you I wouldn't be walkin' out t' no Pikedaw. Not until his lordship has had time t' calm down."

"Calm down?" The scone stuck in my throat.

"While you were out 'im and 'is brother got into it. We 'eard 'em arguin' all the way in 'ere."

"Over what?"

She cast her eyes down. "I couldn't say, mum."

Leaving the room, I hurried to the Great Hall, then to several drawing rooms, and finally the library. I found Trevor at the desk, a handkerchief pressed to one corner of his mouth. As he looked up and saw me, he quickly tucked the bloody linen into his coat pocket.

Cautiously approaching the desk, my eyes on Trevor's bleeding lip, I asked, "What has happened?"

Embarrassed, he looked away. "We argued."

"And he hit you." I closed my eyes. "Oh, my God."

Rising from his chair, Trevor pointed to a stack of papers on the desk. "From Saint Mary's. God in heaven,

Ariel, had I anticipated that he would blunder in on me I wouldn't have had them out." His blue eyes looked blurred suddenly; he leaned wearily against the desk. "Dammit, I hate doing this. But it seems I haven't any choice. You see that, don't you? Adrienne's right. He's not responsible for his actions."

"I'm certain he didn't mean—"

"I'm certain he didn't mean to strike Jane either. He reacts, then he's sorry. But by then the damage has been done." He touched my cheek with his fingers. "Your love and devotion are admirable, but you must understand what sort of danger you are in. No one will think less of you for signing these papers. You are the only one who can do it now, Ariel. For your sake, for our sake, for Kevin's sake, sign them and we will get the proceedings under way."

He pressed a quill into my hands. With my heart pounding in my throat, I stared down at the paper on the desk. "No," I said, dropping the quill. "I won't do it."

Before he could respond, I fled the room, retrieved my cloak from the stairs, then exited the house. I ran down the path, beyond the stables and sheep folds to the open pastures. The wind took my breath away, tearing at my skirts, my hair, bringing tears to my eyes. I struggled onward, my feet occasionally sinking in the mire, until I reached the moor's summit. Below me, my husband and his friend heaved a stone from the ground and swung it atop the crumbled wall. Jim saw me first. He spoke to my lord, then Nicholas spun toward me.

With some uncertainty he lifted his hand in greeting, then began walking up the well-worn sheep path, his eyes never leaving mine. The cold wind had chafed his face. His form-fitting, doeskin breeches were damp and slightly muddy. I stood my ground, hating myself for the betrayal I felt, hating myself for the weakness and desire that besieged me while in his presence. I could not let that daunt me. He would hear me out.

Nicholas stopped some yards from me, his weight shifting from one long leg to the other as he waited.

"How could you?" I asked him. "How could you do such a thing?"

He looked at his hands as he peeled off his gloves. Then he slapped the kidskin against his thigh.

"Do you realize how difficult it is for me to continue to justify your behavior?"

"Am I no longer allowed to voice my opinion without being scrutinized by my wife?"

"Voice!" My control shattering, I clenched my fists and screamed, "You struck him, Nick." I spun and stormed back toward Walthamstow.

"Ariel!"

"Nay," I called back. "I want no excuses. I am tired of hearing them. I am tired of your self-pity—"

He caught my arm and whirled me round. His flushed face had broken into a fine sweat despite the cold. "What did you say?"

"I said, I am tired—"

"You said I struck him."

"Aye. You hit him and for what reason? He has no control over your circumstances any longer. If you wish to take out your anger on someone, then do it on me. *I* will be the one who sees you to Bedlam, not Trevor!"

I turned and ran, but his long legs covered the ground faster than mine. He blocked my escape, towering above me, his eyes like flames. "I did not hit him!" he shouted, catching my shoulders.

The words echoed over the fields, and from the corner of my eye I saw Jim throw aside his stone and cautiously approach us.

"Aye, you hit him. You argued and you hit him. Don't deny it. I saw the evidence all over his handkerchief. His lip was bleeding!"

Dropping his hands, he stumbled backward. I watched his handsome face contort in disgust and frustration, and I felt something crack inside me. I began to weep over the injustice, the act of God that had taken the man I had loved two years ago and turned him into . . . *this!*

"I *did not* hit him!" Nicholas repeated.

"Liar!"

I might have struck him, so stunned did he look, so heartbreakingly desperate. His voice lowered to a husky whisper that was almost lost to me in the wind. "I don't remember hitting him."

"You never remember. It is a sound enough excuse." Calmly I walked around him, noting he did not move.

"Ariel."

I picked up my pace.

"Ariel!"

Lifting my skirt I began to run, unwilling to let his desperation sway me, unwilling to acknowledge the fear I heard in his tone. I knew what it meant. If I allowed him close again, his nearness would dull my judgment and send me melting into his arms, mindless of the danger.

"Dammit, Ariel, come back here."

"No!" A glance over my shoulder told me what I already knew. He had begun to run after me.

I saw him slide in the mire. He fell, cursing, but as he struggled to stand Jim was there, wrapping his brawny arms about my lord's chest in an effort to stay him. "Get on with y', lass," Jim called out. "Quickly, I cannot hold 'im forever."

"Ariel!" came the wounded cry. "Don't! Don't leave me, for God's sake! Ah, damn!"

Then both of them slid to the ground. Covering my ears, tears streaming from my eyes, I ran back to Walthamstow.

I pushed my food around the plate, occasionally spearing a pea or stabbing a bit of pork with my fork. But, having no appetite, I did not eat. Adrienne downed her third glass of wine, her eyes shifting toward Trevor every few minutes. The air was brittle with tension as we each waited for someone to speak.

In that moment my husband entered the room, his sudden appearance shattering the silence. Dressed as he had been on our wedding day—olive-green velvet and ruffled lawn—he strode confidently to the end of the table. "Sorry I'm late," he said. His dark fingers brushing the snow-white tablecloth, he flashed us a smile. "Seems someone forgot to inform the lord of the manor that dinner was served."

"We thought you were still with Jim," Adrienne responded, placing her glass on the table.

"Ah, well, that explains it, then."

I could feel his eyes move over me, and with a volition not of my own, I looked up. The intensity of his gaze brought color to my face. My heartbeat quickened.

"Lady Malham," he said, bowing slightly with the gentle greeting. "May I say you look ravishing this evening."

I tried to speak. Impossible. Calmly placing my fork across the plate, I sat back in my chair.

Taking his chair, he then looked at Trevor. More softly he said, "My wife tells me an apology is in order."

"Your wife, my lord, is a considerate lady," he responded.

"Yes, she is. She also tells me that I struck you."

Trevor looked to me briefly before meeting his brother's eyes. "Yes, you did, Nick."

Nicholas sat back in his chair. "Of course you have the right to call me out if you so desire."

"Call you—don't be preposterous. I don't want you dead."

Matilda hurried to heap Nick's plate with food, refilled Adrienne's wine glass, and, after curtsying negligently for my lord's benefit, darted from the room.

My husband cleared his throat before addressing his sister. "I understand you are considering a sojourn to Paris, Adrienne."

She did not respond.

"Why not to London as well? I think a few weeks in the city—"

"The reason is obvious," she interrupted, lifting one thin brow. "They all know me there."

"You mean they all know *me* there, don't you?"

"Precisely. I don't think I'm up to the gossip."

A grim smile twisted my lord's mouth. He said, "It would benefit us both if you were to face the damned gossips, Adrienne, and deny their accusations."

"How can I when I know them to be true?"

The smile faded.

Pushing her chair back, Adrienne pardoned herself and left the room. Trevor followed with the excuse that he was expecting a patient.

Staring straight ahead, Nicholas asked me, "Haven't you something else to do as well, my lady?"

Placing my napkin beside my plate, I slowly began to rise.

He clamped his fingers over my wrist so suddenly

the movement brought a gasp of surprise from my lips. "Sit down," he ordered. When I had done so, he released my arm and motioned toward my plate of untouched food. "I suspect it is quite good. While you eat, perhaps we can talk."

"I am not hungry," I told him, rubbing my wrist.

"I would appreciate your looking at me when we speak."

I could not do it, but stared more determinedly toward the soup tureen in the center of the table. I heard him release his breath.

"I'm sorry if I hurt your wrist, Ariel. I'm sorry *if* I hit my brother. I'm sorry *if* I killed Jane. I'm sorry I'm alive but right now there doesn't seem to be anything I can do about any of it. Just . . . *talk* to me. Please."

"I have been locked out of Kevin's room," I said. Forcing my eyes to his, I swallowed and finished, "I demand to know why."

"I thought we would eventually get to that little problem." He glanced down at his silver fork, then back to me. "Truth is, wife, I've become jealous. You seem to harbor a great deal of affection for my son. So much so I occasionally believe *he* is the reason you married me."

"Don't be absurd." I looked away.

"Why did you marry me? Simply to be my 'crutch'?"

"Isn't that why you married me?" I snapped. "Because you needed a crutch?"

I looked at him again. His eyes were downcast, and his jaw muscles worked with anger. Unwilling to push him for a response, I stood. "My lord, I have given some thought to moving to another wing."

His head snapped up.

I summoned my courage and continued. "Considering our circumstance, I feel a separation of sorts is in order."

"I won't allow it. You're mine, dammit. My wife—"

"Your possession, you mean. Like Kevin. Like Walthamstow. And God help anything, or anyone, who threatens your authority, my high and mighty Lord Malham." I ran from the room.

I returned again to my own chamber and remained there throughout the night. Such an effort was not easy, for thoughts of my husband constantly plagued me. I felt guilty for deserting him, but separation would allow me to keep my thoughts clear. I prayed throughout the night that he would not come for me, for I knew my body for the traitor it was. And yet, when dawn's light filtered through my curtains, a part of me suffered.

True to my word, after breakfast I took a candle and headed for Walthamstow's closed west wing. Standing at the mouth of the black tunnel, I convinced myself that there was absolutely nothing to be frightened of; then, holding my candle before me, I eased down the dark corridor.

The walls closed in around me. The cold and damp made me shiver and the smell of mildew and rot made breathing next to impossible. Matilda was right. No one in his right senses would move into these rooms.

Deciding to return to my own chambers, I turned just as a gust of warm air brushed my face. I looked back down the black corridor, lifting my candle, still unable to see more than a few feet before me. Compelled by my curiosity over what had caused the unusually warm current, I ventured farther into the house until I was swallowed completely by darkness, until the silence became like a heavy, cold shroud on my shoulders.

A rat scurried along the edge of my candlelight. Then another, and another. Freezing in my tracks, I watched

the tattered sheets covering the furniture flutter in another sudden gust of air. I held my breath, my sudden
fear of the dark coming back to remind me that I had
wandered too far into this black maze. I turned with
the intent of returning to my chamber.

A hooded, caped figure silhouetted against the darkness stood watching me from the shadows. And in that
moment my candle went out.

The warm wind rushed around me, fretting my hair,
my skirts, the fringed shawl I had wrapped about me.
Faint with fear, I waited, my ears straining for a sound.
In desperation I called out, "Who is there?" Moving
aside, I pressed my back against the stone wall, my
fingers clutching each uneven surface for support.
"Someone is standing there," I said. "I can hear you
breathing." It was a lie, of course. I could hear nothing
beyond the roar of blood in my ears. One thought,
however, kept me from losing total control. If I could
not see it, it could not see me.

I inched my way along the wall, praying I met no
obstacle. Deeper into the house I traveled, hoping for
some door, some niche in the wall where I might hide.
I met only another corridor branching off to my right.
I hurriedly stepped around the corner, allowing myself
to take my first full breath in what seemed like
minutes.

Hearing a noise, I listened harder. Silence again.
Gradually I became aware of the dampness at my back,
of water and moss that left my hands slimy and unable
to grip the stone wall. I realized too that for some time
my eyes had been closed; so tightly, in fact, it almost
hurt to open them.

An illumination farther down the hall brought a
strangled cry of relief from my throat. Slipping on the
damp floor, I stumbled toward the light. A warmth

touched my shivering skin as I plunged into the dim halo and through the open door to my right.

Surprised, I looked about the comfortable chamber. A fire snapped in the hearth. A massive tester bed lined one wall, and shelves of books another. It took me a moment to make sense of my surroundings, to realize that someone was secretly residing within the bowels of this house.

Caution crept in on me. Undoubtedly, whoever had happened upon me in the corridor was on his way to this room. Still gripping my candle in one hand, I made haste to light it, then returned to the hallway, eager to make my way back to the main house and report my discovery. Carefully I moved up the corridor, expecting to meet the intruder again. I didn't. No doubt the resident of that chamber had beat a hasty retreat.

Hearing Trevor's voice, I rushed to his office door. I must have appeared greatly distraught, for the look on his smiling face as he glanced up from his patient turned suddenly to one of concern. "Something has happened with Nick?" he said.

I shook my head. "But I must speak with you at the first opportunity."

A nod told me he understood. When he finally joined me, he asked, "What in blazes has happened, Ariel? You look frightened out of your senses."

"I was just exploring the old section of the west wing. Trevor, someone is living there!"

His eyes narrowed in disbelief. "I beg your pardon?"

"I know it is difficult to believe, but I saw it with my own eyes. Someone has set up house in one of the rooms. Have you any idea who it could be?"

Backing away, he shook his head before picking up his topcoat. "Ariel, those rooms are unlivable. They haven't been opened in a century."

"That one has," I told him adamantly. "Come with me and I will prove it."

"All right. But first I have a call to make at Weets Top. Lady Forestier is ailing from gout again and of course she expects *me* to go to her. We aristocrats are a spoiled lot, aren't we?"

I returned his smile, somewhat disappointed.

"Why don't you ride out to Weets Top with me, Ariel? It might do you good to get away from this dungeon for awhile."

I considered his invitation only a moment before agreeing. Within minutes we were on our way to Beck Hall.

I accompanied Trevor only as far as the hallway outside Lady Forestier's bedroom. Sitting in a rose-embroidered fauteuil, I listened intently to the charm in his voice as he greeted his patient.

"My good woman, you don't look sick at all. Your cheeks are blooming like roses."

"It is fever, I declare," she responded gloomily.

I covered my smile with my hand and listened again.

"Tell me, Trevor, if the rumor is true. I understand your brother has married again."

My eyebrows shot up.

"Is that why you had me ride all the way across the grange, my dear? To pacify your curiosity?"

"Is it so? And is it true she is a commoner?"

"Take care," he said, laughing. "She is sitting outside that door."

"Is it that young woman who attended Adrienne here some time ago?"

"Yes it is, now stick up your foot."

"Well, she is a beauty, certainly."

"Yes, she is . . . Your feet are swollen, Melissa.

You've indulged again. I have told you repeatedly to cut back on your mutton."

"I have to eat, my good man—tell me, how *is* your brother?"

His response was a moment in coming. "As well as can be expected. Now, I have something here that may relieve the swelling in your joints. You are to take it twice a day for the next three days."

I listened as he poured water from a ewer into a glass. I imagined his pouring powder from a phial into the water. As he stirred it, the spoon rang musically against the crystal glass. The sound reminded me of something, but at that moment I could not recollect what it was.

Finally the patient declared, "You are a nice young man. A shame you must lower yourself to examining old women's feet to make a living. It doesn't seem fair somehow."

"It is the fate of being born fourth in line for a title, madam. I must cope, mustn't I?"

"But certainly your allowance helps."

"It helps and that is all I will say on the matter. Send for me if the trouble hasn't cleared up in three days."

I left my chair as Trevor joined me, closing Melissa's door gently behind him. Without speaking, he strode past me. When we reached our coach, he threw his medicine bag against the seat.

Startled at his discomposure, I asked him, "Is something wrong?"

He looked at me as if he had somehow forgotten my presence. Finally he smiled. "Remind me to charge her double. Once for the call . . . again for the gossip. Shall we go?"

Once reaching Walthamstow, we wasted little time before taking up candles and venturing into the house's

dreary west wing. My heart skipped with the excitement of sharing my discovery with Trevor. As we
moved carefully into the shadows, I pointed out where
I had seen the "visitor," explained how the sudden draft
of warm wind had extinguished my candle and how,
out of fear, I had backed along the wall until reaching
the corridor to the right. Once reaching that corridor
we walked more carefully along the slippery stone floor
until we came to the room. The door was closed.

I looked at Trevor. He glanced at me, then reached
for the knob. It did not turn at first. Gripping it with
both hands, he leaned onto it until the rusty hinges
sprung and the door released. Slowly it swung open,
creaking in the quiet.

Chapter 20

Cautiously I stepped into the frigid chamber, unable to believe my eyes. The room was uninhabited.

"You are certain it was this room?" Trevor asked me.

I walked to the bed and carefully lifted one corner of the dusty sheet. The mattress beneath was bare. I moved to the window and stared out the broken panes of glass at the courtyard. The twisted trunk and barren limbs of a chestnut tree swayed in the wind. A solitary rook perched on the windowsill, preening its glossy wings and fluffing its feathers against the cold. As it twisted its neck and gazed at me with its glittering eye, a feeling of dread washed over me. My mother had believed such birds were an ominous sign when perched by a window, symbolizing an approaching death. Shivering, I tapped on the glass, hoping to frighten it away.

Coming up behind me, Trevor caught my arm. "Ariel, you've been under a lot of stress lately."

"I know what I saw." Pulling away, I hurried into the hall. "Perhaps it was another room," I told him.

Shoving open the doors along the hallway, we investigated each room, finding them as cold and uninviting as the first. I now understood how my husband must have felt when questioned on a matter he knew—to his own mind—to be the truth.

"Ariel, there has been no one here for some time. Are you certain it was this corridor?"

When I did not respond, he walked up behind me, gently closed his hands over my shoulders, and gave them a squeeze. "It has been a distressing two days and we've both been upset. I think we could use a nice, hot cup of tea and some of Tilly's scones. Perhaps later we'll search the other corridors and question the help. Will that pacify you?"

Without argument, I returned with him to the Great Hall.

I avoided returning to my chamber, thereby avoiding my husband, by spending the afternoon reading in the library. Then I shared dinner with Adrienne and Trevor. When I mentioned to Adrienne the room in the west wing, her lack of surprise was curious. I did note, however, that her eyes went immediately to Trevor, then as quickly back to me. Some instinct told me to drop the subject until later. I did not bring it up again until Trevor had excused himself—this time for an acquaintance from Middlesborough who happened to be passing through Malham on his way to Bradford.

Adrienne appeared quieter than usual as we took our after-dinner tea into the Great Hall and sat before the fire. We stared into the flames several minutes before she spoke.

"Ariel, just over a year ago I too happened upon that room."

My head came up. I blinked in surprise.

Adrienne smiled. "I was shocked as well."

"Whose is it?"

"Now? I don't know."

Placing my tea on the table beside my chair, I said, "Whose *was* it?"

She sipped her tea as if the fragrant brew would somehow calm her nervousness. She then balanced the cup and saucer on her knee and responded. "There was a very pretty girl working for us once. Her name was Samantha."

"I have heard the name."

"I followed her once to that room . . . She had an assignation with one of my brothers."

The blood fled from my face. Dread stirred in my stomach then gripped my heart like a fist. "Nicholas?" I whispered.

"I don't know. Truly. Their voices are close enough in tone that I could not distinguish, and I was afraid to venture closer for fear of being discovered. To be found eavesdropping at the door . . ." Adrienne looked away, her cheeks flaming with the memory. "The very thought of it disgusted me, I must confess, so I did not return there until after Samantha left. Of course I found the chamber as you did this afternoon: as if it had never been occupied."

"But you're not certain it was my husband."

"I can't be certain, no. I must tell you, however, that the young woman was very enamored with Nicholas. And, of course, at that time he and Jane were living . . . apart."

Gripping the arms of my chair, I said, "Dear God, Adrienne, do you think she's come back? Do you think that Nicholas . . ." I closed my eyes as pain washed over me. To imagine him in the arms of his wife was bad enough, but to believe he would hide a mistress in this very house . . .

Adrienne left her chair. Placing a comforting hand on my shoulder, she said, "I'm sorry. Perhaps I shouldn't have told you when I can't even be certain of the facts. It seems so unfair when the evidence always points to Nick and he hasn't the ability to defend himself."

Shaken, I pushed from my chair and left the hall. Samantha. Could the woman who followed me from the cemetery and whom I saw roaming Walthamstow's grounds be the same girl? Samantha. How often had that name come up when talking with Matilda or Polly or Kate? And now Adrienne. A sudden realization made my skin prickle. Samantha had conveniently disappeared the night of Jane's death. Had she, in some way, been involved as something other than a witness?

The door to Kevin's room was open. I stopped in the doorway and watched my son, dressed in a long white sleeping gown, play inside his bed. My eyes filled with tears as he looked up and saw me, lifted his pudgy little hand in greeting, and squealed with excitement. I might have run to him, but then Bea was suddenly there between us, shuffling toward me, her thin face twisted with malice. Before she could slam the door in my face, I told her, "Don't bother," then turned away.

I entered my husband's room. He was not present. I heard him in the studio and walked to the door.

Remaining silent for some time, I watched him paint. I studied his hands, thinking they were the most beautiful hands of any man I had ever known: strong, perfect, able to work magic on my body. I watched his shoulders: the subtle flexing each time he stroked the canvas. I had once believed he could balance the world on one shoulder and the universe on the other. They had seemed that broad, that capable. Why, I wondered, could I not shake that image?

"Who is Samantha?" I asked softly.

My husband turned slowly.

"Samantha," I repeated. "Who is she?"

I stood in that threshold forever, it seemed, waiting, watching his eyes. Finally he put down his brush and said, "Lady Malham. Come here, if you please."

I did so, steeling myself for the touch of his hand on my shoulder. He moved me around so I faced the canvas.

Pandemonium again. I closed my eyes.

His voice came from behind me, lending me an odd sort of comfort. Leaning slightly against him, I found the strength to face the painted nightmare.

My husband said, "I have asked myself why I continually come back to this . . . insanity. Why I continue to paint on it. Ariel, I'm beginning to understand. Will you listen?"

He took my failure to respond as acquiescence.

Nicholas pointed to the canvas, his finger trembling very slightly. "First there was the fire. It is most obvious. As I point to these other things, tell me what you see, or think you see."

"Stalls . . . a horse . . . hay . . . the stable door. A . . . shadow." I felt his warm breath on the back of my neck. Struggling to think, I focused harder. "Red. Blood?"

"But it is here, in the stall," he said.

"From the horse possibly."

"Possibly."

Moving away, I walked to the door before facing him again. I love you, I thought with despair. "Nicholas, who was Samantha?"

He shrugged before picking up his brush again. Rolling the camel-hair tip back and forth in the red oil, he said, "She was a servant here for a while. She left Walthamstow the night Jane died."

"Did you have an affair with her?"

His head snapped up. In that moment I could believe him capable of murder. "Well?" I struggled to ask.

"Would you believe me if I told you that I don't remember?" Before I could form a response in my own mind, he finished. "Your mind was made up, m'lady, before you ever entered this room. Get out."

I did.

That night I never thought to sleep; but I did, fitfully. During moments of wakefulness I reviewed the events of the day. One image dissolved into another, but they always came back to Nick. Nick and Jane. Nick and Samantha. That image disturbed me most, and as I drifted to sleep again, the image of his touching Samantha, holding her, loving her as he had me, brought me upright and weeping in my bed.

At first I noticed nothing unusual in the stillness, but then the slight click of a door closing brought my head around. Blotting my tears with my sleeve, I listened first, then slipped from my bed and tiptoed to the door. Someone walked quietly down the hall. My husband?

I took up my candle and went directly to my lord's quarters. Not bothering to knock on the closed door, I opened it and ventured into the room, my eyes on the bed, hoping to acknowledge his sleeping form. He was gone.

I ran back into the hall, besieged with a kind of madness that I had not experienced even in Oaks. Despite the cold that nipped at my skin through my thin gown, I hurried down the corridor, cupping my palm around the dancing candle flame.

I came to the top of the stairs. How quickly he had escaped. And to where? Gripping the balustrade, I leaned forward slightly and peered into the darkness below me. Was that a movement there? A form in the shadows? Moving around the rail, I took one step down, lifted the light a little more, and looked again. I recognized the form of the tall case clock in the foyer. In the dead silence I could hear its muted *tick-tick-tick* and the shifting of the chime as it prepared to strike the hour.

Silly me, thought I, *letting your imagination get the better of you. Go back to his room and wait. He will come back eventually—*

An unexpected force buried into my spine, and as my body flew forward, I grabbed frantically for something—anything—to save me. My hands opened; the candle flew into the distance, and in that instant I realized what had happened.

I screamed.

My arm hit the stairs first, then my shoulder, and finally my head. My body tumbled uncontrollably down, down, into the darkness. Out of instinct my hands reached out, clawing at images that whirled past too quickly. And then I felt the hard rap of wood against the back of my hand. I grabbed again.

Somewhere in the dulled, whirling recesses of my mind I heard the striking of the clock. Once. Twice. In the intense stillness that followed I gradually became aware that I lay on my back, my feet slightly elevated and my arms out to my sides. *At least,* I thought, *I am not dead.*

But as the pain flooded my body, I thought death preferable to this intense agony. I tried to move, but my body rebelled. Closing my fingers more tightly about the balustrade, I pulled myself around until my head rested even with my feet. Only then did I cry out for help.

Through the haze of my suffering I saw a light approaching, floating down the stairs, and the reason for my laying broken and bruised on the stairwell came back to me in a terrifying rush. My murderer approached, signaled by my cry for help that I was not dead. I struggled to lift my head. I would know the killer and I would take that knowledge to my grave and pray to God Almighty that He avenge my untimely demise.

I suddenly felt colder. The pain left my limbs as I stared up into familiar features. "Oh God," I cried out. "God, no; not you! Not you . . . *husband!*"

I closed my eyes and tumbled headlong into an abyss of darkness.

At first there was pain and nothing else. Then dim light filtered through my lids, and the words came to my mind: *Like God's lamp shining to find me.* I thought: *Perhaps I've died.*

"She's regaining consciousness," came the man's voice, confusing my thoughts. "Lift up her head slightly. This drink will help to alleviate the discomfort she's experiencing."

Forcing open my heavy lids, I focused on the hands stirring the silver spoon round and round the rim of the crystal water glass. It sounded strangely musical to my confused mind.

I felt myself lifted, and it was then that I threw my hand up, knocking the glass to the floor. "No!" I cried. I heard a woman gasp, and then Adrienne appeared over me, her eyes frantic.

"He did this to her," she said. "Oh my God, Trevor, he tried to kill her."

"We won't know that until she tells us."

"But I saw him standing over her. It could be either

of us next time. Certainly she'll see now that something must be done to stop him."

Their voices faded as I drifted again, my mind tumbling with questions.

"Ariel? Ariel?" Someone shook me gently. I opened my eyes. Trevor smiled and kindly touched my cheek. "I've checked you over. Nothing more than some severe bruises; no broken bones. You took a hard fall and you'll be sore for a few weeks ... Can you tell us what happened?"

"Where is my husband?" I asked.

I saw him frown. "Ariel, we found it necessary to lock Nick away."

My heart stopped. Dear God, how long had I been out? Images of Oaks flashed through my mind, nightmare images that made me cry aloud.

"Ariel, listen to me. He was uncontrollable. Dangerous."

"No!" I screamed. "No, no, not Bedlam. Please, have mercy and don't do that to him."

"He's upstairs. I've had Tilly take up something to sedate him."

Panic seized me. "No!" Rolling, I attempted to leave the bed. "You mustn't! He mustn't take anything again."

He caught my shoulders. "My lady, listen to me. He was irrational. It took both me and Jim to wrestle him down and get him to his chamber. Once he's sufficiently calmed—"

I shoved him away, and though my head throbbed and my body rebelled from my efforts, I slid off the bed. "I want to see him. Take me up to see him."

In that moment Brabbs entered the office. With a cry of relief I fell into his arms. "I came as soon as I heard," he said, gripping me to his chest. "Jim had

Polly bring me the news. What in God's name has happened?"

"It seems Ariel had a spill down the stairs."

"I want to see my husband," I said to Brabbs. "They have locked him away and—"

"Did he do this, girl?" my friend demanded. "Tell me the truth, lass. Did your husband push you down those stairs?"

I swayed against him, weakened by my injuries and my own indecision. To my mind he had pushed me—someone—had pushed me—but I was rational enough to realize the consequences of such an admission. I had to know if indeed my husband had tried to kill me. And I wanted to know why.

"I want to see him," I told Brabbs. "Please. They've given him something to sedate him." I looked to his eyes, hoping he would understand my meaning.

With a low curse, Brabbs swept me up in his arms. "Aye, then, I'll take you to see the devil this one last time, girl. Then we all want the truth."

He swept me from Trevor's office, bypassing Adrienne and the gaping servants. Tilly stood to one side, her hands clasped as if in prayer, but her eyes lit when I attempted a weak smile of encouragement. Then there was Bea, watching from the shadows, her mouth twisting with smug satisfaction. Seeing her craning her neck as she watched us mount the stairs, I was reminded of that rook on the windowsill, its very presence emanating doom.

"I told you," came her voice. "I warned you. He'll kill you too . . ."

I closed my eyes and buried my face against Brabbs's chest, blocking the words from my mind, doing my best to block out the pain that splintered through me each time Brabbs took a step. "Hurry,"

I pleaded softly. "I must see him before he's sedated, Brabbs, or he may not be rational." I tried to rid my mind of the knowledge that one ingestion of opium could trigger a damaging response from his system. It could even kill him.

It seemed like hours before we finally stopped before my husband's bedroom door. Brabbs rapped and Jim's voice called out, "Who's there?"

"Her ladyship wishes to see her husband."

A moment of silence passed, then the lock shifted. Jim opened the door, his face full of relief. "Yer all right," he said to me.

I did not respond, knowing I must save my strength for the confrontation with my husband.

The room, as always, was dark and cold. Nicholas stood before the window, a black silhouette against the silver glass. "Get out," I ordered Brabbs and Jim. "I will see him alone."

"I won't allow it," Brabbs said. "Dammit, girl—"

"Get out!"

My vehemence set him back, and with a muttered curse he spun and left the room. Jim followed, closing the door behind him.

I stood in the dark room, my body throbbing with a sort of agony that wrenched more painfully than any injury. Above all, I wanted the truth: Did he shove me down those stairs? And if so, why?

He advanced from the shadows. As the hearth fire lit his features, I noted a desperate and brooding look on his countenance. He seemed uncertain of making any move that might frighten me, yet I sensed that he wanted with all his heart to collect me in his arms.

As he stopped before the fire I saw the flicker of a smile relieve his intense features, then he briefly closed his eyes. "Thank God, you're all right," he said.

As always, the rich timbre of his voice weakened me. I began to sink to the floor.

He caught me. Suddenly I was floating in his arms, drained of all bitter anger and reason. I knew I was lost as he moved to a chair and sat down, cradling me in his lap and tenderly hugging me to his chest as he might have done Kevin.

"My love," he whispered. "Tell me what happened. Did you fall? What in God's name were you doing out there? This is my fault. I should not have allowed you to sleep away from me. Your place is here. With me. I'm going to take care of you, love. I'm better now—look, I didn't take the sherry that Trevor sent me, though God knows I wanted it. Needed it. You don't know what seeing you on those stairs was like for me, Ariel. I thought I'd lost you again. Jesus, I went mad. Truly mad. I know what it's like now— the madness."

"I came to your room," I said softly. "You weren't here."

He stroked my head. "I was painting. Do you remember the portrait I started of you and Kevin?"

I tried to think. It hadn't occurred to me to check the studio. I'd just assumed . . .

"Ariel. They've locked me in here for a reason . . . They believe I pushed you."

I listened to the frantic pounding of his heart against my ear, damning the love that continually blinded me to reality.

"Of course you'll tell them that I was nowhere near you, that you simply fell. Perhaps you turned your ankle. Ariel . . . love . . . they are going to send me away if you don't convince them . . ."

Other voices intruded then. At first I thought I was dreaming.

"Get yer murderin' hands off her."

My husband's arms closed around me.

"She needs rest, Nick. I've brought something that will ease her pain. She's in shock and needs rest."

"I told you it was only a matter of time! Monster! Oh God, he hates us. He'll kill us all in our beds. He's over the edge."

My lord's hands twisted in my hair. I felt the tight constriction of his chest beneath my bruised cheek. Lifting my head, I forced my eyes open and looked at my husband's jury. "I . . . fell," I said. "Now leave him alone. Leave him in peace."

The words faded to an indistinct buzz, an angry sound that made my head ache all the more. I could not reason, and when I felt the cool rim of the glass pressed against my lower lip I no longer struggled, but drank the bitter mixture down, anticipating the lethargy that would follow. Soon the ache left my limbs. I floated downward wondering, in some remote corner of my mind, if I would ever awaken again.

I slept through the next day. The following night I found Belzeebub watching me with yellow eyes from the foot of my bed. Trevor stood above me, running his hands gently up and down my arms. "You're awake," he said. "How do you feel?"

Moistening my lips, I spoke in a thick voice. "As if I've been fed a goodly dose of laudanum."

"It will help the pain."

"Thank you. But I don't think I care to have any more, if you please. It is addictive, you know."

He smiled. "Not if you're careful. But as you wish."

Carefully sitting on the bed, he continued. "I suggest total bedrest for the next week at least."

As Belzeebub jumped from the bed and padded out the door, I closed my eyes for a moment to rest.

"How did it really happen?" Trevor asked.

"I must have tripped."

"You still protect him."

I opened my eyes.

"He tried to kill you and yet you continue to protect him."

"I don't know what you're talking about."

A flash of anger crossed his features. Leaving the bed, he walked to the door before looking back. "If this doesn't convince you that Nick should be put away, the I suspect nothing will."

Minutes after Trevor's departure Adrienne swept into the room. I watched her pace back and forth across the floor several minutes before I beseeched her to sit down. She did so, on the edge of a chair. "You are as pale as a statue," I told her.

Her white hands twisting in the folds of her skirt, Adrienne fixed her blue eyes on the window across the room. "I have just received some distressing news and I am not certain what to make of it. I received a letter from Lady Grey. Her husband has just returned from France . . ." Her words faded as she again looked at me. But I could not respond. The numbing effect of the laudanum was wearing off and the discomfort I felt was growing ever greater.

Adrienne left her chair and stood over me, her smooth face sympathetic, her cool hands soothing as she brushed my hair away from my feverish brow. "Would you like to change your gown?" she asked me. "I brought one in earlier to replace the one you're wearing."

I nodded. Adrienne gently removed my gown, and sponged my arms and throat and shoulders with cool water. She had just begun to dry me when she stopped, brushed her fingers over the inside of my arm above my elbow, and said, "How very curious."

I looked down at the scarred flesh at her fingertips and started.

"It looks like some sort of brand," she said half to herself.

Jerking my arm from her hand, I clutched it to my side and forced myself to explain evenly, "It is a burn and nothing more."

"But it looked like—"

"A burn," I repeated, angry at my own carelessness. Grabbing the clean gown, I said, "Please help me to dress before someone else comes in."

With no further discourse on the matter, Adrienne did just that. After smoothing the coverlet over the bed and tucking it around the mattress, she said, "Matilda is anxious to send up tea and cakes if you're ready to eat something."

I thanked her with a smile, but as she turned to leave the room, I asked, "Where were you and Trevor when I fell?"

Adrienne's face was smooth and her eyes oddly cold. "Playing cards," she said. "We heard you scream, but by the time we arrived we found Nicholas standing over you."

She left the room and I sank again into my pillows, my mind searching desperately for answers. As usual, Nicholas had planted doubt of his guilt in my mind, and though my better judgment screamed a warning I could not find it in my heart to listen. *Someone* had pushed me down those stairs. If I was to believe in my husband's innocence, then I would have to assume that someone other than my husband wanted me dead. But why?

Matilda soon appeared with my tea and scones. "Tilly," I asked. "Where were Adrienne and Trevor when I fell?"

Her face flushed with concern, she placed the cup and saucer in my hands before replying. "They were playin' gin in the Great Hall, mum."

"You're certain?"

"Aye. I were standin' there with 'em when y' screamed."

I sipped the tea while Tilly fluttered about my room, righting this and dusting that. She seemed greatly distressed. Finishing my tea and placing the china aside, I tried to focus on her face and asked, "Is something wrong?"

Wringing her hands, she glanced toward the door, lowered her voice and said, " 'is lordship gave me strict orders, mum, that I wasn't to distress y', but y' should know. We've 'ad a number of the girls quittin' the last couple of days. Kate left yesterday and Polly went this mornin'."

Watching her mouth move, I tried very hard to concentrate on her words. But they came to me like an echo that drifted away before I could grab them. My mind wandered.

"There's been some strange goin's-on, mum. First there was yer fallin', then Trevor found 'is office tore up this mornin, as if someone 'ad been searchin'. All 'is cru-cru—"

"Crucibles," I whispered.

"Right. They was shattered all over the floor and 'is books were scattered about . . . I've 'ad food stolen from the larder. And Polly . . . I know she were always prone to superstition and all, but she swore she seen a woman . . ."

My eyesight blurring, I looked at the teacup and thought, *Oh God. Oh my God.*

Chapter 21

Fighting the opium's effect was futile, or perhaps I had no heart to do it. Time passed. How long I could not be certain, for one hour was just like another, filled with voices and pictures that were too fractured for my confused mind to make any sense of them.

I dreamt once that I awoke to find Bea standing over my bed, her face inches from mine, so close I could count the open pores on her nose and smell the stench of her breath in my nostrils. "I warned you," she rattled, but when I struck out at her she vanished like smoke, leaving me thrashing and screaming for help.

My husband came and went. His cool hands stroked my face, my body, soothing me. Each time I opened my eyes he was there at my side. Odd that I should feel such serenity in his presence when in reality I should still have been crying for help. For here, in all his imposing mien, was, in fact, my would-be murderer. Jane's murderer.

She me some proof, my heart demanded.

I could not, so I chose to believe—hope—pray—that I was wrong. That we were all wrong.

On the third day after my accident I awoke without the groggy after effects of the laudanum to find Belzeebub on the pillow next to mine and my husband in a chair beside my bed, reading a book. I held my breath and watched him.

Something of daylight still lingered: a gentle, misty haze of gray that spilled through the window and silhouetted my lord's features. I might have been watching him again from my hiding place at the tavern, noting the broadness of his shoulders, the width of his noble brow, and the length of his thigh. He wore a loose white shirt with full sleeves and a slashing vee collar. This was tucked into leather breeches and the breeches were tucked into knee-high brown boots. The sight of him made my heart tremble, not with fear— but with love and pride and desire. My veins glowed with an odd heat that brought a flush to my skin.

My lord husband, I thought, it seems I am fated to love you despite everything.

As I lay there watching him in secret, my mind tumbled back over all that had occurred to me since my arrival at Walthamstow: my first *premonition* of danger while I waited in the rose garden, my discovery that Nicholas was being drugged, our marriage and the sudden appearance of the cloaked woman in the cemetery, and the woman and room in the closed wing of the house. The woman hadn't appeared to me until after our marriage . . . Perhaps because until that time I had not been a threat. Perhaps she had been trying to frighten me away, and when that did not work she thought a shove down the stairs would do it.

But who *was* the woman? Bea? Adrienne? . . . Samantha? There was no proof that anyone, other than my husband, might have pushed me down those stairs.

I closed my eyes. When I opened them again, Nicholas was looking at me.

"Enjoying your book?" I asked softly.

"It is most interesting." He flipped it closed, keeping one finger between the pages to mark his place. "Perhaps you've read it: *An Experimental Inquiry into the Properties of Opium and Its Effects on Living Subjects,* by John Leigh. I believe it won the Harvein Prize in 1785, or so it says here." He thumped the cover. "I've learned that it takes very little opium to affect judgment, and that one can become addicted to it after only a few doses . . . Did you know that the majority of addicts are women of wealth? They are the only ones who can afford it, I suppose." He opened the book again and began to read aloud. "Opium is frequently given to dull pain, induce sleep, alleviate cough and . . . to control insanity." His eyes came back to mine. "Of course, not all addicts are women."

Trying to sit up, I asked, "Did you get the book from Trevor?"

"No."

"Then from whom?"

"Your friend."

"Brabbs?"

My husband nodded. "He's been by regularly to check on you."

"And you allowed it?"

He grinned. "You might say we've come to an understanding where you are concerned."

"I hope it is a rather good understanding," I told him. "To see the two people I love most in this world at odds with one another grieves me more than you know."

I saw a softening of his features, and he blinked slowly. Placing his book aside, he left his chair and approached. Did I cower? Nay, I did not, though his presence left me helpless and weak as a leaf in a whirlwind. Dizzy, I rested back on my pillow.

Sitting beside me on the bed, he lifted one hand up to my face, but did not touch me. I watched, disappointed, as those long, powerful fingers curled into his palm. "Are you better?" he asked. "I was about to go prepare me a drink. Shall I prepare one for you as well?"

"Drink, sir?"

"Tea. Not a drop of sherry has passed my lips through this entire ordeal."

I returned his smile and told him I would enjoy a cup of tea.

Without another word he walked to the door, hesitated, and turned back again. "I may be awhile. Matilda is under the weather, and since the help quit—"

"The help quit?"

"Most of them. After your accident . . ." He looked away and without finishing his statement left the room.

I rested, still tired and sore and slightly groggy from my ordeal. Minutes passed. I heard the clock chime the half hour, then the hour. Daylight waned. Darkness encroached, filling the room with shadow. Several times I glanced at the candle on a table across the room, wishing it lit. I thought to leave the bed and light it, but my body rebelled, forcing me back into my pillows.

I heard a noise and lifted my head. Bea stood in the door. A sense of revulsion swept through me at the sight of her stooped shoulders and limp, black dress. The rounded toes of her thick-soled shoes showed beneath her hems, and I noted they were covered in mud.

As if reading my thoughts, she said, "I've been to the cemetery to pay my respects to Jane." She shuffled to the candle and lit it. The flame cast a harsh orange light over her sunken features as she approached me.

Bending over me, she said, "He pushed you, didn't he? Everyone knows it. That's why they've gone." She smiled. "I have something to show you. Would you care to see it? It's proof of what I say." Tottering backward, she crooked her finger at me. "Come along, if you can. I'll show you. Then you'll see him for the monster he is. Quickly! Before he returns."

Her words had an odd, hypnotizing effect on me. Somehow I managed to leave the bed, and force my stiff legs to move. We reached Kevin's room. Shaking, I stood by his bed, watching him sleep while Bea limped to her room. In a moment she was back. I recognized the rectangular, white shape of a canvas in her hand.

I backed away. "I have already seen the abhorrent portrait," I told her. "I don't care to see it again."

She swung the canvas up. "You'll want to see this, milady."

I staggered back as my eyes fixed on *my* portrait, slashed to pieces. Spinning, I ran from the room, stumbling over the hem of my gown. I almost fell, but suddenly there were arms there to stop me, steadying me and righting me on my feet. Only then did I realize I was weeping.

"What's this?" Trevor said. "Ariel, what has happened?"

I looked up then, and saw my husband walk out of our bedroom, followed by Adrienne. When he saw Bea, he sprang for her with a growl, ripping the canvas from her hand and staring at it with fierce savagery that was terrifying to behold. "You conniving bitch," he hissed. "What in the name of God have you done?"

She stumbled backward, her arms thrown up for protection. "You did it! Polly found it hidden among the others you tossed out. She brought it to me before she left. Fiend! Murderer! *She* won't admit it, but you pushed her down those stairs!" She pointed at me.

He looked toward me, his face like white granite as I huddled, trembling, in Trevor's arms. "I didn't do this," he said.

"Liar!" Bea screeched.

Pushing me aside, Trevor sprang for my husband before he could throttle the cowering woman.

I fled to my room, passing Adrienne, threw myself across the bed, and did my best to block out the angry voices in the hallway. How long I laid there, weeping into the bed, I cannot say. Minutes. Hours perhaps. I became aware of the silence just as the door slammed.

Rolling to my knees, I stared at my husband, my breasts heaving with anger and fear. "Stay away from me," I said.

"I didn't slash that portrait."

I covered my ears. "I don't want to hear it. I am tired of the excuses and the lies." He moved toward me and I threw myself back against the headboard. "Stop!" I screamed. "I should have listened to them, but, no, I had to believe you!"

As he moved around the bed, I rolled to the opposite side and jumped to the floor. Sweeping up a teacup from the tray he'd brought up, I hurled it at him. He ducked. I picked up the small pitcher of milk and flung it as well. It crashed against the wall, sending milk puddling on the floor and fragments of glass flying over the room.

Nicholas moved slowly around the bed, his movements cautious. "I did not slash that portrait," he said evenly. "Listen to me. I did throw out some canvases several days back, but I swear to you that portrait was not among them."

"I don't believe you."

"I have rarely left this bloody room since your accident, my lady. Anyone could have taken the canvas at any time by entering the studio through the hall door."

Again I fought that nagging need to believe him, but the deep timbre of his voice and the gentle look in his eyes were having their desired effect on my shattered nerves. The burden of trust fell again onto my shoulders, and I cursed it with all the strength I could muster from my aching body.

The tension swelled and hovered over us like the night's shadows. Then the sound of retching rose up from the darkness at the far side of the room, and my knees turned to water.

Nicholas spun. "What the . . . ?"

Silence. Then a scratching, thumping noise, and a guttural groan that sent ice racing through my veins. Silence again.

Cautiously I approached the place from where the awful sound had arisen, stopping just behind my husband. We both searched the shadows, and in the same moment sighted Belzeebub's grotesquely twisted corpse lying against the wall, his whiskers still covered with milk.

Poison! I backed away, terror choking me speechless as I witnessed my husband's features, grim now and resolute. Whirling, I raced for the door and threw myself against it as if my frail body could somehow obliterate the barrier. Then *his* arms were around me, peeling me away from the door while I kicked and clawed and tried with all my strength to scream.

He clamped his hand over my mouth, and I bit it savagely until I tasted blood on my tongue and heard him curse. He flung me on the bed, and before I could roll away, threw his weight atop me. He pressed his palm over my mouth and nose so forcefully I thought for certain that, having failed with the stairs and poison, he would try suffocating me to death.

I ceased to struggle. My will to live evaporated with the realization that I had been wrong about my husband all along. I had given him my heart while alive. I would yield him my soul in death.

Closing my eyes, I mumbled against his hand, "Go on, then, and do what you will. Kill me."

He remained quiet and I thought I heard his heart pounding in my ears. Perhaps it was mine. Finally, he whispered, "Don't be an idiot."

I looked at him again. Nose to nose we stared into one another's eyes while the heat of his body warmed me to melting. He whispered again. "If I remove my hand, will you promise not to scream?"

"Nay, I will not."

"You will not promise or you will not scream?"

"Take your chances."

He left his hand where it was, biting into my lips. "You will hear me out, Lady Malham, and when I am finished if you care to scream down the rafters you are free to do so. Now, answer me with a nod of your head. Were you pushed down the stairs?"

I nodded and his body stiffened.

"I did not push you," he said.

The narrowing of my eyes told my husband that I did not believe him.

"I was nowhere near you when you fell," he countered. "Trust me."

At that I nearly laughed. Trust is what had gotten me into this perilous predicament in the first place. As he slowly removed his hand from my mouth, I snapped, "Liar!" Then I lunged, nearly toppling him from his position astride me.

Grabbing my flailing hands and pinning them to the bed, he glared straight into my eyes. "For one who practices deception as a way of life, you are hardly in a position to be calling anyone a liar . . . Maggie."

I had suspected that he knew, but to now be sure brought me more fear than a thousand threats of death. I briefly swooned. Then, opening my eyes again, I managed weakly, "How long have you known?"

"I've suspected since I first tried to paint your portrait. I had trouble capturing your likeness because my mind remembered one face while my eye saw another." Releasing my hands, he swept aside a strand of black hair that clung to my cheek. "You've changed, Maggie. The lass I fell in love with two years ago would not have attempted to destroy me by revenge."

"The good lord I fell in love with two years ago would not have attempted to murder me with poison," I countered.

So, there we lay, breast to breast, loin to loin, each having laid our cards on the table, so to speak. Finally he slid to one side, though he kept one heavy leg thrown over my thighs and an arm tossed across my waist. "Maggie," he finally stated. "I want you to listen to me now. It is past time for honesty. We must trust one another. I did not try to kill you. And that means, much as it grieves me to admit, that someone else in this house has tried to kill you. Not once but twice. The difference is, I believe the second time the attempt was directed at us *both*."

I lifted my brow in disbelief and refused to look at him. To do so would be my undoing.

"The tea was to quench the two of us," he pointed out.

"And you prepared it. Will you deny that simple fact?"

"No. Which means that at some time the poison was added to the milk after I poured it into the pitcher."

"I suppose the poison just hovered over your head until you turned your back. Then it dove like a rock into the milk before you could discover it."

"Twit, someone has just tried to murder me. My mood is too foul to tolerate sarcasm."

"So what else is new, sir?"

"You have a bite like an asp, Maggie. I'm trying very hard to remember why I fell in love with you in the first place."

"Because I was the only one who could tolerate your immense conceit, sir."

"Aha. Thank you for pointing that out."

"You're welcome."

I felt him smiling at me, though I continued to stare in the opposite direction. The next thing I knew, his lips were next to my ear, and he was saying, "I left the kitchen for some ten minutes to check on Matilda. I believe I mentioned earlier that she is ill."

"A likely alibi."

Swearing, he rolled from the bed and paced the floor. "Dammit, Maggie, if I had wanted to kill you I would have thrown you over the cliff at the cove."

"You were just lulling me into a false sense of security."

"For God's sake, you sound like Brabbs."

"He thinks you are insane."

"Remind me to thank him when I see him again."

I rolled to the far side of the bed, but from there I could view Belzeebub's stiffening form. Shivering, I crawled to the opposite edge and awaited my husband's next move.

He continued to pace for some time: to the window, the bed, the door. Finally he pulled a key from his pocket and slid it into the lock. My eyes widened as the bolt ground into place, barricading us in.

Well. This is it then, I thought. As he turned to face me, I said, "Will you at least let me see my son again before you do it?"

My lord scowled. "Define 'it.' "

"Murder me, of course."

He muttered something foul before striding to the bed. Time passed very slowly as I looked up through the shadows at his face. I found no anger there, no twisted visage of bitterness as I had so often witnessed since my arrival at Walthamstow. Yet there was pain and confusion and a great deal of worry. I was sorely tempted in that instant to trust him.

When he spoke again, his voice sounded strained and weary. "Maggie, I think you already realize that someone has been drugging me." At my continued silence he cursed again and raked his bloody hand through his hair. "Does it not stand to reason that whoever drugged me would also bend low enough to kill me?"

"Us," I corrected. "And one may have nothing to do with the other. If someone had wanted you dead, why did they not attempt to kill you long ago? Why wait until now, *after* you've married?"

He stared at me again, his eyes black, his look solemn. Then he turned away. "I've so much yet to remember, Maggie. So much is still a blank to me. I may never remember it all. I cannot say unequivocally that I did not kill Jane, or that I have not harmed someone else during my bout of insanity."

I opened my mouth to protest, but he cut me off.

"Aye, insanity it was, or a form of it. The drug drove rationality from me. I might have done anything under its influence. I can remember times when I acted with-

out thought and struck out, if not physically then vo-
cally, to friends or . . ."

He could not bring himself to say it, so I said it for
him. "Family."

I saw him flinch.

Nicholas walked to the window and stared out into
the darkness. I glanced toward the door, then remembered that he had locked it. When I looked at him
again he was watching me, one side of his face lit
by the candle light. "You still don't believe me," he
said softly.

I did not know what to believe.

We gazed at each other through the soft glow of
candlelight. Then he said, "I vowed to you before we
married that I would never hurt you. Do you remember why?"

"You said you loved me."

"Aye, I said that. And I meant it."

"You said it before as well, yet you married Jane."

He pressed his fingers to his temple and closed his
eyes. "I didn't remember, Maggie. *They* were the ones
who told me that I was about to marry Jane."

"They?"

"My mother, Adrienne, and Trevor."

"Adrienne knew why you were traveling to York: You
were going to break your engagement. Why didn't she
say something?"

His eyes came back to mine. "I cannot give you reasons for the madness that seems to have a hold on this
house. Perhaps I am guilty of past crimes perpetrated
during my insanity, but guilty of shoving you down
stairs and poisoning your milk I am not."

He moved toward me so suddenly I fell back in surprise. Looming over me, his broad shoulders blocking
the light from the candle, he looked at me steadily and

spoke in an odd whisper. "That poison was meant for us both. I would stake Walthamstow on it. I will also hasten to add that whoever tainted the milk will be expecting us to be dead as a doornail shortly. It stands to reason that he—or she—will be returning at some time to search us out. Are you willing to wait?"

I agreed, uncertain if the glint I saw in his eyes was some lingering madness or simply determination. Either way I was willing to chance it. It was that damnable trust again, and a heart that refused to harden against him. Hope was like a barbed arrow point in my breast, yielding to my better judgment a final and bitter surrender. Slumping back into the darkness, I waited.

Chapter 22

We talked in whispers late into the night. Nicholas told me something of his life, or what he could recall of it, since he kissed me good-bye at my uncle's tavern.

His loss of memory bothered him greatly, but I assured him that he would likely remember everything once his mind and body were given sufficient time to heal. I explained that the fall into the ice had brought about a certain trauma to the brain that had been greatly exaggerated by the opium's effects. When he asked me how I knew this, I was forced to explain that, while in Oaks, I assisted several of the doctors who frequently practiced there. In turn, I had been treated better than the average patient, and was thus allowed to read many of their medical texts for entertainment.

He encouraged me to talk of Oaks, and I did so as dispassionately as possible. Yet it was a painful monologue; more than once a bitterness edged into my tone as I recalled the unsanitary conditions, the neglect and cruelty of many of the workers. Several times I watched him reach for me. "I'm sorry," he repeated over and over. Once he buried his face in his hands until he could compose himself and face me again.

Little by little my doubts of him subsided, as they always did.

I persuaded him to talk of his nightmares, convincing him that they could, in some way, be related to his memories. As always, he talked about the fire, of hitting Jane, of clawing his way from the stables and watching them burn. Bits and pieces of fact and images of confusion. Was he being drugged before then? He didn't know for certain, but he suspected he was. He also suspected that the opium had somehow affected him the day of his accident. What other explanation could there be for his riding so dangerously close to a frozen pond?

He discussed the voices he heard at night outside his door. Then he spoke again of the ghostly image of a woman he had seen in the hallway, at Walthamstow's tree line, and at the stable. At that my head came off my pillow.

"But that is not illusion, husband. I have seen her myself."

His dark eyes bore into mine. "You've seen her," he repeated.

"Aye. She showed herself at the cemetery. I saw her the next day wandering in the fog outside the house, and again in the closed west wing."

His hands came for me suddenly, lifting me and setting me atop his chest. "Why didn't you tell me this?"

"To be honest, my lord, I did not trust you not to lie. After I found the room—"

"Room? What room?"

"The room where she was living, I assume. I took Trevor to see it, but when we arrived there it looked as if it had never been lived in. At that point I thought I had begun to hallucinate. Then it was explained to me that Samantha had once been kept there—"

"Kept there?"

"Aye," I responded. "Kept there by you or Trevor."

"So says . . . ?"

"Adrienne." I looked hard through the shadows, into my husband's eyes. "Husband," I whispered. "Were you and Samantha lovers?"

He took my face in his hands. "In honesty I cannot say. Maggie, there is so much just before and just after Jane's death that I cannot remember. My madness was at its peak then, I believe. I may have taken the girl as a lover. I can recall that she was a comely lass, small and pale and blond, not unlike Jane. I may have kissed her once—no, don't turn away—you asked for honesty and that is what I've given you. Aye, I did kiss her once, but more than that I cannot say."

Releasing my shoulders, he wrapped his arms around me and hugged me to his chest. "One thing is for certain, Maggie. I haven't been imagining the woman I've seen on the grounds. I do think she wanted me to believe in my own insanity. And I nearly did believe it. I was so close to breaking, Maggie. Then you came and saved me, made me believe in myself again."

In the long silence that ensued, I drifted to sleep, lulled by the heavy beating of my lord's heart against my ear. Once I dreamt that I heard him say, "Maggie, I love you," while he stroked my hair and pressed his lips to my forehead. Then I dreamt he wept.

The sound was so subtle that at first I thought I had imagined it. Then I heard it again: a shift of the doorknob.

I felt my husband tense beneath me, then his hand came up over my mouth in a warning to keep quiet. He gently rolled me off his chest onto the bed, then shifted his legs to the floor. He walked as silently as a cat to the fireplace and picked up the poker.

I too left the bed, driven by fear. If he should leave

this room, he might not return. Throwing myself against him, I whispered as urgently as possible, "My lord, to venture out this door would be foolish. Stay. Wait until the morrow and we will see this nightmare to its completion in the light of day."

Cupping my cheek with his free hand, he smiled and asked as quietly, "Might I take this as encouragement, Lady Malham? Mayhap you've decided to believe me?"

The door again.

My husband nudged me aside and walked on the balls of his feet to the door. He listened.

Nicholas slipped the key from his pocket and eased it into the lock. Then with a quick twist of his wrist he sprang the bolt and flung back the door.

Nothing.

He stepped into the hall.

Nothing.

He hesitated, seemingly formulating a plan, then disappeared into the darkness. I waited impatiently, my ear attuned to any sound, my eye searching for any sight of him. I issued from our apartment, stood in the center of that endless tunnel of cold and blackness, and wondered how the shadows could devour him so swiftly and completely. Then I saw him. He carried Kevin in his arms.

Without a word I rushed back into our room, held my arms out for our sleeping son. Nestling the child against my breast, I looked to my husband and smiled.

His look was reverent.

"I'll go now," he said. "Lock this door behind me and open it to no one but me. You know my signal."

"Where will you go?" I asked. "What do you expect to discover in this darkness that can't wait until morning? My lord?"

He closed the door.

I locked it.

Loathsome solitude, magnifying each sputter of the candle, each scraping of the elm branch against the window. Each *tap-tap-tap* against the glass sent me leaping toward the door, only to discover that my husband had not yet returned.

The candle wick grew short, the light dim. Sitting in the center of the bed, my sleeping son by my side, I watched the yellow halo around us diminish until the last flicker of light danced about the walls. Then darkness.

Outside, the wind rose. I heard the howling of the hounds in the distance. Moving to the window, I looked out on Walthamstow's gardens. A mist crept over the grounds, inching toward the house from the wood. Above it a full moon glowed like alabaster against a black velvet sky.

Fear crept up my spine and prickled my scalp. It turned my blood to ice and my heart into a drum that pounded so loudly and forcefully my head hummed with the pressure. I wasn't alone.

Slowly I turned from the window, searching out each gray corner, each black nook and cranny. I was letting my idiotic fear of the darkness overcome me again. There was no one here. Yet . . .

I could feel it. As I had felt it in the garden, in the hallway, in the cemetery. A presence: an evil so powerful that it transcended mortal boundaries. I shuddered.

Cautiously I pressed my ear to the door and listened. Nothing.

I closed my eyes and listened harder. What was near me? *Something* existed in that vast silence beyond this barrier, I was certain.

Gradually I opened my eyes and watched the doorknob turn. Backing away from the door, I covered my mouth with my hands, certain that whoever was at-

tempting entrance to this room could hear my gasps
for air. Then the knock.

Once . . . twice . . . (pause) . . . a third time.

Relief flooded me; I leapt for the door.

Wait! some instinct called. *This is not right.* Would
he try the door first? He knew I had locked it. And his
knock. That long hesitation between the second and
third rap, as if it had been done with uncertainty. *It
was not my lord's* signal.

Whoever is there must know I am alone.

Stillness, and again the air warmed, the tendrils of
fear seeming to dissolve like mist in the sun. I stood for
some minutes, composing my nerves, and had almost
succeeded when the knock came again, steadily this
time. I tried to move. Again the knock. I forced myself
to walk to the door, to withdraw the key from my
pocket and slide it into the lock. I turned the key. The
bolt shifted. I stumbled back, prepared to beat back
Satan himself if I had to. The door creaked open. My
husband stepped into the room.

With a cry of relief I threw myself against him, covered his neck and face with kisses. He did not, however, return my affection to such degree. Setting me
from him, he locked the door again and walked to
the window.

"Sir," I said, "I thank God you are safe. Did you
discover anything amiss?" I then told him that I had
been visited by someone during his absence.

He responded. "I've no doubts that I was observed.
I did nothing to obscure the fact that I was about."
My lord faced me then. "It'll be dawn soon. Try to get
some rest, Maggie, while I keep a watch."

I dozed. When I opened my eyes again a dim gray
light poured through the window. My husband stood

before the window, his fingertips lightly pressed against the glass, his face as pale as marble. Lifting my head from the pillow, I was about to speak when he ran for the door. I called his name, yet he did not seem to hear me.

I jumped from the bed and ran to the window, searching. Patches of mist moved slowly over the awakening grounds: great gray clouds slightly darker than the dawn light. Then a movement among the trees caught my eye.

I threw open the window, cursing the dreary fog as I strained to see again the object that had sent my husband racing from our chamber. There! A flash of white and . . . the cloaked and hooded figure hurried toward the path leading to the stables. "No," I cried aloud.

I ran for the door, coming face to face with Bea. Her hands came out for me, clutched my shoulders, and I saw her face, drained of blood, look suddenly much older than her age. "Kevin," she croaked. "The lad is gone, milady!"

"He's asleep there!" I explained, pushing her aside. I ran down the corridor, ignoring the pain in my limbs. Reaching the hallway to Adrienne's quarters, I slowed and noted that her bedroom door was open. Yellow light spilled through the doorway.

I had to know. I hurried to her door and glanced about the chamber. Empty.

When I reached the kitchen I found Matilda wringing her hands and placing the chairs upright. She saw me barrel into the room and cried, "Gum, wot's 'appenin'? They've gone tearin' out o' this ole house like the devil 'imself was nippin' at their 'eels."

I grabbed her and said, "Tilly, go to Malham and fetch Brabbs. Tell him it's urgent. He'll understand."

I exited the house without coat or shoes, my white nightdress a frail barrier against the elements. I ran as quickly as my weakened state would allow down the path toward the stables.

At last the ruin rose up before me, all waste and grim black stone. There was the silence of death about it. I could see the door, the stall, the place where Jane had died. There in that corner was a misshapen mass that might have been a saddle. There was a wheel, a brace for a buggy—I shook my head, releasing the memory of *pandemonium*.

Where was my husband?

I left the winter-beaten devastation and returned to the main path, searching frantically both left and right. Then I saw Nicholas as he topped the highest fell, then disappeared on the other side.

Away from Walthamstow's gardens the wind swept more forcefully, whistling between the moor's bracken crags and crevices, whipping away what was left of last night's fog. Finally I topped the rise and looked down toward Pikedaw Cliff. Mist tumbled and swirled before me, caught up in the helter-skelter rampage of the wind. I caught glimpses of the stone wall my husband and Jim had set out to repair those days before. My fall down the stairs had apparently ceased the renovation, for the gaping hole in the wall had yet to be mended completely.

My frantic eye searched the dim and misty landscape for any sight of my lord and the mysterious creature who had led him to this inhospitable place. Why? I questioned. Why here? My gaze traveled up and down the wall and then . . . Realization sprang on me as chill as death as I found my husband backed to the edge of Pikedaw Cliff, and before him, advancing steadily was the cloaked and hooded woman.

Dare I call out? Dare I move? What fear was this
that made my lord back toward that precipice as if
death were more preferable than facing this nemesis?
Yet he backed again. And again. Nearer he came to
the deadly ledge until my fear for his safety lent me
strength enough to stumble down the hill, to mount
the dilapidated wall, and to jump to the other side.

Advancing on the woman, I cried, "Stop!"

The wind rose, sobbing over the gorge and whipping
the woman's hood away from her head as she spun to
face me.

Jane!

Terror reared up inside me, buckled my legs so I
stumbled backward and fell to the ground. Was this
some specter sent back from the grave to redeem her
lost soul? Nay, for as I watched her mane of blond
hair rise like a cloud around her and her head fall back
in wicked, wicked laughter, I knew she was real. I knew
true madness. I had faced it at Oaks. I faced it again
in Jane Wyndham's eyes. Yes, she was real, flesh and
blood and more evil than any demon of hell could
ever be.

She made a quick turn back toward my husband,
whose glazed eyes hinted of shock. Then there was
thunder and the ground shook beneath me. Over the
wall and through the mist loomed a heaving, snorting
monster that seemed to lunge right at Jane. She threw
up her arms and screamed. Horrified, I watched as she
spiraled backward, away from the horse's pawing
hooves, and disappeared over the precipice, her cry of
terror swallowed by the mist.

Moving woodenly at first, Nicholas stumbled away
from the cliff, his arms and legs laden with relief.
Struggling to my feet, I ran to him while Trevor slid
off his horse and approached us.

My lord's arms wrapped around me, held me fiercely against him as he whispered, "God, oh God, Maggie, was it truly Jane or am I imagining it all again?"

"Aye," I cried. "It was Jane, sir, you didn't imagine her!"

My lord opened his arms and took in his brother. "Thank God, Trev, you arrived just in time."

I stood back and watched as my husband hugged his brother in gratitude. I noted that Trevor's slack arms responded with no fondness, and deep in the center of my breast I felt my heart turn over.

Stiff-shouldered, his face without expression, Trevor stepped away.

"No," I said aloud. "Oh dear God."

Nicholas looked at me, then to Trevor. Realization crept over my husband's features, turning his face to stone as he backed protectively toward me.

Trevor looked down at me and smiled coldly. "Hello, Maggie," he said. "Does it surprise you that I know who you really are?"

I nodded, too stunned to speak.

"I didn't until Jane pushed you down the stairs. During the examination I noticed the brand on your arm. Being a physician, I recognized it immediately as the institution's mark. It didn't take long to contact the officials there and learn that an Ariel Margaret Rushdon had given birth to a child. Kevin."

"Then *you* are the bloody bastard who's been drugging me," Nick said. "But Brabbs assured me—"

"I replenished my stock of opium each time I traveled to York. Good God, Nick, are you so damned vulnerable as to believe I could be interested in something so mundane as raising tea in India? That last five thousand quid you advanced me went totally on opium for you and . . . others."

It was I who spoke next. "My lord, it was a simple enough task to slip you the opium so you'd sleep for days, then when you awoke, confused, he would pretend that you did things or said things that, of course, you never did. Like the argument recently in the library. He cut his own lip to make me think you had hit him. It would be an easy enough task with a letting knife. I don't know why it didn't occur to me at the time."

Trevor's blue eyes shifted from Nicholas back to me. "Had you not come along, Maggie, Jane and I might never have needed to resort to murder. We were so very close to convincing everyone, including Nick, that he was insane. But here you come, educated in the ways of insanity, and spoil it all."

I felt my husband tremble with anger. His fists opened and closed at his sides. "Why, Trevor?" he demanded. "What have I ever done—"

"Done? Good God, that should be obvious. You inherited Walthamstow, my dear brother, and I didn't. Coming up with a plan to get my hands on this estate was no easy feat, I might add. Drudging through these last ghastly years pretending to give a damn for the welfare of these peasants has been more than I could tolerate at times. You see, I could not kill you outright. Walthamstow would merely have passed on to George, then to Eugene. So I had to make you appear as if you could no longer function mentally. Then I could have gone to court and requested to be let in charge of the estate. Your accident and short bout of amnesia was a godsend, I might add. It made you look doubly idiot."

"But you had your allowance. I was always willing to advance you money if I felt the cause was justified."

"*You* felt was justified," he sneered. "I am sick to

death of hearing what *you* think, my good Lord Malham. I am sick of living in *your* shadow and sick of crawling to you on my belly each time I need an advance. That yearly allowance is a pittance of what it would take to live in London or Paris, which is where I intend to go once I've washed my hands of you. God, I'll be glad to be rid of this dreary house and these dreary little people . . ."

I looked up at my husband as he asked, "And just where did my wife fit into this?"

"Jane?" Trevor laughed. "Another fool. We were lovers for years, even while our mummy and daddy were arranging your betrothal with hers. I would never have married her, of course, but I convinced her otherwise so she would agree to participate in this scheme. I promised her I would sell Walthamstow when it was mine, take the money and go abroad with her to live, where no one knew us. The plan was without flaw. The argument you had with Jane that night in the stable had been prearranged. Jane goaded you into the argument and struck you, anticipating that you would strike her back. And of course you did. She pretended to lose consciousness and, confused fool that you were, you went roaming about the gardens looking for help. While you were gone we simply set the stables on fire."

"But the body," Nicholas said in a dry voice. "What about the body?"

"Samantha. We lured her to the stable with a note and bashed in her head with a rock. No one was ever the wiser. I hated to do it. Samantha was a more than adequate lover, but business is business . . ."

Trevor looked at me again, even as my husband shifted before me. "Lovely child," I heard him say. "There was a time when I was actually fond of you. I thought of trying to seduce you, but soon realized it would do me no good. Like Samantha, you had eyes only for him. But unlike Samantha, you wouldn't settle for second best.

"You were no threat to me until you married Nick, you know. Then only you could commit him. But you wouldn't. We thought the shove down the stairs would accomplish two things: Either it would get you out of the way, or it would convince you that he was unstable. Obviously it did neither. But then I found the brand, and learned that you are Kevin's true mother. And do you know what that means?" His mouth curled menacingly. "He's legitimate."

Trevor jumped back and pulled a gun from beneath his coat as Nicholas took a sudden threatening step toward him.

Raising the gun barrel toward my lord's heart, Trevor continued. "Had Kevin been illegitimate, Walthamstow would never have passed to him. Now, however, with your deaths, and proof that Ariel is Kevin's mother, it will all go to him. And, of course, he will need a guardian to handle the inheritance until he comes of age. I think it will be simple enough to convince everyone that Nick has again—in a fit of insanity—killed the newest Lady Malham, and himself."

As he cocked the gun, I lunged, hoping the element of surprise would give my husband time to respond. But Trevor was too quick, slicing into my jaw with his elbow so I was sent spinning to the ground.

My world then was a confusing cacophony of sounds, of men struggling and cursing. My head roared with the frightening noises. Suddenly, a pistol shot shattered the air and the bullet buried into the earth just inches from my face.

So close, they were so close to the edge. My husband

struggled but his brother was stronger, healthier, driving him back and back toward the ledge. I tried to stand but my already injured body rebelled, driving me to my knees. I wept wildly, begging for my husband's mercy until fear seized all strength from me and I fell flat into the wet, muddy turf.

I lifted my face. The men struggled and one stumbled backward. I screamed in horror as I watched my husband slide over the ledge toward oblivion. In one last effort his hands came out and buried into the peat and his legs swung from side to side in an effort to gain a foothold. I saw my chance and threw myself over the ground, wrapping my hands over my husband's, twisting my fingers around his wrists in an effort to hold him. Yet his weight pulled him down, dragged at the tender precipice until I was certain that I would witness my lord spiraling into the misty yawning pit that had earlier devoured Jane.

In my struggle to save my husband I had forgotten Trevor. Now I sensed him. Looking back over my shoulder, I watched as he approached, lifting a boulder with nearly superhuman strength.

"Maggie!" my husband called. "Maggie, run! Now, before he can stop you!"

My hands, wet with mire and sweat, gripped his wrists more tightly.

"That's right, Maggie," Trevor snarled, "run while you can and be certain I will eventually find you again." He heaved up the boulder one last time.

"Stop!" came the voice. "Oh dear God, Trevor, I beg you to stop this madness now!"

Adrienne stood at the top of the rise. She pointed a gun directly at Trevor. "Please!" she cried. "Don't make me shoot you!"

He gave a mirthless laugh. "Stupid bitch, where will

you be without me? Who'll supply you with those fine little powders if you kill me?"

"Stop it!" she screamed. "I won't let you hurt them. Oh God, I should have stopped you the moment I suspected. My dear, dear Nicholas, will he ever forgive me!"

My hold burned into my husband's flesh even as his hooked fingers clawed more deeply into the dirt. He wouldn't hold out much longer. Neither of us would.

Trevor moved again, and Adrienne wept, "Don't make me. Please don't make me! I swear to you, I'll shoot!"

He loomed over us, his eyes wild, his face masked by madness.

The gun fired and Trevor spun, staring at his sister in disbelief. The rock dropped to the ground and slowly, very slowly, he seemed to float backward over the ledge and disappear through the mist.

I cried out for Adrienne's help. It seemed an eternity before she fell on her knees beside me and grabbed my husband's arm. Together we pulled him to safety, embraced him in our arms, unable to believe the nightmare was ended.

"Aye, it's over," I told him, kissing his brow and soothing his tremors. "It's all over, my lord husband. I swear it."

And it was, even as Adrienne wept quietly beside us. He took my hand firmly in his, wrapped his arm around his sister's shoulder, and helped us to our feet. Without looking back, we returned to Walthamstow.

Chapter 23

Five years have passed since that wretched ordeal at Pikedaw Cliff. Walthamstow is once again a welcome place, her gardens blooming with flowers, thanks to Jim. Her hallways glow with candlelight and her windows gleam with sunlight, thanks to Matilda.

Bea is still with us. When she learned of Jane's cruelty and deceit she burned the former Lady Malham's possessions and became a loyal, trusted servant and companion to our children. But she grows old and will soon leave us.

Brabbs is still discussing retirement, though I suspect it will be some time before he entrusts the care of his patients to anyone new. Understandable. He is not totally pleased with my marriage to Lord Malham, but has grudgingly accepted it. He visits us regularly. Our children call him grandfather. That pleases him no end.

Adrienne is married and expecting her first child in a fortnight. She lives in York, in a humble cottage whose door is always open to passersby. She seems tremendously happy in her life as a minister's wife.

I will close this journal now, for I see in the distance my husband and two sons approaching, their hands in their pockets, their black hair tumbling in the moor wind. I study my husband's face and know he is well, though he has never totally recovered his memory. Mayhap he never will, and that's just as well. His spirits are high, although I know, when his eyes become distant, that he is remembering. I reassure him with a touch of my hand. His smile affirms to me that all is right.

He is smiling now, so I must go.

Know this: I am happy.

And I am most assuredly loved.

WE NEED YOUR HELP
To continue to bring you quality romance
that meets your personal expectations,
we at TOPAZ books want to hear from you.
Help us by filling out this questionnaire, and in exchange
we will give you a **free gift** as a token of our gratitude.

- Is this the first TOPAZ book you've purchased? (circle one)

    YES   NO

    The title and author of this book is: _____

- If this was not the first TOPAZ book you've purchased, how many have
  you bought in the past year?

    a: 0 - 5   b 6 - 10   c: more than 10   d: more than 20

- How many romances in total did you buy in the past year?

    a: 0 - 5   b: 6 - 10   c: more than 10   d: more than 20 ____

- How would you rate your overall satisfaction with this book?

    a: Excellent   b: Good   c: Fair   d: Poor

- What was the main reason you bought this book?

    a: It is a TOPAZ novel, and I know that TOPAZ stands
       for quality romance fiction
    b: I liked the cover
    c: The story-line intrigued me
    d: I love this author
    e: I really liked the setting
    f: I love the cover models
    g: Other: _____

- Where did you buy this TOPAZ novel?

    a: Bookstore   b: Airport   c: Warehouse Club
    d: Department Store   e: Supermarket   f: Drugstore
    g: Other: _____

- Did you pay the full cover price for this TOPAZ novel? (circle one)

    YES   NO

    If you did not, what price did you pay? _____

- Who are your favorite TOPAZ authors? (Please list)

- How did you first hear about TOPAZ books?

    a: I saw the books in a bookstore
    b: I saw the TOPAZ Man on TV or at a signing
    c: A friend told me about TOPAZ
    d: I saw an advertisement in_____magazine
    e: Other: _____

- What type of romance do you generally prefer?

    a: Historical   b: Contemporary
    c: Romantic Suspense   d: Paranormal (time travel,
       futuristic, vampires, ghosts, warlocks, etc.)
    d: Regency   e: Other: _____

- What historical settings do you prefer?

    a: England   b: Regency England   c: Scotland
    e: Ireland   f: America   g: Western Americana
    h: American Indian   i: Other: _____

- What type of story do you prefer?

  a: Very sexy   b: Sweet, less explicit
  c: Light and humorous   d: More emotionally intense
  e: Dealing with darker issues   f: Other

- What kind of covers do you prefer?

  a: Illustrating both hero and heroine   b: Hero alone
  c: No people (art only)   d: Other_____

- What other genres do you like to read (circle all that apply)

  Mystery   Medical Thrillers   Science Fiction
  Suspense   Fantasy   Self-help
  Classics   General Fiction   Legal Thrillers
  Historical Fiction

- Who is your favorite author, and why?_____
  _____

- What magazines do you like to read? (circle all that apply)

  a: *People*   b: *Time/Newsweek*
  c: *Entertainment Weekly*   d: *Romantic Times*
  e: *Star*   f: *National Enquirer*
  g: *Cosmopolitan*   h: *Woman's Day*
  i: *Ladies' Home Journal*   j: *Redbook*
  k: Other:_____

- In which region of the United States do you reside?

  a: Northeast   b: Midatlantic   c: South
  d: Midwest   e: Mountain   f: Southwest
  g: Pacific Coast

- What is your age group/sex?   a: Female   b: Male

  a: under 18   b: 19-25   c: 26-30   d: 31-35   e: 36-40
  f: 41-45   g: 46-50   h: 51-55   i: 56-60   j: Over 60

- What is your marital status?

  a: Married   b: Single   c: No longer married

- What is your current level of education?

  a: High school   b: College Degree
  c: Graduate Degree   d: Other: _____

- Do you receive the TOPAZ *Romantic Liaisons* newsletter, a quarterly newsletter with the latest information on Topaz books and authors?

  YES   NO

  If not, would you like to?   YES   NO

  Fill in the address where you would like your free gift to be sent:

  Name: _____
  Address: _____
  City:_____ Zip Code: _____

  You should receive your free gift in 6 to 8 weeks.
  Please send the completed survey to:

Penguin USA•Mass Market
Dept. TS
375 Hudson St.
New York, NY 10014